MY SISTER IS GOING TO KILL ME

ALSO BY NINA SIMON

Mother-Daughter Murder Night

MY SISTER IS GOING TO KILL ME

A Novel

NINA SIMON

WILLIAM MORROW
An Imprint of HarperCollins*Publishers*

This is a work of fiction. Names, characters, places, and incidents are products of the author's imagination or are used fictitiously and are not to be construed as real. Any resemblance to actual events, locales, organizations, or persons, living or dead, is entirely coincidental.

HarperCollins books may be purchased for educational, business, or sales promotional use. For information, please email the Special Markets Department at SPsales@harpercollins.com.

hc.com

FIRST EDITION

Designed by Jennifer Chung

Library of Congress Cataloging-in-Publication Data

Names: Simon, Nina author
Title: My sister is going to kill me : a novel / Nina Simon.
Description: First edition. | New York, NY : William Morrow, 2026. |
Identifiers: LCCN 2025053597 | ISBN 9780063478022 hardcover |
ISBN 9780063478046 ebook
Subjects: LCGFT: Detective and mystery fiction | Novels
Classification: LCC PS3619.I56256 M9 2026
LC record available at https://lccn.loc.gov/2025053597

ISBN 978-0-06-347802-2 (hardcover)
978-0-06-356734-4 (international edition)

Printed in the United States of America

26 27 28 29 30 LBC 5 4 3 2 1

For my phenomenal sister, Morgan,
and all the other siblings who haven't killed each other yet

MY SISTER IS GOING TO KILL ME

CHAPTER ONE

LIV LOOKED AT HER watch. Then at the crowd. Then, the abyss.

Her sister was missing.

The response at work when someone didn't show up at an appointed rendezvous was clear: a twelve-step protocol Liv had memorized on her first overseas assignment. The protocol on a sister trip? Swallow the panic and wait.

In ten years, Mandy had never missed one of their annual joint vacations. But she always found a way to show up at the last possible moment, after Liv had mentally notified the National Guard, requisitioned a canine search unit, and completely lost her equilibrium. The one time she'd actually called the authorities—outside a reindeer ranch in northern Lapland—her little sister had come cantering up on an ice-bearded beast, curls bouncing wildly under a hot-pink stocking cap, eyes dancing at the sight of so many members of the Finnish police force deployed to track her down.

It was as if Mandy wanted her to feel off balance. To stumble into their time together instead of marching forward with confidence. And if any place could rattle her, the Grand Canyon was it. Liv had never been a fan of heights, but she hadn't considered this alternative: plunging depths of carved-away rock, a natural wonder that hollowed out the world instead of reaching for the sky.

She forced herself to look over the cliffside railing she was clutching. The South Rim of the canyon stretched down and away from her, forming a greedy, treacherous mouth. If Mandy was here, she'd pronounce it beautiful, throw around words like "ombré" and "perspective," paint a big bright picture of the two of them jaunting down the trail the next morning before the birds woke up. But Mandy wasn't here yet, and all Liv sensed was danger. No matter how she craned her neck, their destination—the Colorado River—was beyond the terrifying zigzag of her field of vision. She couldn't track more than a few hundred feet down to where the footpath dissolved into a gaping wound. But she could trace the bloodred shadows down the cliffside. She could feel the crooked switchbacks pulsing in her knees. She could sense the shimmering heat, which shifted from comfortable warmth at the rim to a blistering furnace down below. She could see enough to know for certain: This time, their sister trip really might kill her.

Liv walked back to their motel room, hoping to find Mandy on the doorstep, jiggling a key and humming a made-up song.

No luck. Her sister was good for surprises, but not the I-arrived-early-and-brought-extra-sunscreen variety. It was Liv who double-checked the packing list and dutifully purchased not one but three sets of Day-Glo strings to keep their sunglasses strapped to their heads as they bucked their way down the Colorado. One for herself. One for Mandy. And one in case of disaster.

She turned her attention to the two careful piles of luggage arranged on the queen beds. The left bed held the contents of Liv's work life, tactical and practical. Three no-wrinkle black suits, one gun holster. A pair of low heels she always kicked off the second she was seated behind her desk. Also her laptop, credentials, and a vintage portable lie detector her boss in Bucharest had given her after her promotion from the visa office. She'd be going directly from the Grand Canyon to her next deployment in Bogotá, joining a smuggling task force as a profiler for the first time. She'd spent the plane ride brushing up on the latest data on human trafficking, exotic animal trade, and new trends in street drugs. This could be her big break into serious investigatory work. The only thing delaying her from it was this sister trip.

For which she was assembling the second bag. Liv stared at the foreign objects she'd bought for the Colorado River. A camp towel. A 50-UPF neck gaiter. Two insulated water bottles, absurdly large, so much so she'd started getting ads on her phone featuring bodybuilders who crushed raw eggs against their foreheads and let the contents drip into their mouths. Cotton T-shirts, which she bought a cheap five-pack of from a street vendor in Bucharest. Cotton seemed outdated compared to quick-dry synthetics—didn't it kill in the backcountry?—but she'd read it could be 120 degrees at the bottom of the Grand Canyon in the summer, which meant the ideal clothing could be dunked in the freezing river and stay wet a very long time. She rolled the T-shirts into a tight tube, sliding them into her duffel between a can of bug spray and a bright blue rain poncho. At least the outfitter had provided a packing list. This was one of Mandy's selling points for the Grand Canyon rafting adventure: It came with a detailed plan and day-by-day itinerary. For once, Mandy had picked a trip that didn't consist of "we'll get there and figure it out." Liv had tried to suggest they could go somewhere with a schedule that also boasted air conditioning, but Mandy had waved her off.

"You get your trips," Mandy pointed out. "I get mine."

Liv hated when her little sister was right.

Their sister trips had started ten years ago, when Liv was twenty-four and Mandy twenty-one, after their dad was arrested for fraud and left them with a shoebox stuffed with hundred-dollar bills and an apartment full of unanswered questions. When the SEC determined the shoebox money wasn't part of their case, Mandy convinced Liv they should keep it. With their mom dead and their dad headed to prison, they only had each other. The money—Liv preferred not to know which of Guy Chisholm's dubious investments it came from—was something tangible they could share, a way to reinvest in their relationship.

Liv suggested a joint savings account. Mandy countered by proposing they quit their jobs, buy a sailboat, and spend the next decade hunting for shipwrecked treasure. After Liv put her foot down—she would not, under any circumstances, abandon her nascent foreign service career to become a pirate—they agreed to use the money for sister trips: once a year, trading off who picked the destination. At first they played nice and considered each other's interests. Then, four years in, Mandy turned an alleged chill-on-the-beach vacation in Costa Rica into a death-defying caving expedition that gave Liv nightmares and foot fungus for months. After that, the gloves came off. Liv frog-marched her sister through Paris. Mandy took them fly-fishing in Idaho. Liv dragged Mandy to Dubai and Seoul. Mandy brought Liv to that Finnish bush village where they ate nothing but reindeer jerky.

Considering some of what Mandy'd put her up to in the past, rafting the lower half of the Grand Canyon was practically a resort vacation. One that would start with a ten-mile, forty-eight-hundred-foot descent at four thirty the next morning.

In the final hour before orientation, Liv tried not to think about the early morning hike, her jet lag, or whether her sister was about to flit through the door with a new vision for the week that involved helicoptering into a pit of javelinas. She focused on the task at hand, packing everything into its respective bag and zipping them up tight. The motel beds now held two black duffels, each stuffed with a different life. For the next week, she would be adventurous Liv. She would be fun Liv. She would be the cheerful big sister Mandy always wanted her to be. Even if it killed her.

CHAPTER TWO

LIV WAS SO GOING to kill her. Mandy made her first flight from Austin by some kind of miracle, but when she got to Vegas, she didn't realize she had to take a bus to a different airport to catch the puddle jumper to the South Rim of the Grand Canyon. Which left her mid-conversation with the Cinnabon cashier about her teenage son's Pokémon addiction when the bus rolled away without her.

Crap. Her phone was at 3 percent. Somehow Mandy's phone sucked up battery faster than other people's, or it just vibed with the way she flew through life's tornado, especially in the summer, when she was no longer coaxing creativity from moody teenagers one fifty-two-minute class period at a time. She'd kicked off June at an all-night bonfire rave where she'd burned her school year planner. Since then, she'd relished losing track of what day it was, let alone the hour. But sister trips required getting back on schedule, or trying to. She found the number for the bus company and took a deep breath. Charm offensives at 3 percent required serious lung capacity.

The call connected, and she plunged in, channeling her inner cheerleader. "Hi! My name's Mandy Chisholm, and I'm here at the Vegas airport to catch your transporter to the South Rim."

"That bus has already left the terminals."

"I'm afraid there was a misunderstanding, a lack of clarity about where I was supposed to meet the driver—"

"Our materials clearly state—"

"You're right. I'm a dingbat and I apologize and I'm sorry if I sound out of breath, but I've been running to try to flag the bus down, and it's really hot out here, and my father—"

"There will be another bus at eight thirty p.m."

"My father, he disappeared years ago, and now all of a sudden he reached out to me, and he says he has something important to tell me, and I *have* to catch this bus to see him because I'm afraid . . . I'm afraid he might be dying."

This was, of course, not true. Technically, it was possible—Mandy's dad was full of surprises, and he'd been living life at double speed since he'd gotten out of prison seven years ago. It was just as likely he was knocking on death's door at a Grand Canyon motor lodge as it was that he was spearfishing off his new girlfriend's yacht in the Maldives. Or did he say Belize? Wherever Guy Chisholm was, he wasn't her concern right now. What *was* her concern was how pissed Liv would be if Mandy missed the welcome briefing for their trip. But she couldn't tell the minibus dispatcher she was scared of her big sister looking at her like the defective peanut at the bottom of the can. There was no upside in a truth like that.

Two percent. She coughed up a sob and gave it one more shot. "This might be the last time I can talk to my dad. Sir, I know the bus has left, but I'm hoping, please, I'm begging you . . ."

There was a long pause on the other side of the line.

"I've contacted the driver. He'll take another lap around."

Mandy gave a grateful squeal and ended the call just before her phone blinked off of its own accord.

"You poor dear." The Cinnabon lady was gazing at her with tears in her eyes. "I know this won't fix it, but sometimes a bit of sweetness helps . . ."

By the time the shuttle pulled up at the curb, Mandy had finished a free caramel pecan MiniBon and trashed the sticky evidence. She gave the driver her biggest razzle-dazzle grin and reached for his arm with a loud, grateful "you SAVED me." Then she beamed her smile all over, like a kid throwing candy at a parade, charming her inconvenienced fellow travelers until they were all smiling about the epic win they had accomplished together.

This was what Liv didn't understand about lying. When you did it properly, it didn't hurt anyone. It was a gift that sprinkled magic on people's ho-hum days. Take this bus driver, who was now pumping Mandy's hand like he'd earned a Purple Heart by circling the terminals. Or the older man who was patting Mandy's shoulder and looking down her shirt and whispering that she was a gem for trying to reconnect with her father. Everyone on the bus was waking up. They were brightening. They were all in on this big adventure together. And Mandy had made that possible.

That was the power of a good lie. It made people feel bigger than their ordinary selves. The truth was dingy. It was complicated. It didn't get you complimentary pecan rolls or extra laps around the airport. The truth wouldn't set you free. Only a lie could do that.

CHAPTER THREE

LIV ARRIVED AT THE South Rim lodge fifteen minutes before the welcome briefing. A quick scan revealed no sign of Mandy. Not a shocker, but it still chafed. At least the crowded cafeteria gave her something to focus on. She sat down by the massive stone fireplace on the edge of the dining room, searching the crowd to pick out possible members of their trip.

She had always thought rafting the Grand Canyon required boatloads of money and years on a waitlist. But Mandy had somehow scooped up two free spots on a trip down the lower half of the Colorado. The details her sister had shared were vague—just a single screenshotted email inviting Mandy on an exclusive "Essence Quest"—but the outfitter was legitimate, and Liv's attention had quickly turned to filling out forms, scrutinizing the itinerary, and absorbing as much as possible about the potential risks on the river. Whenever Liv pressed for more details about who had paid for their spots, her sister simply called it a golden opportunity. Liv just hoped the opportunity didn't come with strings attached. Or if it did, that those strings didn't require them to pose for a sexy reindeer photoshoot. Again.

According to the outfitter's documentation, there were ten guests on their trip, plus three guides. It was a beautiful late-summer weekend, and Liv clocked roughly three hundred people milling around the lodge dining room. Which of them would she be posted with on the river?

She spotted one of the guides over by the bar, his long hair half tamed by a Wild Adventures hoodie. He was early. She liked that. He was flirting with the waitress, leaning so far over the thick wood slab that Liv could see a dark mess of tattoo ink snaking down his side. A clipboard and a stack of papers lay like long-suffering dogs by his leather-sandaled feet. The man looked part feral, part trickster, part business. Liv appreciated how openly he wore his inconsistencies. Everyone had them. As a profiler, Liv was trained to look for what didn't fit, to both construct and obliterate the obvious narratives presented by the information in front of her.

Ten minutes passed. Twenty. Still no Mandy. The guide was now over by the door, calling in a lilting Southern accent for their group to assemble. Liv strode over to join him, forcing herself not to keep scanning the room for her sister. She'd show up. Eventually.

The guide called himself Thor, no last name. His blond mane shone under the fluorescent lights. Thor nodded to the man on his left, and the guests started introducing themselves around the circle.

Some treated the occasion like a cocktail party, while others appeared to be bracing themselves for a grueling tour of duty. For the most part, Liv ignored their words. She was a profiler, not a politician. Occupations, places of residence: All of that would be repeated ad nauseam over the days to come. But this was her only opportunity to form first impressions. To see how people presented themselves in a new situation, with new companions. Some would show up posturing, staking a claim to power unearned. Others would deflect, simper, or hide their teeth in their smiles. She watched for what people hid, listened for what they didn't say.

First to introduce themselves were a middle-aged brother and sister, Charlie and Devon. Both were in hiking gear, but they wore it differently. Devon was tall, solid and weathered, her well-used clothes aged in comfort and pleasure, whereas her brother, Charlie, was a citified bundle of nerves, his brand-new outfit tacked like an itchy costume to his frame. Next to them was PK, another urbanite, a pretty man in his late twenties with a sleek faux-hawk, his pursed lips suggesting a barely contained intolerance for the rustic lodge, the other guests, or the entire prospect of the trip. Dr. Fiona Moon, an exquisite, angular blonde from Los Angeles, made sure to emphasize the "doctor" in front of her name. Liv was just starting to wonder why such slick city people had come to the Grand Canyon when she looked down at her own ill-fitting Romanian slacks. She was a creature of civilization as much as they were.

The last three guests were from other countries. Across from her, a bearded beanpole named Stefan effused about his first time in the great American West, betraying a hint of a Dutch accent. And finally, there was Imogen, a redheaded teenager from Quebec making duck faces at her phone, and her grandmother, Lucinda. The older, birdlike woman watched over Imogen with a mix of care and derision, as if the girl were a lump of bread dough yet to rise.

"That's eight of you." Thor looked down at his clipboard. "We're missing two."

"That would be my little sister," Liv said.

"And mine," Charlie said.

"Ours," Devon amended.

The three glanced at each other, a silent meeting of the unreliable sibling club. But then Charlie explained that their sister Babette would be joining the group the next day for the official launch of the Essence Quest. Devon nodded. It had all been arranged with Thor's bosses.

Thor looked at Liv expectantly, as if she too would have a sensible explanation regarding her sister's whereabouts. But nothing about Mandy was sensible.

"She'll be here." Liv refused to lie on principle, but the truth always bent a bit around her sister. "I'm sure she's just . . . caught up." Whether Mandy was stuck in a tequila shooter contest or backstage at a rodeo was anyone's guess.

Orientation was a perfunctory affair, a flurry of signatures and stern reminders to be at the trailhead early the next morning, bags packed and ready to go. While Thor talked, Liv watched the others. There were no hugs nor cheerful reunions, but some of these people recognized each other. There were subtle nods around the circle, one or two of which were curt enough to suggest past run-ins may not have been entirely positive. Had they traveled together before? Liv wanted to ask what exactly an Essence Quest entailed, but Thor kept rattling through his spiel, telling them any questions unrelated to the next morning's departure would be best answered once they reached the river.

"Four thirty a.m. Or we're leaving without you." Thor directed his final words at Liv.

She resisted the urge to tell him he was wasting his breath suggesting that she had any control, let alone influence, over her sister's movements.

"She'll be here," Liv repeated.

It took a slow lap around the dining room and a disappointingly dry snickerdoodle for Liv to quash the desire to call out an APB on her sister. She was wiping the last of the crumbs into a trash can when she felt something brush her hip.

"Hey, foxy. Miss me?"

Mandy dumped her overflowing backpack on the floor and opened her arms for a hug. Liv stared at the impossibility of her sister, the inevitability of this moment. Her disappointment fizzled into something stickier and more complicated. Mandy looked frenzied and bright, like a handful of Skittles exploded into human form. Her dark curls cascaded over her red leather jacket. Behind her, a young man in a polo shirt hovered with a tray and two frosted glasses filled to the brim.

Liv swallowed her frustration and stepped into her sister's embrace.

The man thrust the tray toward them. "Congratulations, ladies. These are on the house."

"What?" Liv was confused. "You don't have to—"

Mandy squeezed her shoulder once, hard, and beamed back at the man, waggling her left hand in the air. Something sparkled in the artificial light. "Thank you so much. She just asked me this morning, can you believe it?"

"You couldn't have picked a more magical place on the planet," the young man said. He glanced down at the ring, a spray of pimples across his forehead flashing pink. "And, uh, I support you."

Mandy had the courtesy to wait until he left before she dissolved into giggles.

Liv rubbed her temple. "Incest? That's messy even for you."

"Just trying to get into the vacation spirit." Mandy popped the ring off her finger and handed it to Liv. It wasn't even a good fake. Cheap, dinged up, a back-of-the-flea-market find. The band had already started turning her sister's finger green.

"It's great for getting men to leave you alone. Or for scoring free drinks with a cutie. A twofer." Mandy slid the ring back on and handed Liv a glass, raising hers to clink.

"To forever."

"Forever." The lager was crisp and bright, and Liv tried to ignore that a lie had delivered it. Her sister wasn't going to change. No matter how many times Liv asked her, challenged her, or argued with her about the truth, it just wasn't in her nature. When Liv had been trained in polygraph analysis, she'd learned dozens of ways jokers try to beat the test. Deodorant on the fingertips. Thumbtack in the shoe. Mandy used the only technique that actually worked: She lied constantly. She had a full-time, twenty-four seven commitment to making shit up. No lie too small. No story too implausible. She got it from their father. As much as Liv rationalized it, as much as she tried to accept her sister for who she was, Mandy's lies still made her flinch.

She took another long pull of her beer, letting it wash away her discomfort. She could do this. Every year, their trip started bumpy. Every year, they had to relearn how to live together. It always worked out. Mostly.

"You missed orientation," Liv said.

"You can brief me," Mandy said. "You're good at that."

Liv pointed out Charlie and Devon, the middle-aged siblings, who were deep in an argument by the bar. Imogen and Lucinda were trying on hats and rafting gloves in the gift shop. PK and Fiona were nowhere to be seen. She clocked the last of their group near the door, where Thor was still chatting with Stefan, the bearded Dutchman.

Mandy gave an appreciative nod. “Single?”

“I didn’t think to ask about their relationship status.”

“Dibs on blond Tarzan,” Mandy said. “You can have the professor.”

“Thor’s a guide,” Liv said. “There are probably rules against them hooking up with guests.”

Mandy grinned. “I look forward to bending them.”

Liv forced a smile onto her face and told herself not to grimace. She could do this. They could do this. One week of sister time, a chance to shake off the cobwebs from Bucharest, and then Liv would head south to her future helping take down illegal smuggling operations.

She ran a finger over Mandy’s ring, letting its sharp edges poke into her skin.

“Maybe you should take that off before you meet everyone in the morning. Wouldn’t want Thor to get the wrong idea.”

“Some guys are into it.” Mandy drained her glass and pocketed the ring. “If you won’t be my fiancée . . . how about circus performers?”

“I’m not flexible enough for that.”

“Cattle ropers?”

Liv glanced over at Thor and Stefan. “They might ask for a demonstration.”

“How about you be the stick-in-the-mud foreign service officer, and I’ll be the jet-setting woman of mystery you’ve been pursuing?”

“I don’t think I’ve ever met a jet-setting high school art teacher.”

“I’m one of a kind.”

That she was. Mandy’s brown eyes were wide, radiating warmth. She was all curves and curls, sugar and sweat. Liv could feel herself getting sucked in. She could sense other people in the cavernous room turning toward Mandy, magnetized without even knowing it.

“So in this scenario,” Liv said, “I’ve chased you to the edge of the Grand Canyon and intend to extract your secrets as we float down the river?”

"That's right." Mandy's eyes were shining now. "Until the night of the full moon, when I escape from our campsite and vanish up a side canyon without a trace."

Liv hooked her arm through her sister's. "Yes."

"Yes to you tying me to a cactus and letting scorpions crawl all over my body until I reveal my nefarious plan?"

"Yes, I missed you."

She always did.

CHAPTER FOUR

MANDY WOKE UP BEFORE her alarm. The world outside their motel room was pitch-black, her older sister still twisted up in the sheets. Liv went hard on everything, even sleep. For the past few years, Liv's sister trips had all happened in cities where she was deployed. While it was fun to haggle at kebab stands and hit underground nightclubs with Liv's embassy friends, sometimes Mandy felt like she was just another efficiency slotted into her sister's packed schedule.

Which was one of the reasons Mandy had said yes when Babette Botanique had surprised her with two spots on the exclusive prelaunch Essence Quest for their newest product, CareFree. The email from the skin care CEO's assistant said it was in appreciation for her contributions to CareFree, which, as far as Mandy knew, were minor. But she wasn't about to question a free vacation and there was no need to tell Liv what she'd done to earn it. This rafting trip was perfect for her and her sister. There was no cell service in the Grand Canyon, no downtime when Liv could squeeze in a work call on a secure line. There wouldn't even be tents unless the weather looked like rain. They'd spend all day together floating down the Colorado River and hiking up side canyons, all night sleeping out in the desert under the blanket of stars. There were a few things Mandy hoped they'd talk about. But mostly she was excited for the in-between moments, the times that Liv might otherwise turn to her phone, to her ever-urgent emails about Class 2 security threats. Here, she'd have her sister all to herself.

She resisted the urge to jump on Liv's bed and start the bonding right then and there. But her sister was a nightmare before coffee, and Liv had told her the guide, Thor, would have some brewed at the trailhead by four a.m. So Mandy made herself useful. She slipped into her hiking clothes, hauled up her backpack, and grabbed her sister's duffel bags. It was a short walk to the trailhead, and she always felt strong in the morning.

When she reached the trailhead, no one acknowledged her sherpa skills. The glow of her headlamp illuminated a shuffling mess of people. A redheaded teenager in spotless white workout gear with a selfie stick was weaving through the throng, talking rapidly at her outstretched phone, practically vibrating as she navigated the groggy adults and their bags.

"Hey, early birds! I can't tell you where I am, but I'm giving you a teensy peek before I go off the grid for the next week. Seven days without you! I'll have my nana with me. Nana, wave to everyone!" A tiny woman in worn hiking clothes flashed a hand at the phone shoved in her face before the girl moved on. "Seven days in a secret location. A total internet black hole, and everyone here is really"—the teenager glanced over, and Mandy smiled at her—"*old*. So old. Total nightmare, but one thing makes it worth it. I'm getting paid to be here! Just kidding. I mean, I am getting paid, but there's something else special about this trip . . . You'll see. I'll film everything, and you'll get the unvarnished, pure Imogen report when I'm back. Byeeeee!"

She clicked off her phone recording, dropped her grin, and shot a glare at Thor. At his feet, specifically. The guide was standing over a mountain of bags, somehow looking even cuter at four a.m. than he had in the lodge the night before.

"Excuse me, guide man? We have a problem." The teenager kicked a pile of banged-up yellow rubber bags. "I can't shoot with these."

"Look, miss—"

"Imogen," she said.

"Imogen." Thor attempted a placating smile. "These dry bags are the best in the business."

"Not in *my* business." Imogen turned and shouted into the darkness. "PK!"

A man in his twenties jogged over, sporting his own pristine athleisure wear and a surprisingly well-coiffed faux-hawk for a predawn hike.

"I can't work with these," Imogen said, pointing to the bags.

"Ugh," PK said. "They are . . . unfortunate."

"Gingers don't do yellow," Imogen said. "It is *not* on my mood board."

"I get it." PK turned to Thor and assumed a saccharine, fake-friendly tone. "What my dear Imogen is trying to say is that we'd prefer to use our own branded luggage covers on the river. I explained this when we booked this trip. Your bosses were fine with it."

"These?" Thor plucked a thin white duffel bag from an untouched stack on the ground. The duffel had a silver curling *B* painted on one side. "Might as well be tissue paper."

"That would be raw alpaca silk," PK said.

"I don't care if they're made of unicorn snot. These bags wouldn't keep toast dry in the desert. No way they're going to keep your gear safe."

"Safety doesn't boost view counts," Imogen shot back. "I have a story to tell. An image to project. And your bags tell a very depressing tale."

"Here I was thinking you might prefer a story where y'all don't end up whimpering like drowned river rats."

Imogen was silent for a moment, her eyes clicking from Thor to PK to the bags as if she was doing advanced calculus in her head.

"Fix this," she hissed at PK. "It's not just me and my followers. You know she's going to hate it, too. Oh, and next time?" She picked up a white cardboard box and dumped it in PK's hands. "Tell your boss I'm not her errand girl. Somehow this got sent to my room instead of hers."

His boss. Mandy suddenly realized who PK and Imogen were. The man was PK Raghuram, personal assistant to the one and only Babette

Sauvage, CEO of the Babette Botanique wellness empire. PK was the one who'd sent her all the emails leading up to the trip, but despite their communication about Mandy's plus-one and his recommended backcountry skin care regimen, they'd never met. The man was busy. CareFree would be Babette's biggest launch in three years, and in addition to supporting Babette herself, PK ran her company's social media ambassador program. Mandy had seen his posts about a global search for a fresh-faced influencer to represent an exciting new product line in the Babette portfolio. Imogen must have been the lucky winner. And apparently she already had demands.

Imogen whipped out her phone and stalked off, pointing her camera far from the offending yellow rubber and chattering away to whichever of her followers couldn't wait to unravel the mystery of where she was headed at four in the morning. Mandy had no clue how much one influencer's color palette could sway the decisions of a multinational company like Babette Botanique. But Imogen was right about one thing: Babette was fixated on brand. She'd built the company, and she'd built the obsessive fandom around it. Of which Mandy was a card-carrying member.

She leaned forward as PK lifted one flap of the cardboard box Imogen had dumped into his hands. More white fabric, like the bags. Mandy hoped she hadn't missed something in the packing list about a monochromatic dress code.

PK snapped the box shut and turned back to Thor with a decisive nod. "Make the bags work."

"I can't. And you're not going to be happy when your sculpting gel goes down the river."

The faux-hawked man regarded Thor, whose blond mane was more tangled knot than hair. "It's clear we have different priorities."

"We both want y'all to have a great trip."

"I will have a great trip if my boss has a great trip," PK said. "And she's going to want to see these bags on those boats."

"Excuse me." Mandy tried not to let too much excitement sneak into her voice. "Your boss. Is she here?"

"Babette?" A smile teased PK's lips. He was handsome, but in a petulant, pretty-boy way, the kind of man who was used to everyone falling a little bit in love with him. "Darling, of course. It's her big launch."

The prospect of meeting Babette jolted Mandy like a triple shot of espresso. She reached up to fix her messy ponytail. "Where is she?"

"There's a grand entrance planned later," PK said. "A surprise. I promise it will be worth the wait."

But Mandy never waited for someone else to start the fun. She leaned in and dropped her voice to a whisper. "Maybe you could give me a sneak peek."

"Of what?"

"Whatever's in there." She pointed at the box in PK's hands. "Is it the new line?"

"Top secret." He took one more glance inside the box, then sealed it, locking the flap in place.

"Please?"

"When Babette arrives. If I show you before then, I might have to kill you."

"Hmpf." She patted his arm. "You can trust me. And my sister. She'll be here soon. She's an intelligence officer for the State Department. We can help you keep Babette's secrets safe."

PK's smile faltered, and she wondered if she'd pushed too far. But then he winked. "We appreciate your support. But Babette manages her secrets just fine on her own. Keep an eye on the sky."

The sky. It was still dark, but softer now, more charcoal than ink. Mandy dropped their bags on the tarp and took a slow lap around the trailhead, pondering how best to tell Liv about the benefactor of their river trip. Should she wait until after Babette's grand appearance, or break the news sooner? She wasn't going to be able to downplay it—not with Imogen shooting predawn B-roll at the water station and PK handing out Babette-branded chakra-stimulating wristbands to the other guests. What she needed was a stopgap. A half lie. It wasn't so much an issue that a prestigious wellness brand had paid their way to the Grand Canyon. It was *why* that was the problem.

She was still considering her options when Imogen waved her over. Given what Mandy knew about CareFree, Babette's new product line, the girl wasn't an obvious choice as a spokesmodel. She'd imagined someone as wild and untamed as the canyon itself—a big-wave surfer or a rock climber—a symbol of carefree living in an uptight world. But Imogen was practically vibrating with nervous energy. Her skin was milky pale, with only a smattering of freckles to suggest she was a natural redhead. She reminded Mandy of some of her best students in the art studio: twitchy, obsessive, completely focused on their work.

The teenager was standing by a pack of mules roped together in a shuffling line, her gaze grazing across their bristly ears, the dusty leather saddlebags on their backs. A few feet behind the animals, Thor was giving instructions to another man in an identical Wild Adventures tank top.

"Which one is sexiest?" Imogen asked, her voice deadly serious.

"What?"

"Which one?"

Thor was lean and rangy—that desert wildcat vibe—with warm brown eyes and a wave of blond hair spilling over his shoulders. The other man was barrel-shaped, bald, with a chest that seemed ready to tear his tank in two.

"Um, I don't . . ."

"The mules," Imogen clarified. "Which mule do you think is most attractive? I want to shoot one of them carrying our supplies down to the river. I have to bank footage for when we get back to civilization, and charismatic mammals kill it in the Hitch algorithm."

"Oh. The mules." Mandy hoped she wasn't blushing.

She scanned the animals, then pointed. "This one." Mandy grabbed a handful of dry grass and offered it to the long-lashed beast. It had a shock of hair sticking straight up between its ears.

"Careful," said Thor. "Sal likes to spit."

Imogen took a big step back. "Are there any mules that don't?"

"You'll have to consult Marc on that," Thor said, slapping the bigger man on the back. "He's the transport guy on this crew. I got called up to raft guide, which means my mule-wrangling days are over. Marc's head of the herd now."

Imogen grabbed Marc's massive forearm and steered him down the line with her, analyzing the assets of each animal.

"Congrats," Mandy said to Thor. "Mule man to raft captain sounds like quite the promotion."

"I'll be president before you know it." He grinned. "You ready for the rapids?"

"I was born ready. Not that I've ever done it before."

"Open to adventure. Sweet. We could use a little more of that in this group." Over by the pile of bags, a middle-aged man was bent over a white duffel with PK, both of them trying to muscle it shut. "That one, Charlie Sauvage, the CFO, I think? He told me he'd pay an extra grand if I could guarantee we'd get through every rapid without him taking a dip in the river."

Charlie wrestled the duffel out of PK's hands, shoved his foot inside, tried to zip it, got stuck, then toppled over.

"I may be easy, but I ain't cheap," Thor whispered. "I'm holding out for a better offer to dunk him."

Was Thor flirting with her? At four in the morning?

"I just want to know if there are any troublemakers on the trip," Mandy said. "Don't want anyone cutting in on sister time."

"You never know what surprises are in store," Thor said. "Once there was a trio of accordionists who insisted on serenading us every night. It was cool at first, then it was torture, and then it kind of became cool again."

Mandy shot a look at the bags piled high. She prayed there were no polka instruments inside.

"There's plenty of trouble down in the canyon," Thor said. "But mostly not the human kind. The risks here are extreme weather, falling rocks, folks not respecting the power of the natural world. Considering how many millions of people come here, there's almost no serious crime."

"So if we were to rummage through these bags later and someone's accordion went missing . . ."

Thor winked. "We're in the clear."

He looked east, toward the suggestion of sun peeking over the North Rim. "Life on the river is simple. But not smooth. There's always guests who make things challenging. Someone's entitled kid who doesn't want to be here. A couple on their way to breaking up." Thor smiled. "A garden-variety blowhard or two."

"That makes you . . . happy?"

"The pay is lousy and the hours are worse. But big waves make the river worth running." He reached out and scratched Sal behind her ears. "People become their most essential selves on a rafting trip. It's animalistic, you know? Getting to the heart of who we really are. In the canyon, there's no hiding. No lying about how you feel or what you're up for. Law of the wild. It's all real."

Thor looked hungry for it, eager. But his words sent a chill through Mandy. Real was for confession, not vacation, and ever since their mom had died fifteen years ago, she and Liv had kept things on the surface. It wasn't as if that day fundamentally changed their relationship—they'd been on different paths since childhood. But before their mom died, they'd banged against each other, affection and frustration crackling in the same hot pan. After, it was as if they'd discovered that love was breakable. And what broke that day stayed broken. She and Liv started drifting, gliding by each other instead of bouncing off, two satellites on different orbits, avoiding collision at all costs. There were no more shouting matches, but also no more bone-cracking hugs. No more late nights arguing and laughing and shaking instant mashed potatoes into their mouths (okay, maybe only Mandy had done that).

Mandy looked over the rim into the dark fissure below. Fifteen years. No matter how many trips they took, how many rickety bridges they crossed, they'd never ventured back into that canyon of grief together. Was there a river of pain at its bottom? Of love? It had always felt too risky to find out.

CHAPTER FIVE

JET LAG ALWAYS HIT Liv hardest the second day after an international flight. She woke up groggy, and by the time she reached the trailhead, everyone but Mandy and Thor had hiked out, taking the good granola bars with them. At least her sister had gotten her coffee. Liv clutched the hot thermos like a security blanket, letting the caffeine drive her shuffling feet down the Bright Angel Trail.

At first, Liv fixated on every pebble in the path. She'd read the statistics: They were more likely to die walking in the canyon than rafting down the river. And these ten miles formed the steepest, longest hike of their trip. Mandy kept pointing at the looming cliffs and sighing deeply, as if she wanted to inhale the dizzying orange and red towers. But when Liv looked up, all she could see were the dark vertical cracks running down the spires, wide enough to swallow a person whole.

It was so early that even the birds were quiet, though Mandy did break the silence every twenty minutes to proclaim she'd seen a bald eagle, which turned out, every time, to be a rock. Liv focused on the people down the trail ahead of them. Their group formed a spindly line of singles and pairs, occasionally intersecting to share a word. Again, Liv got the feeling there was some connection among the seven other guests that she hadn't yet pinpointed. They were from different places—Charlie, Devon, and PK from Vegas, Fiona from LA, Stefan from Amsterdam, and Imogen and her grandmother Lucinda from Montreal. Plus

Liv, who lived out of her suitcase, and Mandy, who'd been in Austin since college. And Charlie and Devon's missing sister. Liv wondered if she'd made it to the hike.

"Meet anyone interesting at the trailhead this morning?" Liv asked.

"A mule tried to inhale my hair scrunchie. And that guide Thor, the hot one? Turns out he's funny too."

Liv turned and peered into the thin light. The long-haired guide was two switchbacks above them, having stayed behind to break down the coffee setup before hiking to the river. He was taking his time, ambling along in minimalist leather sandals that seemed better suited to a Greek island than a treacherous canyon trail.

"Looks like a goatherd to me," Liv said.

Mandy grinned. "I like a little yodel now and then."

"I don't know, Mand. Pretty sure he's ex-military." Liv could see it in the way he cinched down his pack. "I'd guess Afghanistan. He got discharged, came out here to lose himself in nature, go commando, and forget. I'd steer clear."

Mandy let out an exasperated sigh. "Can you not?"

"Not what?"

"Not do the whole profiler thing."

Liv didn't know what to say. She was a special investigator. It was her job. Her calling.

"I didn't mean—" Liv wavered. "He could be great. I don't know."

She did know. No ex-soldier named Thor was a high-caliber draft pick.

"Whatever," Mandy said.

They fell into silent trudging until they hit a small oasis halfway down. After five miles of bare rock and sky, here was a green breath of trees, a trickling creek, and simple wooden benches that called to Liv's aching back.

"I have to take a break," Liv said.

Mandy smiled at her indulgently. No huff, no sweat—as if this were just a morning stroll to the coffee shop. Liv didn't get it. She hit the embassy gym three times a week, and she still couldn't keep up with her little sister. Maybe the difference between thirty-one and thirty-four was bigger than she'd thought.

"Do you want me to take your pack?" Mandy asked.

"No!" It came out sharper than Liv intended. "I just need some water."

Tired hikers were dotted around the rest area, squeezed into pockets of shade cast by a ribbon of cottonwood trees. Fiona, the doctor from LA, executed an intricate self-misting ritual with a spray bottle. Imogen played with her phone while her grandmother Lucinda fanned herself with her giant sun hat. The family resemblance was clear: Both women were wiry and birdlike, but in different ways. Imogen was a fuzzy, twitchy girl, her pale skin vibrating under a halo of long red hair. Lucinda, on the other hand, was tanned and sinewy, a wild turkey of a woman. Cute little chick. Tough old bird. Liv wondered who had mapped the milestones of human female development to an avian set of axes. Some man, she figured.

The two Canadian women weren't the only ones with a connection. Between the individual pantomimes of self-care, Liv watched the other guests steal glances at each other. No one approached. No one talked. But they were all looking. Waiting. For what, Liv couldn't guess.

"Mandy?" Liv tried to keep her voice as casual as possible. "I don't think you ever told me exactly how you got us on this trip."

Mandy didn't look up from the raven's feather she was braiding into her hair. "Pretty sure I did."

"Remind me."

"Well . . . maybe you noticed some folks have wristbands with a *B* on them."

"Uh-huh."

"The *B*'s for Babette."

"Who's Babette?"

"You really do live under a rock, don't you?"

"If by rock you mean a series of foreign government installations of critical importance to our nation's geopolitical standing—"

"Babette Botanique is a natural skin care line. It's named after a woman. An amazing woman. Babette Sauvage."

Mandy pronounced the name proudly, as if simply saying it was a kind of triumph.

Every time Liv came back stateside, there was a new craze that took her by surprise. One year it was pickleball. Another time it was boba tea. Now, apparently, it was a skin care company that offered river trips on the side.

But that didn't make sense. "Why is this amazing Babette in the business of subsidizing us to come to the Grand Canyon?"

Mandy paused. "It was a gift. Like the wristbands."

"A gift? Are you one of their sales reps?"

Mandy shook her head.

"Is it an MLM?"

"No. It's a wellness brand."

"And?" Liv waited, holding her judgment on a tight leash.

"Babette paid for our spots. I'm one of her followers."

"So it's a cult."

"No!"

"Remember that time Dad told us we were going on vacation in Big Bear and then that bald lady stuck us in a room with one VHS tape and a mountain of homemade fig bars?"

"It's not a cult. Why can't you just accept good things when they show up in your life?"

Because Mandy's explanation didn't hold up. Multithousand-dollar rafting trips did not just drop from the air. Or, at least, not for Liv. From an early age, Mandy had adopted their father's attitude that "if it's free, it's for me," whereas Liv tended to look way down the gullet of any gift horse that seemed too good to be true.

"So they gave us this trip, for free, for no reason?"

Mandy nodded vigorously. "I'm a Babette superfan, okay? I mean, I can't afford most of their products, but I watch all the videos and—I know you think it's stupid—but I started DMing her, and then Babette's assistant, that guy PK, sent me this email invitation, and here we are, with the inner circle!"

The story was a bold one, even for Mandy. Did she really expect Liv to believe Mandy had somehow leapt the corporate ladder from random internet fan to swapping emails with an executive? Then again, here they were, halfway down the ten-mile trail to the canyon's core. It didn't make sense, but that was true of so many of Mandy's—and their father's—schemes. Liv knew expressing her skepticism would result in nothing but a wider gulf between them. If she pressed too hard, Mandy would say she was a killjoy. Ruining the adventure. That wasn't how she wanted to start this sister trip. And she had to acknowledge that sometimes Mandy and Guy found loopholes that actually paid off.

"Okay," Liv said.

"Okay?"

"Thanks for making this happen."

Mandy let out a big breath. "I can't believe we're going to meet her!"

"Babette?"

"She's, like, a goddess."

"A lotion goddess?"

"Her story is amazing. She got her start as an activist exposing cosmetics companies that were lying about their use of animal testing and harmful chemicals. But when Babette didn't see change fast enough, she and her brother, Charlie, started their own all-natural line that took over the industry. Her whole message is about empowerment, women claiming agency to change the world."

"We're going to change the world with her products? How? By having shinier skin?"

"No. It's bigger than that." Mandy unzipped her backpack and started rooting through it. She emerged with a glossy paperback with a giant title in italicized silver letters: *Unleashed* by Babette Sauvage.

"Listen to this," Mandy said, flipping to a heavily highlighted page. "'Inside every woman lives a wild animal. Our company exists to free her.' Powerful, right?"

"You've been hiking this entire time with that brick in your backpack?"

"You wouldn't understand."

Liv didn't. Her sister was a teacher and a talented artist. Their mom had been a commercial pilot. Liv worked for the State Department. And Mandy's hero sold expensive face goop to feed women's insecurities? It didn't make sense.

But it didn't have to. This was one of the maddening beauties of sisterhood, knowing each other so well there was room even for contradictions.

"Have you laid eyes on your lotion goddess yet?" Liv asked. "Did she spritz you with magic hiking toner?"

Mandy stuck out her tongue. "PK told me she's arriving later today."

"How? Is there a service elevator you didn't tell me about?"

"You mean you didn't read appendix B in the itinerary regarding alternative modes of transportation?"

"I read the entire—" Liv said. "Oh. You're joking."

"Want a piggyback ride?"

"I'll survive."

"Of course you will," Mandy said. "Come on. Soon we'll be at the river. Then all you have to do is float."

Liv hefted her day pack, and they started moving again. The heat fell heavy in the last five miles down to the Colorado, the straps of her pack grating against her shoulders as they marched down the winding trail in silence. Or rather, Liv was silent. Every few minutes, Mandy would burst out singing, or whistle, or say something like "did you know lizards smell with their tongues?" It was like hiking with a possessed CB radio that kept turning itself on.

But Mandy said no more about how she won this trip or about the amazing Babette Sauvage. Liv kept thinking about the dog-eared book in Mandy's pack, her sister's rapacious appetite for reinvention and transformation. The big adventure. The quick fix. Maybe that was the draw to Babette, the idea that you could rub a cream into your skin and become someone else. Liv had been trained to separate surface from depth, lies from reality. She looked down the trail to the other guests tromping to the river. Did they all have a connection to Babette Sauvage? What shiny stories had they smeared across their faces, and what blemishes—what scars—might be hiding underneath?

CHAPTER SIX

THEY REACHED THE RIVER before Mandy decided how much of the real story to tell her sister. She'd always wanted to meet Babette, and the chance to spend a whole week with her was too good to pass up. But she hadn't thought it all the way through. Liv wouldn't understand what she'd done, and she'd be even angrier when she found out how long Mandy had been hiding it from her.

Mandy looked out across the Colorado, searching for an answer in the fast-flowing water. The river was more motion than object, thick and viscous, roiling with sediment, a muddy orange fist hooking through the canyon walls. Mandy removed her shoes and slipped her feet into a pocket of quiet water by the bank, letting its chill prick her awake after the tiring hike down. She took a step deeper, flirting with the lip of the current, testing its fearsome shove.

"Not too far," Liv whispered.

Mandy took another step.

The truth was, Mandy liked her sister's protectiveness. So different from her friends back in Austin, the ones who pushed her over the edge to justify their own free falls. They loved concocting cocktails and costumes, making out with strangers at black-light-and-hay-speckled music festivals. Most nights, Mandy loved that too. But sister trips were a time to reset. To strip back the paint and partying and come back to her old self. Even preparing for this trip, waking up early to jog along Lake Austin, she'd felt better.

And now here they were, and Liv's love felt as claustrophobic as ever. Mandy never could tell if Liv worried because she cared or because she didn't trust Mandy to take care of herself. Probably some of both. And so secrets piled up, covering the rough patches where trust ran ragged between them.

She'd tell Liv everything. But not until Babette gave her official welcome. Mandy was a decent storyteller, but Babette had built an empire with her words. Babette could explain everything.

The rest of the guests filtered in slowly, gazing at the river, dunking their feet, tossing off their packs, and tucking into low-lying pockets of shade offered by scraggly bushes along the shore. Every few minutes, PK took a lap around the beach, looking from his watch to the water to the sky, like a dog who had lost his owner. But if he was hoping for a sign of Babette, none was forthcoming.

Finally, there was a whoop from the river, and up came a flotilla: a thirty-five-foot-long barge, with two smaller rafts linked by rope trailing behind. The parade was both rugged and majestic, and it was suddenly obvious that this had been Babette's plan all along: to float in on an inflatable throne, held aloft in a litter by a crew of shirtless, gleaming boatmen, the freshly anointed empress of the river.

Mandy rushed to the bank to watch. There was only one person on the barge, a weathered man in a faded orange life jacket, wielding a pair of oars atop a mountain of bulging tarps. He was towing two rafts, one of which was empty. The other held a young woman with a long braid down her back, using a paddle as a rudder. Babette was nowhere to be seen.

The rafts were bright as sunflowers, blazing above the thick brown river.

"Yellow," Imogen groused. "Kill me now."

The braided woman leapt from her raft, flaked out a rope, and tossed one end to Thor on the bank. Within minutes, the guides had all three boats anchored to stakes pounded into the sand. The oarsman on the barge stood, took a running leap over the bulging tarps, and flew not toward the beach but into the heart of the river. He hit the water with a big splash and a bigger yell. A few sharp strokes later, he scrambled up on shore and shook himself like a satisfied mutt.

"Wild Adventures?" He unclipped his life jacket and took off his sunglasses, revealing a crinkled smile, scraggly beard, and a blue bandana peeking out the collar of his soaked long-sleeved shirt.

"Howdy. I'm Big Pete. Your trip leader. Welcome to the Colorado." Everyone nodded, or waved, or made the absolute minimum effort to demonstrate that they'd survived the hike down. "We'll do introductions tonight at camp. For now, there's me, head boatman. Our other guides are Katy, intrepid boatgirl"—the young woman with the braid rolled her eyes—"and you've already met Thor and Marc. Marc will head back to the rim with the mules today and meet us with the van at the end of the trip. Thor will be on the river with us." The long-haired guide looked positively itching to get on the water, his fingers spidering up the clasps of his life jacket to clip on a knife and a mesh bag stuffed with rope.

"Katy'll talk your ear off about the plants and geology around here," Big Pete continued, "and Thor's our trip medic. If you need anything, holler for any of us."

"Holler?" Liv asked. "Are we piloting the rafts ourselves?"

"Not a chance." Big Pete grinned. "There will be a guide in each raft telling you what to do. Plus one on the supply boat—the big boy we call the chub—with all the gear. Mostly we'll just float along. But we're starting with a bang. These next rapids, a couple miles downriver from here, they're two of the biggest whippers we'll see on the trip. Get ready to hold on."

Liv's hand shot into the air. "Will there be a tutorial?"

"Wear your PFD—your life jacket. Never take it off when you're on the water, no matter how calm it seems. Follow the instructions your guide gives you. When they say paddle forward, paddle forward. When they say stop, stop. Rafting's easy. Until it's not."

Mandy grabbed her sister's hand to keep her from raising it again.

"I know you've had a long hike down," Pete continued. "And there's more work ahead. I promise we'll take good care of you. But more importantly, you ten will take care of each other."

He gave them what Mandy imagined was his best football-coach-before-the-big-game face. Then he frowned.

"I count nine. We missing someone?"

PK swooped in next to him. His faux-hawk was somehow refreshed despite the brutal heat.

"We're not missing someone," he said grandly. He gave a thumbs-up to Imogen. Then PK dropped to one knee on the rocky beach and aimed his phone in her direction. "We're waiting for someone."

Imogen looked up at the sky reverently.

"She's coming," she said.

The girl kept gazing up into the sunshine, not blinking, waging a staring contest with the empty sky.

Liv nudged Mandy. "This is seeming more and more like a cult."

Big Pete frowned and turned to Thor. "I told you to stay with the slowest hiker."

"Dude, I did."

"Shh," PK said. "Look."

Mandy squinted. Way in the distance, a black speck was approaching them.

PK nodded at Imogen, and the young woman lifted her arms in the air, her fingers moving in soft gyrations, commanding the attention of the rest of the group.

"We are waiting . . ." Imogen was practically vibrating. "For that special feeling to arrive. That feeling when your worries just melt away. When the weight of your pack slides off your back. When you feel—" She started spinning in a slow circle in the sand. "You feel—"

"Nope." PK stood up. "Sorry. This isn't working."

"But we practiced!"

"Yeah, we did. You aren't supposed to start talking until the helicopter is above us, and then you throw the biodegradable glitter and—"

"No, I'm supposed to do the speech, then the glitter, and then the helicopter arrives, and then we all kneel down, and then she descends on a long silk rope . . ."

"Cult to the cult degree," Liv whispered.

Imogen's grandmother pulled a pair of binoculars from her pack. "That helicopter doesn't seem to be moving toward us."

"Maybe they're going to swing around," Imogen said. "So we can get better light for the video."

Mandy stared up. It looked to her like the black speck—which sported a white nose and a yellow stripe—was shooting up the far side of the canyon.

"That's not a commercial flight," Katy said. "That's 368, the Park Service search and rescue helicopter. There was a radio call for a hiker off the North Rim with a broken leg an hour ago."

"But . . ." PK looked at his phone. "She should be here."

"When?" Imogen asked.

"Two hours ago."

"Did she text you?"

"No." PK looked around anxiously at the others. "Did anyone hear from her?"

Around the circle, people made a show of taking out their phones, as if they hadn't been told dozens of times that there would be no reception once they got down into the Grand Canyon. One by one, they shook their heads.

"She ditched us?" Imogen asked.

"She wouldn't," PK said. "Something must be wrong. We have to hike back up."

"I'm sure she is on her way," Stefan said. "We have all put a lot of energy into being here."

"She isn't coming." Fiona, the blond doctor from Los Angeles, spoke in a clipped, definitive voice.

"We didn't know *you* were coming," Devon muttered.

"You think I wanted to be here? With you?" Fiona shot back. "Babette called me two weeks ago and begged me to join. I postponed a trip to Seoul, slept in that moth-ridden lodge on synthetic sheets, got up at four in the morning to hike down to meet up with her. All of us made sacrifices to be here. Now we're a mile underground and Babette is . . . where exactly? A conference room? A luxury spa?"

"No," PK said. He looked like a frustrated child about to cry. "She planned to be here."

"This whole trip was her vision," Charlie said.

"Precisely," Fiona said. "You know how relentlessly she pursues her visions. Remember the Raw Essence Quest, when she hired crews to break into our kitchens in the middle of the workday and replace all our cooked food with fresh-pressed turnip juice? Or when she made her assistant hike Half Dome with a fractured humerus during Fierce?"

Stefan frowned. "I thought this was a corporate bonding exercise."

"It is," PK said. "I can't speak for earlier Essence Quests."

"Of course you can't," Fiona said. "You were hired after Fierce, because your predecessor broke his arm in Yosemite, and when it healed improperly, she fired him for having poor alignment."

"That can't be real," Mandy whispered to Liv.

"Not in the autobiography?" Liv whispered back.

"That was a long time ago," Charlie said.

"People like Babette don't change," Fiona said. "She's ruthless. And thorough. She hurts people who get in her way."

"What's your point?" Devon asked Fiona.

"You know your sister." Fiona's eyes were dark. "She isn't late, or lost. My guess is she marooned us down here intentionally, without internet or phones."

"Why would she do that?" Imogen asked.

"CareFree is all about letting go of your worries," Mandy improvised. "Maybe Babette wanted to give us a scare. A before to make the after even sweeter."

"Whatever game she's playing, I'm not interested." Fiona glared at Charlie and Devon. "Babette operates like Vegas. The house always wins."

CHAPTER SEVEN

LIV EYED THE SCUFFED yellow rafts, wondering if they'd ever board them. Once again, her sister's plan had come with a messily knotted string attached. It seemed that the potential for this sister trip to move forward rested on the question of whether Babette Sauvage's absence was intentional or accidental, benign or malignant.

No one seemed to have access to relevant data that might help answer this question, and Liv was still getting a handle on how the others were all connected. Over a simple lunch of sandwiches and watermelon—deliciously cold in the mounting heat—they did what all people do in the face of insufficient information: leapt to conclusions that served their diverging self-interests.

"If Babette's not coming, I'm out," Fiona said. She turned to Marc, who was mid-conversation with Lucinda, and snapped her fingers. "Mule man. Take me to the top with you."

"Me too," Imogen said. "Even if he smells like the back of a barn."

"Imogen!" Lucinda scolded. She turned to Marc. "You smell just fine, dear. But we're not going back up with you. We're here to raft the canyon."

"No, Nana, you're here to raft the canyon," Imogen said. "I'm here to produce video content for a wellness guru who forgot to show up to her own party."

"I doubt she would forget," Stefan said. "Ever since my firm made our investment, Babette has been talking about this so-called Essence Quest. She insisted it was critical to the launch of CareFree."

"He's right," PK said. "We can't do it without Babette. And she might be in real trouble."

Charlie turned to Big Pete. "What happens if we go back up to the rim?"

"This time of year, it's not safe for amateurs to hike uphill in the heat of the day. You'd have to wait until evening to get started. And however long it took you to get down to the river, expect it to take three times as long to walk back up."

Liv did the math in her head. Fifteen hours of hiking uphill. Regardless of what time they started, they'd be walking all night and then some.

Imogen groaned. "I changed my mind. Bring on the rafts."

But Charlie pressed on. "If we hike up and reconnect with my sister, can we have a raincheck? Come back down and get on the boats in three or four days?"

"No," Big Pete said.

"No?" Charlie clearly wasn't used to hearing the word.

"Your trip permit is for a launch today only. This whole season is booked."

"So if we want to go down the river . . ."

"It's now or never."

"Is there a way you can communicate with your colleagues from down here?" Devon asked.

"When we get to camp this evening, I can radio up to our headquarters and see if they know anything."

"You cannot call now?" Stefan asked.

"Sorry. No one's in the office. Everyone's out midday, launching and closing up trips."

Devon turned to Charlie. "What do you think?"

The two executives stared at each other, their eyes flashing their own secret sibling code.

"Do we get a say in this?" Fiona asked.

"What if she's hurt?" PK said.

Devon and Charlie stared at each other again, then over to Stefan, who gave a subtle nod. Liv couldn't decide which of the siblings was in charge, and where the Dutchman fit in. With their CEO missing, maybe the three of them didn't know either.

Finally, Charlie spoke up.

"We're going," he said curtly. He turned to PK. "Was there a script for her grand entrance?"

"It's on my phone. But I really think—"

"No." Charlie clenched his whole body, as if he had swallowed a volcano and was preventing it from erupting by sheer force of will. "Babette is strong. Babette is fine. I'm sure she has a very good reason for being delayed."

"But—"

"But nothing. Even if we start hiking as soon as the sun goes down, we won't get to the rim until tomorrow. We can make contact sooner if we get on the boats, paddle to camp, and use the radio like the guide said."

"It wouldn't be the first time Babette changed her plan," Devon said. "I'm sure she'll join us soon. And if she needs help, she has plenty of resources to draw on back in Vegas."

"I'm going back to the rim," Marc offered. "I can check in tonight at our office after the mules are stabled to see if she's made contact."

Charlie nodded. "If she has, you'll help her sync up with us?"

Marc looked uncertainly in Big Pete's direction.

"We can't make any promises," Big Pete said. "But yes. If your sister needs help getting down to the river, Marc can guide her. We don't have anything else on the calendar for him until he meets us with the van at Lake Mead at the end of this week."

"So that's settled," Charlie said.

"Settled?" PK coughed. "May I remind you that Babette is missing?"

"Delayed," Devon said. "We don't know what's going on. And as you said, this is her Essence Quest. She wouldn't miss it."

Stefan nodded. "Business is business. The show goes on."

"That's right." Charlie was standing beside Devon now, the two siblings fronting a unified confidence, unearned as it might be. "The best thing we can do now is kick off this trip like she would have wanted. You have the script?"

"I can do it!" Imogen volunteered.

PK took a slow look around the beach, as if Babette might be hiding behind a rock somewhere.

"I suppose the welcome should come from someone at the company," he finally said, handing his phone to Charlie.

"If I could have all of your attention," Charlie said. He pulled out a pair of glasses and peered down at PK's phone.

"My sweet unleashable darlings," Charlie read. Cringed. "Sorry. Maybe I'll just paraphrase."

"Don't," Fiona said grimly. "I want to hear exactly what she was planning to say."

CHAPTER EIGHT

CHARLIE'S VOICE ROSE ABOVE the growling river. "My sweet unleashable darlings," he read, "we are gathered for the dawn of a new era at Babette Botanique. We have been Raw. We have been Fierce."

"Those are the last two lines they launched," Mandy whispered to Liv.

"Raw?"

"Root-vegetable-derived rejuvenating serums."

Charlie shot her and Liv a silencing glare. "I have invited you here in honor of our newest, biggest endeavor yet. In three weeks, we will launch CareFree to the world. CareFree will be on the lips of every wellness influencer and in the hands of every person who wants to be liberated. But before we sell it, we have to experience it. This rafting trip is an Essence Quest. A chance to embody the essence of CareFree. Which brings us here, to the heart of the Grand Canyon, where CareFree's potential was born."

Mandy looked at the other guests circled around. PK's eyes were shining, his lips mouthing along as Charlie stumbled over Babette's script. Imogen, too, seemed fixated on Charlie's every word. But the others had more complicated expressions. Devon and Stefan both looked worried. Fiona looked annoyed. And Lucinda was staring out at the water, uninterested in Charlie's recitation.

"This Essence Quest is the final test of our new product line," Charlie said. "No more fighting. No more striving. Now we will be carefree."

If Babette were speaking these words, Mandy might have been inspired. But in Charlie's halting voice, the rallying cry sounded more like a dirge, or a threat. The dry air crackled the hair at the nape of her neck.

"That's it." Charlie looked up from the phone to PK. "Is there anything else?"

"Just this." PK stalked over to the luggage tarp, returning with the white cardboard box Imogen had dumped on him early that morning. He handed it to Charlie.

"A present from my sister," Charlie said. He placed it on the ground and edged back, as if there might be something dangerous inside.

"Want me to shoot it?" Imogen asked. "Like an unboxing?"

Charlie hesitated, then nodded. Imogen handed her phone to Mandy.

"Head-on shot," she said. "Close. Like I'm going to eat the camera."

Imogen took the box, turned, and smiled hungrily, a lopsided, incisor-flashing grin. "Babette Sauvage is full of surprises," she said. "Let's see if this one is worth her absence."

She peeled back one of the flaps and tipped the box toward the camera. Mandy squinted at the screen. The box appeared to be full of ball caps. As far as she could tell, the hats were perfectly white, with no adornment except an index card clipped to each one's brim.

Imogen dropped the smile from her face. "Plain white hats? This is giving design-free, not carefree."

"I wouldn't rush to judgment," Charlie said. He stepped forward, no longer afraid of the theoretical monster inside the box. "There are names on the notecards. They're personalized."

"They're blank."

He took out the hats, calling the names one by one. Stefan Eriksen. Imogen Duvray. Dr. Fiona Moon. Devon Sauvage.

Despite the uniformity of the caps, each person stepped forward with proprietary eagerness, as if the fact that their name was attached to a hat meant that it belonged to them and them alone. Some, like Stefan and PK, immediately secured their hats over their sweaty hair. Imogen started snapping selfies, spinning to find the best light. Lucinda and Fiona seemed underwhelmed, claiming theirs without interest, as if they'd just as soon let the hats float down the Colorado as put them on.

Mandy felt a thrill when her name was called. She clutched her hat and examined it, searching for evidence that Babette Sauvage had singled her out for something special. There was a faint medicinal smell to the brim, and something unusual about the texture of the fabric above it, an aberration in the weave of the crown that she could feel but not see.

"Do you feel that?" she whispered to Liv.

"What?"

Mandy traced a finger over the crown, trying to discern the difference.

"Again, I apologize for my sister's delay." Charlie's eyes flicked down at the last remaining hat in the box, presumably Babette's, and he seemed to lose his train of thought.

Devon deftly stepped forward and took the box from his hand. She turned to Marc, who was linking the mules together in a long rope chain. "When you make contact with our sister, will you give her this?"

The guide nodded and took the box. "I'm heading up to the rim now. I'll call Big Pete tonight from the office if she checks in."

"*When* she checks in," Charlie corrected him. The confidence in his voice had returned. Mandy was surprised how efficiently he and Devon had recast their sister's absence from disappearance to delay. The former was cause for concern; the latter, a simple administrative error.

"Most of you only know me as the company's CFO," Charlie continued, "the name on corporate tax filings. That's how Babette works. My sisters are the geniuses. I just push paper around."

"Geniuses?" Liv mouthed at Mandy.

Mandy nodded and donned her hat. When she pulled it down over her forehead, she felt a slight cooling sensation against her skin.

Imogen raised her hand. "It's, like, tingling me?"

"Tea tree crystals," Charlie said. "Woven into the inner band in a frozen state. As they melt, they emit a cooling sensation that harmonizes with your alpha waves."

"Is this part of the CareFree line?" Imogen asked.

Devon stepped forward. "No. You'll experience that later."

"This is just a token of our appreciation," Charlie said. "If you find the effect wearing off, dunk your hat in the river, and the crystals will freeze again."

"Don't dunk it," PK said to Imogen. "This river's disgusting. That hat has to stay white for your footage."

Lucinda scoffed. "Nothing stays white in a place like this."

When Mandy removed her cap, she could already see where whorls of dust from her fingertips had singed the rim red.

"Please," Charlie said. "The point of this trip is to celebrate our CareFree line. We want you to enjoy the river. To be your fullest, brightest self. To—"

"What is that?" PK blurted out. He was staring at Liv.

"Um." Liv's face was streaked with white goo. "Sunscreen?"

"Let me see it." PK plucked the cheap orange bottle from her hand and squinted at the back. "Avobenzone. Cinoxate. Octocrylene."

He dropped the offensive bottle by Charlie's feet, as if it were radioactive. Charlie, too, was frowning. "My dear. Shall we sign you up for chemotherapy right now? PK, can you get the—"

"On it."

The young man dug into one of his bottomless duffels and emerged with a sleek matte-white tube adorned with a silver *B*.

"Here. This will protect your skin. Without any of those carcinogenic chemicals."

"What's in it?"

"Don't worry," Charlie said. "It's all natural."

"And this one will resaturate those stress lines on your forehead," PK said, offering Liv a small vial and eyedropper.

"I'm good, thanks."

PK pressed the vial into her hand. "You say that now, but you won't be forty forever."

"I'm thirty-four," Liv said.

"You could use a little—" Mandy said.

"This isn't necessary," Liv said.

"You're right," Charlie said. "None of this is necessary. You're here to enjoy yourselves, to bask in the bounty of the great outdoors. And we're here to ensure you have everything you need to have a wonderful, nourishing, carefree trip. To our Babette family, thank you." He awkwardly slung an arm around PK's shoulders. The younger man flinched but didn't move away.

"To our new friends"—Charlie nodded in the direction of Mandy, Liv, Imogen, and Lucinda—"welcome. Allow me to introduce our team. Many of you already know PK Raghuram, my sister's loyal assistant. I know PK wants to do anything and everything to help you have a wonderful Essence Quest."

PK wriggled out of Charlie's grasp. "Babette has personally selected products from our new CareFree line for each of you to have you looking and feeling your best on the river."

"Best is a very high bar," Imogen said.

"I'm sure we'll exceed it. Say hello to Imogen Duvray, here with her grandmother, Lucinda." Charlie tripped over the names but nodded genially at the teenage girl. "Imogen is our new brand ambassador on the Pitch—"

"Hitch—" PK hissed.

"Hitch social media platform. She'll be capturing footage along the trip. You won't notice her, I promise."

Mandy raised an eyebrow. No flaming redhead who'd dedicated themselves to streaming their life one eight-second clip at a time was signing up not to be noticed.

"My sister Devon is also here," Charlie continued. "The brains behind our little family company. She'd prefer if I didn't introduce her, but we dragged her out of the lab for this expedition, so she might as well give you a wave. Dev?"

The tall, severe woman nodded slightly. While Charlie's eyes darted around the group, Devon's gaze was sharp and focused. Like a judge assessing everyone from on high. Her salt-and-pepper pixie cut was swallowed under the white ball cap, casting a shadow over her sun-beaten face.

"Devon discovered the secret to CareFree right here, in the Grand Canyon. A secret we are honored to share with you this week. And soon, with the rest of the world."

Charlie scanned the rest of the group. "And this is Dr. Fiona Moon." His voice went leaden, as if he were reluctant to expend any energy on the blond woman. "She made several contributions to CareFree's development."

Fiona stared stonily back at Charlie, offering only the briefest suggestion of a nod. But she made no further mention of wanting to hike back up to the rim with Marc and the mules.

"Finally, welcome for the first time to Mandy Chisholm, one of the earliest supporters of CareFree, here with her sister, Olivia"—Mandy smiled and held her breath, praying he wouldn't say more—"and Stefan Eriksen, our valued partner on this new line."

Big Pete cleared his throat. "This is all very interesting, sir—"

"Call me Charlie."

"Charlie." The lead guide's voice was laced with an exasperated authority Mandy knew intimately. Big Pete was not a river rat, but a teacher like her, facing an unruly classroom of entitled students. His crossed arms were like braided steel ropes, thick and strong. "We have to launch now. Unless you want to formally withdraw from the trip."

PK stepped forward. "Are you sure there's no way we can contact her?"

"She's just delayed," Charlie said. "This is her party. There's no way she'd miss it."

"You keep saying that. But you don't know, do you?"

Charlie stared down the younger man.

"Our sister will find a way," Devon said.

"All right," Big Pete said. "But once we push off, there's no turning back. The Colorado River isn't an interstate. It only flows in one direction, and there are just a couple places people can hike down from the rim to the Colorado, with trails a lot steeper and more treacherous than what you just did. Let's get to the boats."

PK nodded, but he didn't move. "You're sure we shouldn't wait for her a little longer?"

"Come now," Charlie said. "What's that brilliant CareFree tagline you and she have been working on all these weeks?"

"Let your worries wash away," PK mumbled.

"Exactly," Charlie said. "That's what Babette wants for us. It's what she wants for the world. Let's go out there and grab it."

CHAPTER NINE

THE COLORADO LOOKED QUIET, but Liv knew it held hidden dangers. She'd read about the speed with which the river could flip itself inside out in big rapids, swallowing boats and ill-prepared tourists like herself. While deaths on rafting trips were rare, injuries were not. They could smash into rocks. Get battered by waves. Tumble into a two-story hole of water. She cinched the bottom strap of her PFD tighter around her waist and tried to find something else to think about.

On the far side of the rafts, Charlie, PK, Devon, and Stefan were ignoring the river entirely. They were locked in intense conversation, presumably about their missing CEO. They all wore their white hats tightly fitted, brims straight, like a gang of golf caddies. They looked far from carefree.

"Your skin care cult," Liv said. "They're interesting."

"I told you, it's not a cult."

Liv grazed a finger over the brim of her crystal-lined hat.

"Fine. They gave us swag. But you heard them. It's a business."

"How well do you know these people?" Liv asked her sister.

Mandy scrunched up her forehead. "I know what jobs they do. The siblings are at the top. Babette's in charge. Charlie's the finance and operations guy. And Devon runs scientific research."

"Research?"

"All Babette skin care products are plant-derived. Devon was a botanist at Oxford before her siblings convinced her to join the family business. She goes all over the world discovering rare plants to use in their products."

"And Stefan? Charlie called him their partner. What does he do?"

"No clue. But Babette isn't about its executives. It's about transforming wild plants into healing magic." Mandy rambled on about Babette Botanique's revolutionary serums that cured everything from eczema to chronic fatigue, but Liv kept her attention on the group by the second raft. Stefan looked somber; Charlie and PK, nervous. Devon's face was flushed, her eyes dark blades as she spoke to the men. Maybe she was the one in charge now. Liv had a sudden vision of the tall scientist atop a tractor in the Amazon, clear-cutting rainforest to gain access to an endangered plant whose roots she would grind into antiaging fairy dust.

Liv didn't particularly like these people, but she was intrigued by them. They were a puzzle she felt a growing itch to solve.

"Do you think they really want her to get here?" Liv said.

"Babette?" Mandy said. "Of course. This is her launch. And look at them—they're lost without her."

Liv wasn't sure. Were they lost? Or were they jockeying for power in the absence of their dear leader?

"Charlie and Devon seemed quick to discount the idea that she might be in trouble," Liv said. "Maybe they were just trying to keep everyone calm in a tough situation. Or there's some benefit to them having a couple of days down here without her. Maybe life is easier when their glitter-bombing little sister isn't around."

Mandy flashed her an annoyed glance.

"I'm not talking about you," Liv said quickly. "I'm glad we're here. But could you imagine what it would be like if we worked together? If we had to make strategic decisions every single day? If one of us was the boss of the other?"

"Could be a blast," Mandy said.

It would be a nightmare. But Liv was smart enough not to voice that out loud. "I'm just saying, it sounds challenging. Especially with a CEO as powerful as your Babette. The more I think about it, the more it seems possible that Charlie and Devon knew she wouldn't be here. They argued about it, but every time PK brought up the prospect of going back, they found a way to shut him down."

Liv could feel her sister's eyes boring into her. Whoops. Only three hours ago she'd agreed to put away her working brain. "I'm sorry. I promised I wouldn't go all profiler on this trip."

"No. This is important. What if Babette's missing?"

"We've already established she's missing."

"But what if you're right?" Mandy said. "What if she's *missing* missing? What if Charlie and Devon engineered it, and now they're pretending everything is okay so they can get what they want?"

"Which is what?"

"No clue. Ooh!" Mandy opened her eyes wide. "What if they kidnapped her?"

"And stuffed her in a mule bag?"

"Okay, not that. But what if Charlie and Devon are hiding something, and PK can sense that, and now they're freaking out?"

They squinted over at the other raft. If Charlie and Devon were working together, they were doing a good job concealing it. It looked to Liv like a full-blown power struggle was underway, the waves of authority bouncing among Charlie, Devon, and Stefan. PK was standing to the side, tightening his PFD and watching the others closely.

"I don't think it's easy to make someone disappear," Liv said.

"Easier than you imagine," Mandy muttered. "Just ask my last boyfriend."

Liv considered the evidence: what she knew, not what her sister had invented. There was so little data available to her, and all of it was subjective. Impressions. Emotions. They were as mutable as the river. "We might as well enjoy the trip. That's what we're here for, right? And even if Babette is missing, we're headed downriver. I don't see what we can do about it."

"*We* can't do much," Mandy said, waving dismissively at herself and the other guests fumbling into their life jackets. "But you can."

"I can what?"

"Do your special investigator thing. Find out what happened and where Babette really is."

Was Mandy serious? Just a few hours ago on the hike down, she had demanded Liv put away anything that had even a whiff of her professional life. And now here she was, asking her to trot it out again.

But Mandy was looking at her with expectation, hope even. Liv liked that look.

"Why does Babette matter so much to you?" Liv asked.

Before Mandy could answer, Thor strode over.

"You ladies ready to hit the water? Give me a look-see." He reached out and tugged each of the straps on Liv's PFD. She was glad for the safety review but annoyed by his presumption, the ease with which he manipulated her body without asking.

When it was Mandy's turn, she raised her arms and gave him a ballerina spin. "How big are these rapids?"

"Horn Creek's around the corner. It's a Grand Canyon class eight. At this water level maybe even a nine."

Liv frowned. "I thought whitewater rapids were only rated one to six."

"Everywhere else, that's true. But the Grand plays by its own rules. Here, the ratings go up to ten."

"Which means?"

"Big waves. Fast water." The guide smiled and tweaked the cap on Mandy's head. "Hold on to your hat."

CHAPTER TEN

THEY MAY NOT HAVE worked for Imogen's color palette, but Mandy thought the yellow rafts looked downright cheerful. The two rafts were identical, maybe fifteen feet long, one piloted by Katy, the other by Thor, while Big Pete scrambled back to his set of oars on top of the massive supply boat, now loaded down with all their personal gear. Each raft had three squat rows of inflatable benches, or thwarts, as Thor called them, but he explained that sitting directly on them was a recipe for flying into the river. Instead, he showed them how to perch on the perimeter of the raft, riding the thick rubber tubes that formed the sidewalls, their feet jammed in under the thwarts across the middle.

According to Thor, the front was where the excitement was, so that was where Mandy staked her claim. She and Liv bookended the front bench, then Imogen and Lucinda in the middle, and Fiona on the third bench, balanced along the left outer tube. Thor perched on the very back of the raft, one sandaled foot tagging the spray, his paddle serving as a rudder behind them.

The other raft, piloted by Katy, pulled ahead of them into the quiet heart of the river. Charlie and PK were in front, followed by Devon and Stefan. There was a gap in the third row between the guests and the guide, where Babette should have been. Then again, if Babette had arrived on time, Mandy imagined she'd be commanding the helm of the other raft. *Her* raft. That was how everyone would see it. She wondered which of Babette's compatriots would be displaced from the front when she arrived. If she arrived?

Mandy wished her sister hadn't been so quick to discount her theory about Babette being kidnapped. Not that she believed it, not really, but she wanted Liv to at least acknowledge something strange was going on. Babette's absence had a shape to it, a buzzing energy that elevated the trip from standard-fare excitement to the potential for something bigger. The most likely answer—that Babette was delayed, that she'd join them later—would make it small again. Which was fine. Mandy didn't want Babette to have disappeared. But she wanted the thrill of entertaining the possibility.

But maybe the act of rafting the Grand Canyon was thrill enough. They were a small yellow dot winding through the pumping heart of the river. Their first mile was a lazy cruise in the sunshine, Thor giving a half-hearted stroke every couple of minutes to keep them pointed forward. Everyone else held their paddles like extras on a movie set. Mandy looked up from the water to the sky above them. It was impossibly huge, the canyon walls framing a pale vacancy that made it feel as if she was at the bottom of an endless glass, a vessel filled with light.

"Are we just floating for an entire week?" Imogen asked.

"Not quite." Thor smirked.

A warm breeze tickled Mandy's neck, separating each tiny hair from its neighbor. While she appreciated the free ball cap, she found herself envying Fiona's full-coverage visor, longing for Lucinda's huge straw hat and protective rafting gloves. In Austin, the heat hugged her shoulders like a heavy blanket in summer. Here, it was so dry that the sun seemed to do the opposite, stealing every ounce of moisture from her body.

"That wind you feel, it's the whitewater up ahead." Thor's voice was a smoky drawl, and Mandy craned around to hear him speak. "Horn Creek's no kiddie pool. When I say forward, everyone dig in and paddle. You girls in the front will set the pace. If I say left, people on the left side stroke forward. Same with the right. If things get really dicey, I'm going to yell for y'all to lean in. Let me show ya.

"LEAN IN!" Thor dropped and curled up in the bottom of the raft, head down, like a hedgehog braced for impact.

"When will we need that?" Liv's voice was clipped. Mandy looked across to where her sister was sitting ramrod straight, clutching her paddle tightly.

"Just if we get stuck in a hole. Or a giant wave. Flow's high this week."

"The itinerary glazed over how extreme this is," Liv muttered to Mandy. "We should have trained."

"Relax. We've got this," Mandy said.

"You have no evidence for that." They were still floating peacefully, but Liv's body was rigid, her eyes straining to see the rapid Thor told them was up around the corner.

Pete's giant supply boat pulled up in front of them and took the first position in the lineup. Then Katy's raft. Then theirs. Liv leaned all the way forward, over the front edge of the rubber lip.

"What do you see?" Mandy asked.

"Ripples," Liv said. "But that feels worse. Knowing it's out there and not knowing what it is."

Big Pete gave a whoop and took off. Katy's raft peeled around the corner next. Mandy watched the boats vanish into the unknown and licked her lips.

Finally, it was their turn.

"Forward!" Thor called.

The surface of the river started to feather white in front of them, the sound of it sliding from babble to roar.

"Forward!" Thor yelled again.

They stroked. It felt good. Mandy glanced over at her sister.

Liv's fingers were bone-white around her paddle.

"It's coming," Liv whispered.

"Yeah," Mandy said. But she wasn't scared. She was excited. She was a shaken-up bottle of champagne at midnight.

The boat dipped, and Thor's voice shot out over the roar.

"STOP!"

Mandy lifted her paddle. The momentum of their strokes slammed the boat into its first wave, blasting her with water. It was wild and delicious, colder than she'd imagined. She glanced to her side again. Liv looked sick. Or paralyzed. Mandy needed to find a distraction, something to tear her sister's terrified eyes from the lineup of waves in front of them, a devil's staircase of whitewater.

"Keep your eyes on Katy's boat," Mandy prompted. "Tell me three things you see."

"It's skirting a giant hole of water—are we going to get stuck there?"

"LEFT TWO!"

"Forget the hole. Look at the boat. What do you see?"

The water started speeding up, cresting into waves that rose and fell in place, hungry mouths slurping at the edges of the raft.

"FORWARD!"

One stroke. Another. Mandy strained to pull her paddle through the surging water. To her right, nothing but foam and fury. To her left, Liv was paddling mechanically, barely looking at the waves, her eyes locked on the raft in front of them.

"What do you see?" Mandy asked.

"I see Charlie and Devon."

"FORWARD HARD!"

Mandy dug her paddle in. It felt like the river was tearing her arms from their sockets. She was slipping, and the waves kept building, the raft diving into holes and flying up into nothingness. Sometimes her paddle slammed into a wall of water. Other strokes grabbed nothing but air.

Liv didn't seem to notice the hellscape around them. She was paddling like a possessed robot, unceasing even as a wall of water slammed the side of the raft and drenched her in an icy cascade. "I see her reaching toward him. Is she—"

The front of the boat crashed under the pounding water again, taking whatever Liv said next with it. They popped back up, and Mandy wanted to look over, but a huge wave leapt in from the right and Thor yelled "STOP" and she was holding her breath and clutching her paddle and the small raft flew into the air like a roller coaster without a track. Waves rose on both sides of them, two wild devil horns of water, and Thor was steering them into the biggest ones, driving them up surging walls of whitewater, paddle and stop, paddle and stop. Mandy was trying to keep her feet from sliding out, freezing water was pouring over the sides of the raft, and Liv was babbling about something, but they were marooned on the very brink of life and death and—

"NO!" Liv yelled.

Mandy looked left, worried she'd see empty air where her sister had been. But Liv was leaning forward, her eyes shining. The raft spun and slowed, and the water calmed abruptly, as if someone had switched off its fury.

"We did it," she said to Liv.

Her sister nodded uncertainly, as if she couldn't decide yet if she agreed. Her eyes were still trained on the water. Mandy turned to the others in their boat.

"WE DID IT!"

Lucinda and Imogen looked just as exhilarated as she felt, soaked and smiling. In the back, Fiona adjusted the brim of her visor and gave a crisp nod. At Thor's insistence, all six of them tapped their paddles together in the air in a dripping high five. They'd made it through. They'd all made it through.

And then Mandy heard it. A scream, rising from the bucking waves of Horn Creek.

CHAPTER ELEVEN

"SWIMMER!" KATY STOOD AT the back of her raft, hands cupped around her mouth. The entire right side of her boat was empty.

"TWO SWIMMERS!"

Liv saw them first. Two bodies, floundering and yelling and swirling uncontrollably through the wild heart of the river.

"We'll pick it up," Thor called out. He whipped their raft around so they were perpendicular to the flow.

"Steady, now." He held a rope in one hand, a life preserver in the other. "Left side, reach out your paddles so they can grab on if I don't catch them."

Liv counted the seconds as the bodies moved toward them. One of them, lying face up on the surface in their neon orange jacket, mostly kept their head above water. The other was little more than a muddy Babette hat that bucked and bounced through the waves.

"And . . . NOW!"

Thor knelt down and grabbed the first floater by the PFD with his bare hands. Liv's extended paddle snagged the other. Thor hauled up the first person—Devon—then Charlie, who was clutching Liv's paddle, launching each of them into the raft in a sprawling, soaking cascade.

Devon rose up blinking and gave a shout—was it angry? joyful?—into the wide open sky.

"You okay?" Mandy asked.

"Right as rain." Devon's voice was hoarse, but energy pulsed through it. "I forgot about this."

"What?"

"The way the river makes you feel alive." She took off her hat and rubbed her salt-and-pepper hair, the droplets sparkling as they fell. Then she looked down at her brother. Charlie was still sprawled across the boat, racked with coughing.

"Breathe," Thor instructed him. "You're safe now."

Liv reached down to pull Charlie's PFD away from his neck. "It's okay. We've got you."

His skin was mottled red and white, the adrenaline in his eyes making him resemble a cornered animal.

Liv leaned even closer. "Are you okay?"

He gave her a tight shake of the head.

"Did someone push you?"

"I can't . . . I don't think . . ."

He pushed himself upright and glanced around. While the world felt larger to Liv after making it through the rapid, Charlie looked shrunken. Scared. As if the canyon had trapped him.

"Think of it this way," Mandy said. "Now you don't have to wonder what it might feel like to fall in."

"That's right," Thor said. "You're not a river virgin anymore."

"*River virgin. Dunked for the very first time.*" What Mandy lacked in singing ability, she made up for in enthusiasm. "River vi-ir-ir-ir-gin—"

Charlie clamped his hands to his temples, pressing his soaked Babette hat to his head. Liv leaned toward him again.

"You're fine. It's just a shock."

"She said it'd be safe out here," he whispered. "She was lying."

Liv could barely hear Charlie over the rushing water and Mandy's singing. But she heard the emotion in his voice. It wasn't fear. It was more than that. It was terror.

She bent down close to him. "Your sister?"

"She set this up."

"Did she push you? That's what I thought I saw, but I wasn't sure . . ."

"Devon? She got knocked into me by that wave." Charlie shuddered like a wet dog. "No. It's Babette. She planned this."

The raft jolted left, and Charlie slumped down into the footwell, his face hidden by the brim of his cap. The river had ruined his hat, replacing its pristine white fabric with a smeared mottle of reds and browns. But that wasn't the only thing that had changed. In the middle of the crown, a snow-white uppercase *B* looped across the muddied fabric.

Liv reached up and touched the crown of her own hat. Just as Mandy had noted earlier, there was something raised there, a swooping layer of embroidered thread. She traced it with a finger. An italicized *B*.

Liv looked over to where her sister was playing air guitar with Thor. For all Mandy's frivolous impulses, she was observant. Mandy saw underneath things, rooting out stories she could shape from the little surprises and aberrations of life. As their dad had always said, the best lies are based in something true.

"Your hat," Liv said to Charlie.

"What?"

"It changed." She removed the cap gently from his head and turned it to face him. The bright, looping *B* burst from the dirtied crown like a shout. Like a slap.

He flinched when he saw it. "I'm telling you, she arranged for this to happen. Not showing up. Me falling in. Like Fiona said. It's all part of her plan."

"Her plan to what?"

"To get rid of me."

"Why would she want to do that?"

Charlie shook his head and shoved the cap back down over his eyes.

"I don't think Babette could have anything to do with whitewater knocking you off a raft," Liv said.

"Please. This is a woman who convinced the FDA to issue a short-term ban on Uruguayan snail slime to force a competitor into bankruptcy." Charlie tapped the *B* on his hat. "She's a pro at making things happen."

Liv shot a glance around the raft. No one else seemed to have heard Charlie's wild accusations. Devon was gazing out at the towering cliff walls, the embroidered *B* on her own cap glinting in the sunlight. Lucinda was adjusting her paddling gloves. Imogen was dabbing her face with the bottom hem of her T-shirt, while above her, Mandy and Thor were upright, straddling the middle bench and performing a rousing homage to Madonna, their paddles-turned-air-guitars spraying river water on everyone else in the raft.

"Siblings," Liv said. "They're put on this planet to test us."

Charlie didn't look convinced.

It took twenty minutes of flat water to assure Charlie that it was safe to clamber back into Katy's raft. He crossed and lowered himself onto the left side of the middle bench, his sister settling in behind him, Devon's hand pressed consolingly—or was it oppressively?—to his shoulder. He folded forward, hands on his paddle, brim of his cap pulled down, eyes cast to the river as if resigned to a gruesome fate.

Six more days. Dozens more rapids. And no way out.

Was that how Charlie felt? Back on the beach, Liv had read his reaction to Babette's absence as one of acquiescence. He had taken charge and rallied them to continue the trip. But had his earlier confidence masked a deeper fear? Was there something in Babette's absence that made Charlie think he was under threat? Each time Liv glanced over at Katy's raft, Charlie's eyes were scanning the canyon walls.

If they were being watched, there was nothing to see for the next hour but whitewater. Salt Creek. Granite. Hermit. Boucher. Liv lost track of the names of the rapids as they shot through them, each one bigger than the last. To her surprise, she found herself enjoying it. Each time a wave slammed the boat, she felt the shock of it, then delight. She leaned into her strokes, her ears now tuned to Thor's steady drawl, his insistence that they paddle harder through the turbulent water, the raft rising and falling like they were riding the knobby spine of a giant dragon. It seemed impossible that she and Mandy and the other guests, complete novices, could dig their paddles into a wall of water and yank themselves five, ten, fifteen feet into the air. But they did.

Thor navigated them over the tongue of Crystal Rapid and to the left of a hole big enough to swallow an elephant. Once they'd paddled their way through a rock garden, he spun them into an eddy on Crystal's quiet backside, and they watched as Katy's boat, bucking and falling, followed their line through. As far as Liv could tell, Charlie had locked himself in, his feet clamped under the tubes, one hand clutching a strap on the side of the raft, without pretense of paddling or otherwise contributing to the effort of his fellow rafters.

But they made it through. They all made it through.

Just as quickly as the whitewater had risen, it fell. They paddled easily through a set of small, sparkling rapids—the Gems, Thor called them—and watched the sun tickle the fluted rock on either side of the river, disappearing into sinuous side canyons. Finally, the water went quiet, tiny ripples crinkling along its surface, gossamer-thin and toothless. The only hint of the river's ferocious power was the caves littered along the base of the canyon walls, curves carved into the cliffsides by water shoving its way downstream.

The Colorado sprawled out in the sunshine like a hunt-drunk lion. Liv dropped her paddle and stretched her arms high above her, relishing the contrast between the freezing water drenching her body and the dry, hot air. According to Thor, until they got to camp, they now had nothing to do but float.

"Told you it'd be great out here," Mandy said. She lay stretched out on her back on the outer baffle of the raft, her hat flipped over her face, soaked sneakers dancing on the water. "Even if you think Babette's a cult."

"I don't just think it. Look." Liv reached down and dunked her cap in the river, waving it through the muddy water until the white thread revealed itself.

"See the *B*? The high priestess sent us a message."

Mandy grinned. "I knew there was more to the hats."

"You were right."

Mandy's smile got bigger. "Say that again."

"Don't push it."

"Maybe she isn't missing." Mandy submerged her own hat and waited for the looping white *B* to appear. "Maybe this really is all part of her plan."

"What do you mean by that?" Imogen asked from the second bench.

"I bet Babette has an even bigger surprise. The helicopter wasn't grand enough. She's coming another way."

"A flying mule?" Liv asked.

"Or a submarine. Not yellow, obviously."

It was classic Mandy. One minute, Babette was kidnapped. The next, she was in a silver submersible. Liv knew her sister was just hunting for the best story, the most colorful picture. But the paranoid fear that flashed across Charlie's face earlier was not an invention. There was something going on that didn't add up.

"You really think Babette's coming?" Lucinda asked.

"Eventually," Mandy said. "Babette loves the wilderness."

"Yeah," Imogen chimed in. "She, like, goes camping. For fun."

Liv wondered if the teenager was aware that they too would be camping, or if she expected an air-conditioned villa to be waiting for them downriver.

"Nature is her muse," Mandy said. "Devon may be the scientist, but it's all Babette's vision."

Liv looked across the river to the other raft. Katy had navigated her group into a long shadow cast by an outcropping of fluted schist. Their boat was quiet, the hole where Babette should have been sticking out like a lost tooth. Charlie looked completely shut down. Devon and PK were bickering about something. And Stefan loomed over the rest of them from the back, eyes cloaked by his cap, mouth hidden in his beard.

"Stefan Eriksen. You don't know what role he has with the company?" Liv said.

"He's a money man." The answer came from Fiona, the blonde in the back of their raft.

"Does he work for Babette?"

"The other way around. He joined the board a year ago as a lead investor."

"Is he some kind of Euro-billionaire?"

"Stefan? No. Technically, he *represents* an investor," Fiona said. "His boss is the biggest backer of CareFree."

Liv swung around to face the women on the benches behind her. She'd been so focused on the other boat, Charlie's terror, and the wild wave machine of the Colorado that she hadn't really considered the other guests sharing her and Mandy's raft: Fiona, Imogen, and Lucinda. A doctor, an influencer, and a chaperone. Their boat was definitively the B team. No Babette executives. No power players here.

"What's your connection to Babette, Fiona?" Liv asked.

Fiona's face was all angles, her skin smooth as glass, and she didn't seem to be wearing a speck of makeup, though her white-blond hair couldn't be natural. Even after the long hike, brutal rapids, and pounding sun, she sported a tight, glossy chignon under a wide pastel-blue visor. "I was an advisor on CareFree. Dr. Oz named me the foremost expert on aging gracefully."

"A gerontologist?"

"Dermatologist," Fiona corrected. "I ran focus groups for CareFree and other Babette Botanique products in development."

"In Devon's division?"

"Mm."

"What are you working with them on now?"

Fiona smiled thinly. "I'm no longer directly involved with the company. My career started in plant-based treatments, but these days, I'm focused on something more essential."

"Dirt?" Liv asked.

"The sun. The source of all vitality. I'm opening a light therapy clinic in Seoul."

Liv squinted at the doctor. Fiona's visor was blocking any and all solar energy from reaching her. "But you're here."

"Babette asked me to come."

"Is she interested in Korean light therapy?"

"I doubt it." Fiona looked uncomfortable. "I imagine it has something to do with CareFree. Babette offered to increase my stake if I could help her—with what, she wasn't specific. She said she'd explain everything when I got here. Instead . . ."

Fiona waved her hand dismissively, as if the Grand Canyon was a booby prize at the carnival.

"So you're an investor in CareFree," Liv said. "Like Stefan?"

"Not exactly. Investors come in tiers. He's a whale. I'm a guppy." Fiona held her placid smile, but Liv could feel the tension radiating underneath. "Or rather, his private equity firm is the whale. He represents big money, which gives him power as a board member. But Babette has always been the one to call the shots."

Liv nodded. "Babette's the boss."

"That's how she sees it."

"Isn't it true?"

Fiona eked out another tight, closed-lip smile. "What's with all the questions? Why are you two here, anyway?"

Liv looked to Mandy to explain. If the superfan story was indeed a lie, Liv wasn't going to repeat it. Maybe Mandy had a different explanation now. Maybe she was even ready to tell the truth about her connection to Babette, whatever it was.

"I shouldn't tell you this, but . . ." Mandy winked at Liv. "My sister's on a top secret mission."

Liv wanted to scream. Or slap her. Or both. "I'm not—"

"Don't be modest," Mandy said. "Liv is a profiler for the State Department. She's an international special investigator. Like James Bond."

"And you got assigned to this river trip?" Fiona sounded skeptical.

"To find Babette?" Imogen asked.

Mandy was smiling wide now, giving Liv an encouraging nod. Liv knew what her sister wanted. But she wouldn't. She couldn't. She was constitutionally incapable of telling bald-faced lies. Just thinking about it made her want to jump in the river.

"I'm sorry to disappoint you," Liv said. "But I'm an analyst. I don't work in the field. And I'd never heard of Babette Sauvage before this trip."

"They coach them to go in with an open mind," Mandy improvised. "Blank slate."

"Mandy, please. That's not—"

"They train them to deny everything," Mandy said.

"I've never met a secret agent before," Imogen said.

"Nor have I," Lucinda added.

"I am not a spy," Liv said.

"Bet that's what they all say," Thor stage-whispered to Lucinda.

The older woman nodded.

"Skin care is not an issue of global security," Liv said. She had a full-blown headache now. "And I have no connection with Babette. I'm just here on vacation with my sister."

Her words hit the swirling water and sank out of view. She didn't have to look to know Mandy was disappointed. No matter how far they traveled, they always seemed to find themselves at this same crossroads, where expectation met disappointment from both directions.

Salvation came from an unlikely source. Imogen piped up in a haughty tone. "Babette's lucky we're here, given she didn't have the courtesy to show."

"Imogen!" Lucinda gave her a little swat on the back.

"Nana, I run a business, too," Imogen said. "First, you made us come a day early so you could visit that stupid museum. And now we're in a total media blackout. I'm losing channel followers by the minute. If Babette doesn't arrive soon . . ."

"What's your channel called?" Mandy asked.

"PureImogeNation. On Hitch."

Her words made no discernible impression on the adults in the boat.

"Hitch? The video platform? I review beauty products?" Imogen looked beseechingly at the blank faces. When she didn't see what she wanted, her expression soured. She turned to Lucinda. "I can't believe you convinced me to drop out of the algo for a week to float down a stupid river."

"An opportunity like this will pay dividends," Lucinda said. She turned from her granddaughter to address the others. "Imogen is Babette Botanique's youngest spokesmodel ever. She hit two million followers on Hitch when she announced the partnership." Her tone was even, but there was a waver beneath it. Was Lucinda proud of her granddaughter? Embarrassed?

"How did you get so many followers?" Mandy asked.

"Part of it's because of my background. We're related to the British royals."

"Distantly," Lucinda said.

"They used to call you the laundry queen, Nana."

Lucinda waved it off. "Owning a few laundromats and having a fourth cousin in the peerage hardly constitutes a noble claim."

"It's not like I'm saying I'm a princess," Imogen said. "Just banking on my assets. But frankly, who you are matters less than what you do. To make it big, you need a thing. Something people can get only from you. Like, anyone can unbox swag or make get-ready-with-me videos, but there's something about how *you* do it that's special."

"A catchphrase?"

"Catchphrases are cheesy," Imogen said. "So are pets. We get it: You have a cute dog, or a one-eyed cat, or an albino Komodo dragon that does push-ups on your shoulder. Yawn. It has to be more than that."

"Like a secret," Liv said.

"A secret?" Imogen paused, her fingers tapping her paddle. "Interesting. But risky. No, it just has to be something special you can show hints of, even when you're not talking. And also, like, something people can identify with."

Liv tried to guess what the teenager's unique-but-relatable thing might be. Nail biting? A constellation of freckles in the shape of a Nativity scene? Maybe Imogen recorded all her videos while holding a handstand.

"Mine is radical honesty," Imogen offered.

"Excuse me?"

"Most influencers are positive about *everything*. They have these big grins and permanent jazz hands, like, 'Oh wow! I can't wait to use this juicy melon lip liner every single day!' But people know that's fake. And if they're going to actually follow your recommendations, they deserve to know if a bronzer smells like old cheese. My thing is that I tell you exactly what I think."

"Don't you lose sponsors that way?" Mandy asked.

"I worried about that at first, but it turns out some of the most critical videos I make go viral. Those brands get huge visibility, and they don't care if I tell the world their hair clip made my scalp bleed. You get enough views, and I guess some people want to get stabbed by their accessories."

"So your thing is being mean," Liv said.

"Not mean. Real. And I'm super nice to my followers. It actually came from this book Nana gave me about leadership. It said you should care personally and challenge directly. That's what I try to do."

Liv looked over at Lucinda. "You're mentoring Imogen in this work?"

"Hardly. I gave her the book to inspire her to run for Parliament one day."

Imogen shook her head. "Nana could be a killer granfluencer. One of those take-no-prisoners old ladies. But she won't do it."

"I don't care for the limelight," Lucinda said crisply. "Or the internet."

"Or CareFree?" Mandy asked.

"That remains to be seen."

Liv regarded the older woman. "If you're not interested in social media or CareFree . . ."

"Why am I here?" Lucinda said. "I have no interest in this so-called influencing, but I see Imogen's dedication to her work. Her business savvy. That, I respect. And I've always had a fondness for the desert."

With that, Lucinda took a long swig from her water bottle, adjusted her paddling gloves, and brought her binoculars up to her face.

"I get it now," Thor said. "Y'all are fans and supporters of the company. And the company leaders are in the other boat."

"All but one of them," Lucinda said.

"Until my sister finds her." Mandy winked.

Liv kept her mouth shut.

"They're the heavies," Fiona said. "We're the help. Which is why we get to enjoy the river while they concern themselves about the whereabouts of our dear leader."

"You aren't worried?" Liv asked.

Fiona wrapped her manicured hands tightly around her paddle. "I worry about a lot of things. Babette Sauvage is not one of them. She's a force of nature. When she wants to be here, she will be."

CHAPTER TWELVE

THE SUN HAD DIPPED behind the rim by the time they reached the beach where Big Pete said they'd make camp that evening. There were no tents. No bathrooms. Just a wide expanse of sand and prickly cholla, their brushlike needles glowing in the fading light.

Mandy stumbled out of the raft and looked back across the river. The canyon walls, baked brown at midday by the sun's glare, now held crystalline veins of deep red and purple. Small signs of life popped out at her: the pink, hooked spines of a barrel cactus, the white throat of a duck, a butterfly flitting serenely across the water, as if it wasn't in the raging center of a mile-deep gorge.

"Beautiful," Mandy said.

"I was going to say terrifying," Liv said.

Mandy ignored her. She was still annoyed by how Liv had shut her down earlier in the raft. It had been a brilliant opportunity for Liv to find out what had happened to Babette, and her sister hadn't entertained it, not even for a second.

Where was the CEO? Didn't Liv want to know? Mandy let her eyes drift up the side canyon behind the beach, where the sand gave way to a field of broken shale, like the aftermath of a giant's tantrum. Three thousand feet of rock towered above them. How was it possible they could run into anyone down here? They were tiny human crumbs in a pocket of the earth. The canyon could close in—just a small pinch of the earth's crust—and swallow them whole.

But that was part of what made it captivating.

"We need to talk about what happened on the boat," Liv said.

Mandy wasn't ready for a sisterly lecture. Not here in this glorious place. She could feel the buzz of the long day ripple through her—the soreness of her calves, the damp mineral scent of river water in her hair, the sun still kissing her forearms.

"Later," she said.

"Promise?"

Mandy nodded absentmindedly. She turned away from Liv's sharp voice to smile at the others, holding out a hand to help Lucinda step onto the sand.

"Thank you, dear. I can't wait to take off these wet shoes."

"I am so ready for an adaptogen spritz," Imogen said.

"A chitin mask would be killer," PK said.

"We should face scrape before applying anything," Fiona said. "The microzoa in this river can wreak havoc on your—"

Big Pete let out a long, sharp whistle. "The microzoa can wait. First, everyone helps set up camp. Two assembly lines from the supply boat up to the beach." He unfurled a blue tarp and spread it over the sand. "Gear goes here; kitchen equipment over there, to Thor. Everything must be unloaded before you grab your personal stuff."

"But it's medicinal—" PK protested.

Big Pete raised his voice. "The faster we unload, the sooner you can do your thing. Whatever that thing is."

"What if we have to use the bathroom?" Imogen asked.

"You can pee in the river," Big Pete said. "Just stay near the bank. For everything else, Katy will set up the groover." Down by the water, the young guide pulled a bucket and a battered metal box from the supply boat. "She'll put it over that knoll, behind those rocks, to give you some privacy."

"We are literally going to shit in a bucket?" Imogen asked.

"Yup," Big Pete said cheerfully. "There's chemical powder in the box you can throw on after for the smell."

"I'll hold it," the teenager responded.

"Suit yourself." Big Pete turned back to the rest of the group. "Half of you to the kitchen line, half of you to the gear line. Once all the dry bags are unloaded, you can open them up and find your luggage. Then you can pick out a campsite and get situated."

Mandy followed Thor to the top of the kitchen line. Hand over hand, she passed up two folding tables, a propane stove, and a mountain of food. There were frozen slabs of meat, sacks of rice, jugs of olive oil. Even a box full of fresh pineapples. She could feel hunger rising in her stomach, exhaustion falling on her shoulders. She'd been up and moving since three thirty that morning. Finally, she hefted a massive cast-iron Dutch oven, handed it over, and let herself collapse dramatically onto the beach.

"Can we talk now?" Liv's voice fell down on her from above.

"Shh. I'm making sand angels." Mandy opened her eyes and looked up at the endless sky. The faraway ridgeline of the South Rim nudged a violet silhouette against the blue. It felt as if they'd tapped into the main artery of the canyon, where color was born.

Liv leaned over her, blocking the view. "You're not the god of this place. You don't get to decide who we are out here."

Mandy sat up. "I was making a joke, Liv. Pumping you up. You're going to be a big special agent someday. I was just saluting that future."

"I don't need your salute."

"Don't you ever get tired of being the same person?" Mandy asked. "Isn't this the perfect place to dream? Just a little bit?"

"I don't feel the need to impress a group of strangers by pretending I'm something I'm not."

"We'll never see these people again," Mandy insisted. "Why not have a little fun?"

"Lying isn't fun. It's dangerous."

Their first night on the river, and they were already caught in the sister vortex. It always happened this way. They'd be doing something perfectly normal—or something epically amazing—and then there'd be a wobble, and the universe would dump them back into one of their old traps. There was nothing Mandy could do to catapult them out of it. There was only time, and hoping it wouldn't happen again.

But it always did.

Finally, Liv spoke. "You get our stuff. I'll find a camping spot."

"Fine."

"Fine."

At the luggage tarp, PK was holding court in a sea of Babette-branded duffels, the dinged-up yellow dry bags piled discreetly off to the side. He held a small device that looked like a cross between a light meter and a sci-fi tricorder, waving it in front of Imogen's face. The young woman tipped her chin up and closed her eyes in a pantomime of rapture, her phone held high in the air.

"For you, PureImogen, a 5.8 pH toning diffuser and an oxygenated meta-hydrology mask." PK reached into one of the duffels at his feet and came up with an assortment of white vials. "And this is for the backs of your hands. So you don't get . . . you know."

He tipped his head in the direction of Imogen's grandmother.

"Wrinkles aren't contagious," Lucinda sniffed. "Or dangerous. They're a sign of wisdom."

"In our business, madam, they're a sign of death."

Lucinda shook her head and stalked away.

"What is that?" Mandy said, pointing at PK's device.

"A nanoclimatizer. Proprietary." PK pulled it back to himself protectively. "It analyzes the precise temperature, humidity, UV index, and air particulates in a ten-foot radius and delivers the ideal skin care regimen for your environment. Babette invented it herself."

Stefan snorted. "If only she had invented an alarm clock so she would be here on time."

"She'll be here," PK said.

Imogen opened one of the vials and took a cautious sniff. "Bergamot. Smells like an old lady tea party." She spritzed herself while waving her phone in the air. "Gotta love a mist that burns a little, though. I can practically feel my pores tightening. And when you find yourself in a desert miles away from a humidifier, diffusers can't be choosers."

She clicked off the recorder and turned back to PK. "This footage is mid. A tease. I need access to the real stuff. To CareFree."

PK smiled thinly. "I'd prefer to wait until Babette gets here. Perhaps for now you could focus on capturing carefree moments on the trip."

"Like, strip naked and cannonball into the river? I don't think so."

It sounded pretty great to Mandy.

"Whatever the essence of CareFree is to you," PK said. "That's Babette's vision."

"Her vision, but someone else's money," Stefan said. "My boss and I expect great results from CareFree."

"You'll get them," Charlie said. "The numbers don't lie."

"The numbers depend on your sister sprinkling her fairy dust all over this launch."

Imogen scooped fine sand into her palm and blew it into the air. "How's this?" she called to PK. "Carefree enough?"

PK started coughing and backing away from the redhead while trying to shield the nanoclimatizer from the mini dust storm. "Cut! No!"

"Hey, don't deny my essence. I'm trying to make the best of this pile of rocks and . . ."

Mandy headed down to the river, letting the hum of the water drown out their bickering.

Lucinda was sitting cross-legged on the bank, binoculars trained on the far canyon walls. She put them down and looked up at Mandy. "What do you think?"

"Excuse me?"

"All that hoopla." Lucinda waved dismissively at the chaotic scene behind them. "Against all this glory." She stretched her arms out wide, embracing the majesty of the river.

"It does seem a little absurd," Mandy admitted.

She glanced back at the blue luggage tarp. She should get their gear and find Liv. Mandy knew that. Instead, she joined Lucinda and looked out across the river. The entire canyon was in shadow now, the water inky, cliffs bruised a deep purple in the twilight.

"Do you chaperone Imogen on all her sponsor trips?" Mandy asked.

"No, never. But this opportunity was special. Imogen's mom, my daughter, is a lawyer. She couldn't possibly take this much time off work. And her father"—now Lucinda's warm voice turned cold—"seems to have an allergy to spending time with his only child."

"That's terrible." Whatever faults Mandy's dad had, he'd always been there for her.

"That's family." Lucinda shrugged and pointed up, to where an osprey was circling the narrow aperture of twilight between the canyon walls. "This trip is a gift. An opportunity to share something I love with my granddaughter."

"Rafting?"

"The Grand Canyon."

"You've been here before?" Mandy asked.

"Twice." A canyon wren warbled from the other side of the river, its plaintive whistle falling from the sky. "The first time, on my honeymoon. Then three years ago, after my husband passed."

"Is it like you remembered?"

"Yes and no. Everything gets muted in my memories—heights, colors, the roar of the water. The way the air smells sharp, like a knife held under your nose. The extremes here . . . they're hard to hold on to after you leave."

"Like living inside a dream. You can't quite grab it when you wake up."

"Yes. Quite." Lucinda's eyes were somehow both dark and bright at the same time. "What brings you on this trip?"

"My sister and I—" Mandy looked back to the tarp. Liv had given up on her and was now extracting their bags herself. She'd have to tell her sister the truth. She'd have to tell everyone. She couldn't keep making up stories about winning a raffle or meeting Babette on a yacht and bonding over a shared case of ceviche-borne food poisoning.

"I have an interest in CareFree," she said. "And Babette."

"An investor? Like Stefan?" Lucinda gave her an assessing look. "For what it's worth, I'd wager our missing guest decided she didn't want to rough it."

A spike of indignation shot through Mandy's body. "Babette loves the outdoors. Hasn't your granddaughter showed you any of her videos?"

Lucinda held her ground. "If there's one thing I've learned from Imogen, it's that you can't trust anything you see on social media. It's all a performance. Even her radical honesty is manufactured. Just like Babette's so-called clean beauty business. They promise purity, but plant-based products can be just as dangerous as chemicals. Once it's in a bottle, everything's synthetic."

"Babette would never put out anything dangerous. She cares about her customers. And keeping things real."

"Your insistence proves my point. Babette Sauvage sells a performance of authenticity. Fierce. CareFree. Be natural, but enhanced. Be yourself, but better. Her products are the physical equivalent of Imogen's videos, packaging empowerment as a purchasable good. Maybe she believes it. Maybe she doesn't."

Mandy frowned. "I thought you didn't know or care who Babette was."

"I don't," Lucinda said simply. "But I know this: In any industry, the best salespeople are wholly committed to their performance. It's all blinding surface, with questionable substance underneath."

"Babette has depth," Mandy grumbled.

"I don't doubt it, dear. Anyone who's built a business of this scale must have something beneath the razzle-dazzle. But I wonder if you—or anyone here—knows what lurks down there."

The osprey plunged into the river in a sudden spray, and Mandy startled. A moment later, the bird burst back up with a silver fish in its talons, beating its enormous mottled wings as it ferried its quarry to a perch high on the other side of the canyon, beyond her field of view. The canyon went silent again, as if the violence had never happened. The sun winked out on the water, taking the last of its warmth with it.

CHAPTER THIRTEEN

A LONG, LOW HORN sounded across the beach.

"DINNER!"

Liv could smell it from their campsite. She'd created a sleeping area for two sisters in perfect alignment: two pads squared up in crisp parallel, pillows side by side, bags lined up by their feet. But Liv had set it up alone, while Mandy flitted among the other guests, finding anyone except Liv to talk with.

Even on a sister trip, Mandy was happiest getting lost in a crowd. It was her security blanket in good times and bad. Liv remembered when she'd gotten the call at her college dorm fifteen years ago about their mom's accident. Her sister had been incoherent, babbling, her words knitted with sobs, but Liv caught the basics: her mother driving home late, a truck that migrated over the line. Head-on collision. No survivors. Liv raced to find a flight from Washington, DC, home to Irvine, but somehow, in the fifteen terrifying hours it took to get there, Liv missed the crucial window to fall with her sister into that first shock wave of grief. Mandy had hugged her when she arrived, long and hard, but all week she kept drifting away, floating into the arms of their dad and family friends, the unfocused pain on her face shot through with what Liv could only interpret as recrimination. Because Liv hadn't been there when it happened. She hadn't held her little sister's hand when the first call from the police came in. She hadn't had to identify their mother at the scene.

It wasn't fair. But it was true. The heartbreak that should have been theirs together was theirs apart.

There was no way to reclaim those fifteen hours and pierce the orbit of her sister's grief. Mandy had turned to others, so Liv did then what she did now: She made herself useful. Fifteen years ago, she'd taken out the trash, paid the bills, and organized insurance paperwork. She saved her tears for when she washed the dishes at night, choking out hard, ugly sobs over the sink while no one was watching.

She looked back down at their campsite, then up the brush-scraggled rocks. No one was watching now. Liv headed over the sandy hillock that led back to the main beach. It had been transformed. Where there were once tarps and bags, there now stood thirteen camping chairs in a circle, anchored on one end by a grill, a huge Dutch oven, and a long table loaded with steaming mashed potatoes, green beans, and pineapple slaw. A minor miracle. She'd had nothing but granola bars and a smooshed peanut butter sandwich all day.

Big Pete gathered them inside the circle of chairs. "We like to do something special your first night," he said. "Rib-eye steaks, or tofu if you don't eat meat. German chocolate skillet cake for dessert. There's plenty for everyone to stuff yourselves."

"Babette specified a polyphasic forage-friendly diet for this trip," PK said. "We need ingredient lists."

"And macro counts," Fiona added.

Big Pete smiled wearily. "We make menus, not miracles. What we got is good, hot, nutritious food. I suggest you act accordingly."

He went over the basics of how meals worked: the handwashing protocol, where compost went, and how to sanitize everything at the end. Liv was surprised they were so intense about hygiene. It seemed like a group of scruffy river guides wouldn't care much about that.

"Out here, we take health and safety very seriously," Big Pete said.

"Falling in the river lasts a minute, but an outbreak of norovirus can have everyone laid out puking for days. We can't pick up new supplies midstream, and there's no way to leave the canyon if you get hurt or aren't feeling well. If there's a life-threatening emergency, we have a satellite phone and a radio to call it in. A helicopter can land at one of the medevac locations. But there are only a couple of those. Unless someone is seriously injured, we're on our own until we reach Lake Mead at the end of the week."

"Has Marc contacted you from the office?" Charlie said.

"No."

"So Babette isn't coming," Fiona said. "I knew it."

Charlie looked like he was about to protest, but Devon put a consoling hand on his arm.

Big Pete kept his voice calm. "It's not conclusive. Marc might still be getting back to the rim. He could have had an issue with one of the mules."

"Or Babette might not have arrived or contacted your office at all," Stefan offered.

"Hard saying, not knowing," the guide responded. "Any other questions? Preferably ones I might be able to answer?"

Imogen raised her hand. "I didn't find a tent in my sleeping gear."

Big Pete nodded. "This time of year, you shouldn't need one."

"But what about scorpions?"

"They're out here."

"And snakes?"

"Them too." Big Pete nodded to the long-haired guide behind the grill. "Thor is something of a reptile whisperer."

"Shake out your sleeping bag before you hop in if you don't want a bed buddy," Thor said. Imogen made a face, but Thor grinned back at her. "You're all about honesty, right? This is honest living, plain and simple."

"You'll be glad not to have a tent clogging your view at night." Big Pete spread his arms wide. "Welcome to the million-star motel."

"I was expecting four stars at least," Imogen huffed.

"I'd settle for two stars and a flush toilet," Fiona said.

Big Pete looked around at the group. "Our guides will do everything we can to make this a safe and enjoyable experience for you, but we're a team out here. The more you can pitch in, stay clean, and act smart, the easier this will be for everyone."

Liv followed his eyes around the circle. Mandy and Lucinda looked excited. Fiona and Charlie looked stressed. Everyone else seemed incapable of pulling their eyes away from Thor and Katy flipping steaks on the grill.

For the next week, this was Liv's community. Big Pete, Thor, and Katy. Devon and Charlie. Imogen and Lucinda. PK, Stefan, Fiona. And Mandy.

Liv was by no means superstitious, but she knew there was powerful magic in bringing together a group in an unfamiliar context and applying pressure. It happened in disasters and tribal initiations, in stuck elevators and music festivals. When you leave normal life, there's a brief window of possibility to rethink agreements—to form a new collective identity. Sometimes that leads to greater deviance. People who wouldn't normally do drugs or shoplift might do so in untested environments. Groups in isolation could unlock unprecedented levels of openness and vulnerability. Or, if things went wrong, aggression and fear.

There was a new social contract forming out here, held together by paddle high fives, poop buckets, and the implied promise to protect each other from the worst of the whitewater. They'd hiked deep into the canyon and rafted through its rushing artery. They'd made themselves small under the vastness of the desert sky. Liv thought back to earlier in the day, when Charlie and Devon had tumbled into the river and Charlie had blamed his absent sister for his fall. How could Babette Sauvage find them, let alone wield power over them here? Wherever she was, it was miles and worlds away.

Her sister hardly felt closer. Mandy barely acknowledged Liv during dinner, zipping through the food line before roping Stefan, Fiona, and

Thor into a tight cluster of camping chairs, where they were now playing poker on an overturned milk crate. Every few minutes, Mandy's bubbly laugh rose into the air. Her sister was always touching someone—a hand on a forearm, a punch in the shoulder, a high five with Thor after she took a big swallow from a bottle of bourbon they were passing around.

"Can I talk to you?"

Charlie had snuck up on Liv as she slid a second piece of chocolate cake onto her plate. She couldn't decide how she felt about Babette's CFO. Charlie radiated stress, with an unappealing undercurrent of arrogance. That said, at least he wanted to talk to her. Which was more than she could say for her sister.

Liv turned to him. "What's on your mind?"

He was still wearing his muddy Babette ball cap, despite the twilit sky. He beckoned to her to follow him up away from the beach, beyond the pool of bright light cast by the lanterns in the dinner area.

"I hear you're a secret agent."

Liv flashed a glare back toward Mandy, who appeared to be teaching Stefan how to do-si-do. Her sister was unreachable. Impossible.

She faced Charlie again. "I work for the State Department as an analyst and a profiler. I have a security clearance, but there's nothing top secret about it."

"So you're not a spy?"

"Not a spy." But she knew there was no surefire way to convince him. It was exactly the kind of thing that was impossible to prove: that she wasn't something.

"But you work for the government," he said.

"Yes."

"And I can trust you."

Another impossible statement. If she disagreed, she was setting herself up for an argument. If she agreed, she was open to whatever it was he wanted. But Charlie sounded hopeful, desperate even. And here she was in this burgeoning new society, Liv not-a-spy Chisholm, sister to

Mandy life-of-the-party Chisholm, face-to-face with Charlie possibly-paranoid Sauvage.

She couldn't control what others thought of her. But she could choose how she would behave, how much generosity she was willing to extend to a fellow traveler.

"How can I help?" she said.

"I have something I need your advice on. Discreetly."

He removed the muddied ball cap from his head.

"This is my hat."

Liv didn't feel this statement merited a response.

"You saw how they came in that cardboard box," Charlie continued. "All white, but labeled individually with our names."

"Did you find a difference?"

He thrust his hat at her, and Liv took a quick scan. Charlie's cap was dry, the embroidered white *B* standing out against the streaked mud and silt from his thrashing in the Colorado. Other than its mottled coloring, it looked the same as the other hats, including the one she'd snapped to the belt loop of her pants.

"Take it," he insisted. "Look inside."

Did he want her to appreciate the tea tree mumbo jumbo in the lining? She flipped over his hat, preparing to extricate herself from this odd encounter before she got trapped in a dissertation on the healing power of crystals. But when she looked inside, she saw something she didn't expect. More embroidered stitches—not thick and raised like the *B* on the outside crown, but fainter, barely visible. Bright white thread scratched wispy letters across the inside of the crown, forming ghostly words. The message was only legible because the rest of the hat was so dirty.

CROSS ME AND YOU'RE DEAD TOO

She looked from the hat up to Charlie.

"It's from Babette," he said.

"What does it mean?"

Silence.

"You're dead too?" she prompted. "Has someone close to you died recently?"

"Fourteen months ago, there was an accident. At the business. Babette took responsibility, but she wasn't even there. She didn't . . ."

His voice trailed off, and he dropped his gaze back to his ball cap. Flipped over, it looked just like the others. Which made Liv wonder. She pulled out her own hat and examined it. The fabric was grayed by the river water, with just a tinge of sweat around the brim. She grabbed a handful of crumbly orange sand from the beach and smeared it across the inside of the crown. Nothing.

She looked down at the two hats, one threatening, the other simply dirty. "You're sure these came from Babette?"

"Positive. She buys special gifts for everyone whenever we have an Essence Quest. For Fierce, she got us all custom windbreakers with our moon signs embroidered on them."

Liv wondered if Babette's former assistant had used his jacket as a makeshift sling after he broke his arm.

"She gets them all herself? PK doesn't place the orders for her?"

"As far as I know, Babette's always taken care of them directly. Wants it to be a surprise. She would have shipped that box to the lodge on the rim a few days ahead of our arrival. If we were up in civilization, I could pull the tracking information from our corporate account. But down here . . ."

Liv looked at Charlie's hat, the words *YOU'RE DEAD TOO* plainly visible in thin white thread against the muddy material. She had a thousand questions for him. But there was only one she had a good shot of getting a straight answer to.

"Why did you bring this to me?"

"I thought you were some kind of international hotshot detective."

"I am an investigator. But this is outside my area of expertise."

Charlie persisted. "If someone came to you with a message like this, what would your analysis be?"

She looked from his face down to the hat.

"I'd need more information."

"If this was all the information you had," Charlie continued. "Please."

"I would say you've been issued a warning of some kind."

"Not a threat? She said I'm going to die."

"Not precisely. It says if you cross her, you're dead. Did you cross her?"

Charlie didn't answer.

Liv looked back down at his hat. The rational part of her said what she was feeling was not fear, but confusion. This whole situation was drowning in it. She had fallen into a product prelaunch rafting trip for a reason she didn't understand, with people from a company she'd never heard of, whose CEO had gone AWOL. And now said CEO was sending menacing messages to her brother and business partner via customized hat embroidery.

It sounded ridiculous. But it was the lack of rational explanation that made her shiver in the warm air. Charlie's hat—the planning, the delicate stitching, the sense that he had personally been delivered a threat—was creepy. Fear didn't have to make sense for it to crawl across her skin.

Liv looked at Charlie. "What are you afraid of exactly?"

"I—Devon and I—on this trip, we were going to . . ."

"You were going to what?"

"Can you protect me?" he asked.

"Tell me exactly what this is about."

He stared at her. She stared back. It was the kind of stalemate Liv was well acquainted with: Unwilling informant meets unmoved advocate.

"I think Babette hired someone to come down here," he whispered. "To stop me and Devon from crossing her."

"What kind of person? A lawyer?"

"A hit man."

She stared at him, flabbergasted. "A hit man? You think Babette is going to *kill* you? Why?"

But Charlie said nothing.

"Does she have a history of extreme criminal actions?" Liv asked.

"Not directly. But there have been incidents."

"Fatalities?"

He stayed silent. Liv kept pushing. "Are you talking about that assistant's broken arm? Or the accident you just mentioned?"

Charlie grimaced. "Officially, they were all accidents."

Liv stared at him, willing him to say more, but his lips were clamped shut. "You're making a pretty strong assertion based on a few words embroidered into a hat."

"It's based on a lifetime with my sister," he said. "I know her. You don't."

CHAPTER FOURTEEN

BY THE TIME MANDY stumbled up to bed after the poker game, the sky was lit up with stars, the Milky Way draped like a sheer scarf across their shoulders. Part of her hoped Liv would still be awake so she could regale her with stories of how she'd won them beers from Thor's secret stash for happy hour the next day, plus a promise from Stefan to introduce them to a bona fide duke the next time they found themselves in Amsterdam. But Liv was already curled up on her sleeping pad, her back to Mandy like a silent rebuke.

Mandy unzipped her backpack, rooting around for a headlamp and warmer clothes. From a nearby bush, she heard the scuffle and chitter of small mammals—ringtails, maybe?—and high above, a great horned owl, calling the nocturnal predators of the canyon to the hunt. She pulled a sweatshirt over her head and gazed out at the pinpricked night. This week, the limits were finite: North Rim and South, guides and guests, river and sky. But what wasn't possible within that container? She looked down at her sleeping sister, half covered by her unzipped sleeping bag, a parenthesis of blankets and staccato breath. Maybe this would be the trip where they fully saw each other, where they escaped the well-worn grooves of their skipping record and broke into a new song. Mandy had been gnawing at that hope for a while now, and something about this being the tenth year, their tenth sister trip, felt ripe with opportunity. She'd been only twenty-one when they'd started, Liv twenty-four. She was a different person now. They both were. Maybe here in the canyon, in its mesquite-scented air, they could be different together.

Mandy felt a flutter of contrition. While she'd been playing cards, had Liv gone to bed alone, before it was fully dark? She crouched down to straighten Liv's sleeping bag, but when she did so, her sister's hand bolted up and grabbed her wrist.

"You came back," Liv whispered.

"Of course," Mandy said.

"I was worried."

Worried? About what? From far off, Mandy heard the bright, whistling howls of coyotes, their yips refracting against the canyon walls.

"Something is wrong," Liv mumbled.

"With the campsite? I should have helped you set up." Mandy reached out again to smooth out her sister's sleeping bag, but this time, Liv sat up and shook herself fully awake.

"No. Listen to me."

"What?" Mandy couldn't help the petulance that snuck into her voice. Her sister was looking at her with the urgency she reserved for situations when Mandy had violated the invisible rule book Liv lugged around in her head. "What did I do wrong this time?"

Liv narrowed her eyes, and Mandy squirmed. She hated how this only seemed to get worse as they got older. When they were kids, Liv hadn't been this judgmental—at least, not openly—but when their mom died, her sister took up the reins of the moral high ground and yanked them as tight as possible.

But when Liv opened her mouth again, it wasn't to chastise Mandy. "What I'm about to tell you, you have to keep secret. Can you promise me that?"

"Um . . . sure?"

"For real, Mand."

There was something in her sister's voice—not judgment, but something equally dark—that Mandy wasn't going to mess with.

"Fine. I swear on the light of Venus's moon."

"Venus doesn't have a—" Liv shook her head. "Do you remember how scared Charlie was after he fell into the water at Horn Creek?"

"When he lost his river virginity?"

"Right. He told me he thought Babette was targeting him. I thought he was just stressed from the whitewater and Babette not showing up. But then, tonight, he showed me his hat. It has a message inside it from Babette."

"Something inspirational?"

"Not exactly." Liv looked up at the endless night. "*Cross me and you're dead too.* That's what it said."

"*Inside* his hat?"

Liv nodded. "It was embroidered on the inner crown in white stitches. We could only see it because his hat was muddy from when he fell in the river. I checked mine, too, but there was nothing. Only Charlie got the threat."

A threat. Mandy remembered the excitement she'd felt when she'd claimed her own hat from the cardboard box, and the odd texture of its inner brim above the tea tree crystals. Now, she wondered.

She pulled her cap from where she'd stuffed it in her waistband. "Check mine."

Liv looked confused.

"Just check it, okay?"

Liv scooped a handful of sand from the cold ground and started rubbing it on the inside crown. "There's something here."

Mandy nodded grimly. She leaned in close to her sister, letting a strand of Liv's hair brush her shoulder. Even in the harsh light of her headlamp, she could see the stitches come alive, faint embroidered words inside her hat, barely perceptible in the grainy darkness.

MONEY CAN'T PROTECT YOU

CHAPTER FIFTEEN

"WHAT DOES THIS MEAN?" Liv demanded. Mandy seemed frozen by the message under her hat, which only added to Liv's confusion. "What money? You have no money. Protect you from what?"

"I don't know. It must be a mistake." Mandy looked up at her. "What makes Charlie think Babette sewed the message? Couldn't it have been someone else?"

"Babette was the one to buy and personalize the hats. She shipped them directly to the lodge herself."

"What if it's a manufacturing defect?"

"You think there's a possessed sewing machine somewhere in Guangzhou churning these out?"

"Maybe a fortune cookie company decided to diversify."

But the joke sounded weak even to Liv's ears. Mandy's tone was apologetic. Defeated. Which was not what Liv had expected. She'd assumed there'd be an explanation, an excuse, a defiant wild story. But her sister didn't say anything else.

A flash of heat ran across Liv's forehead. Yet another situation where her sister was ducking responsibility. But this wasn't a classic Mandy mess-up. This wasn't a bail-me-out-because-I-broke-into-the-zoo-at-two-a.m. phone call. This was something else. And that spark Liv felt between her eyes? She realized it wasn't anger. It was fear. Her sister had been threatened, in a way she didn't understand, far from access to information or help.

"Hey." Liv reached out and brushed Mandy's curls back from where they hung over her eyes. "What's going on?"

Mandy seemed to gather herself. "It must be a joke. I can't believe Babette would threaten me. Or anyone."

"Why? Because her skin's too dewy?"

"Because she's all about authenticity. I know it's the internet, and it could be an act. But this is a woman who built her whole life—her whole empire—to fight the status quo. In an industry that's all about facade, she stands for authenticity."

Mandy started to glow the way she always did when she got passionate about something. "Babette tells it like it is. She built her company into something honest and fresh in an industry dedicated to making women feel less than. She talks about skin care like preparing for the adventure that is life. Tools to be exactly who you want to be. The same way a knight would put on his sword or a rock climber straps on all those clippy bits. Or the way you put on your charcoal suit and that flat expression—yeah, that one—the one that says I am a stone-cold government agent and I will take your lies and error-ridden visa applications and grind them into dust. Babette Sauvage makes products that unleash women's full selves, their real selves, onto the world. She wouldn't hide behind threats like this. She wouldn't want to."

Her sister was practically out of breath defending Babette, and Liv wasn't ready for her to whip out the autobiography and start reciting from it again. Everything Mandy was saying confirmed that Babette was a powerful force. But Liv had seen Charlie's terror. She'd heard slivers of darker stories beneath Babette's "all-natural" facade. In Liv's experience, the more power someone had, the more resources they had to shape how others saw them. And when they couldn't mold the narrative to their liking, they sometimes chose more violent ways to control it.

"Fine," she said. "Let's say Charlie's wrong and the messages didn't come from Babette. But someone sent a threat to him, and to you. Is there any way you and Charlie are materially connected?"

Mandy hesitated. She shook her head.

Liv learned more from the pause than the gesture that followed it.

"How exactly are you linked to Babette?" Liv asked.

"I told you. I'm a fan."

"You're more than just a fan. Everyone is here for a specific reason. What's yours?"

"My sparkling personality."

"Please don't lie to me. Not now."

They stared each other down for a long minute.

"Don't be mad," Mandy said.

Those three little words rattled the air.

"I swear there's no reason to threaten me," Mandy said. "Or Charlie! At least, none that I can imagine."

"What is your connection?"

"I've always been a fan, but over the past few years, I've been learning more about CareFree. It's a total game changer for Babette. The prospectus on it is impressive. Zero to ninety. Stratospheric growth potential."

These were not Mandy's words. Had they come from Babette? Charlie? Stefan? Did Mandy somehow have access to Babette's board?

"By Q3 of next year, because of CareFree, Babette will be the dominant player in a multibillion-dollar new wellness category," Mandy continued. "CareFree is going to bridge the skin care–wellness nexus. No one is producing anything like this product. The competition won't exist for another three years minimum."

Liv didn't know if Mandy believed or even understood the bullshit she was spouting. But she'd heard it before. She recognized the pattern. And she knew exactly who was at the root of it.

"What did he do?"

"Who?"

"Mandy. Tell me you didn't pull your pension to invest in one of Dad's schemes."

"I wouldn't. But—"

Mandy's eyes—so bright, so alive—dropped to the dull-red sandstone.

"I'm going to kill him," Liv said.

"It's not a scheme," Mandy insisted. "Babette's legit."

"Fine. She's an angel from skin care heaven. So what's there for me to be mad about?"

Mandy's headlamp dipped to the cold ground. "You know how Dad had that hiccup with the SEC?"

It took all of Liv's training to resist the urge to offer her own interpretation of what had happened when their father got arrested for tax evasion and insider trading ten years ago. She gave a curt nod and waited.

"A couple years ago, after he got out of prison, I told him about Babette. He started looking into it, and he met her and learned about this new development. He got excited about the chance to get in on the ground floor with CareFree. But because of that court ruling, he still has a few years on the clock before he can invest directly. So he came to me with a creative idea, and I . . ."

"You . . . ?"

"I decided to make a significant investment."

"With what money?"

"Not mine. His. Dad set up an LLC. There's a bank account in Nassau. I'm the named investor, but we're partners. It's not a big deal."

"Mandy, this is literally against the law."

"It's a rounding error. No one gets hurt. It's Dad."

"If he's so into Babette, why didn't you invite him on this trip?"

Mandy looked uncomfortable.

"Did you invite him?"

"No!"

"Then what?"

"Babette offered spots to both of us," Mandy said. "Dad and me. We're not the biggest investors in CareFree, not by a long shot, but we were the first. It was sweet of her to invite us. But you know Dad doesn't do wilderness."

"So I'm here in his place?" Liv said. "I'm the pity date you settled for when your first choice canceled?"

"That's not fair. The money is his thing. This trip is ours. Just ours." Mandy looked at her, her eyes pleading for something. Support, maybe. Understanding.

"What you're doing isn't safe," Liv finally said.

Mandy's eyes flashed hot.

"It's safe enough," she retorted. "I'm just . . . helping him."

The implication hit Liv squarely in the chest. The suggestion that all she did was put barriers between herself and their father, while Mandy and Guy had a meaningful relationship. It was true. Liv hadn't even seen her father in three years, since the time he came to Beijing and tried to get her to pose as a US trade specialist with a businessman he was wooing. These days, they traded lackluster birthday voicemails and little more. Distance was the only way Liv could hold herself back from throttling him.

Liv closed her eyes for a moment, breathing in the thin night air. She could smell the chalk in it, the silt-rich mud, the river carrying its own surprises.

"Okay, Mand. Start at the beginning."

"No judgment?"

None she'd share out loud.

CHAPTER SIXTEEN

THE CONSTELLATIONS MARCHED ACROSS the desert sky, tracing age-old myths through the night. Mandy and her sister ignored them. Liv grilled her, and Mandy laid out the details of her and their dad's investment in CareFree, fielding every question thrown her way. Mandy thought it sounded solid. Impressive, even. She'd absorbed more about the project than even she'd realized. The splashy marketing rollout Babette and PK had planned, the financial projections Charlie put together, the extraordinary promise of CareFree's secret ingredient that Devon and her team had developed in the lab. Even this rafting trip, which she described to Liv as part prelaunch deep dive, part celebration of what everyone hoped would be a huge success.

But Liv was too focused to celebrate.

"Who here knows that you're part of Dad's Nassau LLC?"

"What do you mean?"

"If you were their first investor," Liv said, "some of them know that, right?"

Mandy considered it. "Charlie must know who I am. He sends out the monthly investor reports. If PK was in charge of invites for the trip, he'd know. And of course, Babette. She and Dad have met a bunch of times."

"Does she know about Dad's criminal background?"

"I'm not sure. Why?"

"The message in your hat. *Money can't protect you.* Maybe Dad pissed her off somehow, and she's threatening to expose him for violating the terms of his parole. To cancel your investment."

It didn't make sense to Mandy. "Why would she turn her back on her first investors? It wasn't a thousand percent kosher, but we don't have that big a stake. And Dad told me they have a real connection."

"Does he have a connection to Charlie, too? If Charlie is crossing Babette somehow, and Dad is helping him—"

"I don't think so," Mandy interrupted. "Dad only ever talks about Babette. He introduced her to some other prospective investors, and they got at least one hit, another backer who's way, way bigger."

"The one Stefan represents?"

"Maybe? I've never met anyone here before. Honest."

"You've never met them. They've never met you. And yet here you are, with a threat embroidered into your hat."

Mandy realized most of what she knew about the company had come through Babette's autobiography, social media, or her father, all of which employed filters that made things look shinier than they really were. Now she sat with Liv in the rough-edged darkness, their headlamps casting overlapping pools of weak light on the unfiltered sand.

"We don't know for certain that these messages came from Babette," Mandy said. "Charlie was the one handing out the hats. He could've lied about where they came from. It seems convenient to blame the person who isn't here."

"But why would he doctor his own hat to threaten himself?"

"Maybe he's trying to draw attention away from something else."

"Like what?" Liv said.

Mandy racked her brain for anything her dad might have said to suggest a fight or power struggle between the Sauvages. There was nothing. Just Dad's boasts about the big-money investor he had introduced Babette to, and the even bigger payout he envisioned for himself and Mandy. She believed in Babette, but she'd also heard that kind of talk from their dad many times: about a made-to-order omelet delivery service, an AI pet matchmaking app, an mRNA-based drug that cured arthritis. Guy Chisholm had the tendency to talk about investments in the rosiest terms until they went belly-up, at which point he insisted he knew they'd been doomed from the beginning.

Liv turned Mandy's cap over in her hands. "Charlie gave me the impression he and Devon were planning something that was supposed to happen on this trip. Besides the rafting. He didn't say what, but it must be volatile. No matter how scared he feels right now, that message in his hat wasn't enough for him to tell me the whole story tonight."

"So maybe he isn't that frightened?"

Liv shook her head. "Or not that certain. If he's not positive his sister hired someone to cause him harm, he might not want to divulge whatever it is he had planned. Some people defend their secrets to the grave."

"You know," Mandy said, "if one of the Sauvages was going to bail on this trip, I would have picked him."

Liv eyed her curiously. "What do you mean?"

"Devon and Babette both love the outdoors. Devon's been here before, and Babette planned this Essence Quest. But Charlie's clearly not comfortable here. If he's doing something so terrible Babette would want him dead, why would he agree to come out into the wilderness with her?"

"Family. It makes you do weird things."

Mandy looked down at her sister's dust-reddened hands. "How does Charlie think Babette is going to kill him if she isn't even here?"

"Charlie believes Babette planned to ditch this trip," Liv said. "He thinks she hired a hit man and marooned him here in the wilderness, where he'd be a sitting duck."

Mandy stared at her. "A hit man? On this trip?"

"I know," Liv said. "It sounds crazy."

"It *is* crazy." Mandy reached out and rubbed the brim of her hat. "Do you believe it?"

"Charlie seems legitimately afraid. He made allusions to some incidents—deadly ones—where Babette was involved. But he wouldn't tell me exactly why he thought she was after him."

"Maybe he's overreacting," Mandy said.

"If only Charlie had gotten a message, I'd say he was jumping to conclusions. Hurdling over several sleeping elephants to conclusions. It isn't easy to orchestrate a hit on someone."

"And if Babette went to all that trouble, why give him a heads-up about it ahead of time?"

"Exactly."

"So, no hit man."

"Well . . ." Liv re-angled her headlamp. "Things changed when you got a threat too. Even if it doesn't make sense, we have to take it seriously. Though what *it* is, I still don't know."

Mandy could see the wheels turning in that big steel-trap brain of hers.

"Something isn't adding up," Liv finally said. "Charlie gets a threat. You get a threat."

"You're right. It would be a heck of a lot better if Oprah was down here handing out free cars."

"This is no joke. This is a small group. A threat to one of us could be a threat to everyone. We can't just do nothing."

"So what's the plan?" Mandy asked.

"I don't know yet."

Liv looked exhausted. They were sitting side by side, close enough to touch, their bodies separated only by a slender column of night air. Mandy wanted to reach out and comfort Liv, to insist everything would be all right. But it was her choices that had etched the worry lines onto her sister's forehead. Mandy watched as Liv pulled Mandy's cap toward her, flipped it up again, and shone her headlamp on the ugly words.

"*Money can't protect you*," Liv read. "Is there anything about this that makes sense?"

Mandy shook her head. She really, really wished they'd gone to Tierra del Fuego instead.

But they hadn't. And she couldn't run away or stick her head in the river until Liv figured this out. She wasn't willing to be Liv's crusade again. She had grown beyond the little chaos monkey who needed her big sister to swoop in and save her. At least, she hoped she had.

"No. But let's figure it out together." She gently removed Liv's headlamp, brushing a wayward lock of hair from her sister's forehead. "*After* we get some sleep."

CHAPTER SEVENTEEN

LIV MISSED THE FIRST call of the conch shell. And the second. By the time she dragged herself to the outdoor kitchen, Mandy appeared to have already drunk a raftful of coffee. Her sister's eyes shone like a caffeinated chipmunk's, her body draped in a sparkly peacock-print bikini under a sarong with sea turtles floating across it. It was a lot to take in on three hours of sleep.

"Today, we make a plan." Mandy thrust a travel mug at her, but Liv waved her off and trudged to the handwashing station first.

"Step one," Mandy continued. "Find the hit man."

The astringent disinfectant stung Liv's hands. Day two in the canyon, and her skin was already cracking from the dry desert air. Maybe dermal hydration was more important than she'd given it credit for.

"No, scratch that. Step zero point five. Steal all hats. See who got messages. Determine if there *is* a hit man."

Liv accepted the mug now and took a grateful sip. She grabbed two plates, silently handing one back to Mandy, who was juggling a notebook and a fistful of colored pencils. The outdoor kitchen buzzed with purposeful activity, Katy flipping bacon in a pan while Thor sliced bananas. Liv loaded up on eggs, black beans, garlic-roasted potatoes, fresh pico de gallo, and tortillas still warm from the griddle. They might be sleeping on the ground without tents, but these guides didn't skimp on the meal plan.

Not that all the other guests were taking advantage of it. Down by the river, Lucinda, Stefan, Charlie, and Devon had heaping plates of food, but Imogen, PK, and Fiona had gone rogue, whisking moss-green powder from a matte-white bag into glasses of water.

Liv steered Mandy to a pair of camping chairs set apart from the others, on a rocky knoll overlooking a particularly fast stretch of whitewater.

"Maybe first we need to make a list of everyone on the trip." Mandy had filled her plate with tortillas smothered in yogurt and honey. "Everyone who's here and everyone who *planned* to be here."

"We still don't know if Babette ever intended to actually attend," Liv said.

"Right!" Mandy was as loud as ever, and Liv silently thanked the river for its gurgling roar. "Step zero point one. Find out as much as we can about why Babette is missing." Mandy frowned. "That's where we started. And got nowhere."

"Mandy, if we're going to look into this"—Liv reached out and tucked a loose flap of Mandy's sarong back around her—"you have to let me take the lead."

"I thought we could do it together."

Could they? Mandy had no training as an investigator and, more importantly, no aptitude for it. Telling Mandy delicate information was like loading it into a confetti cannon. She was a suggestible, excitable fountain of imagination. Terrific for making art with kids. Not so much for threat analysis.

"We need to be methodical about it," Liv finally said. "Discreet. Make a plan. Follow the evidence. And play it cool."

"I can be cool." Mandy was practically doing a jig.

Liv raised an eyebrow. "Like a cucumber?"

"My cool is more like a hamster with suspenders and a little bow tie."

"Fine. I'll be the cucumber."

"And me?"

"Just try to keep the tap dancing to a minimum."

Mandy waved her notebook dangerously close to Liv's coffee. "I can plan. I can gather evidence. That's why I made this."

She flashed a drawing of what looked like an amateur baseball team. Mandy had sketched caricatures of every person on the trip—Devon fierce, Charlie quaking, Fiona with LED mask in hand. There was Lucinda in her rafting gloves, and Katy with her long braid flipped over her shoulder. Imogen and PK flanked the sides, holding the ends of a team banner that spanned across them. Liv counted fourteen people in the drawing: all the guests, the three guides, and Marc, who had hiked down with the mules at the beginning of the trip and would pick them up in a van at the end. Plus Babette. She was at the front of the pack, swinging a bat.

"This is . . . impressive," Liv said. The pencil version of Mandy was grinning and waving a pennant from atop Thor's shoulders. Meanwhile, the two-dimensional Liv scowled down at a clipboard.

"See what I did?" Mandy said. "I gave everyone a ball cap and wrote the hidden messages we know about real small across the brim. This way, we can keep track of what we learn about whose hat says what."

Liv squinted down at the drawing. "*CareFree Killers*," she read across the banner. "Catchy team name. But maybe a bit . . ."

"Stabby? I know. But I wanted the alliteration."

"I appreciate your initiative." Liv closed the notebook and put it on the rock between them. Big Pete had said it yesterday: If they wanted to survive, they had to play like a team out here. "If we're going to find out who's at the greatest risk—and who might be threatening them—we need to know more about everyone on this trip."

"Where do we start?" Mandy's eyes were shining with eagerness.

"Charlie seems to think Babette has been involved in deaths in the past. If that's the case, someone else here will know about it. You have a natural reason to talk to Babette's team. They're probably curious to get to know their sparkly first investor better. And you already made friends at the poker game."

"Fiona cheats. She hid an ace in her bra."

"We'll keep an eye on her." Liv was still curious about the reason for Fiona's presence on the trip and her stake in CareFree. She wished there was some way she could get access to the internet. She wanted to see annual reports. Earnings calls. Staff directories. Anything that could provide objective background research for analysis.

"What about the hats?" Mandy asked. "Should we ask to see them all?"

Liv scanned the other guests in their camping chairs, metal plates on their laps. Some were wearing their caps. More weren't. She tried to weigh the benefit of getting as much information as possible against the risks. Paranoia was one of the most deadly plagues that could sweep a group, especially in isolation. It was well documented that even smart, high-functioning adults could fall prey to mob riots, phantom outbreaks, and imaginary hit men under the grip of mass terror. Charlie was already infected. If others reacted as strongly as he had, they could put themselves in real danger all on their own, without further intervention from Babette.

Was that Babette's plan? To seed fear and mistrust among her team and let it tear them apart?

"For now, let's be discreet," Liv said. "And focused."

"On what?"

Liv considered the options. "There are some questions we simply can't answer down here. We don't know what happened to Babette, or what she's planning now. We have to devote our energy to information we can learn from the individuals who are here."

"You want to talk with people one-on-one?"

Liv nodded. "But don't scare anyone. Let's keep our questions open-ended, and not just about Babette's disappearance. There's more going on here than a missing CEO. Any guest could be involved."

"What about the guides?"

"Them too. We'll start with the inner circle and expand from there.

I'll touch base with Charlie, try to keep him calm. You talk to PK. See if he can shed any light on the situation."

"Okay," Mandy said. "But when we split up the guides, I want Thor."

"We aren't prioritizing who to talk to based on hotness," Liv said.

"You have your methods, partner. I have mine."

CHAPTER EIGHTEEN

MANDY STRODE TO THE dishwashing station, timing her arrival to sync up with her target. It felt good to start with Babette's assistant instead of Charlie or Devon. Those two were at least a decade older than her, top brass, more likely to be on guard. The best sources were always at the bottom—people who collected information like magpies to help them get ahead. People like PK Raghuram.

"Love love LOVE your shorts," she said. It was true. PK's shorts were bright blue with koalas all over them, chomping away at tiny eucalyptus leaves. He'd paired them with a faded pink tank top and a silvery-white Babette headband that sent his faux-hawk shooting up like a feathery firework.

PK couldn't help it; he smiled back at Mandy. His hands were in the suds, conveniently trapping him at the table at least through rinsing and drying.

"Thank you so much for making this happen," she gushed. "You must have put in a lot of work to get all of us here."

"It's my job." PK looked tired, maybe hungover. Babette was based in Las Vegas, and Mandy suspected he was a creature of bright lights and concrete. She wondered whether his colorful outfit was an expression of joy or a performance, a way to mask the stress of an extended work trip with no indoor plumbing.

She flicked her turtle sarong at him and smiled. "Apparently you and I were the only ones to get the memo about wearing animal print."

He wiped his hands on his koalas. "Honestly? I didn't expect investors to be up for this at all."

"Have you put together this kind of trip for the company before?" she asked.

"Yes and no. This is my first Essence Quest. I joined the team three years ago, after the Fierce line had launched. But we do a board retreat every year in a foreign location, and that's a lot of moving parts—booking reservations, making sure everyone's needs are met. This is different. I don't have to worry about what wine we're pairing with dinner or who wants their board packet printed in eighteen-point font. But there are a lot of things out here I can't control, and in some ways . . ."

"It's worse?"

"Just harder to get a handle on." His cheek twitched.

"It can't be easy without Babette here."

"It isn't." PK's lips clamped into a firm line, and Mandy worried for a moment that she had lost him. PK had been the only one to express real distress about Babette's well-being the day before. Whether he had useful information about his boss's whereabouts or not, he was invested. Maybe even scared. It was up to Mandy to keep him talking before he shut down.

"Do you know everyone here?" she asked.

"Yes and no," PK said. "The family, of course. And Dr. Fiona was around a lot when I first started at the company. Imogen and Lucinda I've never met before. But I knew from the contract negotiations that Imogen would be . . . special."

It was clear the teenager was a flavor of special he never intended to order again.

"And Stefan?"

"Eriksen? This is the first time I've seen him. He became a trustee last year, and he's never even switched on his video for a board call. I was starting to wonder if he was real."

They looked over to where the bearded man was standing with Lucinda, both of them listening earnestly as Big Pete pointed out various sections of the supply boat.

"He seems into it," Mandy said.

"Hopefully that translates to a favorable report." PK twitched again, a reflexive twist of his left cheek. "He works for our biggest investor."

"But they didn't want to come themselves?"

Twitch.

"Well, I'm here to make it better." Mandy raised one hand and touched her pinky to her thumb in her best impression of a Girl Scout. "I solemnly swear to be the lowest-maintenance, highest-fun investor you've ever had to deal with."

"I'm not sure what kind of fun we're going to find here."

"Late-night skinny-dipping? Hot gossip about the guides? I'm here for all of it. Lord knows my sister isn't." She shot a pointed glance over to where Liv was deep in conversation with Charlie, who looked like he'd barely slept.

"She seems kind of intense," PK said.

"So does he," Mandy said. "Hopefully it's not contagious."

"Charlie? He's always wound tight. And especially right now, with Babette not here, it means he's in charge. Not his favorite place to be."

"A behind-the-scenes guy?"

"More like in the shadows," PK said. "Not like a vampire or a mole rat. Just, Babette is the engine. He's the caboose. It works well that way."

"Is she a benevolent engine?"

"Excuse me?"

"I've heard she drives the company with a lot of intensity. Charlie seems to think she can be threatening."

"Threatening? That powder puff. Babette is exactly who she says she is. Raw. Fierce. Her love language is intensity."

"What do you mean?"

PK cocked his head to the side. "Do you know the story of how she got Skinnmilk to stop testing products on baby animals?"

"She keynoted a conference with their CEO, right? She brought a basket of puppies onstage and kept handing them to him as she spoke." Mandy had watched a clip of Babette, smiling ear to ear as the fur balls wriggled all over the horrified double-breasted suit beside her. "Her talk went viral, and the board of Skinnmilk had a change of heart."

"That's the public story. But that CEO?" PK flashed her a sidelong grin. "He's allergic to dogs. Those puppies sent him to the ER in anaphylactic shock. Their stock tanked, he got put on notice, and he changed their testing policy to save his job."

"Babette put him in the hospital? Intentionally?"

PK waved her off. "She motivated a change he never would have made otherwise. It was brilliant. And the guy was fine. Checked himself out three days later. I delivered Babette's get-well dragon-fruit-and-sea-moss bouquet myself."

"Has she ever done something like that to someone who works in the company?"

"Something intense? To inspire them to do what needs to be done?" He rummaged in his pocket and pulled out his phone. "Every day. Look at this."

Mandy accepted the phone and started scrolling through screenshots of text messages he'd received from Babette.

SLEEP IS FOR THE WEAK. GET BACK TO WORK.

WE'RE HERE TO CHANGE THE WORLD, NOT TO TAKE WEEKENDS OFF.

A STONED MONKEY COULD DO YOUR JOB BETTER.

"Whoa," she said.

"Yeah," he said.

"Why don't you quit?"

PK shrugged. "I don't work for Babette because she's my friend. She's a genius. She's my hero."

"But she talks to you like you're disposable."

"She talks to me like I can do better," he said. "And I have the receipts if I need them."

"So your plan is to sue her if it gets too bad?"

"You don't get it," PK said. "Think of a goddess. A beautiful, terrifying, thunderbolt-wielding goddess. You don't want a deity to chitchat with you. You want them to challenge you. Open new worlds to you."

"And Babette does that? Even though she treats you like . . ." Mandy waved at his phone.

"She does that, and more." PK's eyes were shining. "Much more."

He shot a glance up the hillside. "You were the first investor in CareFree. You deserve a first look."

PK motioned for Mandy to follow him up to an alcove in the cliff wall where he had made camp the night before. He had staked a sheet into a makeshift canopy, shielding his campsite from the sun, or prying eyes, or both. He reached into a crack between vertical flakes of shale and pulled out a soft-pack cooler, the word "Babette" sprayed across it in silver.

He unzipped the cooler and pulled out a small cylindrical container. It was like the others: matte-white, unlabeled. Mandy felt a little zing of excitement as he handed it over.

"Here," he said. "A taste of CareFree. A new world of liberation."

She unscrewed the cap, revealing an airy cream with a subtle scent of eucalyptus. It was bright white with a purple halo around the edges, as if it had been beamed down from another planet.

"I recommend waiting until evening to try it out," PK said. "The first time, the effects can be . . . dazzling. Especially in this heat."

"Am I going to forget my own name?"

"Not your name. Just your worries. Temporarily. Which might be more pleasant after we've spent all day barreling down that river."

Mandy took one more whiff. Then she reluctantly handed the container back to him. "Can you keep this safe in your cooler until later?"

"Of course."

He turned to put away the cooler, then froze.

"Everything okay?" she asked.

His back was still to her.

"Shhh." His voice was abrupt, urgent. "There's a—in my—don't—"

His body blocked her view. She couldn't see it. But she could hear it. It sounded less like a rattle than a shushing, like the ill-fated rain stick project she never repeated after the boys turned their instruments into exploding lightsabers.

PK was inching backward, one hand on his cooler, his torso flexing away from his sleeping area as if conjuring a magical force field between himself and a giant, writhing snake.

The snake was creeping out of the seam in the rock behind PK's sleeping area. Its head was patterned in rose-colored diamonds, its body a dark line splitting the synthetic yellow sleeping bag in half. It seemed big. Was it big? What was the standard? She tried to remember if there was any correlation between the size of the rattle and the venomous threat posed, if you were supposed to move or not move, scream or not scream. The snake danced in a hypnotic spiral, coiling and uncoiling, its tiny black eyes boring into her, tongue flickering.

"Should we yell?" she whispered.

PK reached back and grabbed for her hand. "Maybe we should pray."

They took one coordinated half step back, then another. Their bodies fused into a single unit of shuffling fear. His hamstrings, tight muscled ropes, shook the koalas on his shorts out of their tiny trees.

The snake's coils slid and folded over each other, its glinting scales swirling so fast the patterns started to blur. It was much bigger than she'd initially thought.

"Is it just me, or is it pink?" she whispered.

"Matches your sunburn."

Mandy risked a quick glance at his tanned face. "We can't all have little elves who slather us with Babette FeatherLite SPF Perfection every morning."

PK gave Mandy's hand a tiny squeeze. "If we survive this, we're going to be friends."

It was at that very moment he tripped backward, pulling Mandy with him to the ground. She had just enough time to see the rattler match their sudden movements with its own, accelerating from a slither to a dizzying, terrifying blur.

"SNAAAAAAAAAKE!" she screamed.

She dropped PK's hand and started scrabbling backward. Her foot slid on something and shot out from under her, knocking her onto her back.

This was it. Game over. She lay supine, knees throbbing, waiting for the rattlesnake to strike. She could already picture herself being lifted on a stretcher, a handsome paramedic sliding her onto the floor of a helicopter and sucking the venom from her thigh as they flew to safety.

Instead, a flash of blond hair and muscle launched in front of her and crash-landed her reverie.

"Got it!"

Thor thrust a pair of barbecue tongs toward the snake's head and clamped down, pinning it to the ground. He held the tongs steady as the snake bucked and writhed, its furious jaws snapping at the dust. His other hand snatched up its tail close to the rattle, stretching at least four feet in the air.

"Y'all okay?" His drawl held an appealing dash of concern.

Mandy sat up carefully. PK looked dazed, like her. But there was no blood. No bites. They both nodded.

"You got lucky," Thor said. "This here's a Grand Canyon rattlesnake."

Mandy waited for him to explain what *lucky* meant. Maybe it wasn't poisonous. Or perhaps it was especially deadly and her dreamy paramedic would have had to give her mouth-to-mouth in addition to sucking on her thigh.

"These cuties only live here, between the rims," Thor said. "That rose-pink coloring on its scales? You won't see it on any other rattlesnakes in the world. Rarer than pigs in heels." Despite her throbbing fear and pain, Mandy was charmed by the gap between his front teeth, the oddity of this mountain man who didn't get the memo that rattlesnakes are not to be messed with nor described as cuties.

"Anyone want to see a snake?" he called out.

Big Pete, Stefan, and Lucinda hiked up, and Thor started educating them on the features of the rare rattler. PK, whose face was rapidly transitioning from shock to disgust, yanked the sheet off his makeshift lean-to and draped it over his backpack and the soft cooler, hiding them from view.

Mandy rubbed her left knee, which had banged into a rock when she fell to the ground. It didn't seem bad. Maybe a bruise. She reached under her sandal, groping for whatever had made her slip earlier.

It was PK's hat, covered in sand and dust.

Mandy gathered her sarong around her, concealing the hat in the folds of the fabric. "Do you have anything to help with bruising?" she asked PK.

He looked at her, then turned back to the soft cooler, rummaging around. "I think I've got a rosehip calendula tincture in here somewhere . . ."

While he clicked through bottles and vials, Mandy poked her head under her sarong and flipped PK's hat over. There was a message outlined in thread, bright white against the red dust.

EVERYONE IS REPLACEABLE

Maybe they'd gotten mixed up with the wrong goddess.

CHAPTER NINETEEN

LIV KNELT BEHIND A raft, furtively applying sunscreen to her face, while Mandy told her what she'd learned and seen inside PK's hat.

"Thank goodness we aren't allergic to puppies," Liv said. "But I'm surprised Babette would threaten PK. The man dedicates his entire life to her needs."

"Honestly, it didn't seem that brutal after the texts he showed me," Mandy said. "Maybe this is just the way she operates. The weirdest part is that PK seems fine with it."

"Kicked dogs love their masters," Liv said.

"He played it off, but—"

"Maybe your goddess is more of the murderous, vengeful type than you thought?"

Mandy shot her a defiant look. "She talks about this in *Unleashed*. Female leaders are chronically underestimated. CEOs like Babette have to express themselves forcefully to encourage others to do their best work."

"Sending a competitor to the hospital? *Everyone is replaceable? Cross me and you're dead too?*"

"I admit it doesn't sound encouraging."

Liv wiped the last of the sunblock on her pants. "You did good with PK, Mand. More than good."

Big Pete let out one of his long taxi whistles from the bank.

"Time to load up and ship out," he called. "Today's calmer than yesterday. More float, fewer waves. With an option to go on a real pretty hike in the middle."

"Are we not even going to talk about the fact that Babette still isn't here?" Fiona asked.

"The doctor is right," Stefan said. "Has there been no information from the radio?"

"About Babette?" Big Pete shook his head. "Not a peep."

"Then let's get moving," Devon said.

Fiona glared at her. "You still think she's coming?"

"I do," Devon snapped. Her hat was tight over her short hair, and Liv found herself wishing she could take a closer look at it. But Charlie handed his sister a PFD, and the two Sauvage siblings walked away, down to Katy's raft.

Reluctantly, Liv strode over to Thor's raft, staked to a spindly palo verde tree, where Imogen, Lucinda, and Mandy were cinching down their life jackets.

"I can't believe we're going through with this," Fiona said as she approached them. "Sleeping outside with reptiles and vermin."

"Let alone the dry air," Imogen said. "That night serum PK gave me made it worse."

Lucinda turned to Mandy. "Are you okay? That rattlesnake was quite the specimen."

"Thor swooped in and saved us just in time." Mandy looked over at the guide, who was clipping a large knife to his belt. He winked and tipped an imaginary hat.

Fiona shook her head. "If Babette isn't going to show up, the least they could do now is break out the CareFree. That snake situation is exactly what this product line will be good for. CareFree transmutes worry to calm. Takes the edge off nightmares like this."

"Have you tried it yourself?" Liv asked.

"Of course," Fiona said. "We took the formula through many tweaks.

Four rounds of focus groups. Once we figured out what to extract and what to discard, we had a winner."

"Did you lead the focus groups?" Lucinda asked.

"The first three rounds, yes. After the third one, fourteen months ago, there was a major"—Fiona glanced over at Devon and Charlie, climbing into the other raft—"breakthrough. They brought on investors, started to work on production and scale. My input was no longer needed."

There was something the dermatologist wasn't saying. Liv could see it in how her eyes tightened as she spoke, trying to convince them of her words or warn them not to challenge her.

Then Liv made the connection.

"Fourteen months ago," she said. "There was an accident."

"How did you hear about that?"

"Charlie told me."

"No, he didn't," Fiona snapped.

"He did," Liv said slowly.

"These people." Fiona sounded exasperated. "Devon drops me, Charlie shoves a fifty-page NDA in my face, and now he goes around blabbing—"

"He didn't say what happened exactly. Just that somebody died."

Fiona stared at her. Liv could see the furious freight train parked behind her pursed lips, the story she was holding back there. But when Fiona finally opened her mouth, it was to change the subject.

"That's all in the past now." Fiona's voice was back to its clipped, measured cadence. "CareFree is safe and ready for market. Babette sent me a sample of the production-ready formula last week. It's perfect."

"PK said we'd get to experience it on this trip when Babette gets here," Imogen said. "Maybe that's her plan. To wait to show up until we're jumbled up in nerves from a big rapid. She could have even planted that awful snake."

"Pinky?" Mandy clutched her hand to her heart in mock horror. "We were long-lost cousins in the wilderness. He slithered in to protect me."

"From what?" Imogen asked.

"From all of you." Mandy winked.

Liv had to physically stop herself from shaking her head. Or shaking her sister. But to her surprise, everyone else laughed. Mandy was good at getting in with people. It wasn't rational that someone could provoke you, lie to you, and you'd trust them more. But Mandy had it down.

Liv's approach, in contrast, was more like the snake's. Lie in the heat of the problem as long as you can. Listen quietly and sift through the opinions, arguments, and obfuscations. Hold still until you have the answer or, more often, the question that must be answered. Only then, show your muscle. Only then, strike.

She considered the work PK had done to set up this Essence Quest. With Babette absent, he was the one managing access to skin creams, algae powder supplements, and CareFree. Was it possible he was handing out the threats too? According to Mandy, PK and Charlie had spent quite a lot of time fussing over the luggage—including the box of hats—the previous morning before the hike down. Maybe Charlie was wrong, and PK had worked with Babette to get the hats made and delivered. Liv wondered how far his personal assistant role went, and to what extent Babette confided in him about the meaning of the tasks she assigned him.

And then there was Fiona. The dermatologist had mentioned a breakthrough in CareFree's development after the third round of focus groups, fourteen months ago, which was also when Charlie had referenced a fatal accident. Liv didn't like coincidences. Was it possible someone died from that third-round prototype under Fiona's watch? Was that why Fiona was no longer working with the company? And if she was no longer involved, how was she so sure the product was now safe?

As far as Liv knew from a short assignment in Beijing reviewing export manifests, cosmetics were among the least regulated products overseen by the FDA. As long as manufacturers steered clear of certain banned chemicals, they could slap almost anything in a jar and sell it to Americans as lotion. Was there something volatile lurking in the formula for CareFree?

Liv gazed out at the Colorado River. Even in quiet patches like these, the water moved chaotically, individual ripples forming and splintering in the fractured glow. This stage of an investigation was like that, incoherent by design, each new piece of information another shiny object with the potential to blind her to the raging truth to come.

All she had was a messy stream of questions and data points. There was more to juggle than she could attend to all at once, but not enough to reveal patterns suggesting a clear direction forward. Whose words needed to be scrutinized, and whose could be ignored? Which was more important: the CareFree people or the product? The missing CEO or her threatening messages? It was impossible to hold every little observation in her head. But if she culled the wrong information, fixated on the wrong thread, she could lose time wandering down dead-end side canyons. She could end up tumbling through a rapid, losing her head in the whitewater. Or—she glanced at Mandy, busy trying to balance her water bottle on her chin, performing (or being?) her sunny self—she could lose more.

CHAPTER TWENTY

MANDY WAS JUST GETTING the hang of taking a photo without falling out of the raft when Big Pete whistled and waved an imaginary lasso in the air.

"What's that mean?" Fiona asked.

"We're pulling over and circling up," Thor said.

"For lunch?" Imogen sounded desperate. Perhaps her breakfast of powdered moss water hadn't been as nourishing as she'd hoped.

"This next rapid requires scouting," Thor said.

"I thought there weren't any big ones today," Fiona said.

"No nines or tens," Thor responded. "Bedrock's only a seven. But it's what we call a consequential rapid. Look."

Mandy peered downriver. A mountain of rock rose from the middle of the water, the waves wrapping around it and shooting down either side.

"We have to pick our way around that island," Thor said. "Otherwise, we'll get slammed against it."

"And then what?" Imogen asked.

Thor shrugged. "We could flip if we don't high-side in time. The raft could get pinned against the rock by the moving water."

"What do you do in that case?" Liv asked.

"Crawl onto the island and make like Gilligan. Pray you've got enough food and crosswords until someone comes along who can help yank the boat free. One time, I came upon two guys who got stuck for eight hours up there. They'd come up with pirate names and composed an ode to canyon wrens that was surprisingly decent."

Mandy shot a glance at Liv. How long could they last marooned on an island together? Then again, this trip was not much different—they were stuck on this river, with these people and their hats and threats and snakes and whatever else the trip threw at them, whether they liked it or not.

Thor directed the group to back-paddle until they beached on a pebbled spit above and to the right of Bedrock Rapid. The guides hopped out of the boats and started picking their way over the slippery rocks to study the rapid and carve out a plan. Most of the guests followed them, but Liv put a hand on Mandy's shoulder, pulling her behind a cluster of boulders by the rafts.

"I have an assignment for you."

Mandy grinned. They were on this island together. She had a quick, ridiculous urge to find some river grass and make them matching friendship bracelets. Or capes. And a theme song. They needed a theme song.

"What do you want me to do?"

"I need you to get us switched into the other raft with Devon, Charlie, and Stefan."

"That's it?" Maybe Mandy should have waited to hear the assignment before mentally designing their superhero costumes.

"We have to get closer to the power players who know Babette best. If she's behind the messages in the hats, those three are the most likely to be involved. The most likely to be targeted, too."

"Got it." Mandy cupped her hands around her mouth, turned to face the river, and launched into a stage whisper: "ATTENTION! IF YOU, OR ANYONE YOU KNOW, HAS BEEN THREATENED BY A MISSING LADYBOSS . . ."

Liv punched her in the arm, but Mandy was expecting it. She lifted Liv's hand off her shoulder and spun her around like a ballroom dancer.

"Don't worry, sis. Easy peasy. We're moving on up."

"You'll do it subtly."

"Of course."

"Without lying."

Time to move on. "Once we're in their raft, what do we do? Drop hints about Babette's murderous embroidery hobby? Tip the boat so Devon and Stefan fall in and we grab their hats and see what they say? High-side it against the island so they're stuck there answering our questions until dark?"

"No."

"Then what?"

"We listen."

It was just boring enough to be what Liv probably did at work all day.

Mandy sighed. "Fine."

Mandy turned and hopped from rock to rock, passing Devon and Fiona, who were still arguing about Babette; Charlie and Stefan, who were talking quietly; and Imogen, surreptitiously downing a chocolate bar. Lucinda was standing with the guides, soaking up their technical talk about paddle lines and eddies, while PK scowled at the river, as if its essence had proved poorly matched for this quest. Mandy sidled up to him and slid her arm through his. "I've got a proposition for you."

PK stiffened. "Tell me it doesn't involve another reptile."

"I'm hoping for some quality time with the wonder siblings to chat about CareFree."

He looked puzzled. "Is there something that hasn't been covered in the quarterly reports you want to know?"

"The truth is," Mandy said, tugging him closer, "I want to get my sister to invest. She and I have the same amount in trust, but she's always been more conservative with her portfolio than I have." She prayed her words made sense, or that PK knew as little as she did about high finance. "I think she'd be more receptive to a pitch from your team than hearing about CareFree from me."

PK frowned. "Babette's our best saleswoman. No one can tell the story like her."

"I know that. You know that. But for someone like my sister, someone more"—she hunted for a better term than *stick-in-the-mud*—"prudent, I think Charlie and Devon might be a fit. Maybe Stefan too. Get us into your boat. They can shower her with cold, hard data."

"Someone will have to switch into the other raft."

"I was hoping that might be you," Mandy said sweetly. "Imogen has been shooting footage of herself singing songs she wrote. Skin shanties, she calls them. She might need a little more direction."

He didn't look thrilled. Or convinced. But while Mandy's dad had never taken her fishing, he'd taught her how to bait a line.

"If you're the one to bring in a new investor at this level . . ."

PK's eyes widened just a fraction. He nodded. "I'll tell them we need to rebalance the rafts."

When the guides returned from their meeting, PK made a beeline for Big Pete, approaching him with a cockiness that suggested he both feared and relished the opportunity to lord something over the trip leader. Mandy felt a twinge of guilt, stringing him along with the promise of money she knew Liv didn't have and, if she did, would never invest in a skin care company. But PK had received a threat too. This floating confab was for his own good. Even if he didn't yet see it that way.

If Katy was at all surprised to find that her faux-hawked passenger had been swapped out for Mandy and her sister, she didn't show it. She checked everyone's PFDs, and they resettled in her raft: Devon and Charlie in front, Mandy and Liv in the relative safety of the middle, and Stefan in the third row. Katy perched on the back, the hood of her long-sleeved rash guard pulled all the way up. She guided them down the right channel of Bedrock Rapid with precise, confident commands that shot them past the island with ease. The whitewater subsided, and the canyon sharpened around them, slick black rock rising to replace the crumbly sandstone with a tighter, meaner package.

"We're heading into the narrowest part of the canyon next," Katy said. "The granite gorge. That volcanic rock, the Vishnu Schist, is 1.75 billion years old."

Devon nodded. "Dad loved to talk about the ancient mountains that formed this canyon. How the world turned itself inside out here."

"Your father brought you here?" Liv asked.

Mandy could hear skepticism in her sister's voice. Maybe it was just the impossibility of imagining their own dad willingly tromping into the great outdoors.

"He was actually the inspiration for CareFree," Devon said. "Dad got me excited about plants as a kid. He'd always be bending down to snap a picture of a wildflower popping out of the sidewalk or an unusual weed in his tomatoes. Mom joked he was great at taking family photos of our feet."

Mandy looked at Charlie to see his reaction to the family memory. But the man was gazing out at the slick volcanic rock.

"When I was getting my PhD," Devon continued, "my father joined me on some of my scouting trips. Twelve years ago, we came here, not to raft the canyon, but to walk it, rim to rim."

"Not a lot of plants in a desert," Mandy said.

"More than you'd imagine. This canyon crosses five out of the seven biomes you'd see if you walked the US from top to tail. And what grows here, it's magic. The Native people know it. Botanists know it. There's a plant here that showed me what could be possible for CareFree."

"What plant?" Liv asked.

"Datura," Devon said. "Native people call it sacred thorn-apple."

"Why is it sacred?"

"Datura is central to a lot of traditional healing ceremonies in the Southwest. Medicine people brew a version of it as a hallucinogenic. It's a powerful vision expander."

"Datura's all over here," Katy piped up from the back of the raft. "The side canyons are full of it. It's toxic if you don't know how to handle it, but Indigenous people in the Grand Canyon use it for rituals. Kinda spooky, though."

"Spooky?"

Katy nodded. "Datura's a moonflower. It blooms at night, gets pollinated by bats. Witchy. I have an herbalist friend who got deep into communing with it. Smoking the flowers, sucking on the seeds, making tinctures from the root. She said Lady Datura entered her like a murderous goddess of hell."

Charlie coughed. "That's not the way we see it."

"My brother's right," Devon clarified. "We aren't focused on the spiritual side of datura. But its unique properties inspired our product development."

"Datura isn't a product," Katy said. "It's a supernatural being. I drank it once, brewed into a tea. I swear I flew that night."

"Just once? You didn't want to fly again?" Mandy asked.

"I did it one more time," Katy said. "The second trip freaked me out. The plant spoke to me in this deep voice, trapped me in a tunnel of darkness. I think I took a single breath in twelve hours."

Devon nodded. "There are accounts tracing back to the 1600s of people in North America ingesting datura—the seeds, in particular—and experiencing a range of hallucinatory effects. All the records suggest the experience is transcendent, but highly variable. At Oxford, I started correlating different effects that could be traced to dosage, preparation, and the precise strain of the plant. One of the more reliable effects across different strains is a kind of temporary amnesia. A letting go of worry. When you get the right dose, it feels—"

"Carefree," Mandy said.

Devon's mouth twitched. "I didn't love that name at first. But yes. We developed a distillation process to safely isolate that feeling. The sense I had in those earliest tests, it was more than carefree. It was like someone opened new space in my heart."

Her words vibrated through the air, mirroring the easy ripples of the water. Conversation was both quieter and amplified in the canyon, echoing off the high walls and then falling away, slipping under the purr of the river.

"Anyway." Devon shrugged. "I knew there was something in it that could help people."

"So now you're in the drug business?" Liv asked.

"Not at all," Charlie interjected. "We're in the wellness business. Traditional medicine is important, but it's also unpleasant. People see it as being about sickness. You take the drug, you get better, but the road to recovery is studded with chalky pills and scary injections. What we offer is an alternative. An experience of self-care. Of pleasure. It's about building the relationship with your body you want. And this new product? The potential for CareFree is nothing less than personal freedom."

Mandy thought of the little jar PK had offered her that morning, its creamy promise. She couldn't wait to try it later that night.

Liv seemed unconvinced. "You think there are millions of people who want to forget their lives?"

"Not forget. Just take a break. Tap into that openness Devon was talking about. Do you know how rare that feeling is? A few people are lucky enough to do this"—Charlie scooped a handful of river water and let it pour down his arm—"but most don't have the time or money to step outside their lives. They're under constant pressure. Prescriptions for anxiety medications are through the roof. People feel broken, like they need to be fixed. But we believe it's the world that's broken, and you deserve to give yourself a break every once in a while."

"But if datura makes people feel like witches from hell, that hardly sounds like—"

"That's where the science comes in." Devon's voice broke in, strong and sure. "The active drugs in datura, atropine and scopolamine, are neuroblockers, and yes, they can be dangerous. But they can also be used in perfectly safe medical applications, like the patches some people wear to prevent motion sickness. We honed an extraction process that targets a very specific subset of datura's natural properties to tap into that ephemeral carefree feeling. I did years of experimentation, first at Oxford, then at the company, trying different sources of the plant, different strains, different ways to deliver it topically. It's one of the reasons CareFree has been so expensive to develop."

"And worth it," Charlie said. "Now that our formula is safe and stable, this is going to be huge. Like what CBD did for sleep, or retinol for aging skin. CareFree erases worry from your face, smoothing out the hard edges. You can feel it, and you can see it. CareFree's datura formulation has multibillion-dollar potential. And we'll be first to market."

There was real pride in his voice. Or maybe it was greed. Mandy turned to Liv and gave her an encouraging smile. "CareFree sounds pretty great, right?"

"It sounds like you took a cosmic being and neutered her," Katy muttered.

"Neutered is safe," Charlie said. "Neutered is what sells."

"But surely using CareFree comes with some risks," Liv said.

"No risks," Charlie said quickly. "Devon and her team have been meticulous on the science. We've scrubbed the plant of all its delirium-inducing effects. You wouldn't believe how much active psychotropic material we have to discard from every batch of datura to ensure we only deliver the highest quality product to our customers."

Katy frowned. "She won't like this."

"Who?" Charlie said. "Our customers?"

"The plant. The goddess."

The raft fell silent.

"Sorry. What do I know?" Katy said, taking up her paddle again.

"We know CareFree will be a mammoth hit," Charlie said. "Our team believes in this product, and Babette's reputation with our customers is unparalleled. She's a master of selling something new to the world and making people feel like it's exactly what they've been missing all along."

"So where is she?" Stefan's voice was curt and measured. "What is she doing that is more important than this?"

No response. All that salesmanship and bluster, and now nothing.

Mandy couldn't let this opening pass her by.

"Maybe she's plotting to murder the competition."

CHAPTER TWENTY-ONE

CHARLIE GLARED AT LIV. "You told me you were the pinnacle of discretion."

Liv took a long breath, buying herself time to respond. There was no use deliberating over whether Mandy's brash statement had been a brilliant move or a foolish one. Her sister had poked the beehive. Liv's only option now was to see if any honey might come out.

"I told you my job requires me to be discreet," she said. "And I'm off the clock this week."

"What are you talking about?" Devon asked.

"You really don't know?" Mandy broke in.

Devon's face was an iron mask of confrontation; Charlie's, red with anger. Liv had to find a way to keep the pressure on while redirecting the heat.

"Your brother received a threatening message yesterday." Liv shot a look back at Katy before saying more. The guide didn't seem to be paying attention to the conversation in the raft, her eyes tracing the hieroglyphics of the swirling river. So Liv continued. "My sister received a threat too. As did PK. I'm assuming both of you"—she looked from Devon to Stefan—"were threatened as well."

"What was the message?" Devon asked her brother.

When Charlie didn't respond, she nudged him with her paddle.

"You kept this a secret? You got a *threat*, and you told her"—Liv reared back as Devon's paddle swung in her direction—"before you told me?"

His voice was hoarse. "I wasn't sure you'd believe it."

"Why?"

Charlie's voice dropped so low Liv had to slide across the bench to catch his words. "Because it was a death threat. And it came from Babette."

"Oh, please," Devon said. "She's not even here. You're catastrophizing."

"Look," Charlie said. He took off his cap and showed his sister the ugly words inside.

"This doesn't mean anything," Devon snapped.

Denial. Interesting. Liv looked from Devon and Charlie to Stefan, curious how the bearded man might react. Stefan was looking down, as if he were embarrassed by the direction of the conversation. Or was he debating whether to share something?

"Would you please show me your hat?" Liv asked Devon calmly.

Mandy turned to Stefan. "And yours."

Devon hesitated, and Charlie spoke up. "See for yourself. If I'm exaggerating, you have nothing to worry about."

"Fine." Devon passed her ball cap to Liv, and her sister snatched Stefan's off his head with an impish grin.

"Abracadabra," Mandy said, waving his hat in the muddy water.

Once the hats were sufficiently silt-ridden, they flipped them over and lined them up on the middle bench of the boat between them.

"Watch," Liv said. Everyone peered in, as if they were all waiting for a Polaroid to develop.

The murky water had stained Stefan's hat, but otherwise, it remained blank. Liv was surprised. Why would CareFree's first investor receive a threat, but not its biggest investor? Before she could probe deeper, a faint white message surfaced across the inner crown of Devon's. The wording was less threatening than Charlie's, but still aggressive:

THIS IS MY COMPANY, NOT YOURS

"See what I mean?" Charlie said to his sister. "She knows."

"We've done nothing wrong," Devon said.

"You know that isn't how she'd see it." Charlie looked stricken. "If she found out what we're planning, she could be meeting with board members while we're stuck down here."

Devon swung around to face Stefan. "Has she asked for your support?"

"She has not." The investor paused. "And you know where my sympathies lie. But it is your sister's company, as she apparently sees fit to remind you. She may have other sources of information."

"What were you planning?" Liv asked.

Charlie and Devon didn't seem to hear her. They were locked in on each other, speaking a shorthand only they understood.

"We were so careful," Devon said. "But you think she knows."

"I do," Charlie said. "And now she's retaliating."

"Nothing's happened so far, besides these messages."

"We get thrown from a boat and a rattlesnake attacks, and that's nothing?"

Devon shook her head. "I don't see how she could have engineered any of that."

Charlie shot a dark look back at Katy, whose eyes were studiously trained on the ripples in the river. "Maybe the guides work for her," he whispered.

"The *guides*?" Devon sounded incredulous. "Katy tossed you in the water? Thor planted the snake? What's next, Pete poisoning our sandwiches?"

"It's possible. Think about the symbology. A snake. She's calling us snakes."

"I get it," Devon said. "But the snake didn't show up in your sleeping bag. Or mine."

"If she knows what we're doing," Charlie said, "I don't think we can underestimate how she might respond. What she might take from us."

"Our jobs, you mean? The company?"

Charlie shook his head. "Or more."

"What would be more?"

Charlie gave his sister a long, anxious look. "You saw my hat. You know."

"Justine," Devon murmured.

Liv was confused. She shot a glance at Mandy, hoping the name triggered something for her. Maybe Justine was one of the accidents Charlie had referred to earlier. Maybe she was mentioned in Babette's autobiography. But Mandy shook her head.

Devon turned to Liv. "You think these threats are serious?"

"I think . . ." She looked from Devon to Charlie, turning the paddle in her hands. "I think your sister has a history of being ruthless about getting what she wants. I think there's something you three"—she waved her hand to indicate Devon, Charlie, and Stefan—"know that the rest of us don't. I think we're at the bottom of a dangerous canyon, cut off from the outside world. We can help each other, or not. We can lie to each other, or not. My responsibility is to my sister's safety and my own. If you want more from me than that, you're going to have to tell us what's really going on."

At that, the raft went silent. For the next ten minutes, the only sound was the gurgle of the slow-moving river, Katy's paddle dipping to keep them on a straight path.

Then two hard thumps on the back of the raft jolted them all to attention.

"Didn't mean to scare ya." Big Pete waved with his paddle, then maneuvered his raft alongside theirs. He was holding a clunky black object in his other hand. "Got word on the sat phone that our last two guests are hiking down from the North Rim to join us at Deer Creek. In a few miles, your party will be complete."

"She's coming," Devon said. She reached out for her soggy hat, then hesitated, her hand pausing over the brim as if it might bite her.

"Two guests?" Stefan asked. "Who is coming with her?"

CHAPTER TWENTY-TWO

WHEN BIG PETE GAVE the signal, all three boats turned into a wide, flat beach on the north side of the canyon to break for lunch. Mandy dropped her paddle across her lap and stretched her arms in the air, wiggling her fingers in the crackling heat. Ten stories above them, on the south side of the canyon, two huge concave divots in the cliffside bored down on them, like the eyes of a ravenous owl.

"Is this Deer Creek?" Charlie said.

"Not quite," Katy said, leaping from the raft. She started staking the boats to the bank while Thor and Big Pete lifted folding tables and coolers off the chub for lunch. "This is Tapeats. Deer Creek is three river miles ahead. There's a massive waterfall at its base that pours into the Colorado. We'll make sandwiches here, and then you have a choice. You can float to Deer Creek on the boats with me and Pete, or you can hike from here with Thor."

"Shouldn't we all stay together?" Devon asked.

"If you want," Katy said. "But the hike is pretty amazing. It goes to a waterfall called Thunder Spring, then over these big sprawling bowls of rock in Surprise Valley. The last mile links up with the trail from the North Rim to Deer Creek—the one your sister is probably walking down right now."

"Let me get this straight," PK said. "We could float along for three miles to one waterfall, or we can hike for hours in the heat to see a different waterfall and a bunch more rocks?" He snorted. "Easy choice."

"Thunder Spring is unusual," Katy said. "An explosion of water. I promise you've never seen anything like it."

"Pass," PK said. "I'll stay with the boats."

"I will hike," Stefan said.

"Me too," Fiona said.

Lucinda nodded at her granddaughter. "As will we."

"Nana, no," Imogen said. "I need to edit the videos I shot this morning on the raft. And heights make me break out."

Lucinda stared at her. "You hiked all the way down to the river without a problem."

"That was down. Not up and over."

Mandy wondered whether the radically honest Imogen was lying to her grandmother, and if so, why. It wasn't shocking to imagine the teen didn't want to take an optional hike, but Mandy was curious whether there was more to the girl's story. Had Imogen made some recordings she needed to hide once Babette arrived? Or was there a way she planned to meet her celebrity employer—her own surprise grand entrance—that she was preparing to execute?

"Suit yourself," Lucinda said crisply. She adjusted her enormous sun hat and headed toward the lunch station.

Devon and Charlie lingered with Mandy and Liv on the bank as Katy cinched down the last of her knots.

"When do you think my sister will arrive at Deer Creek?" Devon asked.

Katy squinted up to the north. "If they got an early start on the hike down, they might be there soon."

"The boats will reach her first?" Devon said. "Then I'll float."

"I'll hike with Stefan," Charlie said.

"Charlie . . ." Devon's voice was low. "Don't you think it would be wise for us to be together when we greet Babette?"

"When we greet her," Charlie responded, "I'd like to have our biggest investor by our side."

"And your first investor," Mandy added. "I'll hike too." She stepped toward Charlie, then stared at Liv and waited.

It was times like this Mandy wished they were the kind of sisters who knew each other well enough to read each other's minds. She'd always been jealous of siblings like that, the ones who accidentally got the same haircut or yelled, "Fettuccine Alfredo!" during a game of Charades as soon as the other one put a single finger in the air. They'd never had that kind of telepathy. Even when their mom died and Liv had flown across the country to get home and be with her, some part of her big sister never quite made it through the door. Liv was always keeping busy—doing dishes, sorting papers—hovering just outside the crush of grief. She never allowed herself to collapse on the couch with Mandy and wallow in their pain. As if making herself soft was too painfully hard.

Liv's heart was off limits, her brain a steel maze locked in an iron box. You couldn't watch the ball bearings as they rolled through. You could only hear the muffled plinks and guess where you stood with her.

Like right now. Was Liv impressed that Mandy had volunteered to accompany Charlie on the hike, to facilitate a splitting of the Sauvage siblings so they could learn more? Or did Liv think Mandy was hitting the trail just because Thor would be there?

And what would Liv choose?

"I'll float," Liv said.

The words shot a surge of pride through Mandy's chest. Liv believed in her. She thought Mandy could handle Charlie and Stefan on her own. But something else hummed in her heart too. Sadness that they wouldn't be together. A spasm of fear of setting off on her own. And one more note, twanging like a tired guitar string. Regret. She'd had no clue what Liv would choose, or why she'd done it. Her sister was as inscrutable to her as ever.

CHAPTER TWENTY-THREE

THREAT ASSESSMENT WAS EASY when you were doing it from an air-conditioned embassy office. Liv had a much harder time now, standing on the empty beach at Tapeats in the hundred-degree heat, eating a peanut butter sandwich, debating whether she'd made the right call to split from Mandy.

Her sister wouldn't be isolated; in addition to Stefan and Charlie, Fiona and Lucinda had also volunteered to hike to Thunder Spring. And Thor would be watching over them. She still wasn't positive the guide was trustworthy, but so far he'd acted in their best interests. And it probably wouldn't bode well for his job security if he let a guest get hurt on his watch.

The real question was what Charlie was hoping to achieve on the hike. She watched him dig through his day pack, pulling out a long-sleeved shirt to protect his pale arms from the sun. He looked resolved, fierce even, as if there was something he had to do, and no matter how scary or painful, he was going to do it. But what could it be? Stefan had already voiced his support for Charlie and Devon's plan—whatever it was—and Charlie hardly seemed capable of strong-arming the Dutchman if his allegiance had wavered because of the threats.

Liv made her way over to Mandy, who was hovering over the remains of the sandwich table with the guides. Mandy's hand was on Thor's forearm. There was something about it, her sister's fingers lightly touching the blurred grizzly bear he had tattooed there, that scared Liv for a moment. Whether she was worried for her sister's safety, the guide's heart, or her own, she wasn't sure.

"Hey," Liv said, bumping a hip into Mandy's. "Got a sec?"

"For you? Always. But first, help me out here." Mandy pointed to the two-heeled sandwich in Katy's hand. "Potato chips on peanut butter and jelly. Good or gross?"

"Um . . . depends on the chips?" Liv said.

"Doesn't matter," Thor said.

"It totally matters!" Katy crowed. "Regular salty chips, yum. Barbecue, sure. But those vinegary ones, or the spicy ones . . ."

"Dude." Thor shook his head. "You never been out in the wilderness on calorie deficit? One time I chewed on my knife holster just to stay sane."

Liv looked at the salt-stained leather sheath clipped to Thor's belt. Suddenly the leftover chip dust was looking a lot more appetizing.

"Thor's right," Big Pete said. "When you're at the end of the lunch line, and you're oaring that chub all day, I don't care if they're pickle sriracha chips. It's all going in my sandwich."

"Remember Everything Pickles?" Mandy asked Liv.

Of course she remembered.

"When we were kids," Mandy told the guides, "our dad thought it was funny to drop other stuff in the jar with the brine and see what happened. How it affected the flavor. We made penny pickles, chili pickles, grass pickles, even one time he was repping a dog food brand and he dumped some biscuits into the jar just to try it out."

"How'd they taste?" Big Pete asked.

Liv grimaced. Everything Pickles were never about the taste.

She knew Mandy wouldn't tell that part of the story, how he'd send his girls back to the grocery store with the mostly eaten jar of whatever crap he'd thrown in so they could complain there was something wrong with the pickles and get a free replacement. It was a never-ending joke for him and Mandy, a game. For Liv, it was something else. A fermented, stinking lie. Even when she was stationed in Romania, where pickles were works of art—each jar an explosion of flowering dill and fresh-cut horseradish root—she couldn't stand the sight of them.

"I'm with Thor and Pete," Liv said. No more charming Guy Chisholm stories today. "Calories are calories, however you consume them. C'mon," she said, grabbing for Mandy's hand, "let's take a dip before your hike."

Liv guided them down to a quiet stretch of the bank and waded up to her knees in the river. Now that the sun was at its apex, the water sparkled with green flashes of movement, the light tracing every swirling eddy and flickering fish. Next to her, Mandy unwrapped the sarong from around her bikini and dunked it in the icy river.

"Let's talk assignments before we split up," Liv said.

"Charlie seems pretty wound up. Want me to grill him when we're out on a ledge somewhere?"

"I want you to do two things."

"Grill him AND make sure no one pushes him over the ledge?"

"You can watch how Charlie interacts with Stefan, but more importantly, try to get Stefan on his own. He's involved with whatever Charlie and Devon are up to, even if he didn't receive a threat. And buddy up to Fiona."

Mandy draped her soaked sarong over her hair and torso like a nun's habit. "Why Fiona?"

"She ran the CareFree testing for three rounds, until fourteen months ago, when someone died. Then they got rid of Fiona. I want to know why. Maybe she screwed something up. Or maybe there's something dangerous about their use of datura that they don't want her to reveal."

"You believe that witchcraft stuff?"

"It's not just a hippie theory," Liv said. "The State Department has done its own studies on that plant. I didn't make the connection until Devon started talking about scopolamine. In South America, they call it Devil's Breath. Ingesting datura can turn people into zombies, make them willing to do anything. I've seen videos of people voluntarily handing over their car keys and bank cards to criminals under its influence. It's scary."

"But they're using a different strain and part of the plant for CareFree."

"That's what they say," Liv acknowledged. "But the fact that datura is associated with serious crimes . . . I don't like it. Devon says the formula they're taking to market is benign. But Fiona said Babette begged her to come here because of a problem with CareFree. Maybe Fiona saw something different in the focus groups."

"Do you think the person who died in the focus groups might be named Justine?" Mandy asked.

Liv looked at her sister in surprise. Every once in a while, Mandy made a connection Liv hadn't even considered. It was as if the synapses that marched down straight paths in Liv's head did trampoline backflips in Mandy's.

"That's interesting," Liv said.

"*Cross me and you're dead too.*" Mandy sounded excited now. "Maybe Fiona killed someone named Justine. Maybe I can crack the case right now."

"Or maybe it was Babette."

"You don't like the Sauvages, do you?"

Liv hesitated. She could see the frustration on Mandy's face, the implication that she was judging not just the Babette team, but her.

"I don't trust them. There's a difference."

Mandy swallowed. "And you don't trust me to find out Charlie's plan."

"That's not it. I'll push Devon on that. But that's a known issue. Whatever Stefan's up to, what Fiona knows—that's uncharted territory."

"So you get the death threats, and I get the question marks," Mandy said. "You're the deep end. I'm the kiddie pool."

"It's all useful data," Liv said. "Not a competition. And as you said, Fiona could be dangerous. The more we know about everyone, the better we can assess whether the threats are credible."

"What do you mean?"

"A threat is an irrational act. Why inform your target of your intention to hurt them? Why give them information they could use to protect themselves from an attack? The threat is a kind of performance, distinct from any act of violence."

"A performance, huh?" Mandy ran her hands through the water. "And you want to know who's in the audience and who's backstage."

"Exactly." Liv was impressed how quickly Mandy got it. "With multiple threats, it's possible Babette does want to kill multiple people, or has paranoid fantasies of doing so. You'd be amazed how often a disturbed individual sends death threats to the ambassador, the pope, and the manager of their local coffee shop at the same time. But sometimes multiple threats can mean something else. It could be a way of stirring the pot, seeding confusion. Maybe Babette wants to mask who her true target is. Or maybe she isn't trying to kill anyone but is trying to use the messages to extract a piece of information held by someone in the group."

"Maybe there's a threat to CareFree."

"Or maybe CareFree itself is the threat," Liv countered. "That's what I want to find out."

"Hikers!" Thor was up on the bank, waving a water bottle in the air. "Let's get hoofing. Lots of ground to cover before we reconnect with everyone at Deer Creek."

Liv and Mandy stepped out of the cool water and looked up Tapeats Canyon. A faint, scraggly trail snaked up the cliff alongside the fast-moving creek. Within minutes, Mandy would be hundreds of feet above her, tucked into pockets of crumbling rock, invisible from the river.

Liv pulled her sister into a quick, fierce hug.

"Be careful," she said. "Stay away from the edge. Stay with the group. Remember, whether it's real or not, you got a threat. It could have come from any one of them."

For a moment, Mandy's eyes widened. Maybe she was actually absorbing Liv's words, taking her advice seriously. Then she slapped on a sunny smile and wriggled out of the hug.

"Don't worry. I'm an international woman of mystery, remember? We're going to have this all figured out by the time I see you in Deer Creek."

CHAPTER TWENTY-FOUR

FOR THE FIRST MILE, Mandy could barely lift her eyes from the trail to Thunder Spring, let alone ask anyone questions. They walked single file, Fiona and Lucinda setting a surprisingly aggressive pace, with Charlie and Stefan loping close behind. Mandy tried to stay with them, but she kept stumbling over rocks, showering pebbles into the fast-moving creek below. It was clear from the tamped-down path that thousands of hikers had trod through here. But the trail's potential for menace was just as apparent. There were snake holes, scorpion dens, and wobbly boulders ready to slide. She even saw a few places where a fallen rock had punched the trail away, leaving an empty comma of dead air in its place.

"Want me to ask them to slow down?" Thor asked.

Mandy couldn't decide whether Thor was in the rear to watch over whoever was slowest or if he was checking out her butt. In contrast to her crunching lurch up the trail, the guide was moving silently, practically floating over the rocks in his minimalist leather sandals.

"I'm good."

She took a breath and realized it was true. Despite the threats, her burgeoning sunburn, and the potential for each step to send her sprawling, her jittery tension had abated. The intensity and beauty of the hike had temporarily pushed the threats aside. The sandstone ledges they traversed were narrow but navigable, and a light breeze in the paper-dry air kept her sweat at bay. Where the Colorado was a thick greenish-brown, Tapeats Creek ran fast and clear, its music less a roar than a skittering rush as it fell over rocks and lacy tendrils of moss on its way to the river. The higher they climbed, the deeper they seemed to be heading into the side canyon. It was as if they were tucking into a pocket of paradise, a thin seam of the cliffside peeled back stitch by stitch to allow them passage.

"So." A deep male voice jolted her out of her reverie. Mandy had been so focused on the scenery that she hadn't noticed that Stefan had slowed down to join her. "What do you think of all of this?"

His voice was low, his accent and vague words obscuring her ability to interpret his meaning. Was he talking about this hike? The rafting trip? The threats?

This was the perfect opportunity for Mandy to talk to Stefan one-on-one. But the fact that he had approached her gave her pause. Stefan's gaze was intense, and Mandy clocked for the first time how much larger than her he was. He had at least ten inches and fifty pounds on her. He could probably sweep her off the trail, into the abyss, without breaking a sweat.

She looked around. They were alone on a narrow ledge a hundred feet above the surging creek. Lucinda, Fiona, and Charlie were far ahead, ascending an endless staircase of rock. Thor was behind her, scrambling up the hillside toward a line of pockmarked boulders, presumably in pursuit of a rare and dubiously cute reptile.

Mandy sat down against a salt cedar tree, putting as much distance as possible between her and the precipice.

"Pebble in my boot," she explained. She started untying the left one. It would make her vulnerable, being shoeless, but if Stefan was the one behind the threats, she wasn't going to outmuscle or outrun him. She had a better chance if she kept her center of gravity low, the tree backing her up, a heavy object in her hands.

Stefan moved closer, crouching an arm's length upstream from her. She resisted the growing tension in her body, letting her fingers graze the furrowed trunk of the salt cedar the way a child might stroke their worries into a battered teddy bear's fur. Some of the tree's purple blossoms fell into her hair. She brushed them aside. Confident. Calm.

"The messages in the hats," she said. "You don't seem to be as concerned as the others about them."

Stefan looked down toward the water. He seemed reticent to respond, even though he had been the one to initiate conversation. They were exposed out here, on the wavering trail above the creek, the ragged edge of a rip in the earth. She had to find another way to inch along it.

"How did you get involved with Babette?" Mandy asked him.

"It is not me who is involved," Stefan said. "My employer, the Regent Group. I am their agent. I convey their interests with respect to my division."

"What division is that?"

"I represent investments in distraction."

"I'm sorry?"

Stefan smiled. "At my firm, we believe that there are four fundamental human desires that drive consumption. Distraction is one of them. We want to be entertained. We want to escape. People pay good money for this."

"CareFree will help people forget their worries," Mandy said slowly.

"That's right," Stefan said. "To be carefree, this is a child's desire. Americans have quite the appetite for it." He touched the brim of his cap. "Social media platforms like Hitch, where Imogen Duvray performs, these are distractions too."

"You have an investment in Hitch?"

"Distraction is a large portfolio."

Mandy regarded him. She was starting to get a handle on his oblique way of speaking. She wondered if Imogen had truly won the online influencer contest or whether the bearded man in front of her had recommended the girl as the fresh face of CareFree. As Lucinda had said, nothing on social media was as straightforward as it seemed. And she imagined a businessman like Stefan would look for connections across investments where possible.

"So the messages in the hats . . ."

"I see them as distractions as well."

"You don't think they're real?"

"The messages appear real. But I cannot guess at Babette's true intent." Stefan looked at her seriously. "Distraction is a powerful drug all its own. We are all so eager to be guided by the nose—or hat—at any moment. The real question is what we are being distracted from."

A fine cascade of dust fell between them, and Thor hopped down onto the trail from the constellation of cratered rocks above them. "You two okay?"

Mandy nodded. Stefan said nothing.

"We're right around the corner from Thunder Spring," Thor said. "Ready to have your minds blown?"

Mandy laced up her boot and popped to her feet. "Don't tell me. It's a chocolate waterfall."

"Better."

"A secret breeding ground for yetis? I knew global warming was serious, but to imagine them all the way down here with their fur coats—"

"You'll see."

They skirted a long curve—Stefan in front, Thor in back, Mandy comforted by her position in the middle of the sandwich—and over a rocky field. At first, Mandy placed each foot with precision, weighing every step. But her curiosity about Thunder Spring soon outweighed her fastidiousness and she found herself bounding over boulders, scrabbling forward just barely faster than her ability to control her body toward an unseen oasis just beyond the wide gully of rocks before them.

She took one last leap and almost plowed into Stefan. He'd stopped. They all stopped.

An ancient roar echoed through the canyon. Its source was a miracle: a giant waterfall geysering sideways out of an otherwise barren rock face. Water crashed out from two enormous holes punched in the stone, as if a family of cave-dwelling giants had turned the taps on full blast and then forgotten about the bath. Above the falls, the dull orange cliffs rose for thousands of feet, dry and cracked, stretching up to where the sun blazed the top of the canyon gold. Below Thunder Spring, the crumbling edifice gave way to an oasis of lush trees and vines spreading like an old man's beard from the bottom of the falls.

"Thunder Spring," Thor said. "The waterfall from nowhere."

Mandy stood there, dumbfounded. Thunder Spring swallowed up her senses, shoving away all thoughts of hats and human concerns. Mandy gorged herself on its whip-cold spray, its raging growl. This was fury. This was distraction. This was threat.

She could almost drown in it.

CHAPTER TWENTY-FIVE

LIV SPENT THE THREE river miles between Tapeats and Deer Creek in the back of Katy's raft, her T-shirt doused in river water and pulled over her face to shield her from the sun. She feigned drowsiness—not difficult in the blistering heat—and tried to fade into the rubber wall of the boat while Imogen took photos of a family of spiky-crested ducks (mergansers, Katy called them) and Devon and PK debated what lay ahead for them at Deer Creek.

"Who do you think is coming down with her?" Devon asked.

"I'm guessing a board member," PK responded.

"But who?"

"Not Frank," PK said. "He straight-up laughed when I invited him to this Essence Quest. Said he was still recovering from the last one."

"Maybe she convinced Michael to come," Devon said.

"He's in Saint Bart's honeymooning with his fourth wife," PK said. "I messengered them a Fierce couple's basket." He squinted up at the sun for a moment. "Maybe it's someone else who can breathe firepower into the launch. Didn't Babette have dinner recently with Giselle? She'd be a much better spokeswoman than . . . that."

He pointed his chin at Imogen, who was bouncing on the very front of the raft like a bull rider, whooping and waving a selfie stick in the air.

"She does seem carefree," Devon said.

"Brain-free is more like it," PK muttered.

"Do you think it's possible Babette convinced the lead investor to join us?" Devon asked.

Liv noticed how carefully Devon said it, as if it discomfited her even to utter the words. It was becoming clear that PK was closer to Babette than her own sister. Either that, or Devon was out of the loop on the business side of things. Maybe they were the kind of family that compartmentalized, each tending their own garden. If Liv ever ran a business with Mandy—let alone a fast-growing, multibillion-dollar one—they'd need clear delineation of responsibilities to avoid strangling each other every other second.

"Stefan's boss has never shown an interest in personal involvement before," PK said. "No one has even met him besides Babette. Why would that change now?"

Devon dropped her eyes to the water. When she looked up, her tone shifted. It was lighter. False. "We don't have camping gear if she's bringing someone with her. Every spot is taken."

"I'm sure they'll drum up another god-awful yellow sleeping bag," PK said. "Seems like more than enough of those floating around."

He scooted forward to talk with Imogen, and Liv seized the opportunity for a one-on-one with Devon. She pulled her shirt down off her head and slid across to the other side of the raft.

"How are you feeling?" Liv asked.

"About what? The fact that my sister has threatened me and my brother?" Devon's voice was light, but her eyes were sharp.

"So you did cross her."

Devon said nothing.

"It wouldn't be surprising if you were scared," Liv said. "I can help if you tell me."

The older woman regarded her. "My sister and my brother are the emotional ones in our family. I prefer to deal with the facts."

"What are the facts about Justine?"

"Excuse me?"

"Earlier, when we were looking at your brother's hat. You said *Justine*. Who is she? Someone who was killed?"

Devon glanced forward, to where PK and Imogen were huddled over her phone. "Justine Long's death was an accident," she whispered. "An unfortunate consequence of the focus groups we couldn't have anticipated."

So Mandy had guessed right. But Devon's wording gave Liv pause. "It wasn't a sign of potential danger in CareFree?"

"Not at all."

"And Babette? Does she see you as a danger to CareFree?"

The boat rocked, its nose dipping to kiss the river. Katy had shifted into a standing crouch, using her paddle to point forward. "Deer Creek's coming up. Grab your paddles, and let's get to the beach."

"We'll see my sister soon enough," Devon said. "And whoever she's with. It's all going to be fine."

She looked as if she were commanding herself and Liv to believe it.

The beach they pulled up to at Deer Creek was empty. While Katy and Big Pete wrangled the boats, Liv and the others got their bearings on the bank. Babette hadn't made it here yet, but there was another powerful force to contend with: the enormous, pounding cascade of Deer Creek Falls. In the past two days, Liv had encountered more waterfalls in the wild than she'd seen in her entire life to date. They sprang out of cliff sides. They trickled over moss. They cascaded prettily through rocks. Each one was more perfect, more dramatic, so much so that now, staring up two hundred feet at Deer Creek Falls, she was entirely unsurprised.

But then she got closer. The water was falling straight down like a girl's long hair, but Liv could feel the lateral power of it, how it created its own wind system at the bottom, spraying mist outward with enough force to shove her back and make her shiver. Tiny droplets caught the sun in midair, creating a perpetual rainbow that shimmered before her.

Liv walked in beyond her comfort zone, without regard for the cascade's cold fury or the way the spray blasted her full in the face. It stung, but it didn't matter. The sparkling, frigid water was a reprieve from the hot air and blood-and-dun muddiness of the Colorado. The rainbow mist was magic. It was unicorn water. Mermaid water. The kind of water Liv dreamed of as a kid.

When she was eight, their dad had told her and her sister that mermaids were real and living in San Diego. Liv was old enough to question her father's promises, but she wanted to believe in mermaids. When they arrived, however, they spent the whole time in a tiny apartment over a liquor store with Guy's waitress girlfriend and her flatulent dog. The waitress's bangs curled up like a wave, but the ocean nearby was gray and flat, crowded with shipping containers and beat-up seagulls. Every morning while the adults slept, Liv and Mandy would walk along the marina. Whenever Liv yanked her little sister's hand to avoid a splotch of bird poop or a rogue skateboarder, Mandy would squeal and say, "I saw one!"

Liv remembered her five-year-old sister pointing at shattered sparkles on the dirty water.

"You missed it," Mandy said. "She was waving at you."

Liv had given up on mermaids long ago. But now, looking at the rainbows shooting off Deer Creek Falls, Liv wondered if she'd had it wrong. She wondered if it would have been different if they had a dad who took them camping instead of to sales conventions. She wondered again if she'd made a mistake when she split from Mandy earlier, each of them heading to different waterfalls. That was the way they'd always functioned, moving at different speeds, in different parts of the world. That was what worked for them. But Liv didn't want to frolic in the rainbow-misted water on her own. If there were mermaids on this planet, she wanted to meet them with her sister by her side.

"Here it is." The voice floated toward her from beyond the spray. It wasn't Mandy. It was Devon. "Datura."

Liv moved toward her. The older woman had tucked herself in beside the falls, crouching by a cluster of plants with rich green leaves and pale, thin-skinned trumpet flowers.

"This is what CareFree derives from?" Most of the blossoms were closed, but a few had their curled lips parted, their delicate white bells revealing deep purple veins and a ghostly lavender edge.

"Close," Devon responded. "We use *Datura wrightii*. This is a different varietal, *Datura quercifolia*. Don't touch."

"Are there thorns?" Liv couldn't see any.

"Only on the seedpods, not the flowers. But the entire plant is toxic. If you get some on your hand, and then in your mouth . . . it might be unpleasant, especially in this heat."

The flowers looked so innocent. They smelled intoxicating, sweet and metallic, like honeysuckle after rain. There were dozens of them, hundreds, on bushes Liv now noticed winding up away from the pool at the base of Deer Creek.

"What does it take to turn a toxin into a skin care product?"

Devon looked thoughtful, and Liv braced herself for a scientific explanation or a self-aggrandizing speech about the essential lifesaving work of the skin care industry.

But Devon gave her a wry smile and a one-word answer.

"Money."

The botanist rose to her feet, her gaze zooming out past Liv to the pounding waterfall.

"You asked about Justine Long's death," Devon said. "It was regrettable. But Justine wasn't killed by CareFree. She had a reaction to a chemical involved in the datura extraction process, something we remove entirely before making the product. It was a true accident. If anyone was responsible, it wasn't Babette. It would be me. Or Fiona."

"What happened after the accident?"

"We reflected, of course. Babette made a substantial donation to Justine's family, and she personally reached out to help them through the aftermath. I stayed in the lab, where we solved the problem and moved on. Once we could reliably sequester that dangerous material, we knew CareFree was ready for market. Babette found investors. Small investors led to big ones. Which led us to Stefan Eriksen. His company's investment a year ago made it possible for us to scale our manufacturing.

Babette put the charm on Stefan's boss to seal the deal, but all interaction with the Regent Group is now brokered through Stefan. And he's a cipher on his own."

"Had you met him before this trip?"

"Once. I don't get involved on the money side. If an investor wants to visit the research facility, I'll give them a tour. Otherwise, I stay out of it."

"And you haven't met the backer Stefan represents."

"I have not." Devon shook her head. "Apparently an investor that big keeps their name away from the limelight."

"It's a secret?" That seemed odd to Liv.

"For security purposes, probably. Babette signed an NDA when she met them."

"Do you have any guesses on who it might be? Or where in the world they're from?"

Devon eyed her carefully. "I actually wondered if it might be your sister."

Liv dropped her eyes to the deadly flowers, trying not to let her surprise show. Her brain was whirring. Mandy had said she wasn't the biggest investor in CareFree. If one of Babette's top executives thought she was . . . could that be the reason Mandy had been threatened and Stefan hadn't?

But Babette knew who the big investor was. Babette knew it wasn't Mandy. The more Liv learned, the less the threats in the hats made sense.

"I can assure you my sister is not working at that level," Liv said. "What about Charlie? Does he know your lead investor?"

"No. Only Babette. I got the impression maybe even Stefan hasn't met his boss in person."

"That's weird."

"Honestly, it's one of the reasons I stay away from the business side. It's all foreign to me. But I know Stefan is our assigned partner. For all intents and purposes, he's our investor."

Liv thought back to the cryptic exchange in the boat about their plans. "It sounds like Charlie has built a strong relationship with Stefan. One your sister might not approve of."

"It's for her own good," Devon said. "To improve the management of the company."

"*This is my company, not yours*," Liv said softly.

Devon's hand flew up to the brim of her hat.

"It's possible Babette might feel threatened by our work with Stefan," she acknowledged. But she still wouldn't say precisely what that work was.

Devon looked at Liv. "You and your sister, do you compete with each other?"

Liv weighed which version of the truth to offer. "No. We each . . . do our own thing."

"But you're close."

Again Liv wondered what Devon was telling, or asking, her.

"We're different." Liv thought of all the times she'd hunted Mandy down in an airport and found her deep in conversation with the new best friend she'd just met over Bloody Marys at the bar. How many times Liv had supplied her with a phone charger, or clean socks, or on one particularly stressful jaunt through Morocco, a new passport.

"I was different too," Devon said. "I was overseas at Oxford when my siblings started the company. I loved my research, the quiet focus of it, but it was hard to watch them launch and not be part of it. Babette had this huge vision to upend the beauty industry, and she and Charlie threw themselves into making it happen. They built the first entirely green supply chain in skin care, and Babette kept making refinements to ensure every ingredient in every product was pure. And yes, Babette pushed her employees hard, but she pushed herself hard too. She believed in her people. Cultivated them. She even paid for their home garden expenses. And Charlie found creative solutions whenever she went too far. Once, Babette fired a launch team on the spot when they ordered cage-farmed chicken sandwiches for lunch. Charlie hired them all back as contractors under fake names to get the product out the door. Her passion, his focus, their drive. They were a great team."

"And you wanted in." Liv didn't mean to say it aloud. But she could see from Devon's face that it was true. "I mean, I get it. My sister and my dad, they're tight like that. Is that why you joined the company? To be part of what they were creating?"

Devon gave her a quizzical look. "They recruited me. Gave me an equal stake and everything."

But Liv knew stakes with family were rarely equal. And sometimes what worked with two could be shaken by three.

"Do you really think Babette would hurt him?" Liv asked. "Or you?"

Devon pulled a pocketknife and a camp towel from her day pack. She wrapped her hand in the towel and used the blade to carefully separate a few of the closed datura flowers from their leaves. "I think she's under a lot of pressure with the CareFree launch. As is my brother."

"But not you?"

"The stress I deal with is different. Take this plant." Devon took a confident slice down one of the blossoms on the towel, bisecting it cleanly. A clear, oily sap bubbled up, and when Liv leaned in for a closer look, the sweet smell of the flower—heady, almost rotten—overwhelmed her.

"There are at least a hundred different ways to extract medicinal compounds from datura," Devon said, "and ninety-nine of them are dangerous or worthless for our purposes. Getting the science right, formulating stable compounds and delivery mechanisms: It's painstaking, deliberate work. It can be heartbreaking. But it's cold pressure, not hot. It's more about patience and sticking it out than it is about punching through."

Devon tossed aside the ruined flower. She folded the other blossoms into her towel, erasing them from view. Then she turned away from the rainbow-flecked falls and scanned the rocks along the beach.

"Where is she?" Devon sounded tired. "I really thought she'd be here."

"Babette and her guest must still be hiking down," Big Pete called over. He was helping Katy set up a water station on the far end of the beach. Beyond them, Imogen was pointing her phone up the side canyon, while PK dabbed something on his face in a shadowed divot of rock, his body almost hidden by the rare slice of shade. "Or they stopped at the patio."

"A patio?" PK looked up. "Do they serve mimosas?"

"Not quite. But it's a pretty place, lots of shade, just a half mile from here. We'll head up there shortly to wait and link up with everyone. Anyone hiking to the river from the rim or from Thunder Spring has to pass through Deer Creek Patio."

"Want me to come or stay with the boats?" Katy asked.

Big Pete looked at her. "Stay. The last thing we need is for someone to come by and raid our supplies."

"Can I shoot some footage in the falls before we go?" Imogen asked. "I'm doing this mini feature on all the waterfalls, ranking them from best to worst so people don't waste their time."

"Waste their time?" Liv asked.

Imogen waved at the stunning cascade behind her. "You know, with ones like this that are mid."

Liv wasn't exactly an outdoorswoman, but still. Some people didn't deserve mermaids.

"If Babette isn't here yet, could she be up at the patio?" Devon asked.

Big Pete nodded. "It's the first decent stop for shade and water after the long hike down."

"Which way?"

He pointed left, to a stack of crumbly sandstone slabs piled into a makeshift staircase, winding up the steep cliff and over the waterfall.

They were all hot, and sleepy. But Devon's face had shifted, taking on a grim determination Liv hadn't seen before.

"This is still my sister's launch," Devon said. "Let's see what she has planned after all."

CHAPTER TWENTY-SIX

UP CLOSE, THUNDER SPRING was nothing like the other waterfalls Mandy had seen in the Grand Canyon. It didn't drop in an orderly sheet, plunge into pools, or cascade down rocks on its own private waterslide. Thunder Spring did all these things, all at the same time. It was wide and messy and undecided, a crazy quilt of motion, like every waterfall ever created tumbled together into a wild simultaneous eruption.

Surrounding the falls, Thunder Spring had spawned an oasis in the desert, with thick cottonwoods, a shag carpet of moss, and undulating bursts of purple-veined white trumpet flowers. Fiona and Lucinda were sitting in the shade, picking feathery leaves off a bush that gave off a sharp, familiar scent.

"Wild mint," Fiona explained. "Excellent for preventing inflammation."

"And quite refreshing after that hike." Lucinda passed Mandy a sprig, and she took an experimental nibble. Delicious. This was how breath mints should taste. Like redemption. Like rebirth.

"Where is Charlie?" Stefan asked.

"Over here." The CFO was knee-deep in a shadowed pool at the edge of the falls. "Just trying to cool down before I get hiking again." Charlie pulled himself up onto the mossy bank and walked toward them. His hat was soaked again, along with his hiking shirt and the bottom half of his pants. "I'm thinking I'll head out soon."

"But we just got here," Lucinda protested.

Stefan looked from her to Charlie and then turned to Thor. "Is it permissible for us to go ahead?"

Thor shrugged. "It's not protocol, but what Big Pete don't know won't hurt him. If you stick together, you'll be fine. It's a straight shot from here to Surprise Valley. There's a trail junction there with a sign pointing you to Deer Creek. Follow the arrow, and you can't miss."

Stefan gave them a solemn nod. "Then I believe I will press on as well."

"Sure you don't want to enjoy the water a little?" Mandy said. "Looks like paradise here."

"Paradise is a distraction I cannot afford," Stefan said. "I will hike with Charlie. While you enjoy the splashing."

She didn't care if he meant it disparagingly; Mandy fully intended to enjoy the splashing. She approached Thunder Spring, letting the waterfall roar in her face and sting her scalp. Close up, the water was rich with minerals, a pale aquamarine whipped into a sparkling lather. She felt an irrational desire to lick it, to gather its iridescent foam and smear it all over her body. She wondered if this was how Devon had gone from botany to Babette, out of the naked desire to bottle the glory of nature and drench herself in it.

"Magic, right?"

She turned from the pounding cascade. Thor had a cocky smile on his face.

"Want to try something cool?" he asked.

"Cooler than this?"

"There's a secret place. Behind there." He pointed to a break in the falls where the spring ran over a ledge.

She looked dubiously at the water pouring over the rocks, the variable force of it, the way it galloped and gurgled in alternation.

"C'mon. Law of the wild. You'll love it."

Thor was already wriggling out of his long-sleeved shirt and sandals, his blond hair brushing the golden skin of his shoulders. He stepped out onto a fallen cottonwood whose trunk sprouted a line of nascent young trees, spindly sentinels poking up into the sky.

She looked back, but no one else seemed eager to follow Thor. Lucinda's gloved fingers spun across strands of river grass, weaving a braid of thatch. Stefan and Charlie were halfway up the hillside to Surprise Valley. Only Fiona met Mandy's gaze.

"Your funeral," Fiona said. "We'll stay here."

Mandy stripped to her bikini and gingerly traced Thor's footsteps across the dead cottonwood, over a line of slick rocks, and onto a ledge from which water spilled like a milkmaid's pail. The spring moved quickly, but Thor picked out a path that shielded them from the full force of it, dodging the slipperiest rocks and deepest pockets. He stopped at the edge of a shimmering pool backed by a sheet of clear falling water.

"Here we go," he said.

He took a deep breath and jumped in, taking short, hard strokes toward the cascade. There couldn't have been more than three feet to the drop, but the flow was pounding, and he was kicking hard to approach it. When he got close enough to touch the falling sheet, he dove under.

Mandy waited. Five seconds. Ten. Had Thor slipped into a secret cave behind the waterfall? It didn't seem like there was room for that. But maybe the shadows were playing tricks on her.

Twenty seconds. It felt like forever. Then she heard a whoop, and Thor exploded out of the water on the far side of the pool, at least fifty feet away.

She screamed. She couldn't help it.

"How did you . . . ?"

Thor grinned and shook out his hair. "It's called the Maytag. Like a washing machine. Your turn."

"Is it safe?"

"Officially, we don't recommend it. But unofficially? It's freaking awesome."

Mandy hesitated. She could hear Liv admonishing her that this was an unnecessary risk, that Mandy was already in danger, that even being alone with Thor in a sketchy section of a powerful waterfall was beyond reasonable judgment.

Liv wanted her to be cautious. But Thor's dazed smile, his sparkling eyes, the way he practically shone with joy as he shook out his wild mane—that was what Mandy wanted.

She jumped in and started powering her way to the waterfall. The current pressed in on her, but she kept windmilling her arms, ignoring the warning bells ringing between her ears.

"Cover your head when you go under!" she heard Thor call out.

Her fingertips grazed the falling water. She raised her head, facing away from the spray, and took one last deep breath. And dove.

The first thing she felt was the sensation of someone shoving her into a dark cave formed from sharp rocks, their edges banging the soft skin around her shins. She instinctively curled into a ball, wrapping her arms over her head, trying not to panic. She tried to count the flips as the water tossed her around the cave. It was impossible. She was spinning, losing control, alone in the dark. It felt like someone had slammed the door on her from above and she was trapped—forever?—under the water.

Then, just when it felt like all the breath had been squeezed out of her, the water around her elongated, pulling her into a channel. Was she moving up toward the surface? Or deeper? She had no way of knowing. No way of controlling it. It was just taking her. There was a small pop, and then she was shooting across the pool, lengthening out, as if she were a crumpled silk handkerchief pulled from the sleeve of a wily magician.

She surfaced two-thirds of the way across and shook herself free, gasping for air. Thor splashed over and grabbed her under the armpits and swung her around in the water. For a moment, they were no longer guest and guide. They were children, hooting and spinning and reveling in an impossibly cold pool under a perfectly blue sky.

Every ounce of her body had been liberated, reborn in this canyon that delivered terror and bliss in equal measure. If she had to die, let it be like this. Wild and carefree.

CHAPTER TWENTY-SEVEN

LIV PLACED HERSELF IN the middle of the nervous line of hikers up the trail to Deer Creek Patio. Big Pete led them along sinuous curves of sandstone above the creek, the water lapping and falling prettily from one set of rocks to the next. Everyone was quiet, walking silently with their presumed hopes for—or fears about—the reunion with Babette. Finally, they reached what felt like the culmination of the winding path: a cul-de-sac of broad shaded ledges flanking a deep pool. Above the last little waterfall that fed the pool, the view stretched up into Surprise Valley and toward the rim, the orange canyon walls kissing the sky.

While there was no poolside waitstaff to attend to them at Deer Creek Patio, there were people there, five of them, a grizzled group of old-timers scrubbing themselves in the clear water.

It was the first time since they'd hit the river Liv had seen new people up close. The hikers splashed in the sunshine, their backpacks and dusty boots lined up on a far ledge. Liv stared, surprised at how quickly she'd come to feel like the Babette rafting group were the only people out here. There were other cultures in the canyon, other conflicts and mysteries to unravel.

Big Pete gave the hikers a neighborly wave. "Afternoon!"

Two of the women ignored him, busy with their ablutions, but a third, stocky and smiling, waved back, her bare shoulders rising like two pink boulders from the water. Liv was pretty sure she was naked.

"You hiked down from the North Rim today?" Big Pete asked.

"Sure did." A skinny, hawk-nosed man stood and smiled at them. Oh. They were all naked. "Just taking a splash before supper. We're hiking out early tomorrow morning."

Big Pete was unfazed by their natural state. "Run into any other groups on your way down?"

"Just them folks with the mule." This man was huge and bald, a mountain come alive. He wiped his face with a paisley handkerchief, the kind Liv thought had died out with the Gold Rush. "On the esplanade above Surprise Valley."

"Were they coming down?" the stocky woman asked. "I got the impression . . ."

"That's what they said. The lady, she had a hat like yours." The skinny man nodded at Imogen, whose Babette cap was, incredibly, still white. "She gave me this."

He glided away and pressed himself up onto the far ledge in one smooth motion, shining his weathered behind in their direction. Liv kept her eyes on the creek while he rummaged through a backpack before wading back over to them.

"Said it's for forgetting troubles and recirculating hydroadaptowhozies." He held out the white tube, a telltale silver *B* tattooed along its side.

PK grabbed the tube, cradling it as if it were the holy grail. "This is a CareFree tester. No one but Babette would have this."

"You think she's trying to tell us something?" Devon said.

"Probably just being her generous self."

"I don't need it," the skinny hiker said. "My troubles can't find me out here."

"Surprised you haven't seen your friends yet, though," the woman chimed in. "They were ahead of us, just stopped for some water. If they were coming here . . ."

"Shoulda crossed paths by now," the bald man agreed.

"Who was in their group?" Devon's voice was polite but firm.

"That shiny lady with the white hat," the bald man said, "and two men."

"Two?" PK said.

"Big boys," the skinny man said.

"Plus the mule," the woman added. "Long cartoon eyelashes, all loaded down with stuff. Even if they were enjoying the scenery, I'd have bet they'd get here two or three hours ago. No heavy packs to carry."

Devon turned to Big Pete. "We couldn't have missed them on our way up here from the river, right?"

"Not a chance."

To Liv's surprise, Devon turned to her next. "What do you think?"

"What do I think happened, or what do I think we should do?"

"Both."

Liv took a quick scan around the group. Devon looked focused. Big Pete looked concerned. Imogen was combing her hair in the creek, humming at her ever-present phone. The person whose countenance surprised her most was PK. He stood alone, exposed, fidgeting with the CareFree tester. He was practically kneading the tube into submission. Was he worried about his boss out in the wilderness with a mule and two strange men? Or did he know something about Babette's plan? Was it possible she was bringing a hit man—or hit men—down into the canyon with her? If PK had indeed been delivering threats on her behalf, perhaps the knowledge that she was now so close, with the arsenal to make good on her promises, made the improbable all too real.

Before Liv could answer, there was a rustle from above. Three more hikers, but these ones she recognized: Fiona in the lead, with Stefan and Lucinda close behind. The older woman was leaning on Stefan, his forearm jutting out from his body in an awkward approximation of a walking stick.

"Are you okay, Nana?" Imogen asked.

"Did you see Babette?" Devon demanded.

"Where's Mandy and the others?" Liv asked.

Lucinda grunted. "Fine. I'm fine. Just spun my ankle a smidge on the way down. Fortunately Stefan doubled back and helped us out."

She and Stefan shuffled to one of the ledges, and he helped her lower herself beside her granddaughter. Lucinda removed her left hiking boot and sock and plunged her foot into the icy pool.

"That's better," she murmured. She turned her foot in slow arabesques under the crystal-clear water of Deer Creek. Then she looked up. "Is your CEO here?"

"We hoped she was with you," Devon said.

"Haven't seen her," Fiona said.

Liv looked up the trail. "And my sister?"

Fiona smirked. "Thor said he wanted to show Mandy something special."

Big Pete grunted. "So that's what they're calling it these days."

"What about Charlie?" Devon asked. "Wasn't he with you too?"

"Charlie—" Fiona looked to Stefan. "He left Thunder Spring with you, didn't he?"

The Dutchman nodded. "We walked together until the trail junction. I stopped to drink some water at the sign, but he wanted to keep going."

"You split up," Big Pete said. "Thor didn't tell you to stay together?"

"He did. I needed the break," Stefan said. "And I could not imagine that Charlie would get lost. He was on a straight path to all of you."

"And yet he isn't here," Devon said.

Liv felt something itch at her chest.

Charlie.

Babette.

Mandy.

Thor.

There were too many people missing.

She knew better than to jump to any terrible conclusions. But the itch was starting to burn. Statistically, missing people didn't do well in the Grand Canyon. There were too many caverns to fall into, too many ways the sun could leach away common sense. Maybe Mandy was with Thor. Maybe Charlie and Babette had found each other and were having a kumbaya moment. Or maybe . . .

"I changed my mind," Liv said. "I think we should head up the trail toward the junction."

Devon stood up. "Are you worried about your sister?"

"As far as we know, the only person who isn't accounted for is Charlie. My sister is with Thor. Babette's on her way."

"But if Charlie was on the trail, we would have run into him," Fiona said.

"And those hikers said Babette should be here by now," Imogen added.

"We should wait here," Big Pete said. "I don't need to lose any more of you."

He was right. But it didn't feel right. And there was an obvious reason why.

"There's something you don't know," Liv said. "Charlie believes his sister is trying to kill him."

"*What?*" Fiona said.

All eyes shot to Devon.

"Not her," Liv amended, putting a hand on the botanist's stiff forearm. "Devon was threatened too. Several people were. By Babette. Charlie thinks she might have hired someone to confront us on this trip."

"Those two men she's traveling down with?" Imogen asked. "Nasty."

"Are the threats credible?" Lucinda asked.

"I don't know," Liv said. "But she suggested Charlie might meet his end. And now he's missing. Until we find him or talk to Babette directly, we won't know—"

Imogen let out a low, appreciative whistle. "Babette is one bad—"

"This is none of your business," Devon said.

"Of course it is our business." Stefan's voice crashed into the conversation. "It is all of our business. Businesses. We are here because of

Babette. And Charlie. And you. You have made promises about Care-Free. We are here to see those promises fulfilled."

His outburst stunned the group into silence.

"How were they threatened?" Lucinda finally asked. "Babette isn't here."

"They're in the hats," Liv said. "Devon, would you?"

Reluctantly, the older woman took off her cap and showed the group the message on the inside brim, the words glowing in pale thread against the reddish memory of sand.

"*This is my company, not yours,*" Imogen read. "Hardly sounds like a threat to me."

"Charlie's was worse," Devon said.

"Did anyone else get a message?" Lucinda asked.

"Ooh! Did I get one?" Imogen said. "Show me."

She thrust her cap at Liv, who plunged it into the creek before rubbing it with sandstone dust. But there was nothing there.

"Rude," Imogen said. "Charlie was wrong. This hat really isn't personalized at all."

Liv turned to Fiona and Lucinda. "Where are your hats?"

"I packed mine away in case Imogen needed it for her filming," Lucinda said. She touched the straw hat resting on the ledge next to her. "I prefer my own approach to shade."

Fiona adjusted her visor and nodded. "Me too. I can't recall where I put that hat. If I'd known . . ." The blonde looked uneasily at Devon's upside-down hat, as if it were a snake readying to strike. "How was Charlie's message worse?"

"She threatened him with death," Liv said.

"Oh," Fiona murmured. "And now he's missing."

The heaviness of the situation was hitting everyone. Even Big Pete looked rattled now.

PK dug frantically through his day pack. "I don't know what happened to my cap."

"Enough playing find-the-hat," Devon interrupted. "We have to find the people. Charlie and Babette. Mandy and Thor. I don't see how deliberating about my sister's questionable communication choices will help us do that."

"If Charlie's really scared," Liv said, "it's possible he's run off, or gone into hiding. Maybe he decided to sneak back up to the rim while avoiding the trail Babette was taking."

"It's twelve miles straight up from here," Big Pete said. "Ten from the Thunder Spring junction where he left Stefan. And there is no other safe path up to the rim besides that trail."

"Maybe he took an unsafe path," Liv ventured. The landscape flanking the trail was vast and twisted, riddled with thick bursts of thorn bush, dizzying drop-offs, and crumbling rock. She saw a series of pockmarked caves further up the creek bed, a constellation of shallow divots and dark, yawning craters. There were a million places to get lost. A million ways to fall. She only hoped her sister was on solid ground.

"I should have hiked with him," Devon said.

"Can't turn back the clock now." Big Pete spat on the ground and wiped his mouth with the back of his hand. "All right, we've got folks to find. Any other life-or-death revelations before we get moving?"

Everyone was silent.

"This is, like, insane," Imogen said. "You all know that, right?"

"What's the plan?" Fiona asked. "Do we form pairs, send up smoke signals, or . . . ?"

"Pray this is all a horrible dream?" PK said.

"There is no need for hysteria," Stefan said. "I'm sure there is a perfectly good reason for all of it."

"Is everyone capable of hiking?" Big Pete asked.

Imogen looked to her grandmother. Lucinda pulled her bare left foot from the water and turned it in a slow circle. She put her straw hat back on and nodded.

"No more splitting up," Big Pete said. "We'll all head up the trail to the Thunder Spring intersection together. We'll keep our eyes peeled for movement off either side of the path. If we get to the trail junction without running into someone or receiving further information, we'll reassess."

He seemed to grow a little taller as he issued his instructions. "If Charlie is indeed hiding, we need to get him out. He likely hasn't gone far. But out here, too many people get lost or trapped or hurt. They disappear. That isn't going to happen. Not to Charlie. Not today."

He looked up at the sky, where the previously white clouds were now lined in gray ruffles. A few darker wisps trailed behind, edging their way into the perfect blue.

"One more thing," he said, turning to Devon. "Is it possible your brother is carrying a weapon?"

Devon looked confused.

"A firearm," Big Pete prompted.

"As far as I know, he's never shot a gun in his life."

Big Pete gave no indication of whether this was a good answer or a troubling one. "All right, then. Let's get this search party started."

CHAPTER TWENTY-EIGHT

"WHERE IS EVERYONE?"

The cottonwoods and mint bushes surrounding Thunder Spring were eerily vacant. Mandy had lost track of time behind the waterfall, taking not one but twelve dives through the Maytag's underwater tornado before she felt satisfied. The experience was addictive: pain and pleasure, shock and deliverance. It was like getting a tattoo or falling in love. As soon as it was over, she wanted to do it again.

"Hello? Fiona? Lucinda?"

She and Thor picked their way across the mossy rocks to where they'd left their stuff. There was no sign of Lucinda or Fiona, let alone Stefan or Charlie. Just Mandy's sarong draped over a wild scraggle of mint, Thor's day pack resting under the batiked fabric.

"They must have taken off up the trail."

Thor seemed strangely unconcerned about the fact that every one of his other charges had hiked on without him. But if he wasn't worried, Mandy decided she wasn't, either. The last hour—or however long they'd spent spinning in the water—she'd forgotten about the death threats. She'd forgotten about her investigative assignments from Liv, the duties she'd so thoroughly failed to complete. She'd gotten what she'd come to the Grand Canyon for in the first place: an adventure.

It was a shame her sister wasn't with her.

"We've got two options," Thor said. He perched on the hollowed-out trunk of a fallen cottonwood tree. "We can hoof it up the trail to catch up with the others. They can't be too far ahead. Not if we jog."

Mandy craned her neck up. While the trail was clearly visible, it was an unending zigzag of switchbacks through cactus. There was at least a thousand vertical feet of gravelly scree between them and a saddle of mesquite on the horizon. And she hadn't exactly been a speed demon on the first part of the hike.

"What's plan B?" she asked.

He winked. "There's a shortcut."

"A tunnel?"

"Something like that. You trust me?"

She considered what she knew about Thor. He was cute. He was funny. He'd shown her care when she needed it, hiking along with her at the back of the pack up to Thunder Spring. And he'd shown her adventure when she wanted it, swirling with her through the Maytag. Liv probably had a twelve-point matrix for what constituted trust. But Mandy operated on vibes. She was certain Thor would be good at a party, great in a crisis. Was that trust?

"I'm game."

He looked her over for a long moment, assessing something.

"All right, then. Follow me."

She scurried to keep up as he charged away from the hard-packed trail and slipped under a boulder as big as a house. She followed him through a progression of caves, the bright sun blinking in and out of focus as they zoomed forward. Twenty minutes, three broken nails, and a jammed pinky toe later, they stopped.

"Here we are." Thor hoisted himself onto a sun-streaked chockstone sandwiched between two massive towers of rock. He reached down and offered Mandy a hand.

"The back entrance to Surprise Valley."

Mandy looked doubtfully at the narrow sliver of sun that shot through the rocky crevasse. The light traced the outline of Thor's athletic body, illuminating the tiny hairs on his arms. Beyond him, little was visible. The travertine towers flared on either side of him, twisting the narrow space above him into a slender ribbon of air.

Thor unzipped his pack and pulled out a length of bright green rope. He uncoiled it with confident hands, lifting his T-shirt away from his taut stomach and winding the rope around his waist. He tied one quick knot after another. Then he unfurled the rest of the cord, adding a hand-sized loop at the end.

"We'll be able to walk and scramble the first half. Then it gets tight, and we'll have to climb up and traverse. It doesn't take any specialized skills. Just a willingness to press your feet against one side and shimmy your butt against the other."

"This will get us closer to Deer Creek?"

"We'll pop out in Surprise Valley, just above the spring that feeds Deer Creek. Should shave a solid hour off the hike."

She peered again into the dark slot. It didn't look like much of a shortcut. But it did look like one heck of an adventure.

"What's so surprising about Surprise Valley?"

"Guess we better find out."

He turned and grinned at her. The skin splintered at the outside edges of his sunglasses, making her wonder for a moment how old he was, and how it would feel to run her fingers along the lines on his sunbaked face.

Mandy pulled her eyes from his and looked one more time at the narrow entrance to the crevasse in the rock and took a deep breath. The longer Mandy was separated from Liv and the rest of the group, the more alone she felt. But the only way back was through. She clutched the small loop at the end of Thor's rope.

"If you get stuck or need a boost," he said, "just give it a little tug."

He winked, then turned back to the slot, which was looming taller by the minute. "You're in for a real treat."

It was like following the Minotaur into his labyrinth. At first, they were just walking in the cool sand, Mandy trailing her fingertips against the smooth limestone walls that flared out and up to a broken window of sky. After about twenty yards, the gap between the walls grew so narrow they had to turn their shoulders and walk sideways to proceed. Another twenty yards, and Mandy was sucking in her stomach, praying she could squeeze through.

Then it got so tight she couldn't even take a step.

"There's only one way forward now," Thor said. "Ready for your Spider-Man audition?"

Mandy craned her neck up at the slick limestone walls, which widened to a comfortable span fifteen feet above their heads.

"You bet," she said, projecting a level of confidence she absolutely did not feel. "I AM Spider-Man."

Thor demonstrated the technique, pressing his feet against one wall, his back to the other, inching himself up until he was wedged in the flare, his body floating fifteen feet above her. The travertine was cool and buttery, which was a blessing, considering she was wearing hiking boots, a sarong, and a bikini. For the first time, she wished she had a pair of her sister's ugly cargo pants. She'd be lucky if the rock didn't rub the turtles right off her sarong.

"We have to drop the rope here," Thor told her. "Too dangerous. But I'll be right ahead of you as we traverse across."

Mandy pushed herself back into the limestone wall until she felt the tiny pockmarks and perturbations engrave themselves into her skin. She placed one foot against the wall across from her, then the other.

She looked up to where the slot widened. She was a human cannonball, aimed at the sky.

One deep breath. Two. Mandy shoved her palms into the wall in front of her and launched. As she rose, she stretched one leg back, so she was standing with one foot against the front wall, one pressed to the rock behind her, her torso floating in the growing gap between them. She was walking on air.

"THIS IS AMAZING!" she yelled up into the void.

Her words rattled in the slot, the echo sonorous and chaotic.

She felt powerful. She felt dangerous. She started moving up and laterally until she was more than twenty feet off the ground. She followed Thor's path, advancing with just her feet and the lightest kiss of her back against the rock, using the palms of her hands to balance and draw herself forward. She looked up. She looked ahead. She was flying.

And then, all of a sudden, there was no more path. Just darkness.

"Thor?"

Darkness, and silence.

Her left calf started to ache, and she foolishly looked down. It was a long way into the narrowing V of rock below her. She imagined getting trapped there, falling tightly between the rocks and no one coming for her for days.

"THOR?"

They must be close to the exit. He must have popped out the other side and would be waiting for her in Surprise Valley. But musts couldn't help her now. Her left leg started shaking, not from pain, but from nervousness and fatigue. She shoved her foot harder against the wall, trying to impress the nubbly surface of the rock onto the sole of her boot.

Her leg kept trembling.

This was one of those moments when bravado failed her. When she was all alone, without an audience to perform for. A good lie was like an echo: Its power came in how others reflected it back to you.

"I CAN DO THIS," she yelled into the abyss.

Her words tumbled back and fell into the two-story gap beneath her feet.

Thor was gone. Liv was somewhere on the far side of Surprise Valley. Mandy had no choice. She had to keep pressing forward alone.

Did it take ten minutes? Twenty? At first, she was inching along, craning her ears and eyes for the guide, wishing him back into her field of vision. But Thor was beyond sight, beyond hearing. She had to accept it. She started taking bigger straddling steps along the wall, rubbing her fingers raw over the rock as she pressed herself foot by foot, hand over hand, across the chasm.

She prayed it wouldn't get narrower, forcing her to climb higher. She prayed it wouldn't get wider, beyond her ability to brace herself. She kept scooting sideways until she hit a sharp corner. The deep V broke into boulders, and she carefully lowered herself to the sand.

The ground brought stability, but little relief. It was only when she got to the far side and stumbled out of the slot that she started to wonder. It was only when the wall opened and she saw the tight folds of Surprise Valley laid out in front of her that she started to worry. The world before her was all boulders and brush, a stark, twisted beauty, with no discernible trails nor signs of human activity. Was she really getting closer to the rest of the group? And if not, where had Thor taken her?

CHAPTER TWENTY-NINE

BIG PETE LED HIS group up out of Deer Creek Patio in silence. Clouds peppered the sky, but it was still brutally hot. While no one complained, they weren't exactly skipping up the trail either. At a wide creek crossing, Big Pete whipped off his long-sleeved shirt, dunked it in the freezing water, and put it back on.

"Suggest you take this opportunity to cool off." The lead guide stood in the creek, scooping water onto his head with his hat. "This is the last water from here up to the trail junction."

"We don't have time," Devon said. "We have to find them. Before my brother does something rash."

"Or Babette," Fiona said. "Those hat threats are creepy."

"Creepier than what you've seen from her before?" Liv asked.

Fiona nodded. "During the Fierce Essence Quest, she did sew a fake tiger fang into the neckline of everyone's windbreaker. But this feels different. Targeted. And angry."

Liv squinted up past the creek bed, searching the rocks for a sign of movement, of life, in the cracked landscape. "My sister and Thor are still out there."

Imogen giggled. "I bet they are."

"Is everything a joke to you?" PK snapped.

Liv wondered at his harsh tone. It didn't make sense that PK was so belligerent toward Imogen. The girl was annoying. But what teenage social media star wasn't? Surely as the person responsible for influencer engagement at Babette, it would have been PK himself who recruited and invited Imogen and her PureImogeNation followers to the river. And yet he'd been nothing but antagonistic to the teenager for the past two days.

The paucity of information Liv had about these people overwhelmed her. While the Babette guests were new to Liv, they weren't new to each other. She'd only scratched the surface of their relationships, the fault lines that might hold the answer to the threats and disappearances. She didn't know any of them. Not really. Not enough.

If Liv was going to figure out what was really going on with the threats, she had to go deeper. She had to get past first impressions and gross categorizations to understand who was really on this trip, and why.

"Worried?" Lucinda was walking unassisted now, but slowly. Still limping.

Liv surprised herself by nodding.

"Tell me what's on your mind."

Liv was just about to launch in when Imogen gave a little shriek.

"I hear something!"

It was quiet at first, a snuffling whimper. Then, a cry. Liv surveyed the area, homing in on a gray shuffle that sent a shiver through a spiny bush high above the creek.

"Charlie?" Devon shouted. "CHARLIE!"

Another warbling cry. A long, horrible scrape. And then it became clear.

"Is that a pony?" Imogen said.

"A mule," Big Pete said.

The animal was high above them, off-trail. It looked exhausted, its coat matted with sweat. A single saddlebag dragged below its belly, the leather satchel picking up brush as the animal bumped along. Every few paces, the mule would pause, turn, and lumber back the other way. There was no rider in sight.

"Maybe it's the one the hiker mentioned?" PK's voice was entirely too hopeful. "The one with Babette?"

"I don't see any people," Devon said.

"So it's lost?" Imogen said. The mule sashayed forward and back, its drooping head making it look plaintive. As if it had been cut off from any sense of purpose and was just drifting.

"Or its handler is up there somewhere," Big Pete said. Liv followed his gaze up the empty trail. "Maybe they got detained."

"BABETTE!" PK called out.

"Maybe she and Charlie found each other," Devon said.

The mule lumbered into their midst, doggedly pushing to the creek. When it dipped its huge head and began to drink in big snuffling gulps, Big Pete sidled up to it, patting its flank as he approached. Liv grabbed its saddle and pulled what she could from the flopped-open saddlebag. There were just a few items inside. A hair tie. A Raw Power Hydrology Stick, whatever that was. And a piece of mottled white fabric, which unfurled to reveal a spectacular dust-speckled kimono, the word "Babette" blazing across the back in silver paint.

"That's hers." Devon stroked the kimono. There was a touch of surprise in her voice. "She made it."

But where was she?

Liv scanned the horizon. Nothing but rocks and bushes. And a faint, ankle-twisting trail that snaked up to a cavernous amphitheater of sun-baked boulders.

"There!" A hundred yards past the left edge of the rocky bowl, she saw someone. A hiker with hands on knees, bent over and panting.

Devon shot off at a fast clip, charging off-trail up through the boulders. Liv tried to keep pace, flying past the rest of the group behind the older woman. But just as abruptly as Devon started, she stopped.

"Wait."

Liv looked up. The hiker still hadn't moved.

"It's a man." Devon shook her head. "Why would Charlie be with Babette's mule?"

Charlie. Was it possible? Liv couldn't make out the stooped hiker's face, but the silhouette looked about right—slender, in a dark windbreaker and shorts, with a ball cap and a day pack creating a little hump on his back.

Devon cupped her hands around her mouth.

"Charlie!"

The man looked up from his crouch and waved in their general direction. Devon waved back. Liv still couldn't make out his face, but she could see the sharp afternoon light slicing across the canyon, and below it, the wobble in his wave. Was he dehydrated? Or was he just as blinded by the sun as they were?

"I don't know what he was thinking," Devon said. She kept waving, as if her arms could pilot her brother back to her.

"Maybe he got lost on his way from Thunder Spring, found the mule, and followed it back down."

"Charlie doesn't wander. Especially in the wilderness."

Something didn't seem right. The man had turned his back to them now, balancing himself to shimmy down a sandstone boulder. There was something about the recklessness of his movements that didn't sit square with Liv. Charlie struck her as careful and timid, but now, he leapt down from the rock with confidence—overconfidence, even—executing a lurching spin just before he crash-landed on the ground. Was he just desperate to reach them? Was this one of those situations where dire circumstances unlocked a hidden reservoir of strength?

And then there was the mule. She supposed it was possible the animal had come along just as Charlie was returning from some unknown destination. But it had Babette's kimono. When had Babette been separated from the mule? What if this man wasn't Charlie at all, but one of Babette's mysterious hiking companions? What if there really was a hit man and he'd murdered Charlie and was now coming down to . . . what? Kill Devon as well?

Liv stepped in front of Devon. She looked down. Most of the group was still way behind them, which was good. Whatever this man intended, whoever he was, Liv would be the first to confront him. She could feel the adrenaline buzzing in her fingertips. The man was moving faster now, blazing down the trail. His gait was so familiar. The closer he got, the more the itchy sense of recognition grew in Liv's mind.

Not Charlie.

Not a hit man.

Someone else.

Oh no.

"What is it?" Devon asked. Liv hadn't realized she'd voiced her concern out loud. "Is he hurt?"

Of course he wasn't hurt. He was too lucky, too experienced at skating away from pain and responsibility, to ever get hurt. His footwork was sloppy from fatigue, his shins red and scraped. But the look of triumph on his face was unmarred. He stopped, cocked a smile, and put two fingers to his mouth, letting out a whistle loud enough to pull over every taxicab in the state of Arizona.

"That's not my brother," Devon whispered.

The man whistled again.

"I know." Liv's stomach was doing backflips now. Her face froze into a grim, false smile, the kind she would employ if she ever were to face a firing squad.

"Who is it?"

"It's my father."

"Your . . . who?"

His voice boomed across the shortening distance between them. "Livvie Lu!"

Liv closed her eyes. She had no clue how to process Guy Chisholm's presence here, in this wild incorruptible place. But that didn't stop him from bounding over.

"I am so glad to see you, baby."

She opened her eyes. There he was, sunburned and smiling, arms stretched wide, blocking out the sun.

"No hug for your old man?" He chuckled, then lightly touched the sleeve of her gray T-shirt. "I suppose you always were formal."

"What are you doing here?"

"Wild, right?" His smile looked slightly manic, strained. Or maybe that was just the heat. "I know, I know, this is one of your sister shindigs, and I won't interfere, Scout's honor, Dad's honor, but—where is your sis? Who's your friend?"

"I'm Babette's sister." Devon looked wary. "Did you hike down here with her?"

"That's right. Almost killed me, but I made it." He smiled almost shyly at Devon, as if humbled to be in her presence. "Dr. Devon. The botanist. Babette told me all about you. I'm a big fan of your work."

His voice had turned cozy and interested, a bottomless jar of honey.

But Devon wasn't looking for sweetness. She was looking for her siblings. "Where is Babette? And why did she bring you with her?"

"She isn't here?" He rubbed his mouth for a moment, hiding a frown. He'd always told his daughters no one likes to see negative emotions, not even in the mirror. "Huh. And she must not have had the chance yet to tell you about her charming and brilliant investment advisor."

"She has not."

"I'm sure she'll give you a glowing report."

"I don't need a report. I need Babette. Where is she? When did you last see her?"

"She's not here yet? Really?"

"Really," Devon said.

"The guide told me to find y'all. But I got lost. I was sure they'd reach you ahead of me, but I guess—do you have any water?"

It was a classic Guy Chisholm stall tactic. Then again, if he'd been hiking all day down from the North Rim, he really might be dehydrated.

Liv handed him her bottle. "Dad. We need to know what happened."

He put one finger in the air, asking for a moment, his eyes darting between her and Devon as he drank. There was fatigue behind his gaze. Wariness. Even stress. Her dad rarely showed strain. Then again, he had never been one to rough it. His clothes looked shiny but torn, his stiff hiking boots uncomfortably new. His white hat was smudged with dirt and sweat like the rest of them, but it was made of cheaper fabric, and it didn't have the telltale embroidered *B*. Instead, a simple yellow Grand Canyon patch adorned its crown.

When Liv's water bottle was empty, he launched into his tale.

"I never planned to come down here," he said. "This isn't really my scene."

"But?"

"Every couple months, Babette and I meet up to talk business. Two nights ago, we had dinner at the Venetian. We shared some sashimi, some laughs . . . then, out of the blue, she asks me to come down here with her. Convinced me it'd be fun. She booked us one of those prop planes that comes with its own Ken doll pilot, and the kid flew us to an airstrip on a tumbleweed ranch on the North Rim last night. This morning, before the crack of dawn, this guide Marc shows up, no coffee for me, no turmeric matcha for her, terrible service, but he loads our stuff onto this mule and gives us each a hat and tells us we've got a twelve-mile hike down to reach y'all. Babette, she's one heck of a trooper. She set a tough pace for all of us, even the mule."

"Where is she now?" Devon asked.

"That's the thing. She got a little overheated a few miles back. Nothing serious, but it's dry in that valley, and we were running low on water. Marc told me to go ahead with the mule to get more water from you or from the creek and then to retrace my steps back to them. He said he'd help her take a break and get cooled off before they continued down."

He squinted back up the trail, as if he could will Babette and the guide into view. When they didn't materialize, he shook his head. "Then I got turned around. Never found you, or the creek. The guide told me I'd reach a patio within an hour, but it's been four hours at least, and I don't see no cabanas." He flashed Liv a rueful smile. "Can you believe it? Your dear old dad wandering in the wilderness?"

There were at least seven things Liv didn't believe about the story her dad was telling, chief among them the idea that he decided on a lark to hike twelve miles into the center of the earth.

"The last you saw her was four hours ago?" Devon said.

"Thereabouts. I figured they'd be all cooled off and rested and drinking activated charcoal margaritas with your group by now."

So Babette's two companions weren't hit men. The way Guy was talking, it sounded like Babette had come to him for help. That she trusted him. Which meant either he'd lied about what he could do for her or he'd legitimately helped her out in the past. Or both. Guy Chisholm's signature cocktail was a blend of enthusiasm and exaggeration, shaken into stirring performances. Liv was still staring at him, trying to make sense of the situation, when she heard footsteps approaching from below.

"Good. You found him." Big Pete was breathing hard. Then he took a closer look. "You're not Charlie. Who the hell are you?"

Her father winked, bemused. Liv was already exhausted by how rapidly he could flick on the charm. "Guy Chisholm, at your service."

"He was traveling with my sister and your mule guide, Marc." Devon was looking carefully at Guy, assessing him. "But Babette got overheated, and Marc told him to find us."

Liv turned to her father. "Is there anything Marc said about where he would take Babette to rest? Or just that you should look for us?"

Guy scrunched up his forehead in a pantomime of remembering. Liv had no clue if he was actually thinking back or just pretending to do so while he conjured the most profitable story for the moment.

"He told me if I didn't run into you, I should head for Deer Creek Patio. There'd be lots of water there. But he also said something about how a queen like Babette deserved a throne." He smiled at Devon. "Your sister really is extraordinary, isn't she? Even the guide could see it."

Big Pete gave him a quizzical look. "There's a place he could have been referring to. But I didn't think Marc had ever hiked down from the North Rim before."

"Maybe someone told him about it?" Devon said.

"I suppose so. It's close. Right over there." Big Pete pointed across the trail to the cavernous maw where the hillside gave way to blank space.

"Let's get the others and check it out," Devon said.

Guy took off without waiting for the others. Liv followed him. Ten minutes later, they arrived at a broken amphitheater of stone. It was less landmark than vacancy, a cavity yanked from the jaw of the canyon.

"I don't see her," Guy whispered.

Liv kept doggedly moving forward. This whole park was an upside-down world. Every other natural wonder she knew of grew up from ground level. Mountain peaks. Granite towers. Forests of shimmering red pine. The Grand Canyon was the opposite. Instead of shooting up, it plummeted down under the world, tunneling out caves and rivers, absence and emptiness.

Liv peered across the barren void, trying not to question. Trying not to doubt. Hunting for something—anything—in the nothing chiseled away. But it was no use. The fading sun sliced across the empty bowl before her, blinding her to everything but the sharp edges of the orange rocks, bleeding red in the afternoon light.

CHAPTER THIRTY

MANDY STUMBLED DOWN AND away from the mouth of the slot, then caught herself. She was standing on a narrow ledge no more than three feet deep, a fifty-foot drop-off down sheer rock separating her from the rest of the world. She looked left. Ten yards over, the ledge crumbled to nothingness. To her right, the ledge continued, a wavering line of dusty orange sugar ending abruptly at a dark stain in the rock where a trickle of water slicked over the edge and plunged into the sparse valley of brush and gravel below.

She took an anxious look back at the dark slot. Thor hadn't just vanished into thin air, and she seriously doubted he had a wingsuit stuffed in the back pocket of his weathered shorts. If he hadn't turned back and he hadn't flown, he must have continued along the ledge to the right.

It looked like one adventure too far. The ledge was exposed, without enough room for her to turn and walk normally, and she didn't trust herself not to lose her balance. It would be so easy for her shoulder to knock against the cliff, for the edge of her boot to peel down over the lip. She kept her back to the cliff instead, inching along in a shuffling half squat. The sun-warmed rock singed her shoulder blades above the thin sarong, but she didn't care. She wanted contact with the earth. She wanted to touch anything but air.

Had she been an idiot to follow Thor? Why had he left her at the most dangerous part of the slot?

She kept her eyes on her hiking boots, obsessively scanning for pebbles, holes, anything that could cause her to trip. Every few steps, she snuck a look out to the valley below, praying for a hint of a trail that might help her descend safely. But her prayers continued unanswered. The shadows in the desolate valley stretched like dark ghosts away from her, and the adrenaline she'd felt earlier leaked out of her like an old balloon, replaced by fatigue and fear. Her muscles ached, her water bottle was empty, and while the rock against her back was still warm, the fading sun made her shiver each time the breeze tickled her sarong.

She was twenty yards from the dark stain when the ledge narrowed even more. Two feet, maybe. Eighteen inches. Her shuffle slowed to a shambling creep. She tried not to think about the spring she was approaching, how the water would make the ledge slick, how what had looked like a docile trickle from further away now growled menacingly. She took a deep breath and kept moving sideways.

Then a rush of cold air from behind her. Two strong arms grabbed her and yanked her backward.

"Got you!"

She screamed. The sound of it ricocheted around the darkened cavity of rock Thor had pulled her into. Mandy spun to face him, ripping his hands from her sides. She wanted to move away. But there was no away. They were in a shadowed seam in the cliff behind the ledge, protected by a boulder half sunk into the rock. He must have been hiding there as she slinked along the ledge. Or maybe not. Hiding was weird. Hiding was creepy. Maybe he'd been scouting the trail down to the valley and he'd come back to guide her.

He went to clamp a hand on her shoulder, but she shook him away. "Where were you, Thor?"

"I figured you might want to experience the most exciting stretch of the slot on your own. Magical, right?"

"And this ledge? You wanted me to experience that on my own too?"

He cocked his head at her. "I thought you were one of us."

"Us?"

"Explorers. Adventurers. The tribe of the wild."

She gaped at him, annoyed that he'd dropped her into a dangerous initiation ritual for a secret society she'd never asked to join. She loved exploring new things. But she did it on her own terms. And the curses that had run through her mind as she'd stepped out onto the ledge weren't about adventure. They were about recklessness. Abandonment. Danger.

Was that how Liv saw her? When Mandy handed her sister an ice ax and waved at a glacier, when she put a paddle in her hand and whooped at the whitewater, did Liv think she was putting her in jeopardy? Did Liv get that same choked frog in her throat Mandy had felt just a few minutes before?

"Is there a way to get down from here?" she asked.

"Absolutely," Thor said. "We'll be down in Surprise Valley fast as a jackrabbit."

He pointed to a pencil-thin trail she hadn't spotted before, winding down below the dark stain in the cliff. It looked real. It looked better than the ledge. But she felt unsettled.

Still, she followed him. What other choice did she have?

Thor marched downward, leading her into a huge amphitheater of rock a quarter mile across at its base. It looked like a man cave for giants, with boulders big as cars, some of the smaller ones stacked into crude couches and chairs.

"That trickle of water we passed under," Thor said, pointing back up, "it's one of the springs that feeds Deer Creek. But most people call this spot the Throne Room."

From this vantage point, halfway down the amphitheater, Mandy could see how the stain on the rock rippled down to a line of lush plants crowding the creek. In the winter, it might be a pounding falls, but now, in high summer, its flow barely punctuated the dryness of the area. The Throne Room was a red, shining bowl of rock. The empress of the Grand Canyon belonged at its center. Mandy could almost picture a goddess here, perched on a massive slab of sandstone, her scepter the gnarled spine of an ancient ocotillo.

But the best thing she saw had nothing to do with mythic desert queens. It was a cluster of people, real, living people, down in the basement of the amphitheater, heading up into its bowl.

She could hear a man's laugh—was that Big Pete?—and a young woman's screech. Imogen. She hadn't realized how much she wanted the security of the group until she heard them. She turned her head, straining for the sure tones of her sister's voice. But if Liv was there, she was silent. Listening. Observing.

Mandy felt the ridiculous impulse to wave or hoot, to reach out to her sister across the expanse of the Throne Room and let her relief rain down to the rocks below.

But before she could say a word, a foreign sound echoed through the basin.

It was a soft keening, rising from a pile of stones by a thick, yellowed patch of rabbitbrush in the bowl. She squinted down, trying to resolve what was making it.

The sound broke out louder now, a ragged, undulating cry rattling the amphitheater walls, splitting the gem of the canyon into something heartbreaking and terrifying all at once.

She started moving toward it, leapfrogging down the rocks, ignoring Thor's calls to slow down and wait for him to check it out first. Some of the people below were racing up toward the sound as well. The cries didn't stop. Whatever was in that rabbitbrush, it was too focused on its own pain to notice her approach. Which might make it less dangerous. Or more.

"Mandy!"

Thor caught her by the upper arm and wrenched her out of her trance. They were both breathing hard, just feet from the dense cluster of brush. He pulled a holstered knife from his belt and unfolded it, clutching the blade in his hand.

"Follow my lead."

CHAPTER THIRTY-ONE

LIV HAD NEVER BEEN so glad to see her sister fall. Mandy tumbled down the rocky hillside behind Thor, moving so quickly it appeared as if her sarong was a kite cut loose and plummeting to the ground. But it didn't matter. She'd made it back. She was alive. They'd be together in just a few minutes.

But between her and Mandy was the sound.

The sound Mandy was charging at—that all of them were now heading toward—was terrible. It was a ragged, animalistic sound, a siren turned sentient, like the air raid alerts she'd heard sometimes late on foggy nights during her short stint in Ukraine. It tore through the amphitheater, reminding everyone that despite their fantasies otherwise, danger was an ever-present possibility.

"Could it be another mule?" Fiona asked.

Even as the hope hit her, Liv knew that was ridiculous. No animal would make a sound like this. Not unless it was dying.

"It's coming from over there." Lucinda pointed up to a cluster of rocks backed by a yellow thicket of brush.

"It can't be Babette," Guy said. "She was just a little hot. Marc said she'd be fine."

Lucinda shot him a perplexed look. There hadn't been time to introduce Guy to the others yet. But the horrible cries from the rocks suffocated any other immediate concerns. They climbed slowly, some with clenched fists, others with hands open, as if in supplication to the gods for this to be something other than what they feared.

"Babette?" Devon called out. "Is that you?"

"BABETTE?" PK shouted.

Unlike Mandy, Thor's movements were graceful, furtive. Liv watched him snake down through the brush to Mandy's left, pulling a knife from his belt without pausing. Liv felt a faint prick of fear for her sister, but then the guide pushed past Mandy and slowed, holding the knife in front of him, the outstretched blade pointing at the source of the sound.

It was a man, a bent-over, shuddering, howling figure, huddled at the base of a stout tower of rocks.

"Charlie." Thor's steady voice cut through the horrible keening. The guide kept a firm grip on his knife, but he brought it close to his body now, stretching his other arm out in a placating, defensive posture. "Are you hurt?"

The sound coming from Charlie's throat dropped from a wail to a stuttering sob. He was clutching something in both hands.

Devon raced ahead and dropped to her knees by her brother. Liv could see Charlie's eyes—his wild, panicked eyes—flicking from his sister to Thor to the sky above them. The man was in shock. Which meant he was dangerous. Even if he didn't know it.

"What do you have there, Charlie?" Thor said. He was gripping the knife more tightly now. Mandy was practically breathing over his shoulder.

Charlie glanced up, and the two men's eyes met in a swirl of confusion. Liv saw terror on Charlie's face. Terror and pain. He revealed one hand—a dirtied, sandstone-red hand—and Mandy took a step back.

"Good girl," Liv whispered.

Slowly, Charlie rose to his feet. He was trembling hard, the shudder fierce and unceasing, as if this was his new permanent state of being. He brought both his hands up. He was holding a sparkly glass water bottle by the neck.

"It was in her lap. I tried to give her some, but she couldn't . . . she wouldn't—" The bottle tumbled and smashed to the ground, spraying open in a web of cracks that soaked the parched sandstone.

Thor grabbed his arm, but Charlie didn't seem to notice. He had turned away to look at the massive pile of rocks looming over him. Three enormous slabs formed a crude staircase six feet up to a dust-orange throne upon which, Liv now saw, sat a woman. Her head was slumped back, her shirt yanked loose and limbs strewn wildly, as if she'd been impaled there. But there was no blood. Only stillness. She looked like a mangled porcelain doll, beautiful and broken. Nestled in the stone cradle lay the woman they'd all been waiting for, Babette's wide, unseeing eyes taking in the Grand Canyon for the first, and last, time.

CHAPTER THIRTY-TWO

"YOU!" PK LUNGED AT Charlie, who had crumpled back onto the stone steps beneath his sister's body. "You did this."

"Whoa." Devon grabbed the young man's arm. "Slow down. Let's stay calm."

"Calm? Babette is dead, and you're telling me to stay calm?"

Mandy was still processing what had happened. She kept blinking, trying to chase away the impossible horror before her. She'd dreamt of getting close to Babette, but not like this. Never like this.

Thor coolly removed Devon's hand from PK's forearm, angling his body to allow the woman to slide past the wild-eyed assistant and join her brother and their dead sister at the rocks. PK kept trying to shove his way through, but the guide was eerily relaxed, as if he'd prepared for this situation. He stood silent, an implacable wall separating Mandy and the Sauvage siblings from the rest of the group.

PK whirled around, seeking new targets among the others. "It was both of them. Charlie and Devon. Babette knew they were trying to take her down. That's what the messages in their hats must have been about. They've always been jealous, they've never been at her level, and she gave and gave but they took and took until here we are on the worst hike in the history of the universe."

"I cannot believe this," Stefan said.

"My goodness," whispered Lucinda.

"Um." Imogen looked sick. "Are we sure she's dead?"

Lucinda reached out to take her granddaughter's hand.

"Because it would be way better if she wasn't," Imogen clarified.

"She was murdered." PK's eyes had gone black with fury. "By them."

Charlie shrank into Devon, who tried her best to stand up straight, one arm wrapped around her brother. Mandy remembered the message in PK's hat, the way Babette called her assistant replaceable. Was it possible he was pointing the finger at Charlie and Devon to divert attention from his own pent-up desire to lash out at Babette? Could PK have somehow killed his hero? Mandy needed Liv, but she couldn't spot her. Her eyes were still blurry with tears, her body frozen in place in grief and horror.

Thor moved to climb the stairs to the sandstone throne.

"What are you doing?" Devon snapped.

"I'm a wilderness first responder," Thor said. "I can take a closer look."

Fiona stepped forward. "I'm a doctor. I'll do it."

She climbed up the great stone steps to where Babette lay. Fiona checked Babette's neck for a pulse, then put a hand to the woman's heart. She ran her fingers lightly over Babette's entire body, barely touching her. Something about the doctor's tentative, thoughtful movements snapped the edge off Mandy's shock. She watched, letting her gaze follow Fiona's over Babette's broken form. There was no blood. No tear in Babette's clothing. Instead, Mandy caught little suggestions of how recently Babette had been alive. Her cheeks still had color, her forehead broken out. Was it possible the skin care mogul secretly suffered from adult acne? Were there stresses not even the queen of CareFree could wash away?

Fiona gently pressed Babette's eyes closed and turned to the rest of them.

"Is she dead?" Lucinda asked.

Fiona nodded, her smooth skin revealing not even a wrinkle of concern.

"Murdered?" PK's voice was hysterical.

"There's no way for me to know that," Fiona said. "Her eyes made it look like she was afraid of something. She'd popped a blood vessel from strain. But she climbed up on that throne somehow, and there's no obvious wound, no marks on her skin. With her eyes closed, she looks perfect."

"Babette always looked perfect." Imogen fumbled her phone from her pocket. "I should capture something. For posterity?"

Lucinda swatted at her. "Put that away."

Mandy inched out from behind the Sauvage siblings and headed toward her sister. She felt shaky, but Liv locked eyes with her, and Mandy shuffled toward her steadiness, trying to match her sister's solid gaze with deliberate footsteps.

But before Mandy reached Liv, another impossible sight hit her. Her father, rushing toward her.

"Dad? Dad! What are you doing here?"

Guy squeezed Mandy to his chest. His warmth felt good, but also strange. Smothering. She couldn't make sense of his presence, and instead of offering her answers, he was holding her so tight the wrinkles in his windbreaker creased her cheek.

She felt his words more than heard them, a low rumble against her ear. "Babette didn't make it. But I'm here. You're safe."

Mandy gave in to the oddness of it, sinking into his chest and taking big, gulping breaths. In her periphery, she could sense Liv trying to reach her, trying to insist her way into the reunion. But Guy held her so close. And she was sobbing now, really crying, her tears mixing with the sweat and dust on her father's jacket. He seemed to be shaking a little, too.

"*You?*" Stefan took a step toward Guy. "Are you responsible for this?"

"Stefan," Guy responded softly. "Buddy. You know me. I would never—"

"Who are you?" Lucinda asked.

Everyone was looking at Guy now. Mandy felt her father's hand clamp tighter around her shoulder as he regarded them. But when he spoke, he sounded calm.

"I'm Guy Chisholm, Mandy and Liv's father, and Babette's investment advisor. I hiked down with Babette today, as her guest." His words were simple, measured. "Four hours ago, Babette started to get overheated. Marc, the guide, told me he'd help her cool off and get hydrated, and that I should hike ahead to find you and get more water."

"The guide," Charlie hissed. He turned to Devon. "I told you the guides could be behind all of this."

"A guide did not kill our sister," Devon said. "Think rationally."

PK glared at the Sauvage siblings. "Rationally, Charlie was the one with her when she died. We all saw. No one else was here."

"She was already mostly gone," Charlie whispered. He looked frightened. "It couldn't have been me."

Fiona looked at Guy skeptically. "If a guide was with her when you left, where is he now?"

"I don't know," Guy said. "He told me to find you, and that he'd help her. Then I got lost for hours."

"And yet we found you so close to here," Devon murmured.

"I was wandering blind," Guy said. "Couldn't tell up from down by the time you found me. Might have a touch of heatstroke myself."

"Maybe she didn't recover," Big Pete said. "If Babette's symptoms got worse, and you hadn't found us yet, Marc might have felt that he had to get her to a secure location and then seek medical help himself."

Mandy looked around. The Throne Room was wide and cavernous, visible from above and below. The spring was little more than a trickle, but there was shade, and Charlie had found that water bottle in her lap. Maybe this spot had looked to Marc like a safe harbor for an ailing woman.

"So her death was an accident," Lucinda said.

Devon stared at Guy. "If you and the guide both abandoned her, it sounds more like negligence to me."

"Or murder," Fiona murmured.

Next to her, Mandy felt Guy stiffen. Her father's grip was starting to make her shoulder throb. She looked around for an escape, for Liv. But her sister was crouched down on the ground, behind Babette's throne, picking something up.

"Was this her hat?" Liv asked Guy. Mandy could just barely make out the white italicized *B* raised up above the smudges of red dust on the cap.

"That's right."

Liv tucked the hat into the waistband of her pants, then looked up and nodded. Mandy broke free of her dad and followed Liv as she strode across the huddle, stopping in front of Big Pete. The lead guide was swallowing compulsively, his Adam's apple bobbing like a rubber duck in unruly waves.

"What happens now?" Liv asked.

He stared blankly for a few seconds before it apparently dawned on him that he was in charge of this nightmare.

"We have to get back to Katy and the boats," he said. "We'll call the park police on the sat phone from there. They'll send a helicopter to the beach. Rangers. Search and rescue. They'll know what to do."

"How will we carry her body down the trail?" Devon asked.

Big Pete swallowed again. "It's against the rules to move a dead body in the park."

"She has to stay here?" PK asked. "With the coyotes and mountain lions?"

"I'll stay with her." Charlie's voice was low and hoarse.

"Me too," Devon said.

"Like hell you will," PK said. "Probably try and kill her all over again."

"Let's all calm down," Lucinda said. "These accusations help no one."

"That's right. We don't know what happened here." Big Pete sounded more confident now, though his words were still laced with stress. "And no one is taking any more risks today. It's only a mile back to the rafts, but it's getting late and we don't have enough headlamps for everyone. So. We will all walk down. I'll call in the death to the Park Service. Then, if and only if they approve it, two people can hike back up here with Thor and enough camping gear to spend the night. The rest of us will stay down on the beach by Deer Creek Falls."

"Is *he* coming with us?" Fiona said, pointing at Guy.

"Everyone is coming with us," Big Pete said firmly.

"Sure you don't want me to look for Marc?" Thor asked.

"If he went for help and we didn't run into him already, he likely went back up to the rim," Big Pete said.

"I could catch him," Thor said. "I know the backcountry better than he does."

Thor didn't seem shocked or destabilized like the rest of them. His voice held the same buzzy energy as when he'd suggested the shortcut through the slot. As if this were just the kind of adventure he hungered for.

"No." Big Pete frowned at his eagerness. "From now on, we follow protocol. Everyone stays together. As they should have on your hike."

"I think this situation calls for a divergence in protocol," Thor shot back.

"You don't get paid to think," Big Pete said. "You get paid to take guests safely down the river."

Thor flashed him an angry look and spat on the ground. But he didn't say another word.

"How soon can they get a medical examiner and a detective down from the rim?" Liv asked.

"Depends," Big Pete said. "The Park Service has an investigation unit, but they only have a handful of special agents across the entire country. My guess is when I radio it in tonight, they'll broadcast out for help from Coconino County Sheriff's Office, maybe Arizona State Police. FBI, even, if there's a possibility of foul play."

"But if it was heatstroke—" Devon said.

"I'm not sure she died of heatstroke," Fiona interrupted. "Her skin is pale, not flushed. She might have gotten overheated earlier, but I think something else killed her."

Big Pete stared at her for a moment. "Then they'll almost certainly involve the feds."

"Feds?" Guy cleared his throat. "This is a terrible moment. But let's not leap to conclusions."

"Are you suggesting she's still alive?" Fiona asked. "Would you like to check my work?"

"No. This isn't about you. It isn't even about us. It's about Babette, what she would want. I think we should all take a beat and consider that." Guy bowed his head, which might have seemed respectful if Charlie hadn't taken this opportunity to snap out of his stunned grief.

"How do you have even one ounce of a clue what my dead sister would want?"

"You're in shock." Guy's voice radiated compassion. "It's getting dark, and we're in the middle of nowhere. We have to focus on our safety now. Our goddess is dead. Broadcasting it isn't going to help her."

"Guy is right." Stefan seemed to be the only one who had accepted her father's surprise appearance. "We are down here. The world is up there. No one needs to know."

"No." Devon's voice was firm. "Absolutely not. This is my sister. I'm not playing *Weekend at Bernie's: Grand Canyon Edition*."

"Devon, think about it," Stefan said. His voice was as gentle as Devon's had been brash. "We are all, every one of us, invested in CareFree becoming a success. If information gets out that Babette has died, before we know what happened, before the product is launched—"

"It would be a disaster," Guy said.

"It already is a disaster," PK said.

"You can't be serious," Liv said.

No one responded.

"This would mean breaking several laws, let alone some basic standards of—"

"Livvie." Guy put a hand on Liv's shoulder. "It's okay to be scared."

She shrugged him off, but Guy kept going. "Babette was beloved by so many. By everyone here, I'm sure. But sending up smoke signals to the National Guard is not going to bring her back."

"This is not okay," Liv said. "Right, Mand?"

Mandy didn't know what to say. She was still half dizzy from the shock of it all, and she wasn't sure what she thought about when and how to call the cops. But she got the sense Liv wasn't just asking about what they should do. She was asking whose side Mandy was on.

When she didn't respond fast enough, Liv shook her head. "We can't do this."

"Someone didn't love her," Charlie muttered.

"What?" Mandy asked.

"When I found her, she was still alive," Charlie said. His shaking had settled into a faint tremor, but he was still holding tightly to Devon's arm. "She was up on that throne, writhing in pain, clawing at her shirt, yelling at phantoms. Raving about how it wasn't her company anymore, how someone was trying to take it all. And then she just"—he shuddered again, a full-body expulsion of the memory—"seized up."

"She was *alive*?" Fiona said. The perfect skin between her eyebrows puckered. "For how long?"

"I don't know," Charlie said. "It might have only been a couple minutes."

PK looked at him with open hatred. "You really think we're going to believe this? If anyone was trying to take Babette from her, it was you and Devon."

Guy stepped forward. "May I suggest we continue this conversation down by the rafts? Over dinner, perhaps?"

"*You.*" Charlie's voice shifted from terrified to fierce. "You came down with her. You could have hurt her. You had all that time on the trail with her and—"

"Whoa, buddy," Guy said. "Let's think before we speak, shall we?"

"Is that a threat?"

"Enough," Big Pete cut in. His voice was tight. "We're a team. The faster we get moving, the faster the authorities can come to our aid. Let's go. Daylight's fading. And no one else is getting hurt on my watch."

CHAPTER THIRTY-THREE

LIV LOOKED AROUND AT the others, staring mutely at the not-Babette, at the tomb that was once a throne. A brittle, frenetic energy—half shock, half fear—buzzed through the ragged cluster of guests. *Money won't protect you. Cross me and you're dead too.* Liv had assumed Mandy's threat referred to her and Guy's investment, and Charlie's threat to Justine Long's accidental death—both ruthless ways of Babette asserting dominance over her partners. Now Liv wondered if she'd gotten it wrong. Who had really written the threats? Who needed protection now?

When Big Pete signaled for them to hike back down to the river, Liv hustled to the front, falling into step behind the lead guide.

"We should end the trip," she whispered.

"Not my call."

"We don't know what happened, and we have to mitigate the risks," Liv said. "We radio it in, and then we go back to the rim. Maybe we'll run into Marc. Either way, we'll get back to civilization."

"This group is not capable of safely hiking up to the North Rim."

"My dad hiked down," she said.

"So did Babette. And look how well that went." Big Pete shook his head. "Putting aside the fact that it's getting dark and everyone is exhausted, the trail to the North Rim is a beast. It's three miles longer than the trail you took from the south. It climbs fifteen hundred feet higher. It's tough even for the most seasoned hikers."

"Then we helicopter out," Liv said.

"Can't do that from here either. We'll call it in to the authorities. Later tonight, I can find out if Marc made it back to the office. We'll figure it out from there."

"But—"

"This isn't a democracy. Let's go."

Liv fell back and listened to the nervous bickering of the guests behind her. Big Pete was still in charge of the backcountry side of this trip. But who was in control of Babette's company now? By the time they reached the boats, Liv had a partial answer. No one was in charge, but most everyone wanted to be. While Thor explained the situation to Katy on the beach, Charlie, Devon, Stefan, PK, and Guy huddled around Big Pete like eager benchwarmers, each jockeying to direct what should happen next.

"I'm calling it in," Big Pete kept repeating. "And then we'll make camp."

"Don't call it in," PK said. "Not yet. She deserves—"

"Camp where?" Charlie asked.

"Failure to report is a crime. And wherever we camp, we'll all stick together." The guide sounded as exhausted as he looked.

"But you said we could go back up to where she—"

"I lied," Big Pete said. "It isn't safe to hike back up there at night."

"You . . . lied?" Devon looked shocked.

"You cannot call it in," Guy said. "If we're camping, we're stuck here at least another day. The least you can do is let the information stay with us. If you alert the authorities that Babette is dead while we're trapped in this valley of media black holes, there's no way we can craft the message around it. Babette Sauvage is an international icon. Not to mention CEO of one of the biggest private companies in her industry. The news is going to get out—and out of control."

"True," Stefan said. "This is a problem."

"Not my problem," Big Pete said.

"How much money would it take for it to become your problem?" Guy asked.

"Excuse me?"

"Just a little delay. Until we get back to the rim. We'll pay you for it."

The guide looked disgusted.

"This isn't about business," Guy insisted. "It's about honoring Babette. She worked so hard to share her truth with her fans. We owe it to her to take the time to tell her story properly."

Stefan nodded. "It is our responsibility." He turned to the guide. "And your responsibility is to guide us safely through this chasm."

"What's that supposed to mean?" Big Pete said.

"You're part of the narrative, too," Guy said. "When it gets out who died, everyone and their brother is going to scrutinize the particulars. I'd hate to see you report something prematurely that gets twisted to paint you or your tour company in a bad light."

Big Pete stared at Guy and Stefan for a long moment, his mouth opening and closing like a dying fish. Then he turned, took off down the beach, and leapt onto the supply boat. For a moment, it looked like he was going to paddle away and leave them to their squabbles about criminal conspiracy, which would probably serve them right. Instead, he drew back a tarp and hauled out a beat-up lockbox. He clicked the hasps open, and the green metal lid swung up to reveal a radio that looked like it had spent the Cold War hunkered down on a Russian submarine. He started flipping switches and turning knobs to bring the thing sputtering to life.

"Park police!" the box shouted. "What is your emergency?"

The head guide scrunched his face closer to the buzzing radio, as if he were trying to keep the conversation between just him and the machine.

"This is Wild Adventures trip leader Pete Otaro. I've got a private rafting group at mile one thirty-six, Deer Creek Falls."

"Your emergency?"

"There's a dead body."

"Where?" The box squealed and popped, like a toddler with a megaphone. Even over the rushing water, everyone could hear.

Big Pete glanced around nervously. Stefan, Guy, and PK were basically shooting lasers at him. For that matter, so was Liv. But she wanted him to do the right thing.

"We encountered the body up past Deer Creek Patio. In the Throne Room."

"Was anyone else there?"

"We encountered her alone."

"No other injured parties besides the body?" It was ugly, that word "body," the way it reduced Babette to an inert object. A discovery, not a person.

"No."

"Any indication of how she died?"

"No. You'll need to send someone down."

Big Pete's answers were coming out faster now, as if obfuscation was easier once he'd committed to this course. He hadn't lied exactly, but he was leaving out a boatload of information.

Like the hiking guide. Liv wondered again what had happened to Marc. Had he headed up to the rim, as Big Pete suggested? Was he missing? Hurt? Was it possible Guy was lying about when Marc had separated from him and Babette?

The radio coughed, and Liv prayed it would press Big Pete for more information about the dead woman. But the box had other priorities. "Where are you now?"

"We came back down to the beach to make camp before dark."

"You can't camp at those falls."

Charlie looked up, hopeful. Maybe they'd go back up to Babette's Throne Room after all.

Then the box shouted again. "You'll have to cross the river."

"What?" Charlie said. "But she—"

Big Pete cut him off. "I know the rules," he said into the box. "Just wanted to call you first. As per protocol."

There was a long staticky pause from the box, and Big Pete flashed a glance at the group on the beach. Much to Liv's annoyance, her dad nodded approvingly.

"Here's the thing," the box shouted.

Another pause. Now it really did look like Charlie might take a running leap for the boat, current be damned.

"There was a rock slide this morning below Lava Falls, near Hell's Hollow. All emergency personnel have been deployed to that site, and both our copters are fully engaged. Until we know the extent of the damage and injuries, I can't divert resources for a nonemergency situation."

"What about the body?" Big Pete asked. "If you can't send someone, it could get . . ."

Disturbed. Degraded. Eaten. Everything Liv could think of meant more indignity for Babette and her family, and less chance of the park police—or anyone else—ever finding out what really happened to her.

The box had other priorities. "You have provisions to stay in the area another day?"

"Yes."

"Cross the river and make camp," it yelled. "Keep this radio on. We will be in touch by noon tomorrow with an ETA on getting someone out to you. If you don't hear from us by then, reach out."

The box snapped silent. Still, Big Pete stared at it for a spell, as if it might yet provide him a magic solution he could offer the rest of the group.

Then he rose and stood on the edge of the supply boat, facing them. Everyone had inched forward during the radio drama, and they were all clustered there, a pack of scared, tired, angry sheep. Liv was surprised to notice she was clutching Mandy's hand.

"Well," Big Pete said. It was as if he didn't want to come back down to the beach. "Suppose you heard all that."

"You did well," Guy said.

PK shot him an angry look. "Not well enough. No one is coming to help her."

"Or us," Fiona added.

"I want to go back to her," PK said.

"I want to go home," Imogen said. It was a quiet admission, perhaps the most radically honest thing she'd said yet.

Lucinda patted Imogen's arm. The older woman looked exhausted, worn through by the intensity of the day.

"I still do not understand what happened," Stefan said. "You"—he pointed to Charlie—"came upon her, and she was alive? And then, so quickly, dead?"

Charlie squeezed his whole body shut, fists clenched, eyes closed, arms pressed tight to his sides. Then he opened his eyes. "She was delirious. She didn't recognize me."

"Which is a sign of heatstroke, no?" Stefan asked.

"Her skin was too pale for heatstroke," Fiona responded. "It's not my area of expertise, but it looked"—Fiona flashed an apologetic face at Charlie and Devon—"violent."

"Something made her suffer," Liv said. "Something made her die. Something, or someone."

"Snake bite, perhaps?" Stefan turned to Thor. "Your pink friend?"

"Grand Canyon rattlesnakes are docile," Thor said. "They don't bite unless seriously provoked. And the reaction Charlie described . . . that's not how venom hits people."

"Could it have been poison?" Stefan turned back to Charlie. "You said she was seizing when she died, yes?"

"Do we need to talk about this now?" Charlie set his eyes on Devon. "Please. Can we just . . ."

"My brother's right. She's gone. Let's just . . ."

It was as if the Sauvage siblings had fallen in the river again, gasping for air in the surging waves. Liv could only imagine how she'd feel if it were Mandy they'd found up on that throne.

But she also wondered at Charlie and Devon's desire to avoid detailed talk of Babette's death. She cursed herself for not gathering up the smashed glass from Babette's water bottle, the one Charlie had dropped to the ground. Was it possible he'd done that intentionally?

"It matters," Liv blurted out. "It matters how she died."

Devon looked at her. "Of course it matters. But at this moment, I really don't think—"

"If someone intended to hurt your sister, they succeeded. And they could still be down here with us now."

"With us?" Mandy asked. "Like, one of us?"

"Or two," PK said, flashing dark eyes at Charlie and Devon.

"Or the guide," Liv said. "Don't forget about Marc."

"Don't forget your darling daddy," Fiona said.

"Now I really want to go home," Imogen moaned.

"Enough," Guy said. He snapped his fingers at Big Pete. "Hey! Boatman! How much to get a helicopter out of here?"

Big Pete shook his head. "Private aircraft can't land in this stretch of the canyon."

"For the right price they can."

At that, Big Pete exploded. "You people don't get it, do you? Your money, your connections, they can't help you down here. All we can do is follow the rules. Which means we cross the river. We make camp. We eat dinner. We go to sleep. We talk to the park police again tomorrow. We don't split up or hail helicopters or play medical examiner or build a pop-up spa by the waterfall. We wait. That's it."

Clearly Liv wasn't the only one who was tired.

"I don't want to cross the river," Charlie said. His voice was petulant.

"Not your call," Big Pete said.

"I think it is," Charlie said. "I'm the client. And I want to camp here."

The two men glared at each other. Liv couldn't decide why Charlie was taking this stand. Maybe he'd seen how Big Pete had capitulated to Guy's suggestions, and Charlie wanted to assert some control over the situation, too. Or was it possible he planned to sneak back up to Babette's body in the night? Was there someone else on this side of the river—perhaps Babette's killer—with whom Charlie was trying to connect?

Liv looked around the rocky beach, considering their options. Wondering if she had any weight to throw around, and if so, where to pitch it.

"I think we should camp across the river," Liv said.

"Why?" Devon asked.

"There's a wide, flat beach over there. Here it's cramped with rocky caves, and the waterfall is shooting spray everywhere."

She hoped she wouldn't have to spell out why these things mattered. Why it might be not only unpleasant but dangerous for them to stay in a place where they'd have to bed down in individual little coves, where the noise of the pounding waterfall would make it difficult to sleep or hear if someone sneaked up on them.

Lucinda looked at Liv. "If someone killed Babette, then aren't we putting ourselves at greater risk if we isolate ourselves across the river?"

"If one of us killed Babette, perhaps. But if someone else hurt her and then took off, they'll be on this side."

"What if they have a boat?" Imogen asked.

"Do you see a boat?" Liv said.

"It could be, like, in a backpack."

"Then we'll see them when they paddle across," Liv said. She turned to her father. "Marc didn't have a boat with him, did he?"

Guy shook his head. "Just one of those camel packs that holds water."

"Good," Liv said. "And there's one more thing. Lucinda is also right. If one of us is the one who hurt Babette, we need to find a way to stay safe."

"We were all in groups when she died," Imogen said.

"Not all of us," PK said. "Charlie was alone when he found her."

"The damage had already been done," Charlie protested. "And I wasn't the only one alone out there." He narrowed his eyes at Stefan. "You said you wanted time on your own at the junction."

The Dutchman looked surprised. "I just needed some water."

"But you didn't catch up with me," Charlie continued. "And it sounds like you didn't immediately double back to Lucinda and Fiona either."

"What about you and Tarzan?" Fiona said, looking at Mandy. "You took a totally different path. Were you together the whole time?"

"Of course," Thor said quickly. "Stayed close as shadows."

"I think we're ignoring the person who spent the most time with Babette," Devon said. "*Him.*"

Everyone turned to look at Guy.

"How many times do I have to tell you? She was alive and well when I last saw her."

"I thought you said she was overheating," Liv said.

Guy frowned. "Not in a going-to-die way. She just needed water, and a rest. Why are you cracking my nuts on this, Livvie?"

"This is Dad," Mandy said. "He wouldn't—"

"I'm well aware of what he's capable of."

"Enough," Big Pete said. "We're going across the river to make dinner and camp. Katy, Thor, get the PFDs. Everyone else, make sure you have your things."

"Are we taking the mule?" Imogen asked.

The animal had wandered into one of the pools fed by the waterfall and was wallowing in the mud.

"The mule will be fine," Big Pete said.

If only he could say the same for the rest of them.

CHAPTER THIRTY-FOUR

MANDY OFFERED TO HELP with dinner to keep her hands busy. Not that she was very helpful; when Katy handed her a crate of tomatoes, jalapeños, and onions to make pico de gallo, the simple ingredients formed a nine-dimensional puzzle she couldn't parse. She settled instead for warming tortillas on the griddle, letting the hot corn singe her fingertips with every flip.

They'd rowed across the Colorado to this beach in silence. Set up camp—Mandy lining up her sleeping pad in tight synchrony with her sister's—in silence. Grief and fear had rendered the group listless. Katy and Thor prepped dinner while Big Pete radioed up to the Wild Adventures office, but Marc hadn't shown up yet, so there was no new information for anyone to latch on to. Lucinda was icing her ankle. PK dug in the sand with a stick like a little boy. Devon and Charlie were making a small altar to their sister, Devon pulling crumpled white trumpet flowers from her day pack and laying them across a marbled rock while Stefan, Imogen, and Guy looked on. Only Liv seemed engaged, her eyes bright, her big brain likely sorting questions into categories and subcategories and Roman-numeraled lists. It was one of the paradoxes of her sister. Liv shied away from physical exertion. She stubbed a toe on every edge of the great outdoors. But when it came to intellectual challenges or psychological danger, she dove straight in.

Right now, Liv had her sights set on Fiona, who was sitting by the cook site, watching Charlie and Devon make their altar and drinking from a glass thermos that appeared to be lined with charcoal and glitter.

"I think you saw something when you examined Babette," Liv said.

Fiona took a long swig, the minerals in her water bottle swirling into sparkly tornadoes. "As I said, I don't believe she died of heatstroke. Her skin was the wrong color."

Liv nodded. "A useful observation. But I think you saw more."

The dermatologist looked at her warily. "Are you here on behalf of your father? Making sure he covered his tracks?"

"He didn't—" Mandy started.

But Liv talked over her. "As you said, you're not a medical examiner. Not an expert on venomous snakes nor poisons. So my guess is you noticed a reaction on her body you've seen before."

Fiona stayed silent. She glanced back at Devon's altar, her face blank.

Mandy could see Liv wasn't going to get anywhere with this strategy. All Fiona had to do was keep quiet and drink from her cylindrical snow globe, and eventually Liv would have to give up. Her sister was a trained investigator, but she was used to working with the full force of the federal government behind her. Here, Liv had no jurisdiction. No way in. Mandy, on the other hand, had never relied on a badge to get what she needed.

She leaned out over the stove, careful not to let her sarong hit the griddle.

"I saw it too," Mandy said.

Fiona and Liv both looked up at her.

"On Babette's body?" Mandy continued. "I didn't remember until you two started talking about it just now." Tactic number one: Suggest that Fiona was an active participant in a conversation in which she had yet to contribute anything.

"But then something shook loose in my memory, and BAM!" Mandy slapped down a tortilla on the griddle. "There it is in front of me again. You're seeing it too, aren't you?"

Fiona opened her mouth. "I—"

"Crazy, right?" Tactic number two: Cut Fiona off. A weird one, but it almost always worked. An interruption, before Fiona could disagree or shut down the conversation, would only make her more eager to be heard.

"There it is, front and center, clog-dancing through my brain." Mandy snatched up the tortilla and waved it in the air. "I'm even seeing it in these."

The surface of the tortilla was a chaotic constellation of ground corn, char marks, and air bubbles. Mandy didn't have a clue what it might evoke, but it was like a horoscope or a Rorschach test: All that mattered was what Fiona saw in it. And Fiona was staring at her now.

Mandy went in for the kill. "We should just tell her, don't you think? My sister's smart. She might be able to figure out what it means."

"It's not conclusive," Fiona mumbled. Her eyes flicked again to Devon's altar.

"Does it have to do with Charlie and Devon?" Mandy asked.

"Sort of. Not exactly. I've only seen it once before." She looked at Mandy anxiously. "You're an investor; I assume you got to see some of the focus group reports. Is that where you saw it?"

Mandy racked her brain for any clue to what Fiona was talking about. Every three months since she and her dad made the investment two years ago, she'd received an email with an attachment from Babette's lab about the latest tests of CareFree. The document was always hundreds of pages, incredibly boring, and the last one she'd forwarded on to her father without even scanning. Mandy tried to think back to earlier attachments, scrolling the reports quickly on her phone. There were testing protocols, interviews with participants, and maybe . . .

"The photographs," Mandy said.

Fiona nodded. "I'm surprised you spotted it. The stippling on the skin was subtle. I only recognized it on Babette's forehead because I'd seen it in person before."

"Mandy's an artist," Liv said. "She sees things other people don't."

Her sister's words flooded Mandy with warmth. On one level, she knew Liv was just playing into her game—which was remarkable in itself. But the compliment felt real. She hoped it was real.

"What does stippling mean?" Liv asked.

"Tiny bumps," Fiona said. "It looks a little like acne."

Mandy nodded. Now that Fiona mentioned it, she did remember a surprising smattering of bumps across Babette's forehead.

"It was shiny too," Mandy said.

"That's right." Fiona looked somber. "But I don't really understand how you saw those photos. The accident happened after the focus group was over. Devon and her siblings did everything they could to cover it up."

Finally, Mandy made the connection. "Justine Long. The woman who died in the third focus group."

"*After* the focus group," Fiona corrected.

"How did Justine Long die?" Liv asked. "The same way Babette did?"

Fiona glanced one more time to Devon and Charlie. The siblings' heads were bowed now, and each had a hand on the marbled rock. The blossoms before them wilted in the last tendrils of sun.

"I can't be positive," Fiona said quietly. "Not without tests. Tests we're never going to be able to conduct out here."

"Datura flowers," Liv said.

"What?" Mandy asked.

"Those white trumpets Devon laid on that rock. She showed them to me when she picked them earlier today. They're another strain of the datura used in CareFree. A deadly varietal."

Mandy turned to Fiona. "Did Justine Long eat datura flowers?"

Fiona said nothing.

"Hey, Katy." Mandy looked over to where the guide was roasting green chiles with a pair of tongs. "Can someone die from eating datura?"

Katy put down the tongs. "Definitely. It happened here in the canyon three years ago. A guy thought they were grape leaves and tried to wrap them around some beans and rice."

"It's the leaves that can kill you?"

"Leaves, flowers, seeds . . . Any part of it can. My friend, the plant mystic? She calls it a devil drug. Like, death magic. Especially the seeds."

Mandy looked back at Liv. "Do you remember any remnants of seeds or leaves by Babette's body?"

"I don't know," Liv said. She turned to the river with longing in her eyes, as if she'd consider swimming across to scour the Throne Room once again.

"I told you," Katy said. Her voice was low.

"Excuse me?" Liv said.

"I told you the plant wouldn't like it if they tried to commercialize her."

"You think the plant killed her?" Mandy asked. "Of its own volition?"

"Magic is magic. Lady Datura is a deadly sorceress."

The guide looked completely serious. A true believer. But even Mandy couldn't conceive of a scenario where a killer plant witch had come down and slain Babette.

"I think Babette would have known about the dangers of consuming the live plant," Liv said. "And Justine Long wasn't exposed to a bunch of flowers, was she? She was exposed to CareFree."

Mandy turned to Fiona. "Is that what happened? Did Justine and Babette overdose on CareFree?"

"The product is safe," Fiona insisted. "CareFree has always been safe, even when it wasn't working properly. That's not what killed them."

"Then what did?" Liv prompted. "Fiona, if there's something wrong with CareFree . . ."

The dermatologist looked at Charlie and Devon again. They were standing now, heading back to the camp chairs. "The product is ready for market. It's incredible. Transformational."

It sounded like Fiona was telling the truth, even as she was hiding something at the same time.

"Why are you here?" Mandy asked softly.

"Same reason as you," Fiona said. "Babette invited me."

"Why?"

The blond woman looked at her. "I wish I knew."

Fiona flipped her water bottle over and back, over and back. Glittering charcoal spun and danced from end to end, as if the bottle were an hourglass gone haywire.

Finally, she spoke. "After Justine died, I pitched a proposal for how to manage the more volatile parts of CareFree's manufacturing process. Instead of considering it, Devon fired me. Babette and Charlie backed her up. That was a year ago. Since then, I've had no contact with the company beyond the negotiation of my severance package and the reports they have to send to everyone who has shares in the business. Then, out of the blue, Babette called me two weeks ago. She said she needed my help, that she'd tell me everything when I got here. Instead . . ."

Fiona flipped her water bottle over again.

"Babette died in the same way as Justine," Liv said. "Which was?"

Fiona grimaced once, quickly, a razor slicing across her perfect face. "I can't talk about that."

"Do you think the product they're going to release is dangerous?" Liv asked.

"I'm telling you, CareFree is fine. I genuinely believe it's going to change the world."

"And whatever it is Babette wanted to talk with you about?"

"It dies with her, I suppose. Devon sees me as a threat. Charlie does whatever his sisters demand. They aren't going to listen to me." Fiona looked down at her empty, sparkling container. "Now if you'll excuse me, my hydration is calling."

The dermatologist stalked away, clutching her thermos like a weapon.

"Well," Liv said.

"Well," Mandy said.

"Your tortillas are burning."

Ouch. Liv was right. And had returned to her lifelong occupation of pointing out Mandy's undependability. "Tacos hardly seem like the priority right now."

"When you agree to a job, you should do it well."

Then Liv looked her right in the eye.

"What you did there," Liv said. "How you led her in?"

Mandy was on guard now, waiting to be chastised for not following her sister's lead.

"It was great," Liv said. She reached out and tucked in a corner of Mandy's sarong that was flirting with the fire. "Now pay attention to the griddle. If that's how Fiona acts when she's dehydrated, I don't want to see what happens if she goes hungry."

CHAPTER THIRTY-FIVE

LIV SPENT THE REST of the time before dinner mulling over the riddle of Fiona's words. There was something wrong with CareFree that had killed Justine Long and Babette Sauvage. But it wasn't the product, or the plant. Which left . . . what? The packaging? Some other ingredient?

By the time the conch shell blew, Liv decided to recommit her energy to something more pressing: the question of who had killed Babette. No one around the circle of camping chairs gave off the strong impression of having just murdered someone. On the contrary, dinner went surprisingly well. Thor made margaritas that were mostly tequila. Charlie had two, Stefan five, and even Fiona accepted one, claiming the salt around the rim had medicinal benefits. The tacos were delicious, if charred, and the way Mandy drew people out of their funk was downright masterful. Her little sister seemed to know exactly whom to smile at and whom to leave alone. By the time dessert was served—pineapple upside-down cake flipped from a cast-iron skillet, smothered in gleaming caramel—the earlier tension had melted into a fragile peace.

Liv accepted a piece of cake and cracked the brittle shell of caramelized sugar with her spoon. Now was not the time for calm. Someone had hurt Babette. While it was possible the killer was not among them, all the people who had the most to gain—or lose—from Babette's leadership of CareFree were here, and Liv would have bet good money that the person who'd planned Babette's death was one of them. There was more than enough love, greed, and tension on this beach to motivate a murder.

She scanned the group, considering the options. Charlie and Devon, the siblings in mourning. PK, the loyal assistant. Stefan, the secretive investor. Lucinda and Imogen, new ambassadors to the Babette empire. Fiona, cast out and now invited back for reasons unknown. Her dad, who had cadged a beer from Thor and plunked himself down next to Katy, gabbing at her about investment strategy in an overloud, jovial voice, to the apparent discomfort of the young woman.

Her father. What was he doing here? From the furtive looks and whispers around the circle of chairs, it was clear Liv wasn't the only one wondering.

"Dad," she said. Guy beamed at her, and Liv cursed the small, hungry part of her that still thrilled at his attention. "Why exactly did you come down here with Babette?"

"I don't see how that matters now, Livvie." He gentled his smile. "Poor woman. She was so brilliant. Dedicated. Did I ever tell you about the time—"

Liv cut him off. "You don't hike. You don't camp. You turned down the opportunity to come on this Essence Quest when you and Mandy were originally invited. And then Babette buys you sushi, and suddenly you're Mr. Great Outdoors? Why?"

"It was time."

"Time?"

Guy nodded. "I haven't seen you in what, a year?"

"Three years."

"I thought it would be fun to surprise you."

"Here?"

Guy was still smiling, but it looked forced. "Let's continue this conversation down by the river." He motioned to her and her sister to follow him, moving away from the circle of camp chairs and stilted conversations. Mandy fell into step with him, and despite her annoyance, Liv did as well. The further they got from the others, the more her father's body seemed to relax. Whether that meant he was more or less likely to tell the truth, Liv wasn't sure. His presence here was still a shock, and not just to her. No one here knew him, except Stefan, who kept shooting glances their way. According to Guy, he hadn't even known he was coming until the day before. It was the only part of his story Liv sensed was true.

"How long have you been advising Babette?" she asked him.

"Our engagement started informally," Guy said. "It's been a couple years."

"And you never met PK? Or Charlie and Devon?" Liv looked back toward the group, hunting out the Sauvage siblings. Devon was in conversation with her brother, her hand clutching Charlie's arm in a way that looked more controlling than consoling.

"The pressures on a CEO taking on investment for the first time are singular," Guy said. "Babette needed someone experienced. Someone who could be discreet."

"You."

"Me. Is it really so hard to believe?"

His smooth words fell like barbed thistles on Liv's ears. It *was* hard to believe. Impossible, even. But before she could question him further, Mandy spoke up.

"Dad can help us, Liv. He knows what she was thinking in the hours before she died."

But so far, he wouldn't tell her. And even if he did, Liv wasn't sure she could believe him. She thought again about the message in Mandy's hat.

"No one can verify Dad's story about how he got here," Liv said. "And the fact that his investment wasn't kosher might have been what Babette was threatening you about."

"What's your point?" Guy asked.

"Some people might think you hurt Babette to protect your secret."

"That's ridiculous," Mandy insisted. "Dad wouldn't hurt anyone."

"How we got here doesn't matter." Guy put one arm around Mandy, the other around Liv. "What matters is that we're together now."

Liv counted to eight and backed out of his embrace. She considered herself a minor saint for not slapping him.

"And besides," Guy continued. "I have a theory. There's someone here I think might be involved in Babette's death."

"Who?" Mandy asked.

"Stefan Eriksen," Guy said. "I'm the one who introduced Babette to him originally. Two nights ago, in Vegas, Babette told me she was afraid her lead investor was trying to take her company. We thought if I came down here, I could help stop him. I thought he could be reasoned with. Obviously, I was wrong."

"Stefan," Mandy whispered excitedly, looking back up the beach. "He didn't want to call the cops."

"Neither did Dad," Liv pointed out. "And Babette didn't threaten Stefan."

"But maybe the hats weren't really from Babette," Mandy said. "Maybe Stefan wrote the messages to distract everyone, to point fingers at someone else. Charlie said Stefan was on his own for some of the hike back from Thunder Spring, remember? Maybe he killed Babette then."

"He would have had to get extremely lucky on timing," Liv said. "And why would Stefan need to kill her to take over her company? It sounded like he was already colluding with Charlie and Devon on something like that."

"You wanted the truth," Guy said. "Stefan represents a lot of money. A lot of power. And power protects itself. That's the truth."

"Makes sense to me," Mandy said. "What do you think?"

Liv stared at her dad and sister, their arms still linked. Part of her wanted to believe them. To join them. It would be easier that way. But telling stories was what they did, especially when the truth was messy, dangerous, or unflattering.

"I don't know," she said softly.

Guy gazed at her for a moment, then gave her one sharp, dismissive shake of the head. "Come on, Mandy. Your sister isn't going to make them trust me. We have to do it without her."

Liv watched her father and sister turn and head back up to the rest of the group. She wanted to cry. She wanted to run away. She wanted to ford the river and storm up to the North Rim and grill Marc on exactly what he'd witnessed. She'd thought Mandy was on the same team with her, the two of them working together to find the truth in this convoluted canyon of deceit. But Mandy was her father's daughter. She and Guy would always choose whatever story served them best.

Guy strode to the center of the circle of camping chairs and raised the mostly empty can of lager in his hand. "If I could get all of your attention," he announced. Even Liv found herself moving toward his loud, authoritative voice. "I'd like to propose a toast. To Babette."

Fiona glared at him. "First, I'd like to know why she brought you down here."

"Babette trusted me," Guy said. "She knew me."

PK sniffed. "If you really knew her, you'd know a beer is no way to honor her memory."

"You're right." Guy nodded eagerly at the young man. "Absolutely right. If we're going to salute the queen, we've got to do it with royal jelly."

Liv had no idea where her dad was taking this, but that was the rub of it. This was his production now. He wasn't here to answer questions or tell the whole truth or help figure out what happened to Babette. He was here to put on a show. And he did it disgustingly well—conjuring curiosity and desire, making everyone his complicit audience, waiting to hear what he would say next.

"PK!" Guy said. "When times get tough, what do we hope for? When our house is torn apart, when we're lost in the wilderness, when our loved ones abandon us: What do we wish, against all odds, that we could do?"

When the young man didn't answer, Guy smiled. "Let. Your.

Worries," he said, directing each word to a new person in the circle. "Wash away."

"No," Charlie said. "Stop. This is a nightmare. It is not an advertisement for CareFree."

"But don't you see? It is. This is exactly what Babette would have wanted. For us to turn to the revolutionary power of CareFree to give us peace at this time."

"Absolutely not." Liv had to step forward. "You've all been drinking. And from what I understand, CareFree has neurochemical effects."

"It's perfectly safe," Devon said.

"It would ease the pain," Fiona said.

"With a lot fewer calories than those margaritas," PK muttered.

"I'll try anything twice," Thor said.

Before Liv could issue any further protest, PK had dragged his soft cooler over to the circle. Even Imogen, who'd seemed lost in a catatonic state of grief and fear, perked up when he pressed one of the white tubs into her hand. When Liv tried to brush PK off, he insisted.

"It's for Babette," he said.

She shoved the container deep in her pocket.

"Is there a protocol for how to use it?" Imogen had already whipped out her phone.

"Put that away," Lucinda said.

"Nana, CareFree is the entire reason we're here."

"She's right," PK said. Sheepishly, the young man gestured for Imogen's phone and propped it up against a rock on the sand.

Charlie looked stricken.

"You're a loud, arrogant leech," PK said to Guy. "But you're right. Babette would have wanted us to do this."

He hit Record.

"For Babette," PK said. He dipped his fingers into the lavender-tinted cream and started rubbing circles over his cheeks and forehead.

"For Babette," the others repeated. Guy slathered the stuff onto his cheekbones. Imogen made careful dots along her jawline for the camera, smoothing them away one dainty stroke at a time. Even Charlie dipped into the cream, worrying the furrow between his eyebrows. Only Liv, Lucinda, Katy, and Big Pete abstained.

"It's cooling," Mandy murmured.

"The final calibration on the scent is excellent," Stefan said.

"How long before it starts working?" Imogen asked.

"That's the beauty of topical application," Devon said. "It's already sinking into your bloodstream."

"But the full effect?" Stefan asked.

"It peaks in one hour, lasts for two," PK said. "Hopefully by then we can drift off and forget this horrible day."

Forget. Was that what her father had wanted to achieve?

In the first half hour, as far as Liv could tell, everyone just grew quieter. More detached. PK's pupils were dilated, and Devon's skin reddened, but that could also have been a result of the long day in the sun. Thor picked at a ukulele he'd pulled from the supply boat, as if this were just another lazy day on the river.

Liv stood awkwardly with Big Pete, Katy, and Lucinda by the dish station, watching.

"It doesn't look like they're in thrall to a goddess of hell," Liv said.

"It's worse," Katy said. "They neutered the datura plant. Bled the goddess dry. And turned everyone into . . ."

"Lotus eaters," Lucinda said.

"What?"

"In Homer's *Odyssey*. There was an island where everyone was stoned all the time."

"Did something terrible happen to them?" Liv asked.

"Strangely, no. It's one of the few places where Odysseus's crew doesn't torment the locals. They just forget their earthly toil and lounge around."

"But it's dangerous, right?"

Lucinda scrutinized the plate in her hands for spots. "For people like us, maybe. For them . . ."

Liv scanned the beach. Down by the water's edge, Mandy and Guy were sitting together, Mandy's head on his shoulder, singing the Beatles. They swayed gently, losing the lyrics here and there, wandering off-key. It would be so easy to slather on some cream and join them on the sand. To let go of the hurt, the threats, her suspicions about her father's role in Babette's death. If she could only forgive. If she could only forget.

But that carefree dream world was theirs, not hers. Calmly, Liv turned to Big Pete, Katy, and Lucinda. "There are three people who had the opportunity to be alone with Babette today. There's a possibility one of them could have . . ."

"Killed her?" Lucinda said.

Liv still wasn't prepared to say that out loud. "They might have seen something that makes them a target as well. Either way, we need to take care of them. Of all of us."

"How do you suggest we do that?" Big Pete asked.

CHAPTER THIRTY-SIX

IT WAS POSSIBLE MANDY had used more CareFree than recommended. Her skin felt amazing—airy and smooth—but her thoughts slipped and wriggled from her grasp. She leaned back against the sandy bank and stared up at the darkening bowl of the canyon, letting her mind drift as the stars slowly punched themselves out of the sky. She tried to count them.

It felt impossible. It felt normal.

She realized: That was the difference. Despite the insanity of the day—the discovery of Babette's dead body, the shock of her dad crashing the trip, the arguments and uncertainties and potential dangers floating in the river—she felt at ease. Not perfect; all the sharp rocks were still there. But they had been bathed in muddy water. It was as if the tide of her equanimity had risen, blanketing the hard things, making them soft.

Liv's voice floated toward her as if in a waking dream.

"Mandy. I have to ask you something."

"Hmm?"

"Earlier, when Dad—are you okay?"

"Yeah, just . . . you know." Mandy waved to the canyon. The air felt thick, her hand moving slower than usual, sculpting the night.

"Tell me your favorite painter," Liv said.

"Magritte."

"And the name of Dad's convertible from when we were kids?"

Mandy scowled. “What was it you wanted to ask me?”

“Look, I know you think I’m some kind of stick-in-the-mud—”

“More like a stick-in-the—”

“—but that datura plant is no joke. You heard Fiona. It could have been the cause of Babette’s death. There’s something we still don’t understand about that last focus group . . .”

Mandy sat all the way up. The vehemence in Liv’s voice was a buzzkill. “Look, I get it. You’re worried. You get State Department alerts about how criminals use the datura plant to turn people into zombies in Bogotá, and you think the worst. But CareFree is a professional product made by a legitimate company. There are lots of things derived from natural materials where if you took too much, or the wrong kind, it could hurt you. And besides, if there were anything wrong with it, we’d figure it out.”

She really hoped there was nothing wrong with it. CareFree felt too good—and her dad had too much invested—for it to be another flop. Or worse, she supposed. Some kind of illegal poison drug would definitely be worse.

“Here’s what I want to know.” Liv’s voice was soft, riding the quiet desert air. “Do you think Dad is telling the truth about why he came down here with Babette?”

Mandy felt a spike of irritation at her sister’s implication. Then, just as quickly, it melted away. “Honestly? I don’t think even Dad knows why he came down here.”

“What do you mean?”

“We’re not like you.” Mandy tossed a pebble in the river. “You’re a rock. We’re water.”

This seemed to her to encapsulate the situation. But judging from Liv’s confused expression, she had to say more. “We don’t have a fixed plan or position. We go where opportunity takes us, moment to moment. If Dad said Babette asked him and he decided to come, that’s probably what happened.

“And you know what’s weird?” Mandy continued. “Babette changed her plan too. We all thought she'd descend from a helicopter, but instead she waited and brought Dad down with her the next day. It was all a surprise."

"Babette seemed to be full of surprises," Liv said.

"But she wasn't chaotic," Mandy said. "She was a rock, like you."

"Your hero is like me?" Liv's voice was so low Mandy could barely hear her.

"Ex-hero. That puppy thing was messed up." Mandy shook her head. "And don't die, okay?"

"Deal." Liv looked out toward the water. "I could use your help with something else," she said. "Hypothetically."

"Hit me."

"Imagine a situation where you have a group of people. And maybe a couple of those people could be dangerous. Or not. You're not sure."

"Like, they could be werewolves?"

"Mandy . . ."

Okay. Too hypothetical.

"There are a few people who had the opportunity to be alone with Babette before she died," Liv said. "I'm worried they could be a risk to the rest of us."

"Like Stefan," Mandy said.

"And Charlie," Liv said. "They each had time on their own on the trail."

Mandy's mind drifted back to the dark, rough-edged slot she and Thor had navigated as a shortcut around the trail. How long had she been wedged in that narrow place after Thor had abandoned her? Could he have made it down to Babette's body and back in that time?

But Liv spoke again before she could mention Thor.

"They could be dangerous. Or they could be perfectly safe."

"Like Dad," Mandy said. "He's safe."

"Uh-huh." Liv flicked a speck of nothing onto the sand. "What do you think we should do with them? The risk factors?"

"You didn't happen to pack your lie detector, did you?" Mandy asked.

"It's in my other bag, the one that went to the van that will pick us up at the end of the trip."

The end of the trip. It was hard to imagine they'd keep rafting to Lake Mead now. Mandy tried to envision it, the river bucking and breaking for days and miles to come, their group paddling farther from Babette's silent grave. CareFree might offer a respite tonight. But they couldn't forget forever. Could they?

Mandy considered her sister's question. "Let's think of it another way. There were just a few people who could have witnessed Babette's death. If one of them was spotted by the killer, they could be in danger. Maybe they aren't suspects."

"Maybe they're witnesses," Liv said.

"Exactly. Either way, they're all in the same boat. They all need to be protected."

"The same boat," Liv said. "That's it! Thank you."

Mandy felt the delicious shock of her sister's approval, even if she didn't fully understand what she'd done to earn it. Liv's attention had already moved on. Her sister stared out at the dark streak of the river, deep in thought.

"Still want me to tell you what Dad's convertible was named?" Mandy asked.

Liv turned her head.

"Rita Moreno," they said in unison.

"Jinx," Mandy said.

"Remember when he traded it for shares in that goji berry company?" Liv said.

"You're jinxed. Can't talk."

Mandy let herself slip back into the carefree pleasures of the evening: the languid fatigue in her muscles, the warm fullness of her belly, the cool sand under her bare feet. She stood silent beside her sister, all the threads and questions unraveling in her mind.

Below them, the river rushed on, fading to black.

CHAPTER THIRTY-SEVEN

WHEN LIV WALKED BACK up from the riverbank, Big Pete was pacing behind the kitchen area, the clunky black satellite phone clamped to his head. She caught his eye, but he put a finger in the air.

"Where is he now?" Big Pete waited. "I see. Makes sense." Another pause. "No, you can call them off. Yeah. Tell him to call first thing when he gets in in the morning."

As soon as he flicked off the phone, she leapt.

"What did you hear?"

"Nothing new from the Park Service," he said. "That was Jan, in our office. Marc made it back to the rim thirty minutes ago. He went straight to Wild Adventures and told Jan we needed a medevac sent down. Apparently Babette did indeed get worse after your dad left them. Jan called me for coordinates for the medical team." He sighed. "I told her they aren't needed anymore."

"Did Marc say anything specific about her condition when he left her? Anyone else he ran into?"

Big Pete shook his head. "I didn't get to talk to him directly. Jan said he was about to collapse from exhaustion himself, so she sent him back to his trailer for the night. I told her I want to talk to him as soon as possible tomorrow."

Liv felt a spike of disappointment at not being able to interview Marc herself. But if the guide had hiked twenty-four miles that day, she supposed he deserved some rest. And her sense of letdown, she realized, ran deeper than that. A piece of her had been holding on to the hope that Babette's murderer was the guide, or someone else far from their small beach, no matter how little sense that made. Now she had to confront the reality that the killer was most likely here among them.

It was enough to prompt her to put into action the idea Mandy had sparked. While the others lolled in their canvas chairs, inventing constellations and passing around tubs of CareFree for reapplication, Liv pitched her idea to Big Pete. The conversation was shorter than expected. The lead guide seemed hollowed out by the events of the day, and he had few questions to contribute. Once they'd agreed on the basics, Big Pete stepped out from behind the kitchen into the circle of camping chairs.

"Folks, I have an announcement to make."

It was dark enough now that Liv could make out only the brightest features of each person—PK's frosted tips, Mandy's toothy smile—as they turned toward Big Pete.

"I've decided to appoint Liv as our safety officer for the rest of the trip."

Liv braced for resistance, but she was met only with dazed puzzlement.

"Like, CPR training?" Fiona asked. "I'm a doctor. I'm good."

"You want a vest?" Thor asked. "Or a badge?"

"My sister's a federal agent," Mandy said. "She already has a badge. And a gun."

A few sets of eyes turned anxiously in Liv's direction.

"My gun isn't here," Liv assured everyone. "There aren't any guns here. Right?"

Big Pete and Thor exchanged a look.

"We have one gun," Thor said. "In case of mountain lions. But it's locked up tight on the supply boat."

"We don't typically need a security protocol on a rafting trip," Big Pete said, "but this is anything but a typical situation. So I've asked Liv to take this on. And as her first order of business, well, why don't you tell them?"

Liv inhaled deeply. Her sister had given her the inspiration, but she wasn't going to like it. No one was going to like it, even if they were half doped on CareFree. Liv didn't have Mandy's gift of gab or her dad's ability to conjure belief out of fairy tales. All she had was the truth. She exhaled and went for it.

"For everyone's safety, we are going to separate Charlie, Stefan, and Guy from the rest of the group for the night," she said.

"Separate?" Devon asked. "How?"

"Why us?" Guy said.

"You were the only ones with the opportunity to spend time alone with Babette before she died. We're going to ask you three to sleep on the supply boat," Liv said. "It will stay staked in the cove on the other side of these rocks. The guides will remain onshore, and you can sleep on their kits on the boat. The guides will take turns keeping watch from the rocks," Liv continued. "To ensure no one gets hurt or crosses over."

"You're saying one of the three of us is a killer, and the other two have to sleep next to him?" Charlie said.

"Not next to, exactly. The supply boat's thirty-five feet long. The sleeping kits are on three different sides of the boat, with all that equipment stacked in the middle. You won't be able to see each other, let alone reach each other. This is for your safety, truly. I'm not accusing any of you of hurting Babette. Maybe you saw something. Maybe you heard something. This is as much for your protection as ours."

Charlie wasn't having it. "If one of us wanted to, we could take two steps around the supplies and jump the others before the guide even got down to the water."

"I have a plan for that."

"Of course you do," Guy said warily.

All Liv could do was say it plain. "We're going to tie you to the boat. For your safety."

"What?!" Mandy said.

"For our safety?" Guy said.

"We'll be sitting ducks!" Charlie said.

"No, you'll be safe from each—"

"Let us alone." Stefan spoke in a low, slow growl.

"This is totally unacceptable," Mandy said.

Liv frowned. "We need to—"

"Let us alone," Stefan's voice intoned again. "What is it that will last? All things are taken from us, and become portions and parcels of the dreadful past."

"I can explain—"

"Let us alone!" Stefan was practically shouting now. "What pleasure can we have to war with evil?"

"Is he speaking Dutch?" Imogen asked.

Thor squinted at the raving investor. "That's Lord Tennyson. A poem from the 1800s about Odysseus. The lotus eaters." Thor turned to Liv and Lucinda. "Weren't you two talking about them?"

Liv gaped.

"What?" Thor said. "I spend weeks in the backcountry, just me and the bighorn sheep. I like to read classics. Is that a crime?"

Stefan stumbled away and continued spewing poetry, lurching down the beach and addressing his recitation to the black, shining river.

"Have you seen this happen with CareFree before?" Liv asked Devon.

"Quoting old English poems? This would be a first."

"He drank five margaritas," Liv said.

"I might have given him double shots," Thor added.

Devon winced. "That isn't recommended. But the CareFree won't hurt him. I think mostly this is just his way of dealing with"—she waved her hand around, encompassing the darkened river, the looming canyon, their ragtag crew on the beach—"all of this."

Liv remembered the message in Devon's hat. *This is my company, not yours.* Was it possible Stefan and not Babette had written it? Had Babette's lead investor killed her to take control of the company—and was he now cracking up after doing so?

"The lady has gone too far!" Stefan cried. "She disposes without care plans well-crafted, rips asunder that which all hold dear. Her violence has no place in this affair."

"He's right," Katy said.

"About what?" Liv asked.

"Datura. I told you, she's a demon goddess. A destroyer of false idols."

"Great," Imogen said. "He's not nuts. He's possessed by a devil plant."

"Maybe someone should follow him." Liv glanced over at Devon's altar to make sure Stefan hadn't made a snack of the datura plants she'd harvested. The white trumpets looked untouched. "And, Devon, those flowers? They shouldn't stay out in the open."

"You're right. It was sentimental. But Babette wouldn't want anyone to get hurt." Devon moved to wrap the wilted flowers in a paper towel, tucking them into her pocket. Then she turned to PK. "Keep an eye on Stefan, will you?"

He shot her a sour look. "Fine."

"I'll join you," Lucinda said. "I don't mind poetry."

The two of them took a few careful steps down the hillside. They stopped well short of Stefan and spread out to flank him, watching at a cautious distance as Stefan continued his raving soliloquy to the riverbank and the night sky. Apparently Lord Tennyson wasn't one for brief poems.

Guy stepped forward. "Can we go back to the whole 'tie your dear old traumatized dad to a boat' proposal?"

"It's not personal," Liv said. "I just think everyone will sleep better if the people who were in one-on-one contact with Babette are contained."

There was a loud splash from the river.

"He's throwing rocks," Imogen said.

"I see the Lady mad for blood! No good will come of this sorry business. We should come like ghosts to trouble joy!" Stefan shouted at the water. PK took a big step back toward the group.

"Was there a Lady Tennyson too?" Fiona said.

"Definitely," Thor said. "She was his proofreader."

"Yeah right," Katy grumbled. "She probably wrote the poems that made him famous."

"I can understand tying up Vincent van Weirdo over there," Guy said. "But me and Charlie? Her brother and the trusted advisor she brought down here? You really think one of us would hurt her?"

Charlie stiffened. "Don't put yourself in the same category as me. You hardly knew her."

"I knew you were trying to steal the company out from under her," Guy snapped back.

"What?" Devon said.

"And you," Guy said.

"I knew it!" PK said.

Guy nodded. "So did Babette. You two were going to—"

There was another splash, and a shout.

"Enough," Liv said. "There's a lot to hash out about what might have led to Babette's death. But it's late. The priority now has to be to get us safely through the night."

"Not all of us," Guy muttered.

"The guides will trade off watching you throughout the night. You couldn't be safer."

"Couldn't Dad just sleep next to us?" Mandy said.

"It's not personal," Liv repeated.

"You keep saying that," Devon said. "But it is personal. Someone killed my sister."

Stefan came bounding up the hillside, soaking wet and grinning. Lucinda and PK trailed, giving him a wide berth.

"I feel better," Stefan announced. "CareFree is good, but that river! It has true healing powers. Perhaps we can commercialize that."

Liv looked at Stefan carefully. His eyes were shining, pupils dilated. "You sure you're feeling okay?"

"That was quite the recitation," Lucinda said.

"The poem?" Stefan's voice had swung from droning monologue to a rapid, almost chatty tone. "My boss made me memorize it when I was brought on. A condition of employment."

"Bankers are into some strange stuff," PK said.

"It's not strange," Stefan said. "It's foundational. Our investment group makes money off modern-day lotus flowers. Social media. Reality TV. Face serums and sleep aids and hope."

He nodded at Imogen. "We were the first backers of the platform where you are famous. Videos that last exactly eight seconds? They are petals of a digital lotus flower melting on viewers' eyeballs. Like Lord Tennyson said: Surely slumber is more sweet than toil."

"I don't put my fans to sleep," Imogen said.

"No. What you do is better. You invite them into suspended animation, onto your own little raft on the vast river of consumerism. You take their attention. You distract them. You make them love you and yearn for what you have. It's perfect."

Imogen just stared at him.

"Right," Guy said. "I definitely vote to tie him up."

"Nobody's voting," Liv said. "Unless someone has information they want to share right now about how Babette died, we're sticking to my plan."

"What if it wasn't any of us?" Charlie said. "What if it was the guide?"

Big Pete looked insulted. "Can you please stop blaming the guides?"

"Marc made it back to the Wild Adventures office this evening," Liv said. "He hiked all the way to the rim to seek medical attention for Babette. If he meant to kill your sister, I don't know why he'd check back in at the office and try to send a team down to save her."

"Maybe because he succeeded," Charlie mumbled.

"You three each had the opportunity to be alone with her." Liv crossed her arms. "We have to take appropriate safety measures."

"This is hardly appropriate," Guy retorted.

"Dad's right," Mandy said. "We can't tie anyone up. It's inhumane."

"What's inhumane is what happened to Babette," Liv said.

"And the fact that we left the mule behind," Imogen muttered. "That was messed up."

"Well." Guy clapped a hand on Mandy's shoulder. "There's one thing we agree on: We need to get some sleep. Plenty to discuss when the sun comes up. Mand, you got a patch of sand picked out where we could roll out the old sleeping bags?"

There was a loud click, and everybody froze. Across the circle, Liv could see the metallic gleam of a pistol wavering in the twilight.

"Do what she says," Katy said. Her voice was hoarse. Maybe a little desperate. She was holding a gun in both hands, pointing it at Guy. Her legs were planted, arms stiff, fingers vibrating. Without seeing the guide's eyes, Liv couldn't guess at whether she was more angry or scared.

"Katy," Big Pete said, "put that down."

Thor came up beside the girl, but she swung the pistol in his direction, and he froze, opening his hands. "Whoa, girl. There's no need for that."

Now Liv could see her eyes. Katy was furious. She glared at Thor, then spun back and trained the gun on Guy, more confidently this time.

"The woman who died," Katy said. "Babette. I wasn't there. I didn't see what you saw. But I've heard enough to know that someone here hurt her. Someone killed her. That's a real and present danger to all of us." She looked around the circle. Everyone was quiet. Even Guy had quit posturing.

"Pete's right," Katy said. "We're professionals." She turned to her boss, her eyes still hot. "And I'm not just your supply girl. I'm a trained guide just like you. Our duty is to keep these people safe. If you want me to keep watch over a bunch of might-be murderers? Either I'm using this"—she waved the gun in the air, and everyone flinched—"or we're getting out the rope."

No one said anything. No one moved. Liv could hear her heart pounding in her throat.

Then Charlie broke the silence. "You can tie me up." His voice was tired, resigned. "Just keep me on the other side of the boat from him." He shot an angry stare at Guy.

"Me as well," Stefan said. "Though I would prefer to change into dry clothes first if that is permissible."

Big Pete moved to take the gun, but Katy brushed him off and shook it one more time in Guy's direction. "And you?"

Guy gave her a long, lazy smile. "You can tie me up anytime, darling. Just as long as you lock that pistol up and throw away the key."

"I'll get the rope." Katy dropped the gun into Big Pete's outstretched hand and stalked away.

"I'll put this in a more secure location," Big Pete said.

"You better," Guy said. "There's all kinds of crazy wandering this beach." He winked at Mandy and stretched out his arms. "Can your poor dad get a hug before they truss me up for the night?"

Mandy shot Liv an angry glare before turning to their father. "You said the scenario was hypothetical."

"And you said I needed to protect everyone."

Mandy turned her back on Liv and folded herself into their father. Liv watched them embrace. Guy's arms would be strong around her little sister, his chest pumping out heat. Guy's warmth wasn't on offer to Liv, and Liv didn't want it. But she was well aware that the decisions she'd made to protect herself and Mandy over the years—choices made in canyons, embassies, and dingy apartments—had kept her out in the cold. Mandy and Guy shared a connection that didn't fray in the face of lies or broken trust. Their kind of love was unreasonable. Nonsensical. Irreplaceable. Liv both longed for it and shoved it away with all her heart.

CHAPTER THIRTY-EIGHT

MANDY WOKE BEFORE THE sun again. She'd slept well, despite everything—Babette's death, her dad's strange arrival, her sister's betrayal. She'd ended the night annoyed with her father, pissed at Liv, unsure what to believe about the others. But still, she'd fallen into an easy, unencumbered sleep, bundled in the cocoon of her sleeping bag and CareFree's light, eucalyptus-scented touch.

From what she could see in the glow of her headlamp, everyone else had slept like the dead as well. Dark lumps spread across the sand like beached sea lions, each in their familial cluster. Imogen and Lucinda were curled up back to back. Devon, PK, and Fiona formed a three-pointed star, sleeping heads in slapping distance of each other, feet stretching out and away. The guides' bright yellow air mattresses were down by the water, two occupied, the third presumably the property of whoever was currently on watch.

Not that she could see the Colorado at all in the inky breath before dawn. But she could hear it growling.

She suddenly felt a need to see her father. Not to wake him; just to remind herself that he was there. That he was safe. Mandy slid on her shoes and stepped around Liv's rigid, dormant form, walking past the empty circle of chairs, beyond the kitchen setup, and over to the rocky embankment that separated camp from the cove with the boats.

The cove looked quiet, but the roar of the river filled the space. It was a furious highway, letting through only the sounds it didn't swallow in its wet mouth or crush against its rocky jaw.

The light of her headlamp picked up the sway of the supply boat floating high above the water, an empty raft flanking it on either side. Thor was sprawled on the beach above the boats, passed out, an empty tequila bottle in one hand. She stepped around the guide and into the shallow water, putting both hands on the outer rubber tube of the stern so she could press herself up onto the supply boat. It wouldn't be easy. The rubber wobbled under her palms, and the river sucked greedily at the bottom of her pajamas, turning her bare feet and ankles to ice in the dark.

Three.

Two.

The boat lurched toward her, the inflated rubber tube bumping hard against her hip.

Just the river, she told herself. She looked down at the little eddy she was standing in, where the water seemed eager to shove itself into the shore. It moved; the boat moved. Nothing surprising about that.

She put her hands back on the tube and braced herself to leap again.

Three.

Two.

Something was wrong. The air was dry. Her left hand was dry. But her right hand was wet.

She adjusted her headlamp to look down. Her hand was stuck to the yellow rubber baffle, outlined in a dark, sticky liquid.

She wanted to remove it. She wanted to plunge it into the river and erase whatever she'd touched there. But her eyes and headlamp moved unbidden, tracing a path past her hand, past the tube, onto the boat.

Stefan Eriksen was lying in a jumble of duffel bags and tarps, his head lolling toward her, his beard coated in a mess of black goo. There was no movement. No breath. The goo traced a ragged collar around his neck, staining his shirt and spreading out under his head, pooling on the tarp and spilling over onto the rubber baffle where she'd placed her hand. Stefan's hands were still tied above his head to an eyebolt at the tip of the stern, his feet lashed to a crate in the middle of the boat. His ball cap had fallen beside him on a tarp, slathered in more reflective goo.

Blood. It was his blood.

Mandy swallowed hard. She yanked her hands from the tube and plunged them into the river, letting the icy water numb her to what she'd just seen. But it was no use. The memory of Stefan's bloody throat shone against the dark water, sending bright green shock waves across her field of vision.

Something hard and slippery rolled under her left foot. A finger? She prayed it wasn't a finger. She let the headlamp drop to the shallow water and reached down for the object. It was a slender metallic cylinder, like a mascara wand or a fountain pen. But when she pulled it out and shone the light on it, she saw she was wrong. It was a folding knife, an old silver one, with a rough pattern of leaves and vines worked along its edge. It took her three tries to figure out how to extract the blade. When she released it, it was shiny, edged in blood.

She turned to run, to wake Thor, and her sister, and the whole damn world if she could. Then the boat bumped her again.

Her father. Had he been hurt too?

She clumsily folded the knife into her pocket, took a deep breath, and flung herself up on the supply boat, training her hands and eyes to the right of Stefan's terrible outline. Her knees slipped against the rubber, and she almost fell back into the river, but she found one more ounce of strength in her shoulders and thrust herself all the way up on the baffle.

She crawled forward until her headlamp caught the corner of her dad's sleeping kit: a blue hammock stretched between two ratchet straps, a yellow sleeping bag slumped within.

But her father wasn't there.

"Dad?" she whispered.

There was a rustling sound below her.

She froze.

"Mandy?"

She peered down. The ropes that bound her father's wrists and ankles were still attached, but somehow he had rolled or slid down from his hammock. Guy was wedged beneath it in a pile of camping chairs and PFDs. It couldn't be comfortable. But he showed no eagerness to get out.

"Are you alone?" He cringed in the bright glare of her headlamp.

She flicked it off. "There's no one else here."

"You sure? The lady's gone?"

"What lady?"

"Did she hurt him?" Guy asked. "I heard Stefan arguing with some woman. It sounded bad. Real bad. So I rolled over to hide down here."

Mandy peered down at her father in his burrow of life jackets. "Stefan is dead," she whispered. "Someone . . . someone slit his throat, Dad."

Her father went very still. "We have to leave. Now."

But there was nowhere to go. Mandy didn't move. Didn't turn on her headlamp. Somehow it felt safer in the dark.

"When did you hear them?" she asked.

"Thirty minutes ago? I can't say for sure. I heard a woman's voice saying something about how she couldn't tolerate being disrespected. That Stefan was being replaced. Then she must have—"

"Did you see who it was?"

"He just kept calling her *lady*."

"*Katy?* The datura thing?"

"No. Maybe. Just—*Lady, don't do this. Lady. Lady.* Then there was this awful groan, not loud but raspy, broken, and . . . I just tried to be as quiet as I could."

Mandy could see the whites around his irises now. "Think, Dad. Was there any clue in her voice, in what she said, that might tell us who—"

"Babette told me—" But then his voice cracked. "We have to go."

"But if we figure out who did it, we can wake everyone up and—"

"No! Don't you see? Babette asked me to come down here to help her. She said someone here was out to get her, trying to take control of her business. I thought she was talking about Stefan, but obviously I was wrong."

Mandy stared at her father. "Why didn't Babette tell you who she thought was out to get her?"

Guy shook his head. "She said if she told me who it was, I'd be in danger too."

There was something he still wasn't saying. But she'd heard enough. "Devon," she said. "She's a lady. Or could it have been Charlie, disguising his voice?"

"Charlie? But he was tied up too. Unless . . ."

Mandy shot a look past the crates to Charlie Sauvage's sleeping quarters, her shallow breath echoing in her ears. She tried to open the folding knife, but her fingers were shaking too badly.

She crept toward Charlie. The man hardly looked like a threat. He was cocooned in a hammock, trembling, the thin fabric shivering around him as he moved. Only his eyes were visible. They were wide open, imprinted with terror.

"Charlie?" she whispered.

He burrowed deeper in his cocoon.

She carefully peeled back the edges of his hammock with her free hand. Her headlamp picked him up in pieces: misbuttoned shirt, dirt-caked pants, wrists and ankles still tied to the ratchet straps. She didn't see any blood or sign of a struggle.

"It's me, Mandy. Did you see what happened to Stefan?" she asked.

"Heard it," Charlie whispered. "I pretended I was asleep."

"Do you know who did it?"

He shook his head.

"Mandy!" Her father's voice shot across the pile of equipment between them. "Let's get moving."

"Where?"

"Away. In a raft. It doesn't matter."

"I'm coming, too," Charlie said. "They're going to kill me next."

"Who is *they*?" Mandy asked.

"I don't know. But they killed our CEO and our lead investor. I'm next in line. Whoever killed Babette and Stefan is probably out to get me too."

Mandy was usually all for running away from problems, but this time, it didn't seem like the best idea. She'd never attempted escape on a literal life raft, and she suspected Charlie and Guy were even less capable than she was of navigating the fast-moving river. But she wasn't the one who'd received a direct death threat. She wasn't the one who'd lost a sister. She wasn't the one who'd been forced to listen to a man get murdered while tied up just a few feet away.

She stood up, straddling the crates between the two men. "We should call the police."

"No," Guy protested. "You heard them on the radio yesterday. It could take days for them to get down here. And then they'd probably just point the finger at me. I know how it looks. I was the one who had the most time alone with Babette. I was the one who accused Stefan. And now, with his death—"

"He's right," Charlie said. "The cops can't move fast enough to help us now. We have to get away."

"So we go to Liv," Mandy said. "You tell her every single thing Babette said to you. We can figure it out. She can come up with a plan to keep us safe."

"Your sister won't believe me," Guy said. "And her plan is the reason Stefan Eriksen is dead."

Her dad was talking about the present, about the urgency of what they did next. She knew that was important. But the recent past was wailing and waving its arms too. Babette, dead on that rock. Stefan, dead on the supply boat. Had Stefan murdered Babette and then someone took revenge on him? Or had someone else killed them both?

"I'll untie you," she said. "If you have to go, go. You can take a raft and some supplies. But I won't leave Liv."

"Can you convince her to go with us?" Guy asked.

Mandy glanced up the hillside. She tried to calculate what it would take to sell Liv on leaving. The math wasn't promising. She knew Liv wanted to protect her. But she wasn't sure Liv trusted her and their dad enough to do it in the way Mandy needed.

"Just leave without me," she finally said.

Before Guy could respond, a gravelly voice jumped at them from the beach.

"What's all this talk about leaving?"

"Thor," Mandy whispered. "Be careful."

"Why?" His voice was throaty, almost flirtatious. "You got a big surprise for me?"

His headlamp clicked on, the beam running across Charlie, her, and Guy. Then he pulled back, and the illumination fell on Stefan.

"You . . . you killed the poet?"

"No!" Mandy said. "We found him like that."

Thor's light dangled on the dead man, the blood shining around his neck. Mandy looked away.

"Is there a weapon?" Thor said.

"This." Mandy showed him the folded-up knife with its engraved handle. "I found it in the water, by the bank."

"Why would they drop it here?" Charlie asked.

"Maybe they got scared?" Mandy said.

"Or they didn't know the river," Thor said. "They might have tossed it, thinking it would sink or get swept away. But an eddy this strong just pushed it right back to shore."

"It wasn't one of us," Charlie said. "We're still tied up."

"And my girl got here after he died," Guy said. "She wouldn't hurt a fly."

"That so?" Thor ran his light over the two hostages, reaching out to give a sharp tug on one of the lengths of paracord linking Guy to the boat. Then he focused in on the knife in Mandy's hand. He reached for it, then stopped.

"Open it," he said to Mandy.

"What?"

"I want to watch you open the blade."

She shot a glance at her dad, who nodded. Her fingers were numb now, her sweatshirt sleeve muddied with water and blood. She fumbled with the mechanism, trying not to shake. The knife was old, tarnished under the light of Thor's headlamp, and it took four tries before she applied pressure to the handle properly, from both sides, to flip the blade open from its hiding place.

"Right." Thor turned abruptly to Guy. "I believe you. She's never fooled with that thing in her life."

The guide took a long, slow look back toward the beach. "There's a murderer up there, huh?"

"Someone who snuck down while you were on watch," Guy said. Mandy could almost hear the implication sinking in. "We need your help. We'll pay you to take us out of here."

"Sorry. I've got a code." Thor flicked his light back toward Mandy. It almost blinded her. "I don't ferry fugitives for cash."

"Five grand," Guy insisted.

Mandy wondered how Guy intended to make good on this promise, given that his cash situation was precarious even in the best of circumstances. But she knew what her dad would say: That was a later problem.

"We aren't fugitives," Charlie said. "We're victims."

Thor said nothing.

"Seven grand," Guy said. "But we leave right now. Untie us, grab supplies and a raft, and we're out."

"And I'll go back to camp," Mandy said. "Back to sleep. I'll pretend I didn't know anything about this. It'll buy you time to get away." Liv would be furious at her, but she could handle that.

"Mandy," Guy said. "I'm sorry."

"About what?"

"We can't let you go back up there. You might wake the murderer and then who knows what. It could be a bloodbath. If we sneak away, we can get to help faster."

"But—"

"Your dad's right," Charlie said. "If we're suspects, we can't do anything. But if we go get help, we could be heroes."

Mandy glared at Guy. "I won't leave Liv."

"If you want to protect her, we have to."

A desperate feeling rose in the back of Mandy's throat. "No." She turned to Charlie, who was now looking at Thor. "I can't leave my sister. And you can't leave yours. You and Devon both got threatened."

Charlie didn't take his eyes off the river guide.

Mandy tried one more time. "*Cross me and you're dead too. This is my company, not yours.* Whoever murdered Babette and Stefan may be after you, Charlie. But they could be after Devon too. If we leave, and she dies—"

"Our only shot at saving everyone is to leave now," Guy interrupted.

"Ten grand," Charlie said to Thor.

"Deal."

Before Mandy could protest further, Thor wrapped a wiry arm around her shoulders. It felt boa constrictor tight, locking her in place on the sand.

"Sorry, sunshine. You're coming with us. Law of the wild. We'll keep you safe."

CHAPTER THIRTY-NINE

IT WAS THE SHOUTING that woke Liv up.

It was just before dawn. The air was cool and thin, the canyon walls washed in sepia like old tea. The voices were coming from directly below her, by the boulders that separated the cove with the boats from the sandbar where everyone had slept. Big Pete and Katy were standing on the rocky outcropping, yelling and waving their arms at a raft in the middle of the river.

Liv sat up and squinted down at the dark water. Were the park police here already? The boat didn't bear distinctive markings that suggested official duty. In fact, it looked remarkably similar to the rafts they'd paddled in for the past two days. There were three people in the raft—no, four—the middle of the boat loaded high with gear. Were they bringing specialized equipment to handle Babette's body? Evidence processing kits?

Liv started mentally sorting the questions and information she wanted to share with the authorities. But before she could dig into her bag for a pen and paper, she heard Big Pete's shouts from below take on a furious pitch.

"Hey! Stop!"

She looked again. The raft was riding low in the water, weighed down by its cargo, moving fast. Too fast. The navigator at the back was paddling hard, shooting past the sandbar where the others were starting to rouse.

The yellow boat bucked over a patch of whitewater before swirling into an eddy, and Liv assumed it was going to whip around and approach the beach on its far end. But then, it shot downriver into the yawning granite canyon, and the shadowed cliffs swallowed all sight of it.

Just before the raft disappeared, Liv caught the words stamped in red across the back.

Wild Adventures.

"Is that another tour group?" she shouted down to Big Pete. "Are they going for help?"

Big Pete didn't acknowledge her. Instead, he said something to Katy, and the two guides hopped down the rocks to the cove where their boats were tied up. Headed for the radio, she bet. There must have been a conversation—or hand signals, maybe?—before Liv had woken up.

Even if she'd wished for an opportunity to speak with the people on the raft directly, it felt good to know that someone else had an inkling of what they were dealing with. It was too easy to feel isolated out here, thousands of feet below the surface of the earth. If they were going to get through this, they needed others. The more people got involved, the less likely their problems would be crushed by the rocks or washed away down the river.

She hurriedly dressed, then headed down to join the guides by the boats. But Katy stopped her on the hillside before she made it to the shore.

"We need a minute," Katy said.

"For what?"

Big Pete was approaching the stern of the supply boat, moving cautiously, as if it might bite him. Had Charlie, Stefan, and Guy slept through the shouting? Liv couldn't see the second raft on the other side of the chub, but the raft in front of it bobbed merrily in the water.

She heard movement from behind her. The other guests were beginning to rouse, some clambering groggily to their feet. Oddly, Mandy wasn't among them. Their fight last night had been regrettable, but her sister was quick to forgive, and she was unreasonably chipper in the morning, which, for once, Liv craved. She wanted to see Mandy's wild hair and frenetic smile. She would accept whatever colorful curses her sister might lob at her. She was ready to try again to figure things out properly together, as a team. As soon as Mandy saw Guy untied and unharmed, Liv wouldn't be the bad guy anymore.

Liv hiked over to where they'd camped the night before. Her sister's backpack was still there, unzipped and spilling over with spangly bikinis and sarongs. There was a sketchbook and a small tub of CareFree by her inflatable pillow. But no Mandy.

Liv turned and ran down to where Katy and Big Pete were standing by the supply boat.

"My sister," she said. "She's gone."

"She's not the only one," Big Pete said. "Your sister, your dad, Charlie, and Thor. That was them in that raft, with a lot of our equipment. Total jailbreak."

"Why didn't you go after them?"

"The river only flows in one direction. If I'd taken the other raft to follow them, there's no way I could have come back. And then y'all would be even more stranded."

"What about Stefan? He didn't go with them?"

"He didn't make it onto the raft," Katy said stiffly.

Liv puzzled over this. Guy, Charlie, and Stefan had all been tied to the same boat. Thor had been on watch, and Mandy had been . . . Who knew what Mandy had been doing. But why hadn't Stefan left with them? Did they decide Stefan was the killer and that they all had to escape from him?

The more she thought about it, the weirder it seemed. Given the little she understood about the relationships and alliances at play, it was hard to imagine Guy and Charlie trusting each other. It would have made more sense if just Guy and Mandy had left, or Charlie and Stefan. And Liv couldn't even begin to guess how Thor fit in the picture.

"Did you ask Stefan if he knows why they left?"

Big Pete shook his head. "Didn't get the chance."

"Do you want me to speak to him?"

Liv started to move toward the back of the supply boat, where they'd tied Stefan to a twenty-gallon barrel of filtered water the night before.

"Wait—" Katy put her hand out to stop her, but Liv pushed past.

It took her a moment to parse what she was seeing. The back of the boat was piled with kitchen supplies. Between the crates, a blue tarp was pulled up and over a line of foreign objects. But they weren't objects. They were parts of a person—a knee, a head, an unmoving chest. A German hiking boot sticking out one end, a shock of dark hair peeking out from the other.

"Is he . . . ?"

"Dead," Big Pete said.

"His throat was slashed," Katy added.

Liv swallowed hard. "This is bad."

"You think?" Big Pete said. "I'm the trip leader who tied a guy up and let him get murdered. I'm the one who said we could wait for the park police to figure everything out. My job is over. My life is over."

She heard him, but the meaning of his words didn't pierce her focus. She was still fixated on the outline of the dead man under the tarp.

"Was he covered up when you found him?" she asked.

"I did that," Big Pete said. "It just seemed more respectful."

"Right. Yes. But we need to . . ." Liv took a deep breath and pinched the tiniest corner of the closest edge of the tarp, making sure her fingers touched nothing but blue plastic. She peeled it back slowly, lifting the fraying sheet high and away from Stefan's body, hoping it wouldn't catch on anything.

The tarp billowed away smoothly, which was a kind of blessing.

But that was wrong. There were no blessings here. Stefan was lying on his back, his throat muddy with half-dried blood. The wound, while fatal, wasn't a gaping mess. It was a long, deep slit, a tight cavern across the mottled skin of his neck.

Liv scanned the rest of Stefan's body. His eyes were closed, his face holding a clenched, terrible strain. His hands and feet were still tied to the boat, but his elbows were wide, knees jutting out in a butterfly position. He must have jerked against the ropes in his last traumatic moments. But he hadn't come loose.

His clothing looked undisturbed, and she couldn't see a knife anywhere on his body or the tarp around him. But there was his hat, overturned, the white *B* on the outer brim dredged in blood.

She turned away, forcing herself not to gag. Stefan hadn't received a threat, but he'd still been murdered. She scanned the beach, looking for a weapon or some other piece of evidence among the rocks and sand. There was a dented metal box twenty feet up the beach, an empty bottle of liquor, and, closer to the water's edge, a rainbow pom-pom hair scrunchie. She recognized it immediately as one of Mandy's homemade craft explosions. She bent down and riffled through the ribbons of fabric—damp, but thankfully, she discerned no blood. There was a small folded piece of paper sandwiched between the bright scraps, ink peeking through the folds. She ferried the hair tie and the paper into her sleeve, burying them from view.

"Find anything?" Big Pete asked.

"No," she said. "Nothing."

She replaced the tarp over Stefan's body and took a step back. Then it hit her. Horror at what had happened to Stefan. Fear for her sister, Charlie, and Thor. Heck, even for her dad. And behind it, shame. Liv had just knowingly lied to Big Pete. He was one of the few people here who likely wasn't involved in the murders, perhaps the only person who could pilot them safely out of this nightmare. And yet she'd lied to him.

She could tell herself the scrunchie and the folded paper were meaningless, sentimental, or that her choice to withhold information about their existence was tactical. Two people had been killed. She'd have to weigh every movement carefully now, vet every disclosure. She'd have to strategize over what to share, with whom, and how far it might travel.

But the truth was, she didn't have a strategy yet. She'd lied reflexively. Automatically. She'd lied for her own gain and self-preservation.

She'd lied like a Chisholm.

CHAPTER FORTY

IF MANDY HAD TO be taken hostage, she wished it could have been under more exciting circumstances. Pirates. She could get down with pirates. Or a band of sexy fighter jet thieves. Instead, she was in a raft with her dad, an accountant, and an anarchic river Tarzan. Three selfish, scared men. Not that she was much better than them. She could have fought harder to stay with Liv. She could have run over the rocky beach and woken up Big Pete before they got away. But the truth was she'd been terrified too. She'd allowed herself to believe that she had no choice but to go with them. It was only once they launched the raft downriver that she realized she'd betrayed her sister and the others.

The river. It was maddening how similar the Colorado felt to the days before, burbling along, unconcerned by the conflicts among the people it carried downstream. The breeze off the water was cool, and the high cliff walls boasted a predawn hangover of purple and blue shadows. The rock was dark, the river black, their little yellow raft a speck of cheer in a canyon of gloom.

Inside the raft, the mood was decidedly more gloom than cheer. There was no idle banter. No chitchat about CareFree. No one commented on the quavering cry of the canyon wren nor the ghostly outline of three desert bighorn sheep sure-footing across the knife-edged granite. Charlie's head was on a swivel, looking back upriver every few seconds to check whether they were being followed. Mandy couldn't tell whether he craved the sight of another boat or feared the possibility. Thor was stoic in the back, hat pulled down low, contributing minimal adjustments with his paddle and even fewer words to the conversation.

And then there was Guy. At first her dad talked a blue streak, trying to keep the energy up, assuring Charlie and Thor they were doing the right thing, the best thing, not just for themselves personally but for Devon and Liv and the rest of the group. They'd get to help faster this way, unencumbered by fears and suspicions—their own of the others, the others' of them. There was no radio signal or satellite phone reception in the narrows, but Guy knew a guy—a whole raft of guys—who could swoop in to help the moment the sat phone was back in commission.

Mandy wasn't so sure. The faster Guy talked, the more his words knocked emptily against the granite walls. Eventually even he stopped talking. He knew the power of words, and the danger of not being listened to. He had taught Mandy never to love the sound of her own voice past its utility to help her get what she wanted.

What did she want?

She wanted to be safe, and alive. No doubt about that. She wanted her dad and sister in those categories as well. Beyond that, she wasn't sure.

Her sister. Mandy wondered what Liv was thinking now. Did she assume Mandy had taken off with their dad intentionally? Was she terrified or furious? Or simply relieved not to have to deal with their shenanigans any longer?

No. Even if Liv blamed Mandy for leaving, she loved her. She'd do anything to try to help her. And what had Mandy done? Marooned her with a killer, without so much as a goodbye.

The only shot she'd had to communicate with Liv was right before they left. Her dad and Thor wouldn't let Mandy leave the cove—too afraid she might alert the others—so she'd had to improvise. After she cut Charlie and Guy free with that horrible folding knife, she'd helped her dad and Charlie grab a mess of supplies, handing them down to Thor, who stacked them in one of the rafts. Just before they were ready to take off, she pulled her silly baseball sketch out of her pocket, along with her scrunchie and a pen that she'd stuck in her bun that morning.

She flipped the sketch over to the blank side.

I'm sorry, she wrote. Then she hesitated. She almost crossed it out. Why was she apologizing? If Liv hadn't tied their father up, none of this would have happened.

Mandy wanted to be clear: She wasn't sorry she was being kidnapped. The thing she was sorry about was too big and undefined to contain in words scrawled on a scrap of paper. She was sorry her sister's sanctimonious confidence had put them in this position, sorry that Liv couldn't make any of it better, sorry that a part of her expected Liv to do so. Most of all, she was sorry that they'd gotten to this point, with her wanting to punch her sister in the face and crawl into her sleeping bag and curl around her like a koala at exactly the same time.

The first two words stayed.

What else should she write? Something about the killer. *Dad says it's a woman*, she thought, but that sounded like a baby announcement, and she wasn't sure Liv would take anything Guy said seriously, even if he was a thousand percent sure about it.

Mandy thought about what she knew. The tiny pebbles of information she had and the hundred-ton boulders she didn't.

Watch out for the lady, Mandy settled on.

What else? She wanted to write something like *You find her, I'll get help*, but she wasn't sure she could promise that.

I didn't want to leave you. But I know you'll figure it out, she finally wrote.

Then she folded up the paper and tucked it into the scrunchie on the shore.

Now Mandy cursed herself for all the things she didn't write. When she'd been scribbling the note on the supply boat, it had been easy to imagine she and Liv would be reunited soon, swallowing the hurt, pouring more coffee into each other's mugs. But now, as their raft slipped down the dark river, she felt herself falling further and further away. What if Liv couldn't figure it out? What if the murderer struck again? Why hadn't she made one more attempt to convince her dad and Thor to let her stay with her sister?

And why hadn't she written *I love you* while she still could?

CHAPTER FORTY-ONE

BETRAYAL. THAT'S WHAT LIV was looking at.

It wasn't just that Mandy and Guy had run away and left her with a dead man. It was what they'd taken that hurt the most.

The catalog of supplies no longer available to Liv and the others was dismayingly comprehensive. Her dad and sister had stolen the radio and satellite phone. Also the water filter, the crate of energy bars, and, for reasons Liv didn't care to examine, an entire braid of garlic.

Then there were the boats. Fortunately, they'd left the second raft tied up, and the supply boat appeared to be intact. The same could not be said for the critical items needed to operate the watercraft: paddles and PFDs. They'd left exactly none of each. Only the huge set of oars lashed to the supply boat remained.

"They stranded us," Liv said.

"I was supposed to radio the park police again this morning," Big Pete said.

"And we were going to talk to Marc."

"But now . . ."

"We can't go anywhere," Liv said. "We can't call anyone."

"Those hikers might have a sat phone," Katy said.

"They said they were moving on early this morning."

Big Pete rubbed his temple. "Then our best shot is another rafting group stopping at Deer Creek Falls. But that might not be until this afternoon."

"Not good enough," Liv said. "By then, they'll be far downriver. And we don't know if the park police can help. We weren't their priority last night with one dead body, and we still might not be with two. We need a plan. And clean water. Unless we figure out a way to seriously increase the output from Fiona's rainbow sparkle water filter, we're going to get thirsty."

"We have iodine tablets," Big Pete said.

"You think this group is going to drink iodine?" Liv asked.

"I don't know what this group is capable of anymore," Big Pete said. "Or why those four were the ones who left."

Why had they left? A tree diagram sprouted in Liv's head, branches forking to different conclusions. There were the bad options, the a-murderer-has-my-sister options. If one of the missing four had killed Stefan and been seen, maybe they'd taken the others hostage. But who could the murderer be? Not Mandy, obviously. Hopefully not her father. That left Charlie and Thor. Charlie had been tied up. Was it possible he had a secret background as an Eagle Scout or a wannabe Houdini? Not likely. Thor, on the other hand, was a former soldier, a risk-taker, a feral wolf in the wilderness. And he had—

"Where's the gun?" Liv asked.

Big Pete looked at Katy. "I locked it in a gang box yesterday after this one's Annie Oakley routine."

"I should have fired it," Katy grumbled. "Maybe then no one would've—"

"That box?" Liv asked, pointing to the rusted metal case she'd spotted on the beach.

Big Pete nodded.

The case was scuffed and heavy. Liv tried to leverage open the lid, but it didn't move. "Where's the key?"

"When I came off watch at two thirty a.m. and woke Thor to take over, I gave it to him," Big Pete said. "Just in case he needed it."

Liv shook the box and heard muffled clanks, but nothing she could confidently identify. "We'll have to pry it open. See if the gun is still there." She tried to keep her voice even, shoving away unwanted images of Thor holding a pistol to her sister's head.

She looked up the hillside, to where all the other guests were stirring on the other side of the rocks. They hadn't figured out what was wrong yet, but they would if they ventured over. She needed more time.

"Do we have supplies for breakfast?" Liv asked.

Katy nodded. "They didn't take the eggs. Or the fruit."

"Why don't you get that going with the group. In the meantime"—Liv turned to Big Pete—"we should take a full inventory of everything that might be missing."

Big Pete looked uncomfortable. "We can't go into people's bags without permission. Pretty sure that's in the Constitution."

"We're not cops," Liv said. Though she did have a fleeting worry about what her boss at the State Department would say when this was all over. She shook it away. The only priority now was to get to that conversation alive. "We have no idea when the police will get here. We don't know where the gun is. And somewhere there's a knife that was used to murder Stefan."

"Thor has a knife," Big Pete said.

"I assume you have one as well."

The look he flashed her was shocked and angry in equal measure.

Liv kept her voice calm. "We just need to know if there are any more surprises traveling with us."

She looked up the hillside, where Katy had distracted the rest of the group with various fruit-salad-related tasks. It was what she'd asked for, and it was a nightmare. Each and every person had a knife in their hand. Fiona was stabbing a cantaloupe, Imogen slicing bananas, Lucinda using a paring knife to peel an apple in a continuous spiral. Liv had a fleeting vision of the beach blanketed in deadly knives, blades under every rock, in each of Devon's zippered pockets, hiding in PK's faux-hawk. She swallowed hard and blinked it away.

"What is it?" Big Pete asked her. "Do you know who did this?"

"No. Not even close. I don't know if the killer is here with us or if they're paddling down the Colorado with my family. But if we're going to have a chance at figuring it out, we've got to open everything up. Every locked box. Every crumpled pillowcase. Every secret in every bag."

"You aren't in charge, you know."

Liv didn't like the challenge in Big Pete's voice. "We've been working together."

"No. My priority is keeping people safe. Not finding a murderer."

"Isn't that the same thing?"

"Can't say. Not anymore. You told those men they'd be safest lashed to a boat. Now Stefan's dead and a raft is gone. If you go commando now, tear through everyone's stuff . . . I wouldn't be surprised if they tie you up next."

At that, Big Pete headed up toward the kitchen area. Another betrayal. Soon enough, he'd break the horrible news to the others, and gathering evidence would get trickier. Liv wondered if Pete had something to gain by resisting her suggestion. Maybe he had a secret that he didn't want exposed. Maybe all of them did.

But it didn't matter. Big Pete was right. She'd taken a gamble the night before and lost. It was impossible to say now what might have happened if they hadn't tied up Stefan, Guy, and Charlie. It could have been better. Could have been worse. But it had been her idea, and now Stefan was dead.

A new feeling was hitting her: guilt. Her brilliant plan to keep everyone safe had done the opposite. She'd pushed Mandy away, into their feckless father's arms. She'd restrained Stefan so someone could slash his throat with ease. She'd sent her sister running—or hostage—on a raft downriver, moving deeper into the dark heart of the canyon.

She heard Stefan's voice again, reciting that eerie poem. *What pleasure can we have to war with evil?* She needed to turn things around.

She headed over to the relative privacy of her campsite and fished out the note she'd found in Mandy's hair tie. She could see her sister's fingertips imprinted in the whorls of red dust on the tightly folded paper, and for a moment, she resisted opening it. As long as it stayed shut, she could tell herself it contained everything she needed. The name of the murderer. Forgiveness from her sister. A way out of this nightmare.

Of course, it revealed so much less than that. It was Mandy's baseball sketch, with a quick message scrawled on the back. *I'm sorry. Watch out for the lady. I didn't want to leave you. But I know you'll figure it out.*

Liv swallowed and cursed herself for imagining the impossible. She scanned the baseball sketch, the tiny horrible messages lettered on the figures' caps. PK had received the vaguest one: *Everyone is replaceable.* Mandy's seemed to refer to her investment, and perhaps their father's crimes: *Money can't protect you.* Devon's suggested an executive power struggle—*This is my company, not yours*—and finally, there was Charlie's, simple and brutal: *Cross me and you're dead too.*

Each message suggested a rift between its recipient and Babette, giving Liv the impression she was looking at a laundry list of motives and suspects who might have killed the CEO. But she couldn't ignore the possibility that someone else had sent the threats, a killer trying to cast suspicion on others. She, Stefan, and Imogen all had blank ball caps, and Fiona and Lucinda claimed not to have needed theirs. Could one of their hats be hiding a threat they didn't want the others to see? She wondered if she should push to look inside Fiona's and Lucinda's hats, but that didn't feel like the top priority now. Everyone was at risk at this point. And if one of the two women was the killer, it seemed too obvious to conveniently ditch the item that could have enabled them to masquerade as victims alongside the others.

There was one more person in Mandy's drawing whose hat was blank. Front and center, smiling enigmatically: the magnetic, elusive Babette. Liv dug out the white ball cap she'd found by Babette's dead body the day before. In the hubbub since then, no one had asked her for it, and she hadn't had time to examine it.

Babette's hat looked like the others. Liv rubbed dirt against the inner crown, hoping against hope that a message inside would reveal the answer, or a hint in the right direction. But she found no embroidery. No threat. The red dirt clung to the empty fabric, mocking her.

Liv turned back to Mandy's note. *Watch out for the lady.* Who was she referring to? Did Mandy have information about the killer concealed behind this riddle? She felt a flash of anger at her sister for abandoning her with this terrible puzzle, as if she was a rat and Mandy the mastermind of a maze of granite and whitewater, dangling cheese in the form of cryptic notes and sketches. But that was ridiculous. Even if she did run away, Mandy was just as trapped in this nightmare as she was.

Trapped. Liv had constructed her life to never feel that way. Every other investigation she'd been part of, she'd worked methodically, gathering evidence—often for months—and lining up the resources to take down her target at the exact right moment, showing her work meticulously so no target could come back at them on appeal. But here there was no due process. Here there would be no appeal. She was on a beach with a dead man. Her sister and dad had disappeared. She prayed they were alive and simply doing what they did best—improvising a way forward, dancing over coals, whether toward greater danger or away from it.

Liv had to think like them now. Mandy and Guy wouldn't be caught dead waiting for authorities or hoarding enough redundant data to make the highest-percentage decision on what to do next. She had to move like them: fast, half blind, without all the information she needed. She had to be willing to conceal the information she had, or even—though it was hard to imagine how she'd pull this off—twist it into something else.

She looked down at her backpack. Inside it was the unwanted gift from PK, a foreign object she'd intended to hand back to him this morning. Now Liv regarded the little tub with its silver-on-white logo and nearly invisible seal. It was everything she abhorred. A crude shortcut around responsibility, trumped up in bogus claims about what it meant to lead a fulfilling life.

Liv screwed open the container and regarded the lavender cream inside. She could almost hear the whispered promises emanating from the jar: a life free from hyperanalysis, a billion-dollar market potential, a blissed-out, destressed world. And then there were the other voices: Mandy chastising her for prioritizing work over family; Fiona's warning that the substance might be more reactive in the hot sun; Stefan reciting Tennyson and raving in the dark. She thought of all the times in the *Odyssey* the boatman took what he wanted and suffered the consequences, until he staggered naked into the arms of Nausicaä, burner of ships, to tell his strange survival tale.

No sensible person would choose to forget right now. No rational person would want to. But deliberate, considered action wasn't working for Liv anymore. She needed to unleash something wilder, to tap into the energy her sister would bring to an unprecedented situation like this.

Liv scooped up a tiny crescent of CareFree and dabbed it experimentally on her cheekbone. Then she plunged her hand in, like a bear discovering honey, and smeared it all over her face.

CHAPTER FORTY-TWO

IT TOOK THREE MELTED protein bars for Mandy to decide she needed to make a plan. It wasn't her strong suit—not by a long shot—but if she didn't do it, no one else would. They were drifting. Her dad was paddling sloppily in the front of the raft, guarding the radio at his feet as if it were a flighty girlfriend he suspected of cheating on him. Charlie was silent, his paddle seemingly propelled by a windup toy jammed under each shoulder blade. And Thor only seemed to care about the frequent reassurances he sought from Guy that he'd be paid for his services.

The morning light sluiced over the North Rim, slapping the waves with brightness that alchemized the whitewater into foamy diamonds. Mandy tried aiming her fake engagement ring at the sun, hoping it might create a flash of light she could use to signal a plane or helicopter. But cheap tricks wouldn't help them now. The discount ring just bit at her tired hand.

What was her goal? To reunite with her sister. Scratch that: to *safely* reunite with her sister. Which meant she had to do two things: figure out what was really going on with the murders and stop the raft's forward movement.

Which was more important?

Mandy thought about how her sister would evaluate the question. Liv would know which information was crucial and what could be ignored, and if she didn't, she'd invent a nine-dimensional prioritization matrix to figure it out. Meanwhile, here Mandy was, sorting through scattered marbles rolling across the floor and hoping she might pick up the right one at random.

She had to do better. She had to think like her sister.

"It's time to call for help," she said to her father.

"Give me a few more minutes," Guy said. "This is delicate. Gotta get the right people on the bus."

"Raft."

"Can't we just call the police?" Charlie said.

"No cops," Guy responded. "That'll only add to our problems. They're tied up in red tape, and they'll ask questions we can't answer. This will be faster. Better."

"Better for you," Charlie grumbled.

"It's not like the park police jumped to the rescue last night," Guy retorted. "And now that we're a bunch of fugitives, if they do show up, it'll be with handcuffs. We need our own team now."

Mandy bit her lip. Her dad did have a knack for charming people into helping him, and she knew he cared about Liv. But she didn't love the fact that they kept paddling further away from her.

"Sounds like we should stop," she improvised. "You can focus, and we need a rest. We've been paddling all morning on barely any sleep."

"She's got a point," Thor said. "Upset Rapid's coming up in a few miles. And I'm starting to see double."

"Then we'll pay you double," Guy said.

"Dad. If we could just stop for a bit—"

"Can't stop," he said.

Why? she wanted to scream. But that was a Mandy impulse. Liv would keep the question from coming out. She would turn it over in her own head first.

Why was her dad so insistent on barreling down the river? Was he racing toward something, or away from someone?

Away, she decided. He didn't know anything about the Grand

Canyon or what lay ahead. But he knew what he was escaping. She wondered if he planned to tell his contacts that a world-famous entrepreneur and her lead investor had been murdered, whether dropping Babette's and Stefan's names would sweeten his ask or make it harder to secure help.

Stefan. If they couldn't get help or stop yet, she'd work on her other goal: securing information. She put down her paddle and leaned forward.

"How long did you work with Stefan Eriksen?" she asked Charlie.

He didn't even turn his head. "A year."

"And the business he was in?"

"The Regent Group is a private equity firm."

"Based in the Netherlands?"

"Their investments are global. I don't know where the home office is."

This interrogation was going nowhere. Charlie was boring, and Mandy didn't waste her time on boring people. But then she remembered whom she was trying to emulate. Liv wouldn't see Charlie as boring or not-boring. Liv would see him as useful.

She tried another way in. "You know, when I got that email from PK inviting me to be your first outside investor, I thought it was a joke."

Charlie kept paddling.

"It was a dream, totally," Mandy continued. "I just never imagined she'd consider an investment from someone like me."

"That was Babette," Charlie said. "She wanted our first outside investor to be a fan. Picked you out of her DMs. She was always doing things her own way."

"What made you take on investors in the first place?"

"CareFree."

There was a pause, and Mandy feared she'd hit another dead end. But then Charlie kept talking. "The first twelve years, it was just her and me, bootstrapping the business with money we'd inherited from our parents. Then social media and direct-to-consumer blew open our industry, and Babette's dreams got bigger. The last four years were breakneck. The Fierce line. Raw. Her book."

"She became a star," Mandy said.

"A supernova. Shining so bright it blinds you, pushing our team to the max. She's one of those people who makes an absurd ask, and even if you know it's impossible, you still want to hunt it down and bring it back to her wriggling between your teeth. We all want to do that."

Wanted to, Mandy thought. She didn't have the heart to say it out loud.

"Babette was making promises we couldn't deliver on," Charlie continued. "We needed more of a science foundation behind her claims of transformation. So I roped Devon in. She told me about datura. That's when everything tipped."

His eyes brightened, and a wisp of a smile graced his face.

"For the first time," Charlie said, "*I* was the one with the dream. I was the one who saw the potential for CareFree. This isn't just another face cream for us. CareFree is the next Xanax. It's the next CBD. But we didn't have the cash to live up to that opportunity."

"So you decided to raise investment," Guy piped up.

"Right. But Babette insisted on doing it backward. No banks. No consultants. She wouldn't even go on *Shark Tank*. Instead, she put out a wide open call on her socials, inviting anyone who wanted to to get in touch. No screen for qualified investors. No screen at all. We were flooded with ridiculous offers, kids with their piggy banks, fans with the Babette logo tattooed on their thigh."

"She sought investors who really care about your company," Mandy said. "What's wrong with that?"

"Nothing's wrong with it," Charlie said. "It's brilliant, really. Amateurs are easy to control, and they make for great press. Look at you—wide-eyed high school teacher, aspirational customer—socials eat that up."

Mandy bristled at the idea that she might be nothing more than a prop in Babette's campaign. But it was her dad who came to her defense.

"Not everyone who got involved was an amateur," Guy said.

"Oh, right," Charlie said. "There were criminals too."

"Hey," Guy objected. "I connected Babette to Stefan."

"True." Charlie searched her dad's eyes for the answer to a question he didn't ask. "And look how that turned out."

"I'm not the one who killed her," Guy snapped back. "Or him."

"Neither am I."

A note of tension hummed in the air between the two men. But Charlie's story wasn't over. Mandy still didn't understand how everything was connected. She needed to loosen the wire.

"How did the investments change things?" she asked.

"It meant more money, of course. The investors we brought in—and yes, Stefan represented the biggest—turbocharged our development of CareFree. Renovated labs, bigger marketing budgets, more sophisticated supply chains. We went from growing fast to growing huge. But investors have expectations. Babette's seat-of-her-pants management style wasn't as popular in the boardroom as it was on the internet."

"Stefan wanted a more conventional captain, didn't he?" Guy was smiling now. "And you saw an opportunity to take a spin at the wheel."

Charlie stiffened.

"I get it," Guy continued. "Your sister gets the sunshine while you're sweeping up broken glass in the back alley. Then you get this billion-dollar idea for CareFree. And she takes all the credit."

"I didn't care about credit," Charlie said.

"Of course not," Guy said. He could be generous when he needed to be. "You just wanted to protect what you were building."

Mandy could see what her dad was doing, and still she was taken aback by his glib adaptability. Guy had admired Babette. Mandy remembered how he'd raved about CareFree, and her, and how this time, a CEO truly appreciated his skills. They were both risk-takers, and Babette had been the rare businessperson who met Guy's maverick energy with her own unorthodox methods. Just yesterday, he'd hiked down into the middle of the earth to help her fend off a threat to her business. And now here he was, commiserating with her backstabbing brother about how she'd blocked him from achieving his dreams.

"There was nothing secretive about my work with Stefan," Charlie said. "His firm made a major investment in our company. And yes, he preferred a more data-driven approach. Like me."

"So you suggested you might do a better job running the show than your sister."

"Not the show. Just the shop. Frankly, at first, Stefan wasn't interested. Then he called me a few weeks ago, talking about a succession plan and a smooth transition so Babette could still have a role as spokeswoman."

"What changed his mind?"

"Can't say. Maybe it was because Babette switched the launch location to align with the position of the moon? Or when she fired our marketing director two days before the campaign was set to start? Whatever his exact reason, Stefan said it was time for the business to mature. He drew up the papers and brought them on this trip, so we could break it to Babette here, far from cameras and media. To give her time to acclimate before the rest of the world found out. Between Stefan, me, and Devon, we had the board votes to push it through."

"You were going to fire her here?" Mandy asked. "On her own Essence Quest?"

"We were giving her a promotion. To chairman. An opportunity for her to focus on what she does best."

Now Charlie was the one lying, in the crudest way. Not inventing a story or flipping the narrative—just telling a version that suited him. Even if Mandy didn't know Babette personally, she was certain taking away the CEO title would have killed her. Breaking the news deep in the Grand Canyon wouldn't have been compassionate. It would have been a form of damage control, a way to prevent Babette from fighting back with the full arsenal of her loyal following.

Babette had always ferociously defended her work and grown her business. Maybe she didn't do it in exactly the way Charlie would have, but there was no question that she'd been more than just a well-moisturized face. She'd built an alternative to the corner-cutting, planet-harming corporations that controlled the cosmetics industry. Under Babette, CareFree would have been a liberation cry. With Charlie and Stefan at the helm, it sounded like just another way to make a buck.

Maybe that was extreme. Charlie had been Babette's partner since the beginning. But old scars could open fresh wounds, especially between siblings.

"What will you do with CareFree now that you're CEO?" she asked.

Charlie's response surprised her. "I'm not the new CEO. I was never going to be. Like your dad said, I work best in the background. It would be Devon. She was just as frustrated with Babette as I was."

Devon. Mandy thought back to how the steely older woman had consoled her brother after Babette died. How she'd steadied him after they fell into the river that first day and applied aloe to his sunburned neck later that evening. Every time Charlie struggled, Devon planted herself like an iron rod beside him. Mandy had seen her as a caring older sister, but maybe that was misguided. Maybe Devon hadn't been supporting Charlie but forcing him to stay in line.

"Was Stefan's boss involved in this plan?"

It was Thor who asked the question. The others turned to the back of the raft in confusion, as if they'd forgotten the guide was there.

"Stefan told me he wasn't the investor," Thor continued. "He worked for the big money person. Said he was hired help, like me."

Mandy seriously doubted any multinational firm would employ someone whose chief skill seemed to be diving headfirst into waterfalls.

"I don't know." Charlie turned to Guy. "Did you ever meet Stefan's boss?"

"No. My connection was with Stefan, and their firm was set up such that the investments he managed were air-gapped from the rest of the business. Every department at the Regent Group works that way. I met him a few years ago when we were both vetting an IQ-boosting candy company. Ultimately, I didn't invest—the value prop didn't set me on fire—but I liked Stefan. He was always looking to make big moves. With his boss's money, of course."

"Is it typical for big investors to have someone like Stefan who manages their business?" Mandy asked. "I thought part of being a shark was getting to show your teeth."

"That's just how it looks on TV," Guy said. "Big money is whale money. And whales like to hide way down deep." He looked at Charlie. "Of course, with Babette and Stefan dead, that whale's going to come sniffing at you now. CareFree's in your hands."

"Devon's hands," Charlie corrected him. "But I don't know that the whale will choose to get involved. As you say, they compartmentalize everything at the Regent Group. We were lined up to make the leadership transition this week. I assume they'll assign a new representative from Stefan's division and we'll move forward as planned."

Mandy wondered if Charlie was aware how this sounded, like he was already getting back to business as usual. He'd presented himself as a humble ambassador striving to make the company the best that it could be. But what if he was lying? What if there was no transition planned? If Stefan didn't want to replace Babette, if he'd resisted the ouster, it could be a good reason for Charlie—and Devon—to shove him out of the way.

She thought back on what she and Stefan had discussed on the hike to Thunder Spring, hunting for anything that spoke to his intentions. But all she remembered was the strange comment he made about the threats, his sense that the messages in the hats were intended to misdirect. "Stefan told me he managed a portfolio on distraction."

"That's right," Charlie said.

"He said it was one of a few divisions at their firm. Do you know what the other ones are?"

"There are four of them," Charlie said. "Hard to forget, because they're so odd. Babette liked the idea that our chief backer had a creative streak. The Regent Group focused on four different investment areas: love, attention, distraction, and yearning. Apparently their founder believed that each could be a gold mine."

"Smart whale," Guy said.

"What do you mean?" Mandy asked.

"Anyone can invent a product worth selling," Guy said. "But the thing that lights up buyers is the promise, not the product. It isn't the pen, the condo, or the face cream. It's the letter they're going to write with that pen to win their lover back. It's the home that makes them feel secure for the first time. It's the cream that's going to take their pain away. It's the promise that makes it worth buying. And those four departments—what were they again?"

"Love, attention, distraction, and yearning," Charlie said.

Guy licked his chapped lips. "All fundamental human desires. When a product's promise matches a universal desire, BAM! You've got yourself a hot ticket."

Her dad kept riffing on his grand theory of no-lose investing. But Mandy ignored his bloviating and thought about what he and Charlie had just said.

Love, attention, distraction, and yearning. CareFree was in the distraction department, poised to help millions of people forget their worries. And Stefan had also invested in Hitch, the social media platform. It made sense.

Distraction was one heck of a drug. But the Regent Group's other departments sounded just as powerful.

Love.

Attention.

Distraction.

Yearning.

There was something else there. It was only when she fully tuned out her father's rambling that she could see it.

"Remind me," she interrupted. "What was it Stefan repeated when he was dying?"

"Huh?" Her dad was midway through a story. "Oh. *Lady.* He seemed to be arguing with a woman who was accusing him of being disrespectful. A lady."

With that, Guy turned back to the other two. While he riffed on the power of yearning and an investment he had made in a podcaster-slash-spiritual medium, Mandy focused on what he'd told her.

Lady, Stefan had said. Love, attention, distraction, yearning. *L-A-D-Y.*

She didn't think the acronym could be a coincidence. The question was: What on earth did it mean?

CHAPTER FORTY-THREE

AT FIRST, LIV TRIED to chart her experience of CareFree scientifically, consulting her watch every thirty seconds and waggling her bare hand in front of her to check if her perception had changed. But after four minutes, she decided she didn't have time for that. Her skin felt refreshed, as if the cream had peeled back some of the stress of the past twenty-four hours. And all her fingers appeared to maintain their proper proportions.

She looked up to where the others were staring at the breakfast they'd made but had yet to touch. Big Pete must have broken the news. They looked numb and scared. They wouldn't want hard questions, terrifying truths, or a plan to find the killer in their midst. They would want reassurance or, at minimum, the semblance of it. They would want a lie.

And Liv? She wanted Mandy. But she felt almost loose enough to emulate her sister. She was ready to throw out the book. Burn the ships.

She decided to start with a small act of liberation: destruction of evidence. Liv took Mandy's note out of her pocket and wadded it up. Then she paused. It wasn't enough to bury it in her bag or under the sand. She'd memorized its contents and didn't want anyone else to see it.

What would her sister do in this situation?

It was obvious. And disgusting.

Liv stuffed the note into her mouth and chewed the paper gummy, letting the sandstone dust grit her teeth. One hard gulp, and it was gone.

It was surprisingly satisfying to fully commit to the obstruction of justice. Liv felt lighter now. She was on the CareFree path. She wiped her mouth with the back of her hand and marched up to the group with their perfectly sliced pineapples. She resisted the urge to scan their knives for traces of blood. She opened her mouth—so empty, so full of possibility—and began to speak.

"I have an announcement to make," she said. Her voice sounded unnaturally buoyant, as if she were conducting a circus instead of a murder investigation. "As you know, sadly, we lost our dear friend Stefan Eriksen during the night."

Dear friend? Where were these words coming from? And why had she placed her right hand against her chest? But it seemed to be working. Everyone was paying attention to her, and they looked, if not happy, not angry either.

"I have sworn an oath to tell the truth." She could feel her heart beating under her fingers. "And the truth is that Stefan was murdered."

Honesty: That was in her wheelhouse. But here came the lie. A lie to encourage everyone to let their guard down and, hopefully, let her in. The best way to find a killer among them, she'd realized, was to tell them the killer wasn't there.

"The harder truth is that we know the person who murdered him." A twitchy murmur rippled across the group. Fiona took a step back, and Devon switched the grip on her fork to a decidedly stabby position. Even Lucinda, who had been placidly peeling an apple, stopped moving.

Liv imagined a lonely scapegoat, cast into the wilderness under the burden of human sins. She'd never liked goats, but they had their uses. She took a breath and dove in.

"It was Thor. He killed Stefan Eriksen before dawn. Then he took Charlie, my dad, and my sister hostage in one of the rafts. Thor stranded us here with Stefan's body, no radio, and not enough supplies to get help. At least, that's what I think happened."

She'd added that final caveat on a whim. It was a risk. It undercut the story she was trying to sell. But it was also an opening, an invitation for others to join her in discovery instead of cursing her for the terrible certainties she'd presented.

"A guide?" Devon said. "My brother was right?"

"How do you know it was Thor?" Fiona asked. She sounded worried, not confrontational.

"Stefan's throat was slashed. From the wound, I could see that the blade that cut him had an unusual pattern, an irregular notching that matched the bowie knife Thor carried."

This was a bald-faced lie. Liv had only gotten the barest glimpse of Thor's knife sheathed in the holster on his belt, and she had spent even less time looking at Stefan's throat. She waited for someone to call her out on it, but not too long. Silence was the tool of the investigator. Nonstop talking was the tool of the liar.

"I spent four months training on exotic street knives with the State Department in Thailand," she said. Liv had never been to Thailand. "If you know what to look for, every blade has a fingerprint all its own. That first day on the river, Thor couldn't resist showing me every feature of his knife, how he'd carved a tiny notch near the blade-tip to help him break lines quickly when he was fly-fishing. When I saw Stefan's throat, it was all right there."

"Mandy told me Thor left her in that slot above Surprise Valley for a while," Fiona said. "Maybe he snuck down and killed Babette too."

Liv was momentarily frozen. Mandy had shared information with Fiona that she hadn't told her own sister. It stung to realize that, but more importantly, was it true? Could Thor have actually—no. She was inventing a killer, not investigating one.

"That fits," she said, nodding at Fiona.

Big Pete frowned. "Why the heck would Thor have any reason to—"

Liv cut him off. "I don't know. But my family's heading down the river with a killer while we speculate about his motives. We have to do something. We have to save them."

"She's right," Devon said. "My brother's with them too. We have to protect them."

The older woman drew her into a tight hug from the side.

"We're going to get them back," Devon whispered. She turned toward the rest of the group and stiffened her spine. "With my siblings gone, I am responsible for the company and this Essence Quest. We will move as quickly as possible to rescue my brother, and her family, from Thor. We'll call the police, then we'll get in the boats and go find them. We will find them alive. We will do what needs to be done."

There was nothing to add to this, so Liv settled for nodding enthusiastically. Her heart was beating faster now. She felt warm—too warm—and she wondered if it was possible she'd overdone the CareFree and put herself in danger. But the pleasure pulsing through her felt too good for that to be the case. It was one thing to get others to listen when she was telling the truth. It was a thousand times more satisfying to get them to believe a story she'd made up. She felt powerful. And hot. She took off her sweatshirt and didn't even feel embarrassed when she realized she only had a river-stained sports bra on underneath.

"Nice speech," Big Pete said to Devon. "One problem. Two, actually. Your brother and the rest of the desperadoes took our radio and sat phone. So we won't be calling anyone. Also, they took all the PFDs and paddles."

"Can we go downriver without them?" Liv asked.

"Rafting without PFDs is against Park Service regulations. It's also a recipe for drowning."

The old Liv would have stopped right there. But the new Liv batted away the threat of a watery death and stormed ahead.

"And paddles? Can we raft without paddles?"

"Raft? No. But the supply boat has fixed oars. We could all pile on there, but . . ."

"But what?" Fiona asked.

"Stefan's body is on that boat," Liv said.

"So we take him off and leave him on the beach," PK said.

When no one answered, PK doubled down. "What? It was okay to abandon Babette on the rocks, but Mr. Eriksen gets to go with us?"

"It's illegal to move a body in the Grand Canyon," Big Pete said. "And Stefan died on that boat. We have to keep him with us."

"No way I'm riding on the supply boat, then," Imogen said.

"Me either," Fiona said.

Big Pete looked like he was reaching the end of his rope. "Well, unless any of you have secret rafting paddles packed in those coolers full of eye cream—"

An opportunity. Liv saw it, shiny as a gold-plated ring on the carousel, dangling there for her to grab. "Great idea," she said. "Let's get the bags and open them up. Between all of us, there's got to be something we can work with."

She felt Devon stiffen next to her. Was there something in her luggage she didn't want others to see?

"I do have an extendable tripod," PK said doubtfully.

"Sounds like a paddle shaft to me!" Liv wasn't sure where this chipper maniacal energy was coming from, but she was riding it. "My family and her brother are relying on us. Come on."

She clapped twice, like a kindergarten teacher. It worked. Even before the echo shot back off the canyon walls, people started to move.

Katy laid out a tarp on the sand, and it started to fill with luggage. There was too much motion for Liv to pick out the subtleties of who brought their bag willingly to the tarp and who seemed uncomfortable with the proposition. The important thing was that the beach was soon empty, the tarp full. Big Pete even unloaded the supply boat, or everything he could that wasn't directly under Stefan's body.

All the material possessions the group had were now laid out in front of her. Now what?

"You two start looking for things we can use to make paddles," Liv said, pointing to PK and Fiona. She turned to Imogen and Lucinda next.

"You work on anything we can use for emergency flotation. Devon and I will look for any other useful equipment."

Bag after bag exploded under the others' hands. The frenzied activity reminded Liv of a team bonding exercise she'd been subjected to by the head of station in Beijing, a man with a passion for suspenders who believed his employees' fullest potential would be unlocked by constructing towers out of dry egg noodles. That had been one of the longest mornings of Liv's life. But maybe he'd been on to something. A group effort—a real project, not a noodle-gluing exercise—could bring people together. The crew on the tarp was working through their stress and fatigue. PK even cracked a hopeful smile when Fiona lashed one of her light therapy masks to a pole with strips of a battered Babette kimono, creating a totemic glowing scarecrow that could possibly—whoops, no, definitely not—propel them down the Colorado.

They had a purpose. They had a goal. They were no longer on a trip that had gone horribly, disastrously wrong. They were on a mission to make it right.

Liv ignored the expanding chaos on the tarp and focused on the bags no one touched: Charlie's, Mandy's, Stefan's, and Thor's. She started with Thor's knapsack. If by any chance he'd left his knife in there, she needed to sequester it to keep her story alive. But there was no knife, just flannel shirts and a couple thick paperback novels. She moved on to Stefan's backpack, which was mostly German hiking gear, along with a worn wool sweater wrapped around a file folder. She snapped it open. Papers. Her eyes skated over the many pages of legalese. She slid the folder into her sweatshirt to review later, when reading once again felt like an attainable skill.

Charlie's bag held gray and khaki clothing, Mandy's every bedazzled color of the rainbow. Liv felt a sharp pang while fingering the rhinestoned top of a flamingo-print bikini. Then, just like that, the feeling floated away.

Devon crouched beside her.

"Is that Stefan's?" she said, pointing to the backpack.

Liv nodded.

"May I see it?"

Liv watched as Devon conducted her own search of Stefan's bag, pulling out all the clothing and turning it over, as if she were searching for a hidden zipper or secret compartment.

"What are you looking for?" Liv asked.

"Nothing," Devon said. "I just thought . . . he'd mentioned . . ."

Did Devon know about the file folder Liv had taken? Liv's inclination was to stay silent and keep the evidence to herself, but time was of the essence, and if she was going to understand the legal papers she'd smuggled out of Stefan's bag, Devon might be well positioned to help. It was possible Devon was a killer and something in the papers would trigger her. But Liv couldn't imagine she would physically hurt her in broad daylight with everyone else around. After breakfast, Liv had insisted Big Pete and Katy squirrel all the knives away.

"I wasn't sure if I should tell anyone," Liv said, "but now—"

"What?" Devon asked.

"Stefan gave me something. The first morning at camp," she improvised. "He asked me to keep it safe."

The lies were getting easier now. Liv stacked them like bricks, each new story bolstering the deceit she'd already laid. She pulled the file folder out and opened it, setting the pages on the sand one by one.

She and Devon stared down. The papers made no more sense to Liv now that they were all spread out before her. They didn't seem to have to do with putting money into Babette's business. There were no tables of expected returns nor language about investment tranches. These looked like something else.

"This doesn't make sense," Devon said. She started arranging the papers into two separate piles.

"How so?"

When Devon didn't answer, Liv kept talking. "Look, I know you run a complex business, and there might be private information in here. But if it can help us save your brother and my sister . . ."

Devon sighed. "Charlie and I were in talks with Stefan about taking over management of Babette."

"Taking over from your sister? Did she know?"

"No."

The word hung in the air, neither one of them choosing to poke the wasp nest of sibling betrayal.

"Stefan said he'd bring the documents to finalize the leadership transition on this trip," Devon said. "These pages"—she pointed to the stack on her left—"are all about that. But these other ones"—she indicated the papers to her right—"are something else."

"What?"

"It's odd. This is a vendor contract Babette canceled a few weeks ago," Devon said, touching the papers on her right. "A waste management company we were working with to dispose of excess material generated in the production of CareFree."

"Was there a problem with the vendor?"

"Not to my knowledge," Devon said. "ADD Inc. specializes in startups that use unusual ingredients in research and development. We didn't have any issues with them in the lab. As far as I knew, they showed up on time and took reasonable precautions with the more volatile material."

"Volatile? You mean, the psychotropic elements? The—"

"Scopolamine, yes," Devon said. "It's a controlled substance, and the CareFree waste is hyperconcentrated. We can't just throw it out or pour it down the drain. The waste has to be managed by professionals."

The information was moving too fast for Liv. She scanned the papers for bold type, capital letters, something she could understand. "ATTENTION TO DETAIL DISPOSAL INC.," Liv read. "Babette canceled this?"

Devon nodded. "Maybe a month ago. I don't know why."

"Did she often get involved with vendors on the science side?"

"Babette had her fingers in every little thing. Sometimes for a brilliant reason. Sometimes just the flavor of the day. When she wanted something different—poof. It changed."

Liv could hear Devon's bitterness, even now, after everything that had happened.

"You and Charlie were hoping to run the business differently," Liv said.

"We will," Devon said. "And we'll do it in her memory."

Was it possible this was always Charlie and Devon's plan—to get rid of their sister and take over? It didn't make sense that a scientist as analytical as Devon would speak so carelessly if she had in fact orchestrated Babette's murder. But maybe it was like what Liv was learning with her stack of lies: The more you believed your own tall tales, the more true they became for you.

All kinds of people were capable of self-deception. It wasn't just losers deluding themselves with personal mantras and lottery tickets. The most visionary people she knew lived deep in the belly of beliefs that ran counter to common sense. They had to. They saw things other people didn't. Sometimes their intense commitment to a dream enabled them to do things no one thought possible. Other times, their obsessions blinded them to how far from reality they were traveling. The difficulty was assessing when they were right and when they were lying to themselves.

Which was Devon? Right about her sister's shortcomings as CEO? Or so deluded by that belief that she'd go to any length to take over the company?

"Why would Stefan bring a canceled waste contract with him to the Grand Canyon?" Liv asked.

"No clue. As far as I know, Stefan wasn't even aware ADD Inc. existed." Devon looked downriver, then shook her head. "Charlie might know more. He processed all the final contracts."

Liv slid the papers back into the folder.

"Let me keep that," Devon said.

"Why?"

"Because you're right. It doesn't make sense that Stefan brought this down here. If I have more time to look at it, maybe I can figure it out."

Liv didn't like it. If the papers held important information Devon wanted to hide, it would be easy for her to stash them out of sight or simply toss the folder into the river.

But Liv also knew there was no way she'd uncover the import of the contract on her own. If the management of CareFree's waste material was germane to the murders, her best bet was to hope Devon could figure out why. That, and that the woman wouldn't lie to her about it. Liv was discovering just how easy—and useful—deceit could be.

CHAPTER FORTY-FOUR

BY LATE MORNING, THE heat, nonstop paddling, and exclusive diet of caffeinated energy bars had worked Mandy into a buzzing, uncomfortable silence. Her plan wasn't working. She hadn't stopped the raft, her dad hadn't launched a grand rescue plan, and she was no closer to knowing who killed Babette and Stefan. Maybe the mysterious Lady was Devon, who wanted control of the company. Or Fiona, who seemed to have a deep hatred for all things Babette. Or maybe . . .

"Thor?" she said. "How well do you know Katy?"

The guide squinted. "Why?"

"Seemed like she was pretty confident with that gun."

Thor snorted. "You should see her throw an ax. She annihilated a group of truckers at a bar in Flag last summer. Fastest two hundred bucks I ever made."

"Is she some kind of Wild West kid?"

"More like a trust fund kid. She came out here five years ago from the East Coast. Lives in an old horse trailer. But you can tell she came from money."

"Do you know what business her family was in?"

"We don't talk about past lives out here. It's for the best."

Past lives. Was it possible Katy came from a wealthy family and was the whale behind Stefan's firm? It seemed like a stretch for a young outdoorswoman who spent weeks at a time on the river to have a second life as an international investor. And Katy had never gotten close to Babette—she'd been at Deer Creek Falls watching the boats while all that had gone down. Unless she knew a secret way to hike to the Throne Room? There could be hidden slots and tunnels all over the side canyons like the one Thor had taken her through.

Speculation was getting her nowhere. Further from Liv. Further from help.

She looked over to where her dad was sitting on the other side of the raft, picking at his cell phone, his long legs straddling the cold radio. Earlier, when the canyon had narrowed between tight columns of granite, Thor had told them the satellite phone would be out of commission for a few miles. But now they were floating on sluggish water under an open sky. It had been like this for at least an hour. Why hadn't Guy called his contacts?

"Dad," she said. "No more planning. We have to get help."

To her surprise, he nodded. "Right you are. And I've got the guy." He looked up from his phone. "At first I thought we'd need a team, but this situation calls for maximum discretion, laser-sharp skills. Paulie's our guy."

"Who is Paulie?" Charlie asked.

"An ex-cop I met in prison—not dirty, just light-fingered. Smart. Very capable. He was this close to retaking the detective exam when he got pinched, and he's got contacts all over the west who owe him favors."

"A convict?" Charlie said.

"Ex-convict. He's rehabilitated, like me." Guy nodded. "I'm thinking I make the connect, you put up the cash. A hundred grand should do it, and I won't take a nickel for referral. I can call him on the sat phone right now."

Mandy stared at him. They all stared at him.

"Dad. No."

"How about a little faith, Mand? A little belief in your hardworking dad?"

"We have to call the authorities," Mandy said.

Guy scoffed. "You sound like your sister."

Weird. Good. She kept going. "We need to take this seriously. I'm not the one who forced us to flee. I'm not the one who ditched my sister on a beach with a murderer."

"That's not fair," Guy barked. Then he seemed to physically collect himself, as if he recognized that showing anger might endanger his position. "You know Livvie wouldn't have been willing to come with us. Secure your own oxygen mask first, right? That's what we're doing. So we can help her."

"Help her how? By not using that radio? By not getting legitimate help? And no one really does that, Dad. Flight attendants say it in their spiel, but no parent is going to watch their own kid choke for air and not do everything they can to help them breathe again. That's how real people actually behave around folks they love."

"So real people are willing to make irrational sacrifices? If that's the case, excuse me for trying to make sure we get out of here alive." Guy shook his head. "Liv can take of herself. I'm confident—"

"When is that not the case?" Mandy was losing control now, but she didn't care. "Fake it till you make it, right? You taught me that. But we're not in the magical-thinking kiddie pool. Your sketchy friends aren't going to fix this. People have died. We have to stop. We have to go back. At the bare minimum, we have to call the police."

Her words were met with silence. Guy looked annoyed, Thor unreadable, and Charlie hadn't made eye contact with her since she'd started ranting. Was this how things went when you told the truth? Mandy thought of all the times Liv had come off as sanctimonious, how many times she'd batted away her sister's objections and kept storming forward. Her dad had shown her how to do that, too.

"He doesn't want to call the cops," Thor said. "And frankly, I don't want them involved either. We've broken all kinds of rules today."

"I won't go back to prison, Mand. I can't." Guy's hard edge softened, and she could hear the fear and sadness behind it.

Charlie crumpled a protein bar wrapper in his fist and tossed it at Guy.

"Why you?"

"Why me what?"

"Of all the people in the world my sister could have turned to, why did she come to you?"

"Thanks," Guy said. "Thanks a lot."

Charlie appeared unfazed. Mandy's outburst had rattled the power balance in the boat, and Guy was no longer their captain. "Babette had all kinds of powerful people in her life. She was strategic about keeping in touch, sending little gifts, so she could always go back to someone if she needed them. You're a criminal with no meaningful resources. What did she see in you?"

"I helped her out with investor strategy," Guy said. "And I believed in her. Her methods, her vision, all of it. Unlike some people." Guy gave Charlie a pointed look before continuing. "She and I had dinner the night before she was coming down. Babette told me all about the Essence Quest and how I was missing out. I told her to give Mandy and Liv a hug and a howdy but camping just wasn't my bag. And I was busy, anyway. I was resolving an issue with another project I'm working on, a line of gold-infused weight loss shakes. Vitamin Au was doing great, growing fast, until the idiot board president replaced the CEO with his defective nephew last month. Now it's tanking. Babette got real interested. She asked a million questions about how I was addressing it."

Mandy turned to Charlie. "Was your sister into weight loss products?"

"Not at all. She called them indoctrination devices in the cult of female perfection."

"I didn't get it either," Guy said. "Thought maybe she wanted to pick up the distressed asset. But then, early the next morning, she showed up at my hotel room."

Thor smirked. "She wanted a taste of your shake?"

"She told me CareFree was under threat."

"What kind of threat?" Charlie said.

"All I know is it had something to do with the Regent Group. Maybe that's why she came to me, because I'm the one who introduced her to Stefan. I thought he was legit, but investors have a bad habit of screwing over founders. Babette was terrified they were going to do something to ruin CareFree. To ruin the whole business."

"Our family would never let that happen," Charlie said.

"That's the thing," Guy said. "She thought you and Devon might be part of it. That you might turn on her and ally yourself with Stefan."

Now Charlie was silent.

"Right about that one, huh, brother?"

"I'm confused," Mandy said. "Even if Babette was afraid the Regent Group was going to take over, or that Charlie and Devon might be part of it . . . what could have possibly changed between when you had dinner and the next morning to make her worried enough to show up at your hotel and beg you to come down with her?"

"All she said was that there was someone on the trip who wasn't supposed to be there," Guy said. "And she didn't beg. She demanded. She promised she'd make it worth my while."

"So *that's* when she tasted your shake," Thor said.

"Ew. Enough." Mandy swatted the guide, then turned back to her dad. "Who wasn't supposed to be on the Essence Quest?"

"She didn't say."

"Fiona," Charlie said. "It must have been her. Devon and I were shocked when she showed up at orientation."

"But how would Fiona even know about the orientation without an invite?" Mandy asked. "She made it sound like Babette bribed her to come. She clearly wasn't excited about roughing it."

"Maybe she lied," Guy said.

"Maybe." If so, Fiona must have had guts of steel. To crash her ex-employer's Essence Quest and insist she'd been invited by the CEO herself—a CEO she had to believe was going to show up at some point. Was Fiona planning to ambush Babette in the canyon? And then, when Babette didn't show, did she improvise somehow?

Something else occurred to Mandy. "Babette wasn't at orientation.

She wasn't at the South Rim at all. If Babette was in Vegas the whole time, how would she even know someone crashed the trip?"

"Maybe PK told her," Charlie said. "They were in constant touch."

"But if PK called or texted her the night of orientation—if Fiona or someone else showed up uninvited—don't you think that would have been fixed before we hiked down to the canyon the next morning?"

"It was chaotic at the luggage drop," Charlie said. "And so early."

Mandy remembered the cranky people milling around in the predawn haze. PK and Thor arguing over the duffel bags. Imogen with her camera, live-streaming everything, demanding that Marc strut out with mule after mule on display.

"You're right," Mandy said. "We started hiking by five. If there was something strange at the luggage drop that PK messaged Babette about, she might not have seen his text until we were way down the trail."

Charlie turned to Guy. "What time did she get to your hotel room that morning?"

"Early." Guy shuddered.

"Six?" Mandy asked. "Seven?"

"Nine thirty," Guy said.

"We were halfway to the river by then," Thor said. "Zero reception. There's no way she could have reached PK or anyone in the group."

Mandy looked at her father. "Why wouldn't she tell you who it was?"

"I don't know. She said she couldn't."

"But she convinced you to come down with her anyway?"

"I told you, she made me a promise."

"What promise?" Mandy asked.

Guy glanced at Charlie, then back to her. "She said if I could help her retain her role as CEO, I could name my position in the company."

Charlie scoffed. "You're a convicted felon and a fly-by-night investment advisor. What position could you possibly be qualified for at Babette?"

"I was thinking yours."

Charlie's face went red. "She would never—"

"Just like you would never steal her company from her?"

"You don't—"

Mandy gave her paddle a flick in the river, splashing them into silence with the icy water.

"Focus," she demanded. "Babette brought my dad down here because she was worried about a threat to the company made by someone on this trip who wasn't supposed to be here. But she couldn't, or wouldn't, tell you who it was."

"Maybe it was one of the guides," Charlie said. "Maybe she didn't know their name."

Katy? But she and Big Pete hadn't met them until they reached the river.

"Marc?" Thor said. "Could he have been who Babette was stirred up about?"

"Couldn't have been," Guy said. "When Marc met us at the ranch yesterday morning, Babette was all smiles and handshakes and can I pet the mule. She'd never seen him before, I'm sure of it. When she started feeling hot and Marc told me to hike ahead for help, she didn't even bat an eyelash."

"Maybe she should have," Charlie said.

"Maybe," Guy said grimly. "But even if Marc did kill her, he wasn't the one she wanted my help dealing with."

"Then who was?"

Before anyone could speculate further, a whoosh of energy hit the front of the raft. The breeze, a wandering trickle in the warm morning air, folded into a sharp, driving wind. All around them, the river erupted into swirling boils, bubbling like a witch's cauldron.

"Upset Rapid," Thor said. "Time to strap in."

CHAPTER FORTY-FIVE

"WE DID IT!"

Imogen leapt off the tarp, arms raised triumphantly. Her waist was ringed with empty Babette water bottles strung together with yellow paracord, punctuated by three Babette soft coolers duct-taped to her back.

"Watch this." The girl strutted down the beach, her waist-belt jangling. She pressed her phone into Liv's hand. "Take a video, okay?"

Liv gamely held up the phone. The effect of the CareFree was fading, and she could feel her good cheer melting in the prickly heat. Imogen gave a theatrical shriek, slid her feet into the cool mud, and lowered herself into the river. She slipped all the way under the water, shooting Liv a dazzling smile as she descended.

Then the teenager started to rise. The bottles around her waist came up first, bobbing in a yellow circle, giving the impression of a last-minute Halloween costume of the floating island of plastic waste in the middle of the ocean. The zipped-up soft coolers on Imogen's back kept her aloft, but she kept flopping from side to side like a dead fish.

"Ta-da!" The girl popped back up to standing and flipped her hair dramatically behind her. "I floated!"

"You floated," Liv said. Sort of. For a few seconds. In calm conditions. One of the Babette coolers taped to Imogen's back unpeeled itself and started drifting.

"So we'll just make six more of these, and we'll be good to go!"

"Imogen, I don't think—"

"And we've got paddles now," PK added. He waved something in the air that looked like a junkyard snow shovel. Upon closer investigation, it was the skeleton of a camping chair, stripped of its fabric and lashed into a bundle of poles, a baking pan duct-taped to one end. PK and Fiona had five such chair paddles assembled, each with a different kitchen implement secured to its head. The cast-iron skillet had a promising shape, but it was so heavy Fiona could barely lift it. The last three paddles were outfitted with a matrix of spatulas and wooden spoons. They looked like the world's worst pitchforks, and try as she might, Liv could hardly imagine them propelling a raft anywhere but ruin.

The CareFree had definitely worn off. Now she could see the situation for what it was: a disaster. Liv had done the first part right, selling them a story that pushed them from terror into action. But it was useless action. Even Imogen, the internet's poster child for radical honesty, had deluded herself into embracing the color yellow. If Liv told the truth now, it might crush them. Their frenzied hope would sour and flip. They wouldn't just go back to fear and uncertainty about Babette's and Stefan's deaths. They would go lower, into raw anger, paranoia. Terror. The crash would be worse than where they started.

"This isn't going to work." It was Lucinda. She didn't sound upset about it. Just matter-of-fact.

Devon agreed. "We're stuck here," she said. "We're stuck on this beach while my brother gets paddled to his death—"

"Maybe Thor isn't the murderer," Liv impulsively blurted out. "Maybe they were going for help."

"I thought you told us it was his knife," Lucinda said.

"You were so confident," Devon added.

Terrific. Now Liv had broken the cardinal rule of lying. She'd smashed her own story for no good reason but panic.

"I'm just saying we can't give up hope," Liv said.

It sounded weak even to her own ears. Liv thought of all the times her sister had spun up an audacious whopper of a dream and sold it to her, all the times she'd gotten fed up with Mandy for skirting the truth and taking the easy way out. But Mandy's way wasn't easy. Conjuring up a world better than the one they were stuck in, fabricating and finagling her way into that dream—that was no shortcut. It was a survival tactic. And Liv had failed miserably in trying to execute it.

She had to find another way to survive.

Big Pete came striding up from the beach before she could come up with any brilliant ideas of how.

"There's something I have to tell you."

No good conversation ever started that way.

"While you all were playing dress-up, I used a crowbar to lever open the gang box." He grimaced. "It wasn't there."

"What wasn't there?" The question came from Lucinda, who was gathering up dislodged bottles from the failed flotation belt experiment.

Big Pete glanced uneasily at Liv, the question of whether to answer written plainly on his face.

Liv weighed her options. She looked from Big Pete to Lucinda Duvray. Both were competent. Both had no prior connection with the Babette empire that Liv knew of. If she was going to trust anyone here with the truth, it was going to be these two.

"You can say it," she said.

"The gun," Big Pete said. "It's missing."

Liv remembered what Big Pete had said earlier, about how he'd locked it up but made sure to give the guide on overnight watch the key.

"That means Thor has it?" she asked.

Big Pete nodded. "I'm sorry."

Lucinda put a hand on Liv's arm. "We'll find them. They're going to be just fine."

"You don't know that," Big Pete said. "Thor's a funny one. He knows his way around a gun. And he's burned bridges before."

"What do you mean?"

"Nine years ago, I met him down here in the canyon. He was alone, wearing a sheepskin loincloth he processed himself. He had a pistol, a fishing pole, a bunch of old books, and a laminated guide to desert leaves and berries that are safe to eat. He made it a whole year before he wandered into our office looking for a job. He's a skilled wilderness guide, but he's not big on following the rules. Start of every season, I'm half surprised he comes back."

"Where was he before the canyon?" Lucinda asked.

"Wherever it was, he wasn't going back there. We got certified mail for him once from Virginia. He taped it to a beer can, took it out to the desert, and unloaded a full clip into it."

Liv felt a little rip inside her chest. "We have to go after them. Now."

"No can do," Big Pete said. "Not without PFDs."

"He has the gun," Liv said. "And my sister. We have to take the risk. How dangerous is the stretch of river ahead?"

Big Pete looked toward the looming cliffs to the west. The obsidian rocks were lit by the sun, shining like mirrored skyscrapers.

"A couple moderate rapids ahead. Then there's Upset thirteen miles downriver. It has a hole at the bottom that can flip a boat and tear it to pieces. A guide, Shorty Burton, died there years ago. *With* a life jacket."

Maybe Mandy's raft wouldn't get that far. Maybe they'd have the good sense to stop before Upset Rapid. Or not. Liv pushed on.

"But the supply boat can hold all of us, right? And you've got lots of experience on these rapids."

Big Pete sighed. "It's possible."

"The boat wouldn't be too heavy?" Lucinda asked.

"Not if we take out anything we don't absolutely need."

They all glanced at the tarp holding Stefan. In the gathering heat, his body was going to become harder to ignore. In just a few hours, Liv imagined the smell would be unbearable.

"Well, then," Lucinda said. "We will leave Stefan on the beach, and we'll all get on the supply boat."

"We can't make people get on a boat without life jackets," Big Pete said. "And we can't move a dead body." He was emphatic. "That's bigger than PFDs. It's a serious crime."

"Ferrying him down the river might also be a crime," Liv pointed out. "We don't know which would be worse according to park police standards."

Even as she said this, she cringed. Liv did know. Moving Stefan from the exact place where he was killed was likely to destroy evidence. Let alone what would happen if they left his body on the beach for the mountain lions and turkey vultures to find.

"No," Big Pete said. "Babette was in the gray zone, because she hadn't yet joined the trip. But Stefan Eriksen is squarely my responsibility. I have to stay with the body and wait for the police. We'll just have to wait here and flag down another party to use their sat phone."

But no other boats had passed them all morning.

"You have a responsibility to all of us," Lucinda said. "Not just Stefan. Leave Katy here with a raft, and food, and anyone who doesn't want to take the risk of getting on a boat without a PFD. You can take the rest of us in the supply boat to try to catch up with the others."

"And Stefan's body?"

"We'll bury it," Liv said.

"That's a crime," Big Pete said. "I won't—"

"I'll do it," Liv said. "I'll move him. If the cops ask, I give you and Katy full authority to say I forced your hand. That you had nothing to do with it at all."

Big Pete stared at her. Liv stared back. Swallowed hard. She was about to commit a crime. She was signing her own pink slip. No more State Department. No more global jet-setting. But this decision would take her to the one place she needed to go.

"Fine," Big Pete said.

Liv turned to Lucinda. "Do you think those paddles PK and Fiona made could be used as shovels?"

"I'll find out," Lucinda responded.

Liv nodded. "Okay. We need to dig a hole. A big one. Then we're getting out of here."

It took forty minutes before they had an acceptable trench. No one said anything when they pushed Stefan's body in. The whole affair was silent and horrible, everyone's eyes sliding away from the tarp as soon as it was covered by sand.

"I'm sorry. You deserved better," Liv finally said. She was speaking to the fresh mound on the beach, to the big sky, to all of them.

The quiet held them for one more minute, and then they had to make their choices. Devon and Liv were the first to commit to going, but in the end, all the guests chose to climb on the supply boat beside them. No one wanted to stay and wait with Katy and Stefan's dead body on the beach. Katy stood at the helm of their mountain of discarded gear, saying nothing. It was impossible to know if she was angry to be left behind or glad to be rid of them.

Imogen let out a single whimper when she saw her phone battery bank and all the Babette products they were abandoning. "Couldn't we—"

"Come on," PK said. For the first time, he spoke gently to Imogen, a sad half smile on his face. "When we get home, I'll send you so much CareFree you won't remember any of this."

"I can't imagine there will be a CareFree without Babette," Fiona said.

Devon looked at her sharply but said nothing.

Big Pete launched them into the water, working the giant pair of oars at the top of the supply boat. Katy watched them blank-faced from the shore. No one waved. No one talked. Whereas the rafts were small and nimble, the supply boat was more like an inflatable barge, rising high above the Colorado on its massive tubes, with everyone huddled close to the center. The spray barely reached Liv's sneakers, but the distance from the water didn't make her feel safe. Quite the opposite. She had no flotation device, and her bench was a wobbly plastic cooler that threatened to chuck itself into the water with every ripple.

Even in the slow sections, the Colorado never stopped roaring. Liv had thought she'd tuned it out, but that was a lie. Its growl was constant and unrelenting, unbothered by their frenzied decisions and crimes. She was trapped in its capricious violence, its ability to surge without warning. It soaked the edges of her thinking, dousing her surety in fear. When she looked down at the water, at the muddy rush below her, all Liv saw was how hard and far she could fall.

CHAPTER FORTY-SIX

THE COLORADO YAWNED WIDE as Mandy's raft drifted toward Upset Rapid, a long tongue of muddy water lapping at the foamy peaks ahead. She could feel the muscle of the river underneath their little boat, pressing them toward the roar.

"Listen up." Thor back-paddled them into a swirling eddy on the right, arresting their forward momentum. "There's a big old lion's den of a hole at the bottom of this rapid. If we get stuck in it, we flip. If we flip, there's no rescue boat to pick us up."

"Meaning?" Guy said.

"Don't get stuck in its roar. If you fall in, grab one of the lines around the outside baffles and stay with the boat. Doesn't matter if the raft is right side up or where it's pointing: Just hold on. Otherwise, you could get eaten by the hole, or the tail waves might pluck you up and spit you downriver faster than we can catch up."

"How do we avoid the hole?" Charlie asked.

"We'll take the line on the right. It's rocky, but we can make it." The cliffs were still in shadow, but the river was sparkling in the sunshine. Thor swung his paddle back into the water and took three hard strokes, pivoting them into the current. "Let's rock and roll."

The river swept them into a tight tunnel of waves. Mandy listened for Thor's voice, trying to follow his instructions, but up front, her dad was confronting his first rapid ever with unstudied chaos. Guy paddled when Thor called for it, but also when he didn't, digging into the whitewater in a ceaseless frenzy.

The raft wobbled and smacked the water as they headed for a long line of rocks and waves. The boat leapt over the first two waves, then shot right and buried itself in the third.

"Guy! Stop!"

Mandy whipped her head around to see Thor brace against the back of the boat as the whole thing tipped, the prow shooting to the sky.

The raft slammed back down and spun wildly. A full circle, another half turn, and now they were hitting the waves sideways, each bigger than the last. The water frothed like chocolate milk, spraying muddy geysers twenty feet in the air before raining down on them. She could hear her dad cry out as the boat hurtled sideways downstream, slamming into wall after wall of water. But he kept paddling, his frantic movements shoving them closer to the rocks on the right.

The rocks got bigger the closer they got. A pile of ancient stone, millions of years in the making, opening its jagged mouth to her.

"STOP!"

Guy let go of his paddle, and it launched into the air. The raft spun again, and Mandy screamed. Thor dug in and yanked the boat downstream. The river kept raging. They spun left, crosswise to an enormous boulder, and Mandy started to feel the weight below her fall away. The raft was tipping, sliding sideways. Its rubber bottom shot up the rock, Mandy's side of the boat rising into the air like a carnival Tilt-a-Whirl. She grabbed a strap and clenched it to keep from falling down across the boat into the churning whitewater.

"We're pinned!" Thor shouted.

There was no way to escape. The boat was pressed against the boulder sideways, with Mandy and Thor straddling the high-side baffle seven feet in the air, while Charlie and Guy sputtered at the water level, blasted by the full force of the waves. Between them, poorly secured gear shot out of the boat—PFDs, paddles, the braid of garlic—looping in the air before plunging like diving birds into the whitewater.

All Mandy could do was bear-hug the rubber tube and pray. Each surge of water shoved the boat against the rock again with a terrifying jolt. Thor urged her dad and Charlie upward, stretching out an arm to help them crawl one by one to the high side. Guy had lost his shoes in the driving whitewater, and Charlie was crying. But they inched their way upward, until all four of them were squished together on the high-side baffle.

They were safe for the moment. But they were also stuck, marooned above a swirl of angry waves against a sedan-sized boulder, their only form of escape the yellow raft flipped up on its side. The boulder was just big enough that they could probably crawl onto it, but it was uneven and slippery with spray, hardly stable or comfortable enough to stay long. And what would happen if they let go of the raft to move to the rock? Would it stay shoved against the boulder forever? Or would it unwrap itself and shoot downriver with the rest of their supplies?

"Now what?" Mandy shouted.

"We have to unpin the boat," Thor said.

"How?" The river was still pounding the lower edge of the raft below them, jackhammering it in place against the boulder.

"There's a little pocket of water back here," Thor said. He pointed to a strap at the front of the boat. "I'm going to grab this end. You're going to give the back a shove. With luck, it'll catch the pocket, come loose, and we'll jump on."

"Jump?" Charlie asked.

"Yes."

Charlie moaned and clutched the baffle tighter.

"How do we push it?" Mandy asked.

"Get up on the rock and line up as close together as you can. Hold the baffle and put your feet against the boulder for leverage."

Carefully, Mandy heaved herself over the tube, pressing her shoes back against the rock. Her feet slid against the slimy surface, scrabbling for purchase, but the rock held. It felt solid. Charlie and Guy swung over as well, lining themselves up shoulder to shoulder with their hands on the back edge of the raft. She could feel Charlie shivering next to her.

"On my count," Thor said. "Three . . . Two . . ."

On one, Thor yanked, and they leaned all their weight forward. But the raft didn't budge.

Mandy looked down in the space where water was shooting up between the rock and the back of the boat. "I think there's something caught."

"Here!" Thor handed her the silver folding knife, its blade open and facing out.

She leaned down to take a closer look at the gap, shielding her eyes from the spray. One of the ratchet straps looped around the raft was snagged on a chicken head of rock. "You sure it's okay if I cut this?"

Thor nodded. She took a deep breath and swiped the blade across the webbing. Her first cut missed, but on the second attempt, she sliced a screaming rip that split the strap in two with a bang, throwing it into the air. The old knife was sharper than she'd thought.

She gave Thor a thumbs-up, and he started shouting again. "Three . . . two . . ."

This time when they shoved the baffle, the high side of the raft came clear of the rock, the whole boat hanging in midair for a fraction of a second before it flipped upside down and started spinning away from the boulder.

"Jump!"

"It's upside down!" Charlie yelled.

"JUMP!"

Just before the raft flew past them, they dropped onto its underside.

"Hold on!" Thor shouted. He was spread across the upside-down raft, digging in the river behind them with both hands. "We're coming to the hole!"

She could see it. A deep, hungry mouth, sucking water fifteen feet down and shooting a wave at least thirty feet high. This was no washing machine. If they fell into that hole, there was no getting out.

Mandy clutched at her dad, at Charlie, at whatever straps she could find.

She held her breath.

They shot past the hole.

"Woo-hoooo!" she screamed as they bucked through the tail waves, the raft racing toward calmer water. "WE DID IT!"

The boat spun one last time when they hit the softer part of the river, no longer chaotically, but like a sleepy drunk, slowing with every rotation.

"We did it." Thor was grinning wildly, soaked head to toe, his face sporting a fresh scrape that drew an angry red line across his forehead.

"I am never going rafting again," Charlie rasped.

"Me neither," Guy added. Both men looked stunned.

"Please," Mandy said. "That was awesome. *We* were awesome." She flopped on her back across the upside-down raft, letting the warm air prick her soaked, exhausted skin.

"Good little knife," Thor said.

"It did its job." Mandy realized she'd been gripping it tightly ever since she'd cut the strap. She sat up and carefully folded it shut. Engraved lines ran up its handle in a rough suggestion of leaves, the sun outlining the knife's blunt, terrible beauty.

When she went to hand it back to Thor, he waved her off. "Keep it."

Then he leaned forward.

"What is it?" she asked.

"That pattern. I didn't notice it this morning, in the dark. But I reckon maybe I've seen that knife before."

Charlie peered over. "Huh. I think I've seen it too."

"What about you?" Thor asked Mandy.

She took a closer look at the knife in her hand. "No. Never. The first I spotted it was in the eddy, by Stefan's body. Where did you see it, Charlie?"

He shook his head. "I can't remember."

Mandy didn't have time to deliberate over whether Charlie was lying. "What about you, Thor?"

The river guide closed his eyes.

"It was Marc." When Thor looked up, a drop of blood slid down from the scrape on his forehead, tingeing his left eyebrow red. "The mule guide. He had it with him the night I met him."

"How many years ago was that?" Charlie asked.

"Not years," Thor said. "Days. I met Marc two nights before this trip started."

Mandy was surprised. "Had you been on different work schedules?"

"Nah. Marc was a canyon newbie. Last month, a boatman took off for a private gig on the Flathead, up in Montana. Big Pete told me if I could find a new mule wrangler, I could guide the river the rest of the season. Marc bought me a beer at a bar in Flag last week, we got to chitchatting, and . . . that was it."

"Did he have guiding experience?" Mandy asked.

Thor shrugged. "You don't need it to run mules. He was interested, and I knew he could tough it out. New to the Southwest, he told me. Retired JTF-2. Worked the same part of Afghanistan where I was ten years earlier."

"JTF-2?" Charlie said.

"Canadian Special Forces," Thor replied. "Like, Army Rangers of the north."

"He did seem a little martial," Guy said. "Not sure you get muscles like that running mules."

"Yup," Thor said. "I remember thinking the knife seemed a little out-of-date. I wondered if his great-great-grandfather used it to liberate Canada from the Brits."

Mandy thought back to that first morning up at the rim, the two guides standing together, Thor a rangy mountain goat, Marc a silent bull. But Marc had only come down to that first beach with them. He hadn't set foot on a raft or in the water. Presumably, he'd hiked the mules back up to the rim that afternoon, and then gotten the call to take Babette and Guy down the other side the next day.

And then Babette died. Marc hiked back to the North Rim for help. But somehow his knife crossed the river to kill Stefan.

She couldn't see it. All the pieces of the puzzle floated in her head in discrete chunks, and Mandy wished Liv was there to line them up properly. But all she had was her instincts, and the hazy sense that she was missing something.

She turned to her dad. "Marc didn't bring a raft or a kayak down with you, did he?"

"No," Guy said. "He only had a little pack for water. All of Babette's and my stuff was loaded on the mule."

"If Marc didn't cross the river, how did his knife end up killing Stefan?" Charlie asked.

"You." Thor pointed at Guy. "He must have given it to you or Babette. You were the last people to see him."

Guy shook his head. "I swear to you, I never saw that knife before this morning. I don't even know if Marc had it when he was hiking us down. He could have given it to the lady who killed Stefan at another time."

Charlie snapped to attention. "Wait. I remember now—"

But Thor interrupted him, turning on Guy. "Why should we believe you? How do we know you aren't lying about this whole a-lady-killed-Stefan business?" Thor came up to kneeling and pushed himself closer to Guy, who was sitting on the front edge of the upside-down raft. The boat wobbled, sending a sheet of river water pouring across its back. "You convinced us to get out of there. You said we'd get help. But that was a lie. How do we know you didn't kill Babette, and Stefan, maybe even Marc too, and now we're just your escape route?"

Guy's eyes were fierce. "That's not what happened."

The boat dipped again, and Mandy scooted back, trying to keep them from tipping. "My dad was tied up when Stefan died. There was no way—"

"You got proof, buddy, or just talk?" When Guy didn't respond,

Thor started to reach toward his belt. Toward his knife. "That's what I thought. I don't believe a single word out of—"

Mandy flipped open the silver knife and plunged it into the dead center of the upside-down raft. There was a huge explosion of air, and the boat slumped, folding in on itself and letting out a horrible hissing noise. Guy shouted and tumbled into Thor, who hit Charlie, all of them crashing into the center of the deflating raft. Mandy stayed high on the back tube, holding the blade tightly in her hands, instinctively defending herself from what might come next.

"Take us to shore," she demanded. "And stop threatening my dad."

Thor stared up at her from the shallow pool of water in the middle of the upside-down raft. His eyes were hot, and Mandy braced herself for another tirade, or an assault.

Instead, the guide started to laugh, his braying chuckle chopping across the sunken boat.

"Looks like you've picked up the law of the wild after all."

Thor hauled himself over the back tube and reached down into the river with both hands, swinging them around to face the North Rim.

"Where are we going?" Guy fumbled to his knees, pulling himself up against the left baffle and trying not to slide back into the ruined middle of the boat.

"Only place we can." Thor's powerful arms dug into the river, steering them into a fast slip of water that pushed them diagonally to the right. The upside-down raft started limping toward shore, still bleeding air from the middle. Guy had to grab one of the ropes lining the edge of the boat to keep from flipping out. He glared at Mandy. But she'd saved him. Even if she'd sabotaged their escape in the process.

"Where are you taking us?" There was real alarm in Charlie's voice.

"I'm beaching us." They drifted to a spit of land on the north side of the river that was more boulder than beach, with long, flat terraced slabs of rock licking at the water. "It's called Bloody Ledges. We'll stay until the others arrive. Or don't. We'll stay as long as we bloody need to figure this out."

CHAPTER FORTY-SEVEN

LIV WAS SWEATING, AND not just from stress. In the frenzy to get back on the river, she had somehow neglected to grab her cap.

It was ridiculous to worry about her hat when there was a murderer with her on the supply boat. She knew that. But it was the hottest day of the trip—105 at least—they were low on drinking water, and her sunblock had been jettisoned by the Babette skin care police. She kept squinting down at the river, wishing she could dunk her head, a hand even, but the water was at least two feet below the baffles of the boat. Without a life jacket, she didn't dare even get close to the edge.

All the guests had bundled themselves in the middle of the barge, ringing Big Pete, who worked the giant oars from a perch above their shoulders. The only exception was Lucinda. The older woman was at the very back of the boat, her paddling gloves on, dangling one of the deconstructed camping chairs in the water like a crude rudder.

There weren't many of them left. Devon. PK. Fiona. Imogen and Lucinda. And Big Pete.

His powerful oars drove them down the Colorado much faster than they'd gone in the rafts. There was no bumbling chitchat, no amateur paddle strokes to nowhere. Even the rapids passed quickly, the bucking waves tempered by the massive size of the supply boat. They were going deeper into the canyon whether she liked it or not.

Just like the canyon, Liv's investigation, while riddled with side trips, was fundamentally about narrowing. If Stefan's killer was indeed a lady, as Mandy's note had suggested, the pool of possible suspects was small. PK and Big Pete were out. Imogen didn't seem clever enough to plan a scavenger hunt, let alone a double murder. And Lucinda had no connection to Babette's business. So Liv homed in on the two women now sitting on opposite sides of Big Pete's perch: Fiona and Devon.

Fiona sat ramrod straight against a stack of crates, eyes closed, LED mask switched on, the glow from it an eerie blue that matched her wide-rimmed visor. Devon was a few feet closer, poring over Stefan's papers under a shade covering she'd rigged up from a sleeping mat and a Babette kimono.

Shade. That was a good idea. Liv looked around for her own source of relief and, finding none, settled for pulling her thin T-shirt up over her head.

Fiona and Devon. Could either of them have pulled off both deaths?

She'd put money on her theory that Babette had been poisoned with whatever had killed Justine Long. That required specialized knowledge from CareFree testing that both Fiona and Devon had. But it wasn't at all clear how either of them could have delivered a deadly substance to Babette on the day she'd hiked in. Perhaps it had been stashed in Babette's luggage, in a personal item they knew she would reach for during a long hike in the sun? That suggested a level of closeness and proximity that pointed to Devon . . . unless Fiona had offered Babette a new skin protection doohickey and had buried the poison within it.

Stefan's slashed throat seemed bolder, but easier to execute. As a dermatologist, Fiona had likely performed minor cosmetic surgeries, and Devon, a botanist, was skilled with a knife. Liv remembered how deftly she'd split the datura flower to show Liv its insides, the confident way Devon ran the blade down the delicate surface of the plant.

Each woman had the means to kill Babette and Stefan. But did they have motive? Devon wanted to take over the business with her brother, and it was possible a coup might not be as bloodless as she had led Liv to believe. Meanwhile, Fiona, while invested financially in the success of

CareFree, seemed to have little trust in Babette's leadership to put out a safe version of the product. Maybe she wanted to take the company down. Or take it over. Perhaps the two women were even working together.

A two-person team. Liv felt the ache where her own partner should have been. Where was Mandy? Had she been compelled to leave, or had she left Liv behind?

If Liv was honest with herself, this was the riddle that plagued her most. Not who killed Babette and Stefan, but where her sister and dad were. Visions of Mandy flooded Liv's brain. Mandy as a little kid, scarfing down orange dust from the mac and cheese box and begging Liv to tell their mom a stray dog had stolen the noodles. Mandy as a teenager, sneaking out to concerts with a fake ID she'd conjured from a library card and laminate. Mandy after their mom died, stunned, in pain, and drowning in her first confrontation with the fact that sometimes life's magician had terrible tricks up its sleeve. Mandy in her twenties, skittering from job to job, apartment to apartment, accumulating hand-thrown ceramic bowls and bedazzled sunglasses. Mandy tugging Liv up a tree; into a bar; down a trail; or, just the day before, paddling beside her through walls of water, a riotous grin on her face as they smacked the river and rose again.

The memories hit Liv like heat waves, making her woozy. She pulled her shirt down off her head. The truth was that Mandy had never run away from her. It was Liv who had done that, with her judgments and foreign service assignments, her unwillingness to leap into the unknown. Mandy always wanted to be closer, to go deep with her. Liv was the one who had pushed her sister away.

Her face burned with the realization. The guilt. The loss. And the heat.

"What's going on in that big brain of yours?"

Liv squinted up at Lucinda Duvray. Could she be a useful thought partner? Liv didn't want to scare her, but Lucinda had handled herself calmly and capably so far. And she'd been a businesswoman before she retired. Maybe she could be some help now.

"Have you ever been involved in a corporate takeover?" Liv asked.

Lucinda looked puzzled. "A million years ago, yes."

"Do you know of any that have gotten . . . violent?"

"You think someone killed Babette and Stefan to gain control of their skin care company?"

"Maybe," Liv said. "But I don't see why they would have to go to criminal extremes to do it. I thought those things were usually bloodless."

Lucinda smiled. "You've never been in a boardroom, have you?"

Liv shook her head.

"They have dark hardwood tables," Lucinda said. "Mahogany. Teak. You might think it's for aesthetics. But really, it's to hide all the blood spilled in the name of 'business as usual.'"

"Things can get ugly," Liv said.

Lucinda nodded. "In my experience, family companies are the worst. I never did business with my family. There's something precious about the opportunity to love someone without expecting them to produce. Business is business. Family is family. Bad things can happen when you mix the two."

Lucinda looked to the front of the boat, where Imogen was shooting a video about "survival skin care" using a spatula as a mirror. Liv could see the barefaced pleasure the older woman took in her frivolous grandchild.

"You own laundromats, right?" Liv asked.

Lucinda waved her off. "Owned. Some retail as well. Direct sales. Vending machines. Cash businesses. Simple stuff."

"You must have gotten good at assessing what might be a worthwhile investment."

"Those businesses didn't require much analysis, dear."

"But you did well."

"I did."

Liv liked that she owned having achieved something with her work.

"Sometimes, the simple companies are the most lucrative," Lucinda said. "Imogen says I should get interested in these new platforms, the power of social media. But companies like Hitch or Babette always seem like paper tigers to me. I can't tell where their roar is coming from, or if it's real. Give me a cash business with a one-sentence value proposition. That I can understand. That I can make money from."

"Do you think it's possible there's something wrong with CareFree?" Liv asked.

"What do you mean?"

"What you just said about paper tigers . . . I've been narrowing in on the person behind these murders, assuming whoever killed Babette and Stefan did so to capture the value of the new product line. But what if there is no value in CareFree? What if the value is somewhere else?"

Lucinda stared at her. "I'm not following."

Liv shook her head. "You're right. I just keep talking myself in circles and not getting anywhere. I'm sorry. It's too hot."

Her hands were turning pink in the heat. She looked longingly at Lucinda's long sleeves and paddling gloves. Covering up was the smart thing to do.

"Do you want a hat?" Lucinda asked. She reached between two coolers and dug out a pristine Babette ball cap. "Imogen ended up not needing mine after all."

"Are you sure?"

Lucinda nodded. "Let me help you."

Liv wanted to peek at the inside brim, but Lucinda was already smoothing the hair back from Liv's forehead, pressing down the hat, and cinching the back closure to a snug fit. The tea tree crystals felt good where they pricked Liv's skin. Whether it was a placebo effect or not, she was already cooling down.

"Thank you," she said. "I just wish I could figure this all out."

"Don't be so hard on yourself," Lucinda said. "We're alive. We're moving."

"For now."

"For now."

CHAPTER FORTY-EIGHT

MANDY'S VICTORY FELT SOUR. She had achieved one of her goals: She'd stopped their raft from traveling further from Liv and the others. But she hadn't considered how much stopping would feel like being stuck. She'd destroyed their boat, infuriated her father, and beached them on a pile of cracked rocks that, according to Thor, was not named Bloody Ledges because of a Wild West showdown, but in honor of all the rafters who'd stubbed their toes on the brittle slabs, dotting the sandstone with blood.

"Cuts don't heal easy in the desert," Thor said. He was the only one who seemed unfazed by their new situation. "Hard to put you back together when the heat and the dryness want to rip you apart. Watch your step."

Guy, still barefoot, plunked himself down with a frustrated groan. Mandy offered him the water filter and a dented thermos. At least those had been securely strapped in with the crate of energy bars and the radio. But her dad waved her off without a second glance.

"So, Captain," Thor said to Mandy, "what's next?"

"Yes," Guy said. "Please illuminate us on your brilliant plan."

"Well," Mandy said. "We've got food and water. And the radio. I'm assuming it works even if it's gotten wet. We can call the park police."

"And tell them what?" Guy asked. "That we stole a raft and left two dead bodies and a murderer behind us?"

"I was thinking we could do one better."

"What's better?" Charlie asked. He looked tired, but less jittery than he had on the river. Maybe being on dry land—even a bloody sandstone ledge—felt safer to him than the motion of the water.

"We're not just going to report a crime," she said. "We're going to report a criminal. If we can tell the police who the killer is, they'll see us differently."

Guy let out a dry bark. "Now you know who the killer is?"

Mandy stared at her dad in frustration. She hated to see him this way, biting and bitter, especially when it was directed at her.

"I don't know who murdered them," she said deliberately. "But I've narrowed it down. And I think, with all of us"—she gave Charlie a small nod—"we can figure it out."

Before Guy could protest further, Charlie leaned forward. "What do you know so far?"

"I was thinking about what Stefan called the killer. Remember, Dad?"

"Lady," Guy grumbled.

"That's right. *Lady.* The Regent Group was organized into four departments. Love, attention, distraction, and yearning." She took a breath. "I think the secret investor is the person who killed Babette and Stefan. The lady behind *L-A-D-Y.*"

To her surprise, her dad burst out laughing.

"A woman! I should have known." Guy turned to Mandy, his face shining now. "You know, that investor gave Babette an eight-foot pink salt healing crystal as a gift. I assumed it was a woo-woo dude, but this makes more sense."

"You think this lady is on our rafting trip?" Charlie said. "She showed up, what, in disguise?"

Mandy nodded. "Or under false pretenses. Your whale is famously secretive, right? Anyone who met her had to sign NDAs up the wazoo. Maybe that's why Babette wouldn't tell anyone who it was she was afraid of. She couldn't."

"There are no investors on this trip besides Stefan and you." Charlie looked at her pointedly. "And you're not a whale."

"I'm not even the investor, really," Mandy said. "It's my dad's money. I'm just the front man. Like Stefan was."

Charlie whipped his head around. "You're our first investor?"

Guy gave him a sly grin.

"I'm sorry I was rude to you earlier," Charlie said mechanically.

"Water under the bridge." Guy smiled again. "You can make it up to me by rescuing CareFree."

"The product is not going to be impacted," Charlie said.

"Really?" Mandy asked. "Even if it turns out your biggest investor murdered two people?"

Charlie dropped his eyes back to the mushed energy bar in his hand.

"Who do you think it is?" Thor asked.

"A woman on the trip who has a bigger stake in CareFree than they're letting on. Someone with a huge pile of cash and the ability—and desire—to keep their investing secret."

Guy looked at Charlie. "How much did you and your siblings inherit when your parents died?"

"You think I'm the secret investor behind all of this?"

"No," Guy said. "You and Babette put your money into starting the company. But I wonder what Devon did with her share."

"I'm not sure," Charlie said. "We never discussed it."

"It could be Katy," Mandy said. She turned to Thor. "You said she was a trust fund kid."

"I know who it is." Charlie looked upriver, his face set. "Fiona."

"The blonde with the blinky masks?" Guy asked.

"*Cross me and you're dead too*," Charlie muttered. He took off his Babette hat and let it rest upside down on the ledge, the ominous white words marching across the filthy fabric.

"I'm lost here," Thor said.

Charlie swallowed. "Fiona Moon was involved in the early development of CareFree. She had good ideas, but she hated reporting to Devon. She wanted to be in charge. A year and a half ago, she went to Babette and told her Devon was steering the product in a direction that would never be safe to go to market. Babette came to me and Devon. We disagreed. Fiona didn't like it. And then, fourteen months ago, the third focus group failed."

"Failed?" Thor said.

"There was an accident. Justine Long, a twenty-six-year-old test subject, was exposed to unsafe materials. She died. Everyone was upset, but I always wondered . . ."

"What?" Mandy said.

"I wondered if Fiona was happy it happened. Because she thought it would stop the project."

"You think Fiona killed Justine Long intentionally?" Mandy asked.

"Maybe not. But I do think she came on this trip to confront us. There's no other good reason for Fiona to show up now. Devon fired her after Justine died, and Babette gave her plenty of shares to stay quiet. It worked. None of us have heard from her for months. And now, suddenly, she shows up, saying Babette invited her? She must have been lying. You saw how she reacted when the helicopter didn't drop Babette on the beach. Fiona wanted to go back to the rim right away. But then I guess she found another way to get what she wanted."

"How?"

Charlie looked out at the gurgling river. "The water bottle. The one I found in Babette's lap. Fiona has the exact same one. Maybe she doctored it to poison my sister."

"Hold up," Guy said. "If Fiona didn't think CareFree was safe or if she didn't trust you, I could see wanting to kill the product. But if Fiona was secretly Stefan's boss, she's the biggest investor in CareFree. Why would she put all her money behind a product she didn't believe in?" Guy shook his head. "And how does a dermatologist have a secret second life as a multinational investor?"

"Fiona comes from serious wealth," Charlie said. "Her dad was one of the pioneers of the microprocessor boom in South Korea. I don't think she does much doctoring these days."

"So you think . . ." Mandy said.

"I think there are two reasons to make a big investment in a company," Charlie said. "To make money off of it or to bleed it dry. Whoever killed Babette and Stefan wasn't doing what was best for CareFree. They were doing what was best for themselves."

CHAPTER FORTY-NINE

ONCE LUCINDA'S BALL CAP had helped her cool down, Liv was back on track. She rose from her perch, shook out her numb legs, and crept around to where Devon was holed up under her makeshift tent.

"Knock, knock," she said. It sounded stupid. For the thousandth time, she wished she had her badge. Or a chaotic, extroverted sister who could get the conversation going.

Devon pushed the kimono away from her face, and for a moment, Liv had the impression that she was removing a veil, like a fortune teller ready to spin stories about the past and future.

"Any joy?" Liv asked, nodding at the papers.

"Not really," Devon said. "It's the contract we signed with ADD Inc. a year ago, when we started ramping up production of CareFree." She peered more closely at Liv. "You feeling okay?"

"Just a little hot," Liv said. "The hat's helping."

Devon nodded. "Fiona gave me one of her masks. The science on them is questionable, but these blue ones are cooling. You want to try it?"

Liv glanced down at the alien object by Devon's side. She pressed it against her face for a few seconds. It wasn't a discernibly different temperature, but it did make her cheeks tingle and tighten. She shivered. She put the mask down.

"I'd rather take a look at that contract."

"Be my guest."

Liv started flipping the numbered pages. "Any idea why Stefan would bring a canceled vendor contract on this trip?"

"No. But there is one thing I remembered. I think Stefan was the one who recommended this vendor to us in the first place." Devon stared at the papers, as if they could speak their secrets aloud. "When Fiona first identified the risk associated with the datura waste material, she had a disposal vendor she wanted to use, owned by a friend of hers from Seoul. Very pricey. And complicated. Engaging them would have involved an overhaul of our manufacturing process—maybe a two-year delay. She tried to convince me to do it, but I wasn't sure. Then a few weeks later, Babette secured the Regent Group investment, and Stefan came forward with this company, ADD Inc., that they'd worked with before. ADD came in cheaper, so we went with them."

Devon shot a glance over to where Fiona was offering PK a sip from her sparkly glass water bottle. "Fiona was pissed."

"Because her vendor wasn't chosen?"

"Because of . . . all of it."

Liv thought about the dates. The ADD contract was signed twelve months ago. A couple months before that would have been fourteen months ago, when the third focus group went wrong.

"Is that what Justine Long died of? The datura waste material?"

Devon nodded. "At the time, we didn't know how volatile the waste was. Justine got some on her hand, and she must have touched her face."

"What form does the waste material take?"

"It's a sap-like resin. Highly concentrated scopolamine."

"Deadly?"

"Yes."

Liv remembered how the dirt had clung to the blank inside brim of Babette's hat, and the rash of bumps across the dead woman's skin. "Who has access to that waste material now?"

"No one. ADD Inc. has a proprietary machine process to sequester the scopolamine into sealed containers that are removed directly from our labs. There's no way anyone can get hurt by it anymore. And even at the time . . . Fiona knew the risks. She should have been more cautious in the testing environment."

"But you still gave her a stake in CareFree to keep her quiet."

Devon was silent for a long while.

"My sister did what she had to do."

Liv wiped the back of her neck. The tea tree crystals in the hat had stopped working, their effect likely blunted by the sweat on her forehead.

"Just to clarify," Liv said. "The creation of CareFree generates a dangerous byproduct that killed someone. Fiona recommended an expensive waste management process to deal with it. After Stefan's firm invested, he suggested a different approach. You paid Fiona off and went with Stefan's suggestion, ADD Inc. Then a year later—a few weeks ago—Babette canceled the ADD contract. Did she sign on with someone new? Or could she have been in conversation with Fiona about reopening the question of how to process the waste?"

"As far as I know, Babette and Fiona hadn't talked in months," Devon said. "Though Fiona did say Babette invited her here." Devon looked out to the edge of the river, where a flock of mergansers were diving for fish. "Babette made business decisions on instinct. She didn't feel the need to tell us why she fired someone or didn't renew a contract, and the reasons she did share rarely made sense. For all I know, she decided ADD had bad vibrational energy, or the owner's astrological chart was suspect. She just told me and Charlie she'd canceled it. The implication was that we'd have to figure out a new option."

"Did you?"

"Charlie sourced some bids, but frankly, we had bigger issues to deal with. This was just another instance of our sister acting impulsively and expecting us to clean up her mess."

Liv looked back down at the contract in front of her. She flipped past lists of chemicals and waste sequestration specifications, hunting for something she could grab on to, something she could understand. She got to the very last page. White space surrounded two signature blocks: one for the head of ADD Inc., and one for the CEO of Babette

Botanique. The black line above ADD Inc. was signed in blue ink, a jagged scribble she couldn't even begin to guess at. The signature line for Babette was vacant.

Then she saw it. Under the ADD Inc. signature, also in blue ink: a hand-scrawled date.

This contract was not a year old. It had been prepared just a week ago, days before they'd all met at the lodge to begin this godforsaken trip.

She narrowed her eyes at the signature page. Stefan had brought this contract with him to the Grand Canyon alongside the papers for Babette's leadership transition. Were the two contracts linked? What would make this waste subcontractor so important to Stefan?

The papers that had struck Liv as dry before now seemed to be pulsating with energy. The heat that had felt so oppressive just minutes ago now felt like the portal to a breakthrough.

Liv stacked up the papers. "With your sister dead, who signs contracts on behalf of the company?"

"Charlie," Devon said. "Or if we move forward with the CEO transition as planned, it would be me."

"Would you reenter a contract with ADD Inc. for CareFree waste management?" Liv asked.

Devon looked puzzled.

"Stefan's boss—your big investor—if they asked you to reinstate the contract," Liv said, "would you do it?"

"I'd sign it right now," Devon said. "Charlie and I deal in outcomes and data, not signals from the universe. And ADD did nothing wrong. Even if we don't know why Stefan had this with him, it must have mattered to the Regent Group. If working with ADD is important to our biggest investor, especially at a precarious time like this, then it's important to me too."

CHAPTER FIFTY

"SO, FIONA?" GUY SAID. "A secret investor turned killer?"

Charlie nodded somberly. "As much as it pains me to say it, it makes sense."

"All right, then." Guy clapped his hands together. "Let's fire up the radio and call the police. Then we can get on the same page about our own story and get rescued."

"Now you're willing to call them?" Mandy asked.

"If we know who did it, we aren't suspects," Guy said. "We're heroes."

Mandy looked over at Thor, who hadn't weighed in. He was whittling a coyote willow branch, trying to approximate a needle they could use to patch the raft.

"I don't like it." Thor flicked his blade, shooting slivers of wood into the late afternoon air. The guide pointed his knife at Charlie. "I think you don't like Fiona. I think it would be convenient for you if she was the killer. Disgruntled ex-employee, no connection to what you're doing now. It would take her objections to your product off the table."

"The product is safe," Charlie said.

"I can't fathom it being Katy, neither," Thor continued. "Though I suppose she's the only one I could imagine taking the gun."

"The gun?" Mandy asked.

Thor nodded. “She handed it off to me when I went on watch last night.”

“And you don’t have it anymore?” It was a silly question. She wasn’t sure how it would change things if Thor had a gun. But just talking about it scared her enough to ask.

The guide shook his head. “I had it when I went on watch, but I had that bottle of tequila too. And, between us chickens, I’m a lightweight. By the time y’all woke me up with your goings-on down at the supply boat, the pistol was gone.”

Mandy thought back to when she’d crept by Thor that morning. It felt like a million years ago. She could see his passed-out sprawl, the empty liquor bottle in his hand. But no matter how hard she squinted, she couldn’t recall a gun.

“Whoever killed Stefan probably took it,” Charlie said.

“Then why didn’t they shoot him?” Mandy asked.

“Too loud,” Guy said. “They never would have got away with it. The knife was quieter.”

“The knife,” Thor said. He turned to Mandy. “You still got it?”

She pulled the slim blade out of her pocket.

Thor nodded. “Let’s go back to basics. If Marc never crossed the river, how did that knife end up killing the Dutchman?” He turned to Guy. “You said you didn’t see it when he was hiking down with you.”

“We’ve already gone over this.”

“He wasn’t wearing it on his belt?”

Guy held up his protein bar. “I swear on this peanut butter monstrosity. I never saw that knife before.”

Then Mandy remembered something.

“You saw it,” she said to Charlie. “You said so in the boat.”

“I must have been mistaken.” Charlie shrugged. “It’s Fiona. It’s done.”

Thor’s hand darted out, fast as a snake, grabbing hold of Charlie’s long-sleeved hiking shirt. There was a swishing movement. His whittling knife. The long, sharp blade. One of the buttons from Charlie's shirt fell into Thor's sun-cracked hand.

"It's not done until I say it's done," Thor said. "Not until we know everything about what happened."

Mandy gulped. She didn't want to see Charlie in danger. But they needed the truth now.

"When the raft was upside down," she said in a quiet voice. "Before I beached us. You said you'd seen that knife before."

"Yes, but—"

Another swishing breath. Another button dropped.

"You did say that," Thor said. "She's right."

Charlie clutched the gaping fabric of his shirt where the buttons had been. He was trembling now.

Finally, he spoke. "Can I see it?"

Mandy held it in her outstretched palm toward the jittery CFO.

"I could be wrong," Charlie said, "and I don't want to get anyone in trouble."

Mandy resisted the urge to roll her eyes. This was how accountants killed people, with an abundance of caution.

"But I think I saw Marc showing it to someone that first day, down at the beach, before we got in the rafts."

"Who?" Thor asked.

"Imogen and Lucinda. I first noticed them chatting at the luggage drop, now that I think about it. Imogen had her phone in the air, streaming everything. She was arguing hard to bring a lighting bank along with her tripod. Marc told her there wouldn't be electricity down in the canyon, and she flipped out."

"I was with Marc that morning," Thor said. "I don't remember any of this."

"You were flirting with this one," Charlie said. "I believe you and Mandy were swapping tips about backcountry hair care."

Touché. The accountant had some nerve after all.

"Anyway," Charlie said, "once Imogen got over her disappointment, she stalked off, and the other two repacked the bags together. It seemed like they knew each other."

"Marc and Lucinda?" Thor asked.

Charlie nodded. "When she told us she'd rafted the Grand Canyon before, I assumed maybe Marc had been a guide on another trip she'd taken. But then you told us he'd just been hired a few days ago."

"Marc was green as a Muppet," Thor said. "Told me the only desert he'd ever seen was on active duty in Afghanistan."

Mandy tried to picture Thor at a dusty bar in Flagstaff surrounded by hikers, thrill seekers, and wannabe desert cowboys. Thor said he'd recruited Marc, but maybe it was the other way around. She imagined the hulking bald man approaching Thor, talking him up, buying him a beer or five. Marc must have profiled Thor. Tracked him. It took a level of professionalism and focus that made Mandy very uncomfortable.

Then she realized something.

"The military group Marc was part of, JT whatever it was . . . that's Canadian Special Forces, right?"

"So?" Thor asked.

"Lucinda and Imogen are Canadian," Mandy said.

"Canada's a big place," Guy said.

"I know," Mandy said. "But Imogen said they're related to royalty. Lucinda Duvray might really be a lady. With a capital *L*."

"The lady in the poem!" Thor said. "I knew it wasn't Tennyson."

"What?" Guy said.

"When Stefan was reciting that poem on the beach," Thor said, "he repeated this line, like 'the lady has gone mad, the lady has gone too far,' and I remember thinking, there's no lady in that poem. I mean, it's about the lotus eaters, and probably some of them were women, but it's not like when Odysseus gets trapped by Circe or Calypso or when Nausicaä helps him. The lotus eaters are just generic opium fiends. There is no lady in that part of Odysseus's journey across the water."

The water. Mandy turned to Charlie. "You said you saw Marc and the Duvrays talking down by the river too?"

"That's right." Charlie's words were coming faster now. "When we were eating lunch and waiting for Babette. It was just the two of them, Marc and Lucinda, feeding watermelon rinds to the mules. That's when I saw the knife. Maybe he gave it to her."

Mandy nodded. It fit. If Lucinda and Marc had a plan to kill Babette, they would have had to scramble when the helicopter didn't show up. They would have had to improvise.

It was time to put her cards on the table. "It's Lucinda. She's the whale. She's the killer."

"The grandma?" Guy asked.

"How could she have killed Babette?" Charlie asked.

"I think she directed Marc to do it on the hike down."

"A guide." Charlie shook his head. "I knew it."

"I don't think Marc was truly a guide," Mandy said. "He was a plant. A mercenary. I think Lucinda planned it all. Think of the hats. Imogen said they got accidentally delivered to their room at the lodge, and they came to the rim a day early. Lucinda probably embroidered the threats in them herself."

"Not mine," her father said. He adjusted the cheap Grand Canyon ball cap on his head.

Mandy nodded. "Marc brought Babette's custom hat back up to the rim for her. But he had to buy a souvenir one for you, because no one knew you were coming."

"Do you think Babette's hat had a threat in it?" Charlie said.

"If there's something in that hat, Liv will find it." For the millionth time, Mandy wished her sister was here with them, but this time, she didn't need Liv to save her. If anything, she wanted Liv to see what she'd accomplished on her own.

"Imogen was streaming everything that morning up at the luggage drop," Mandy continued. "She even gave her grandmother a quick shout-out on her last post before we started hiking down. If Babette watched Imogen's post when she woke up, she would have seen Lucinda on the video. The person who wasn't invited was Imogen's chaperone, and CareFree's secret investor. Babette would have known Lucinda showing up without telling her meant trouble."

"So Babette went for help," Charlie said.

"Me," Guy said.

"You," Mandy said. "But she signed that intense NDA, so she couldn't tell you who you were after. And she never got a chance to confront Lucinda. Marc killed Babette on the hike down, and Stefan figured it out. When he was raving on the beach about how the lady had gone too far, how the violence wasn't necessary, maybe Lucinda felt threatened. Or just disrespected. And she killed him with the knife Marc had given her."

"It's a lot of ifs," Charlie said.

"But it fits," Mandy insisted. "Stefan mentioned that he invested in Hitch, the social media platform Imogen is on. If Lucinda is the money behind the Regent Group, it makes sense that she could pull the strings to get her granddaughter selected as the fresh face of CareFree. Lucinda could plant who and what she wanted for your new product, and for her own purposes.

"And her company is called the Regent Group," Mandy continued. "A regent is an agent of the king, like a lord or a lady. Like Lucinda."

No one said anything for a long moment.

"What purposes?" Charlie finally asked.

"What?"

"You said she could plant who and what she wanted for her own purposes."

"To make money, I guess," Mandy said. "Can we focus on what's important here? Our sisters are trapped with a murderous grandma."

Guy snorted.

"What?" Mandy said.

"You have to admit . . . it is kind of a wild accusation."

"But the knife, and Marc, and Hitch, and—"

"You've got a lot of interesting points," Guy said. "But what I don't hear is the reason *why* Lucinda Duvray would want to kill Babette. Let's imagine you're right. Let's say this little Canadian lady is the brilliant investor behind CareFree, and Hitch, and a slew of other companies. Let's say Marc works for her and he killed Babette, and she got pissed when Stefan said she was nuts and she killed him for that. Which means she's also a secret knife aficionado or a former ninja. But let's put that aside. If Lucinda is the big money behind CareFree, why would she murder Babette? What purpose would that serve? Why would she kill the woman who was going to sell CareFree to the world?"

He was right. It didn't make sense. Regardless of her management skills, Babette Sauvage was a born saleswoman. Even in a world where everyone was replaceable, a spokeswoman like Babette was not. She was the brand. She was the megaphone. She was CareFree.

"I don't know," Mandy admitted. "But if Lucinda is a killer whale—as strategic and ruthless an investor as you say—she must have a reason."

CHAPTER FIFTY-ONE

NIGHT WAS UPON THEM, but no one on the supply boat considered rest. Big Pete drove the oars through the water well past sunset, the geological strata darkening and peeling back millions of years of canyon formation with every mile they sped downriver. Something didn't feel right. Despite the dark slate sky, Liv could still feel the sun beating her in waves. The water—once sparkling Technicolor, now a jumble of somber grays—seemed to be rising toward her, its roar growing more distinct and variable, as if it were speaking a language she only knew in dreams.

The roar got louder, and the boat spun sideways to a halt.

"Upset Rapid's ahead." Big Pete's voice was swallowed by the growling river. "We can't go on."

"But my brother—" Devon said.

"I'm sorry," Big Pete said. "I thought we'd catch them by now. But Upset's too dangerous. The hole at the end of it is big enough to drown all of us."

"You can do it," Devon said. "You're a professional."

Liv pulled herself upright to join Devon's campaign. "Please. I know it's scary, but think how scared they are right now."

"We don't know what they feel right now," Big Pete countered. "But they'll feel a lot worse if they get through this and find out we didn't. We'll beach the boat and start again at first light."

That was it. It was over.

As Big Pete paddled them toward the right bank, Liv cursed herself. She'd failed. They'd come far, but not far enough to save her sister. And she was still feeling strange. The pincushion of stars crowded the sky, but she hadn't cooled down.

"Are you okay?" Fiona asked. "You look queasy." She was wedged in by the crates, grasping a taut ratchet strap an arm's length away from Liv.

No, she wanted to shout. She wasn't okay.

"Do you want a sip of water?" Fiona said. "Or one of my masks? At least take off that hat. It's dark. I don't think you need it anymore."

"It's fine," Liv said. She couldn't show weakness. Not to a suspect.

Above them, Big Pete uttered a single low grunt. Then another. It sounded like he was wrestling with something, his shoulders straining as he worked the massive oars.

The river's chattering voice gathered into a howl. The boat jolted left, Big Pete cursed again, and Liv fell, nearly knocking Fiona over in the process. Her brain was spinning. What was wrong with her?

The front of the boat dipped.

"We're getting sucked into the rapid!" Big Pete yelled. "Find something to hold on to!"

Fiona yanked Liv down into the narrow gap between the crates. Spray soaked the bucking boat, and Liv closed her eyes for a moment, relishing the icy water, the cool relief. The river ran wild around them. It was her enemy and her salvation. She couldn't see the massive waves, but she could hear them calling to her like deadly sirens.

"Hold on!" Big Pete shouted, and the boat flew into the air.

Liv turtled into her little cubby, Fiona trembling beside her. The blond woman looked just as unsettled as Liv felt. Just as vulnerable.

Think, Liv urged herself. *Find something to ask her.*

Her brain, usually so quick to race down multiple paths at the same time, felt sluggish. Clogged. The boat smacked the water again, and she could feel the synapses knocking inside her skull. She wondered if the CareFree she'd used earlier had interacted with the day's heat somehow, if it was boomeranging back on her now. She couldn't wrap her head around the minutiae of an arcane contract, let alone her tongue. So she grasped for something simpler.

"Babette's death?" she said.

"What about it?" Fiona asked.

The boat dipped, and Liv fell into the blond woman.

"We're past the hole!" Big Pete yelled.

Fiona's face loosened, but Liv felt no relief. She scrambled for the words she needed.

"The waste material," Liv said. "The . . ." She lost the word then, running the fingers of her mind over the bumps on Babette's forehead. "Stippling. Did the resin kill them? Justine Long and Babette?"

The boat spun and slowed in the tail waves, the whitewater disappearing behind them. But Fiona didn't speak. It looked to Liv as if the dermatologist was physically gathering her words, like apples. Like sheep. Sheep? She had to focus.

"Yes," Fiona finally said. "The waste material is lethal. Far worse than the raw plant, and fast acting. I believe it killed them both."

"Who knew what happened to Justine Long?"

"All the Sauvage siblings. And Stefan." Fiona looked back at her now. "He must have known. The Regent Group closed their investment weeks after that focus group, so Babette would have had to divulge it. I thought it was messed up how Babette jumped from Justine's death to a huge cash infusion. Like a deal with the devil."

"The devil," Liv breathed. Katy's stories about datura burbled up in her brain, swirling with the briefs she'd read for her upcoming assignment in Bogotá. "Devil's breath. The zombie flower."

"Are you sure you're okay?" Fiona asked again. "You don't look—"

Liv nodded. She could feel her chin bobbing like one of those plastic birds that drank from a cup.

"I think you need to cool down," Fiona said. She held out her water bottle.

The doctor was right. Liv glanced at Fiona's glass bottle, but it was too sparkly. Too small. She closed her eyes.

"You need to cool down now," the voice said.

Yes. She needed water. She could smell it. She could hear it. It was calling to her.

Liv rose to her feet, ran to the edge of the supply boat, and dove into the pitch-black river.

CHAPTER FIFTY-TWO

THE SKY WAS BLACK, the water darker. Twenty hours of caffeinated energy bars had left Mandy exhausted and wired at the same time. At sunset, they'd called in their theory to the park police. While the voice on the other side of the radio sounded skeptical, they were convinced to send a helicopter to the stranded group at Deer Creek Falls. If that beach was empty, they'd keep flying downriver to Bloody Ledges.

As night descended, the canyon reverberated with strange movements. A parade of bats emerged from a crevasse near the water's surface, crisscrossing the river in a fluttery jumble. There were hoots and scratches. Yips and howls. A scream, high and sudden, rattling down the walls before drowning in the Colorado.

Mandy clutched her water bottle a little tighter.

She sat on the lowest set of sandstone slabs, using two life vests as cushions against the crumbly rock. Her bare feet kissed the river, and she let the cool air and colder water keep her just on the functional side of conscious.

Behind her, Guy and Charlie talked in low voices, their conversation unraveling in clumsy circles as the night went on. Farther down the beach, Thor was still whittling coyote willow, a steady shuck-shuck rustling the air.

"Got any CareFree?" Guy asked Charlie.

"Sorry. Didn't think to pack it when we were running for our lives this morning."

If Guy took offense at Charlie's tone, he didn't let it show. "I was just thinking it would hit the spot right now."

"Maybe that'll be our new marketing campaign. CareFree: for when you're stranded in the middle of the earth escaping a murderer."

"Niche market," Guy said.

There was a long silence, and a splash. Mandy craned her head upriver, where something—a hunting bird? a fish?—was scrabbling in the water. Then her father's voice rose again.

"Just between us," Guy said. "Is it addictive?"

"It's legal," Charlie replied.

"Not what I asked."

There was another splash.

"The line between attraction and addiction is hard to measure," Charlie said. "Take lip balm. There's no ingredient in it you can become dependent on, like nicotine. But it's habit forming. Some people fall in love with the feeling of it. And then they can't stop buying it."

The splashing was closer now, cut through with sharp cries, like a dying bird.

"The better something works, the more you want it," Guy said.

"Shh," Mandy said. "Listen."

Two voices, people, shouting something. She stood up. A boat was coming toward them, illuminating the river with a reedy beam of light from a headlamp a few feet above the water.

"Hey!" Mandy shouted. She didn't care if it was the police, a pleasure cruise, or another group of knife-wielding weirdos. She was done. "Over here! We need help!"

"Swimmer!" the voices called back. "In the water! Help!"

The splashing was not a bird. It was a person. A flailing, fading person. There was no bright life vest keeping them afloat as they rose and fell in slivers illuminated by the thin light from the boat. Just strands of hair. A crescent of pale skin.

The headlamped person was yelling down, jiggling a thin line of cord attached to a floating bag tossed in the water. But the swimmer didn't grab the rope. Didn't even seem to know it was there. They were just a flutter of fingers, a billowing dark shirt.

Thor crashed past Mandy, grabbing a life vest from behind her.

"Come on!" he yelled.

His long hair streamed behind him as he leapt into the river. He swam hard, churning through dark water, grabbing for glimpses of the drowning person. Mandy hastily clipped the other PFD around her and started swimming out behind him.

The river was chaos, everything in motion: the body, the swirling water, the tiny light blinking erratically across the surface. Something brushed Mandy's hip, and she screamed. She tried to kick it away. But it wasn't a fish. It was too big. She scissored her legs around it, feeling its weight threaten to sink past her.

"Thor!" she yelled. "Under here!"

The guide flipped, reaching down as deep as his life jacket would allow.

"Got him!"

Thor popped up with an arm around the swimmer's torso. Mandy reached down and grabbed for a hip, a foot, whatever she could find. Thor tugged the person onto their back, but still, Mandy couldn't see a face. The head kept slipping below the black water.

They hauled up onto the beach, Thor sputtering, Mandy's eyes streaming with silt. Even before she could make out the swimmer's face, she knew.

It wasn't a man.

It wasn't a killer.

It was Liv.

They lifted her sister onto the first set of ledges, and Thor swept her mouth with his finger while Mandy hunted for a pulse. Nothing. Liv wasn't coughing. She wasn't breathing.

Thor started chest compressions. Mandy watched as if in a dream, a nightmare, though the thing that flashed in her brain was the first time she'd gotten her CPR certification, which Liv had insisted they do as teenagers, because Liv was already a million years old, even then. The mannequin they were assigned was so janky that its head kept popping off. Liv had her fingers laced together, her hands driving into the self-decapitating piece of plastic, and Mandy kept making jokes about how Liv was killing the patient and Liv kept scowling at her, and was she never going to see her sister glare at her like that again? Were they never going to perform their stupid duet, their push and pull, thrust and parry, hug and throttle, again?

Thor kept pumping. Mandy administered the rescue breaths, shoving air into her sister's body, praying for it to come out again as carbon dioxide, as river water, as anything close to hope. She was vaguely aware of the supply boat coming to shore, other people crowding the ledges, her dad putting his hand on her back. But they were all just paper cutouts, shadows in the dark. The only thing she could feel, the only thing she could hope for, was Liv.

On the twenty-fourth breath, her sister's eyes flashed open, just for a second, the whites around her pupils shining over the dirty water smearing her face.

They fluttered shut again.

Thor kept pumping. Mandy kept counting. Every time he got to thirty, she gave Liv two more breaths. Two more chances.

Six breaths later, one of Liv's legs started to shudder. She groaned and twisted. Mandy looked to Thor, unsure what to do.

"Keep going," he said.

Finally, on the thirty-sixth breath, Liv shot up to a seated position, coughing and puking river water everywhere. She looked wild, ragged and raw, streaked with mud and God knew what else. But she was alive.

"Ashhhh."

The sound creaking from her sister's mouth was more ragged exhalation than word. It was the sweetest thing Mandy had ever heard.

"Breathe, Liv. Just breathe. You're okay. You're okay."

"Cashhhh," Liv said. She shuddered and jerked in Mandy's arms.

Then Liv retched again. "You know what the best cash business is?" she croaked.

"Shhh."

But her sister wrenched around and grabbed Mandy's wrist.

"Drugs," Liv rasped. "She's using it to make drugs."

"What?" Charlie asked.

She whipped her head around and pointed at Lucinda. "She poisoned me. She poisoned Babette. With the hats!"

Lucinda shook her head calmly and stepped forward, unfurling a sleeping bag to put over Liv's shoulders.

"You're delirious, dear," she said. "Here. Poor thing."

"Get away from us," Mandy hissed.

"I'm just trying to help."

"Like you helped Babette and Stefan?"

Lucinda held her ground. "What on earth are you suggesting?"

"You're the one who killed them," Mandy said. "You're the lady. The secret lead investor behind CareFree."

"It's true," Guy added. "We figured it all out."

"Oh really?" The older woman looked almost bemused, as if Guy was a colorful moth flitting around her garden.

"You're the one who made those threatening messages in the hats," Mandy said. "Imogen said you got to the lodge a day early, and that box of hats was in your room. You had plenty of time to sew in those threats. I think you wanted to make us all believe Babette was out to get us. But really it was *you*, out to get her."

"And then there's the knife you used to kill Stefan," Guy said. "Charlie saw Marc give it to you, your first day on the beach."

Mandy looked over at Charlie, hoping for verbal affirmation, or at minimum, a nod. But Charlie shrank back, staying silent.

Lucinda cocked a puzzled smile. "I'm sorry, but I don't have a clue what you're talking about. Who is Marc? What knife?"

Guy motioned to Mandy, who passed him the old-fashioned knife, latched shut.

"This knife," Guy said. "My daughter found it in the water near Stefan's dead body. It belonged to Marc, the guide you hired to hike down with me and Babette to the river. The guide who killed her on your orders."

"This is all very interesting," Lucinda said. "But I recall spending our extra day at the museum, not messing around with hats. I don't remember hiring a guide, or him giving me a knife. It seems like you're the one with the knife. You, and your daughter."

Liv jerked in Mandy's arms.

"Lying," Liv rasped out.

"Yes, dear," Lucinda said, "I'm sorry but I'm inclined to agree. It seems you've done your best to avoid the family predilection for deceit. But your father and your sister continue to tell their tall tales, don't they?"

"Lying," Liv repeated. "I hate it."

Mandy stiffened. But she didn't pull away from Liv. She could feel her sister's heartbeat right up against her own.

"Unfortunately, I fear lying is the least of your family's offenses on this trip," Lucinda said. "Your dad got one thing right. I am the investor behind the Regent Group, the chief backer of CareFree. No one here is more committed to this product, and this company, than I am. No one had more to lose from Babette's and Stefan's untimely deaths. But someone had something to gain."

Mandy was vaguely aware of Charlie and Devon drawing closer to each other on the beach.

"You," Lucinda said. But she didn't point at the Sauvage siblings. She was staring straight at Mandy. "You and your dad."

Lucinda swung her attention to Guy. "You used your daughter to invest in CareFree. You saw its potential. You wormed your way in. But you couldn't stand that someone else was going to make more off of CareFree than you. I know you, Guy Chisholm. I've heard your big talk and seen how little success has accompanied it. With CareFree, you found something that could actually hit. And you wanted all of it."

"No," Guy said.

"Yes." Lucinda's voice had power now, reinforced steel. "You were the one who hiked with Babette to the river. For all we know, you hired Marc—"

"I hired him," Thor said.

"Fine." Lucinda didn't miss a beat. "You hired him. Not me. And we don't know how far Marc hiked with Babette and Guy, do we? We don't know what happened after Marc turned back."

Mandy could see the faces turning to her father with questions in their eyes.

"Dad . . ." she warned.

"And you," Lucinda said. "The bubbly little minority investor. While your dad was dispatching the CEO, you had your sights set on the big money. On Stefan, and by extension, on me. When your sister decided to tie Stefan up, you saw your opportunity."

"It's not true," Liv wheezed. "Mandy didn't—"

"I'm sorry, dear, but it is. She stabbed him, and then they escaped. I know it's difficult to accept the truth sometimes. Especially when it's family. That's probably why you threw yourself in the river."

"No," Mandy said. "You're the one who's lying. Distraction: That's where CareFree falls in your portfolio. And here you are trying to distract us with a story. But this time, we actually know the truth." She swallowed. "Stefan knew it too. When he was raving on the beach about a lady who'd gone too far, he was talking about you. You didn't have to kill Babette. Charlie and Stefan had a plan worked out to take over the business without bloodshed. When you killed Babette, it must have infuriated Stefan, or scared him. Or both. So you decided to silence him too."

"You're embarrassing yourself," Lucinda said smoothly. "Why would I kill Babette if Stefan could replace her by other means? Why would I remove—let alone kill—either of them at all? They were both critical to CareFree's success."

Lucinda sounded calm. Rational. And for once, Mandy didn't have a good answer.

"You did it," Guy said. "You coldhearted—"

Lucinda turned coolly away from him, facing the rest of the group. She gestured back at Mandy and Guy. "Think about the time you've spent with these two. Have they said anything that was actually true?"

Mandy cringed as silence swallowed the beach. Fiona, Charlie, and Devon backed away. Even PK shook his head.

Was this it? Was Lucinda going to convince everyone that she and her dad had murdered Babette and Stefan? Even more than her fear for her own survival, Mandy hated the idea that Lucinda might get away with it. That Lucinda's stories might be more powerful than her own.

But there was nothing she could do to fight back. Any word she said, any attempt she or her dad made to right the wrongs, would be looked at with suspicion. She was muted. They were done for.

Then Liv dragged herself up and out of Mandy's arms. She staggered, not quite to her feet, but to a kneeling position under her own power.

"You're right," Liv said. "I hate how they lie."

She half shuffled, half crawled. One step. Then two. Toward Lucinda. Away from Mandy.

"But truth requires proof," Liv said. "Thank God I held on to the letter."

"What letter?" Lucinda asked.

Liv pulled herself up to standing.

"The letter I found in Babette's hat. The letter where she explained that CareFree's lead investor was actually a criminal who planned to use the waste material from the product to create a deadly drug that turns people into suggestible zombies. Or kills them. Like roofies, only worse. Because the target is conscious while they're being controlled."

"This is ridiculous," Lucinda said. "You're delirious."

"It was a brilliant business plan; I'll give you that." Liv's voice was hoarse but sure. "You're the lead investor in CareFree, and Attention to Detail Disposal—ADD Inc.—is under your control too. CareFree assured you an unlimited, unregulated supply of highly concentrated scopolamine. ADD got paid to take it away, and you'd make even more from the skin care products that kept the psychotropic waste material pumping. But Babette connected the dots, found out what you were doing, and canceled ADD's contract. That didn't work for you. You couldn't risk being exposed, and you wouldn't let the scopolamine go, either."

This was the piece Mandy had been missing. While she'd been tracking down Marc and the lady behind him, Liv had found the motive.

"You told Stefan you needed the CareFree waste contract reinstated," Liv continued. "But you also had to remove the possibility that Babette would tell her siblings—or the feds—what you were up to."

"Babette saw you on a video Imogen posted, that first morning up at the rim," Mandy said. "She thought you were coming down to steal her company and turn it into a front for your criminal activities. She went to my dad for help."

"That's right," Liv said. "Babette didn't know what would happen to her when she confronted you. But she knew enough to write it all down."

There was a click, and Mandy stopped breathing.

Lucinda was holding a pistol, pointing it at Liv.

"Give me that letter," Lucinda said.

"I don't think so."

A blast shook the air, and Liv fell to the ground.

Mandy screamed and ran to her. Behind her, there were shouts. It sounded like someone had tackled Lucinda. There were grunts, then a soft thump. But no more gunshots. No more victims.

Only Liv.

And so much blood.

The rocky ledge beneath her sister was wet and slick where Mandy knelt. She whipped off her sweatshirt and pressed it to Liv's chest, to her shoulder, squeezing until the fabric was black with blood. Behind them, she could hear Thor and her father shouting at Lucinda, presumably as they wrangled her into submission.

She leaned down. She let the rest of them go. She put her face as close as she could to her sister's.

"She showed us who she really was," Liv whispered. She grimaced then, her whole face contracting. "It hurts."

"She shot you in the shoulder," Mandy said. She held her sister tight, tighter than she ever had, letting the blood and sweat and tears all mix together.

"Then I don't want to paddle anymore."

Somehow this stupid joke made Mandy burst into tears.

"What happens now?" Liv rasped. Her voice was growing fainter.

"The police are on their way," Mandy said. She took a quick glance over her sister's shoulder. Thor had reclaimed the gun and wrapped a length of webbing around Lucinda, tying her to a boulder. "And Lucinda's not a threat anymore."

"She did it," Liv croaked.

"I know."

"What do you know?"

"I figured out who and how," Mandy said. "But not why."

"All I had was why." Liv closed her eyes, and Mandy's heart jumped back into her throat. Had her sister lost too much blood already?

But then Liv came alive again. "We're a good team."

Relief. Gratitude. And one thing that confused Mandy.

"The letter," she said. "Why didn't you tell me about it when you found it?"

Her big sister looked up at her, eyes glazed, and time stopped again. Mandy knew Liv might not remember this night. But Mandy would. She quieted her brain and locked in on this moment, this little pocket of hope deep in the heart of the earth.

"There is no letter," Liv whispered. "I made it up. I lied."

CHAPTER FIFTY-THREE

Las Vegas, One Year Later

LIV SCANNED THE BUSTLING hotel ballroom for a hint of her sister. Nada. It didn't seem possible that she could have lost Mandy between their suite and the party—what had she done, run away with the blackjack dealer who'd smiled at them in the elevator?—but here they were. Here Liv was, in her least favorite city in North America, in a silver-and-white dress Mandy had insisted she buy for the occasion. Sleek, glossy people milled around the room, sipping cocktails filled with pastel elixirs and flower petals. While everyone else glittered, Liv felt like a crumpled piece of tinsel ten days after Christmas.

"Nice cult they got here, don't you think?"

Before Liv could respond, Mandy wrapped her in a hug, as if it had been months and not minutes since they'd last seen each other. She always did this now. Every week, her little sister bombarded Liv with rhubarb muffins and triple-texts and last-minute invitations to quiet dinner parties that turned out to be karaoke rodeos. Maybe Mandy had always had it in her to be so persistent, so giving, so eager to dump the whole jar of sprinkles onto the cake. But these past eight months, living in Austin, it was the first time as an adult Liv experienced it up close.

It wouldn't last forever. Someday Lucinda would be convicted, Liv's interminable administrative review would end, and she could get back to the business of international diplomacy. Liv nodded at Casey Ito, the gangly special investigator in his ill-fitting suit, who was watching the crowd from the corner with a bottle of water in his hand. He nodded back.

"How is Double-O-Boring?" Mandy asked, following her gaze.

"Busy."

Casey had generously kept Liv in the loop on the investigation's progress. The international team was still working through all the evidence against Lucinda, but Liv was optimistic. It seemed more of a jurisdictional puzzle than anything else at this point. Marc had flipped on Lucinda in exchange for immunity, and Imogen's copious videos from the trip had bolstered many of Liv and Mandy's suspicions. The teen had even captured her grandmother daubing what was presumed to be scopolamine resin on the spare hat—Lucinda's rafting gloves insulating her from the deadly substance—before offering it to Liv.

Perhaps the most surprising witness to Lucinda's crimes was Babette herself. While Liv had lied about the imaginary letter, it turned out Babette kept meticulous notes in her office detailing what she'd discovered about the links between Lucinda, the Regent Group, and ADD Inc. As Devon had mentioned, Babette was obsessed with the purity of her supply chain. She'd traced a dizzying array of shell companies linking CareFree's deadly waste material to Lucinda and a major international drug cartel and written it all up in a little notebook. She'd planned to ask Fiona to rejoin the company and reengineer the CareFree waste management plan once she confronted Lucinda. But Babette never got that chance.

It had taken months to gather enough information to build a case, and it might be several more before the various international authorities decided where to charge Lucinda, for what. In the meantime, Liv was on hold with the State Department and making decent money as a contract polygraph analyst for the Texas attorney general's office. She had an apartment that was close—but not too close—to her sister's. And she was learning to say yes to a life she couldn't entirely control.

Mandy's dress was a deep emerald, with silver interlocking snakes she'd appliquéd onto it herself. Liv had to smile at the way PK shied back when Mandy greeted him and pointed out the one she'd named Pinky after their shared ordeal. It had turned out in the investigation that despite Lucinda's careful planning—the embroidered threats, the implantation of Marc, the scopolamine smeared on the hats that killed Babette and poisoned Liv—the rattlesnake had crashed the rafting trip of its own accord.

"I thought you'd disappeared," Liv said to Mandy.

"Just had to go back to the room for a little something." Mandy held out her closed fists to Liv. "You pick."

Liv eyed her sister carefully. "Are they different from each other?"

"One will turn your heart to iron. The other will turn it to jelly."

"What kind of jelly?"

"Grasshopper."

Liv nodded seriously, looking intently at her sister's closed hands. Ever since her recovery from the gunshot wound, Liv had taken a new interest in anatomy, in the way bodies were stitched together and could fall apart. She saw the strength in Mandy's fingers, the tiny flecks of paint on her nails, and a recent scab that Mandy had attributed to a late-night piñata incident. This was what they were made of: meat and muscle and blood and bone. Hope and pain. Desire and limitation. These past few months, going through the healing process, spending more time moving outdoors, Liv felt more acutely how her body worked and where it could take her. It didn't hurt that the physical therapist she'd been assigned to was a total fox.

Said fox had told her there are more ways our bodies can change than we can imagine. But could anyone really change? Liv had heard from an old colleague that they were trying to close cases against Lucinda for seven unsolved deaths by poisoning in three other countries—and Liv could only imagine how many near-miss poisonings, like her own, might add to Lucinda's victim count. She still didn't know whether she'd gotten lucky because Lucinda hadn't had sufficient scopolamine to kill her or whether leaping in the river somehow disrupted its deadly course. Katy swore later that it was the datura goddess herself who had chosen to spare her life. But Liv disagreed. Any credit for her survival was surely due to the maddening, loving, flesh-and-blood sister standing before her now, waggling her fists impatiently.

Liv looked from Mandy's trickster smile down to her hands and deliberated over her choice. Before she could decide, a tinkling sound filled the air. Dozens of people were clinking tiny silver spoons against their martini glasses. An amplified voice, warm and serious, washed across the room.

"Welcome."

Devon looked younger than when Liv had last seen her. She still sported a tight salt-and-pepper pixie cut, but her face looked ironed smooth, her eyes brighter. Devon Sauvage would never be the poster child for Babette that her sister had been. But by all accounts she'd embraced her new role as CEO, and it appeared she was using the company's products accordingly.

"We are here today to announce a new product line at Babette Botanique. To share it with all of you, our dedicated friends and supporters."

Imogen was standing to the side of a gaggle of other influencers, phone held aloft. Her follower count had skyrocketed after the Grand Canyon trip, when she pivoted from peddling beauty tips to eight-second exposés on her grandmother's exploits. Turned out being the innocent princess of a crime family was a boon to business. And Imogen was, apparently, innocent. Lucinda was still fighting the conspiracy and murder charges, but she refused to speak ill of her granddaughter, even as Imogen released one explosive video after another. According to the prosecutor, they were still piecing together the dizzying collection of shell companies, offshore accounts, and unregistered operations Lucinda employed to conceal her illegal drug cartel's deadly business. They'd turned up a few criminals like Marc who accepted deals to talk, and more unlucky employees like Stefan who no longer could. But they hadn't found a single family connection. Even Lucinda's laundromats—a perfect front for turning dirty money clean—traced back to her and her alone.

But now was not the time to wonder how long it would take for investigators to navigate through the maze of Lucinda's crimes. Today, the name on everyone's lips was Babette's. On the stage, Devon gestured to Charlie, inviting her brother forward.

"As many of you know," Devon continued, "we had been working for the past several years on a line inspired by our dear sister's fervent belief in all people's right to be free. Free from worry. Free from regret."

Across the ballroom, Guy nodded tentatively at Liv. They'd seen each other more since Liv had moved stateside, mostly at Mandy's prompting. But her dad was spending much of his time these days hopping between Vegas and Seoul, helping Fiona expand her light therapy face mask business. According to Guy, it was going to be a total game changer.

Charlie cleared his throat and leaned into his sister's microphone. "In the wake of our sister's tragic death, CareFree no longer seemed like the right product for the future of our family's business. Babette had a gift for unleashing the wild spirit of our community. But her loss has focused our attention on other gifts. Other possibilities."

Devon held up a simple bottle, matte-black, with the telltale silver *B* emblazoned across it. "Welcome to the first offering of Care. A new line from Babette, dedicated to enhancing the bonding power of love. Care starts as a lotion, and is coming soon as a fragrance and a serum. Care will not set you free from obligation. Care will bring you home to the connections that matter most."

Devon raised the bottle as if in a toast or a salute. From the back of the stage, PK gave a subtle nod, and a blanket of silvery flower petals fell from the ceiling onto the crowd.

"To Care."

Amidst the oohs and polite applause and phones tipped upward to capture the moment, Liv turned to Mandy.

She tapped her sister's right fist.

Mandy opened both her hands. Each held the same thing. A ring. A pearly, opalescent stone, with a delicate trumpet-shaped blossom etched across the surface.

"Is that a datura flower?"

"It is. On a moonstone."

Liv looked closer at the flowers engraved on the shimmering gems. She imagined her sister tracing them with an X-Acto knife, the pink slip of her tongue sticking out between her lips.

"That scab wasn't from a piñata incident, was it?"

Mandy grinned. "If I tell you, I might have to kill you."

"Then I guess I'll never know."

There were so many things she never would know. So many choices Mandy would make that were not to her satisfaction. Liv looked at her sister, who would never stop lying to her. Who would never stop loving her.

"Thank you."

"Here." Mandy gave Liv her ring and slid the other one onto the pinky of her left hand. "So we never forget what's important."

ACKNOWLEDGMENTS

FOR THE FIRST FORTY years of our relationship, my sister and I never went on a trip together. We love each other and are incredibly close, but that closeness hasn't always translated to ease. We're the kind of sisters who can finish each other's sentences, but we can also set each other off with a single word.

Three years ago, we dealt with a series of major family health crises. We did a bang-up job supporting each other and tag-teaming care for our parents, but it was stressful, emotional work. We decided to balance it out with our first-ever sister trip: a rafting vacation in the Grand Canyon.

That trip was one of the best experiences of my adult life. I was amazed at what I learned about my sister and myself on the Colorado River. We traveled as a unit—branded "the sisters" among the guests—and our paddles both propelled us forward and resurrected childhood patterns of relating. Morgan and I are quite different from Liv and Mandy, but the sister bond at the heart of this story is fueled by our connection and all its loving, complicated, messy, beautiful aspects.

Thank you Morgan for paddling down the river with me, for saying yes when I asked if it was okay for me to write this book, and, most of all, for being my brilliant, caring, powerful sister. I also want to thank my mom, Sarina, who was once again my first reader, generously reading draft after draft and encouraging me to keep going. I feel so lucky to have these strong women beside me, always.

Thank you to all the friends and loved ones who helped make this story shine. Thank you Sarina, Morgan, Sibley, Carson, Beck, Peggy, Susan, and Kiera for providing feedback on early drafts. Thank you Will and Rocket for our inspired brainstorming sessions. Thank you Ian for backpacking with me into the canyon and agreeing to stretch our food so I could watch the birds and boats at Deer Creek one more day. Thank you Jeff, Mike, and Franny for sharing your rafting guide wisdom; thank you Lee for describing your rich experiences with datura; and thank you Jessica for shedding light on life at the State Department.

Thank you to the team of publishing superstars who made it possible for all of us to enjoy this book. I feel lucky and grateful to collaborate with my wonderful editor at William Morrow, Liz, and my terrific agents at Janklow and Nesbit—Stefanie, Molly, Alysse, and Adam. These people are creative partners in every sense of the word. Thank you Kim for the stylish cover art, and thanks to Kathleen, Chris, and Martin for helping this book reach as many readers as possible.

Finally, for all the Grand Canyon lovers out there… This book is informed by my deep love for the canyon and many joyful experiences rafting, hiking, and backpacking through it. While I tried to honor and bring to life the specific realities of the setting, there are three changes I made in service of this story:

1. The place I call "Thunder Spring" is technically "Thunder River." In editing, we decided this was unnecessarily confusing—and let's face it: it *is* confusing that a river feeds a creek that feeds a river—so I changed the name. I also made the hike easier than it would actually be to accomplish in high summer. I promise you that Thunder River is every bit as magical as the fictitious Thunder Spring, and highly worth a visit in the spring or fall.

2. The final showdown occurs at a beach with the evocative name of "Bloody Ledges." While Bloody Ledges does indeed exist, it is at river mile 158, and this showdown more accurately occurs at "Ledges," a beach at mile 152.
3. There are incredible canyoneering secrets hidden all over the Grand Canyon. However, there is no slot traverse that connects Thunder River to the Throne Room under Surprise Valley—or if there is, I haven't found it yet.

Nina Simon writes crime fiction about strong women. She is the author of the *New York Times* bestseller *Mother-Daughter Murder Night*, which was a Reese's Book Club pick, an Anthony Award winner, a Golden Poppy Award winner, and a "best of 2023" selection for Amazon, Barnes & Noble, CrimeReads, and *Library Journal*. Before turning to fiction, Nina wore many hats: NASA engineer, slam poet, game designer, museum director, and nonprofit CEO. Her work on community participation in museums, libraries, parks, and theaters has been featured in the *Wall Street Journal*, the *New York Times*, NPR, and the TEDx stage. Nina lives off the grid in the Santa Cruz Mountains. More information can be found on her website, ninaksimon.com.

[illegible] Simon [illegible] for [illegible] the [illegible] that [illegible] and [illegible] Rutgers [illegible] [illegible] [illegible] [illegible] [illegible] [illegible] [illegible] [illegible] [illegible] [illegible] [illegible] [illegible] [illegible] and [illegible]